Heartbreak in the Valleys

Heartbreak in the Valleys

Francesca Capaldi

hera

First published in the the United Kingdom in 2020 by Hera Books

This edition published in the United Kingdom in 2021 by

Hera Books
28b Cricketfield Road
London, E5 8NS
United Kingdom

A CIP catalogue record for this book is available from the British Library.

Print ISBN 978 1 80032 357 5
Ebook ISBN 978 1 912973 41 5

Look for more great books at www.herabooks.com

Printed and bound in Great Britain by Clays Ltd, Elcograf S.p.A.

To the mine workers of the Welsh valleys and their families, particularly those in World War One who dug out that 'good steam coal' for the war effort. And to my family, the Morgans, the Joneses and the Jenkinses, who were part of that.

Prologue

3rd August 1914: The day before war is declared

Anwen Rhys stopped by the railings, overlooking Whitmore Bay on Barry Island. The beach held a throng of day-trippers, taking advantage of the blue skies and warm air of the bank holiday. She closed her eyes and breathed in deeply.

'You all right, *cariad*?' said her fiancé, Idris Hughes. His arm, tucked around her narrow shoulders, gathered her in a little closer.

She looked up at him, towering above her. He was smiling. His eyes, the colour of dark chocolate, crinkled with pleasure. How lucky she felt, with her kind, handsome man beside her, his coal-black hair shining in the sun.

'I'm more than all right,' she told him, returning the smile.

'How about going on the Figure Eight roller coaster?' He looked inland, at the huge scaffolding-like edifice of the newest addition to the resort. 'Looks exciting.'

'Looks frightening to me,' she laughed. 'Didn't you hear people screaming as we walked past it?'

'Just excitement, that is.'

'The Switchback railway is more to my liking.' She looked behind in the other direction, past the buildings, at the undulating rail of the fairground ride.

'That's very tame. I bet Sara and Jenkin would go on the Figure Eight with me,' he teased.

'Oh, I have no doubt. As quiet as she is, Sara likes a bit of excitement. Pity they've gone off for a cup of tea with our

I

parents. Perhaps you could take them on when we meet up again.'

'Aye, I'll do that...Is your mam all right? She seemed a bit down on the train coming.'

'She and Da had a bit of an argument before coming out, that's probably it.'

More like a blazing row. It was over the money he'd left her short of this week, as usual. He'd threatened not to come on the trip, relenting when Mam had told him, 'Fine, we'll have a better time without you.' At least he was better behaved with Meg and Isaiah Hughes around. She wondered how long it would be before he proposed a trip to the public house with the other men, leaving the women and Jenkin to their own devices.

Idris didn't comment on her reply. She knew he'd heard them arguing before so was unlikely to be surprised.

'So what's it to be then? A walk to Friars Point?' He nodded his head west.

'What, so you can watch the ladies bathing in the pool there?' She put on a mock scowl.

He went bright red and stuttered, 'N-no, I didn't even think of it. Only of the view over the coast.' When she giggled he said, 'Oh, you're pulling my leg. Perhaps you'd rather go the other way, to Nell's Point, where the men are bathing?'

She pushed him playfully. 'I only have eyes for you, Idris Hughes, always have done.'

'And I for you. Just think, under a year now until we're married.'

Her heart gave a leap of joy. 'We've waited long enough, thanks to our parents.'

'I suppose they only want what's best for us.' He pointed to the beach, where several donkeys were being led across the sand. 'Let's have a ride, eh?'

'Yes, I do love a donkey ride. Then maybe go on the Switch-back afterwards?' she looked hopeful.

'Of course, *cariad*, anything you want to do. We've got plenty of time before the grand band competition on Nell's Point.'

'One moment, while I adjust my hat.' She pulled away from him to pluck out the pin and relocate it. 'There!' She linked her arm through his and they set off towards the sand. A warm stream of contentment flowed from her head to her toes. She was the luckiest girl alive.

Chapter One

5th November 1915

Anwen Rhys pushed open the door of the newsagent's on James Street and stepped in. The pungent aroma of tobacco was mingled with the treacly scent of sweets, for the shop also served as a tobacconist and confectioner's.

'Good afternoon, Mrs Davies.'

'Hello Anwen. Just finished your shift, have you?'

'I have.' She rubbed her back, irritated as it was with the gritty coal from the sorting machines.

'Your father's paper as usual is it?'

'Yes please.' Looking around at the sweets on the shelf, noting the depleted jars, she wondered if she should get some for her sister as a treat. No, there wasn't money for that today.

Mrs Davies placed the paper on the counter and Anwen dropped some coppers next to it.

'I guess the men will be out from the early shift soon and dropping in here for their baccy.'

'Yes, the first cages were coming up as I came out of the gate.' She picked up the paper and left.

Looking down the hill towards the pit, she saw the men start to tramp through the gate, tin boxes and bottles tucked under their arms. They were chatting and laughing, no doubt relieved to be in the light and the clean air once more. Anwen paused a while, imagining Idris among them. They'd often walked up Station Road and Jubilee Green together after the shift, arm in arm, even though Idris had been teased by the other men for it.

She was due another letter from him, for he tended to write once a week. It must be eight or nine days since she'd heard from him. The last three or four letters had become ever shorter. Normally he was full of humorous observations about the jumped-up little sergeant in charge and the funny mishaps he and his friends had suffered. She loved it best when he recalled the wonderful times they'd spent together, making it clear how much he missed her. The dwindling content of the letters might well indicate how hard they were training now, as the time of their departure grew ever closer.

She set off once more, rounding the corner onto Jubilee Green, envisaging Idris next to her. She fancied she could almost hear his voice, its deep, lilting rhythm, soothing her after the exhausting hours of work.

The illusion was broken as she came face to face with her oldest friend, Violet Jones, who'd just exited Schenck's book-shop on the corner. She was carrying Benjamin in one arm while balancing a basket in the other. Beside her was little Clarice.

'You look busy,' said Anwen.

'Thought I'd see if Mr Schenck had a nice second-hand book for Benjy. He's been a bit tearful. Reckon he's missing his da.' She pinched her lips together.

Anwen knew exactly what she was thinking. Why had Charlie enlisted in the war when he didn't need to? She'd thought the same thing, over and over again, about Idris. But at least they weren't married with two little kiddies.

'Now I've got to call at the greengrocer's,' said Violet.

'Would you like some help?'

'No, I'll let you get home. Your father's just coming up Station Road.'

Anwen looked down. Sure enough, Madog Rhys was striding up, gesticulating wildly as he spoke to a work mate.

'Yes, I'd better. I'll see you at chapel on Sunday.'

As they parted and Anwen carried on up the hill, she wished more than ever that Idris was here beside her. The war hadn't been over by Christmas 1914, as had been predicted. Idris had enlisted, with a group of other Dorcalon men, in March this year. They were still at the training camp but it couldn't be long now before they'd be sent off to France. Or further.

Reaching the top of the village, she stopped in front of the Workmen's Institute. The road here split into two: left onto Alexandra Street and right onto Edward Street. It would have been where she and Idris would have parted, at least until one of them visited the other's house. She recalled their various activities over the five years of their courtship; the visits to the picture house, the plays, musical shows and talks at the Workmen's Institute. They'd sung in the choir together. Every remembered moment was now precious to her. Would they ever happen again?

She wrapped an arm around her waist, holding in the pain. She couldn't bear the idea of him in mortal danger.

Perhaps the war would be over by *this* Christmas. She pictured him returning to her, marching up the road with his mates, each of them peeling off in turn to their own homes and loved ones. He'd spot her and come running up, throwing his arms around her. The image in her head brought a warm glow, blocking out the bone-cold chill of November.

'What you standing round for, you daft bint?' Her father stood on the pavement next to her, his hands on his hips and his eyes narrowed.

So taken had she been by her own imagination, she hadn't realised how long she'd been standing there.

'Sorry Da, just trying to remember something.' It was the best she could come up with.

'What you need to remember is to get home sharp, like, to help that halfwit of a sister of yours get my dinner ready. Been looking forward to that bit of mutton. Working bloody 'ard all morning, I've been.'

6

An old woman passed them in the road, tutting at Madog's bad language. He ignored her.

'Now run along before my boot helps you along.'

She didn't need telling twice. Lifting her skirt a little, she headed right down Edward Street and home.

–

Anwen dragged herself across the garden with the bowl of potato peelings. She'd been in a despondent mood since her walk home, unable to shake off the feeling that the war would not end well for Idris. She reached the compost heap and emptied the potato peelings absent-mindedly onto it, observing the slope of Twyn Gobaith, where it rose up steeply beyond her garden, the grass a deep green from the recent rain. A sigh from deep within signalled her reluctance to return to the stifling house, despite the icy breeze.

She'd taken but two steps backwards when she was brought to a halt by the sight of a figure trudging over the brow of the hill. She squinted, shielding her eyes against the sun. The knapsack slung across his back gave the unusually tall carrier a pronounced stoop. It could only be a soldier on leave. Her heart raced. Normally a few of them came together from the Rhondda Pals, the battalion the young men here, in Dorcalon, had joined.

The figure stopped to lower his load, straightening his back and stretching. It couldn't be, could it? No, it couldn't be Idris; it was her vivid imagination, sparked by having him so much on her mind today.

A voice, just audible from where she stood, hollered from the scullery. 'What the hell is it you're doin', girl!' Her father. 'Get in here now.'

She ignored the voice. It *was* Idris, her sweetheart, home on leave.

Anwen threw open the gate and struggled with the long skirt up the wet grassland. Idris leant down to pick the knapsack up again. Her voice, calling his name, was blown away by a whistling wind. He started tramping through the grass once more, staring straight ahead. She was only a few yards from him when she called again. 'Idris, Idris! Are you on leave? Are you being sent to the war soon?'

He did now perceive her, his eyes widening, and not, she feared, with the pleasure of seeing her.

She came to a halt beside him. 'Idris, *bach*, what's wrong? You didn't write to say you were coming. Where are the others?'

'Anwen.' He looked like he was about to step forward, but instead looked down at his feet. 'I'm sorry, I need to get home to sleep.'

She was stunned when he tramped on past her, not even stopping to kiss her, his trousers flapping around his legs. It was then that she noticed how thin he'd become. She followed him, two paces behind.

'Is it ill you are, *cariad*? You're so pale.'

He came to a sudden stop. Removing the cap, he pushed his fingers through his hair, disrupting the centre parting.

His deep brown eyes were hollowed, the surrounding skin dark, as though bruised. A shudder went through her. 'Idris, what on earth has happened?'

His Adam's apple bobbed up and down as he swallowed. It appeared strangely large. 'I'll explain – later.'

Her heart stirred for her intended, who bore an air of defeat. She leaned towards him, stroking his sleeve. 'How long on leave are you?'

He rubbed his forehead, squeezing his eyes tight shut. 'Not now.' He set off once again, his steps more purposeful.

'Idris? When shall I see you then?'

He took several strides away from her before half turning round to face her. 'I dunno,' he replied, before carrying on across the hillside.

Madog was sitting at the table, his arms crossed, when Anwen slipped through the kitchen door.

'You took your bloody time, girl.'

'I was talking to Idris, Da. He's just arrived on leave.' The worry of his cold reception coursed through her once again. Maybe he'd call round later, when he'd had a sleep.

She checked the pot over the fire to make sure the meal wasn't burning. Her father had performed a small miracle in getting hold of the mutton, which he'd brought home yesterday night. Her fifteen-year-old sister, Sara, had added potatoes, onions, carrots, leeks and stock to make a cawl.

'So that streak of bacon's back, is he? Don't see him and the others enlisting has made any bloody difference to the war.'

She offered no opinion. Where there should have been warmth in her heart at the prospect of seeing her beloved, there was a frosty anxiety.

Sara came through the door from the front room, her long hair, the colour of a hazelnut, loose. She was less pale today, her increased energy confirmed by the amount of housework she'd achieved that morning.

'Did you say Idris is on leave?' Sara placed the feather duster into a brass box on the floor and looked up, wide-eyed, at Anwen. Her dark brown eyes were stark against her fair complexion.

'Yes.' Anwen glanced at her father, but he was scrutinising the newspaper she'd picked up for him.

'When are you seeing him, then?'

'Oh I dunno. I'll let the poor lad have a good rest first. He looked fair worn out.'

Madog flicked the paper to straighten it. 'He should have been down the pit as many years as I have, then he'd be *fair worn out.*'

Anwen checked the simmering pot once more. 'The cawl's ready. Sara, would you take some up to Mam, please?'

'Of course.' She took the offered bowl and left the room.

Madog folded the paper noisily, slamming it on the other side of the table. 'About bloody time.'

Anwen served her father first. When Sara returned, the sisters sat together. Madog sat at the opposite end of the table and was already eating. There was no saying Grace before meals in Madog Rhys's house these days.

'Does Mam want any help?' asked Anwen.

'No. She insisted she could manage fine.'

Madog ignored the conversation, slurping at the stew before barking, 'Where's the bread?'

Anwen sprang up. Heading towards the larder in the scullery she said, 'There's only a bit left. I was hoping to make it stretch till Friday, when I can afford the sixpence it now costs.'

'A bit's all I want.'

She brought it back with a serrated knife and wooden board, putting it down in front of him.

'Where's the margarine?'

'It's finished, Da.'

'Then buy some more.'

'Mrs Brace at the grocer's had run out, Da,' Sara said.

He grunted, tearing off half the bread in a chunk. He dunked it in the stew, shoved it through his lips and chewed it with his mouth half open.

'*Ych a fi!*' he shouted, spitting bits everywhere, throwing the remainder towards the fire. The bread was consumed by the flames.

Anwen wanted to protest about the wasted bread, but she knew better. 'It's dry Da, that's all. There's not enough bread now to buy it every day.'

Madog emitted a deep rumble in reply. 'It's about time you got a job,' her father bellowed, pointing his spoon at Sara, mouth bulging with cawl. 'Your sister's been workin' since she were fourteen. Seven year she been workin'.'

That hadn't been Anwen's choice. She'd wanted to continue at school, maybe train for teaching. Not that she could have taught once she'd married Idris, but there had to be something useful she could do.

'Well? Cat got your tongue?'

Sara swallowed the food she'd been eating. 'I'll go down the village, see if there's some work in the shops.'

'There's plenty of work at the mine, sorting coal.'

'Da, that's not—' Anwen started.

'I don't want to hear from you. Nothin' wrong with mine work.'

Anwen remembered an idea she'd had, when she'd seen her mam's brother in the grocer's the day before. 'Da, Uncle Hywel is searching for new lodgings, on account his landlady, Mrs Price, is moving her mother in.'

The mumbled, 'So?' was barely audible.

'Well, we've got three bedrooms. Sara and I could move in together. We wouldn't mind, would we, Sara?'

Her sister's face lit up. 'No, not at all.'

'He could have a room, and that would really help us out with money, and—'

'No.'

'But Da—'

'I said bloody no! I don't want your mother's brother snoopin' around here, you understand?' He pointed the dripping spoon at her.

'Yes Da.'

Madog slurped at the stew once more. Sara took hold of Anwen's hand under the table and squeezed it tight.

Chapter Two

Going round the back of the village, slipping home unseen, had seemed like a good idea to Idris at the time. Why had fate put Anwen in the back garden at that moment? He loved her rosy cheeks and the full lips that often smiled, displaying her big-hearted nature. There'd been sadness behind that smile today though. Her hair, reaching her waist on the rare occasions he'd seen it down, had been dishevelled, yet had only served to make her more beautiful. His longing to see her had grown into apprehension in the last few days, because… If he couldn't bear to think it, how was he going to say it, even to Mam and Da?

He should have gone to Merthyr, to Da's relatives. There were mining jobs everywhere since men started enlisting. But no, his family needed him. *You didn't think of them when you signed up*, he heard his friend Gwilym's voice admonish him.

He dragged his feet over the hill, behind the houses on Edward Street. He shivered, despite the coat. It had been kind of Colonel Williams to give it to him, even if it was, as he'd explained, an *old one*.

The hoarse rasp of the pit wheels, a sound he was once so used to he was mostly unaware of it, jarred his nerves.

At the end of Anwen's terrace he turned slightly right, to head behind Alexandra Street. It continued at the opposite angle to Edward Street, making them together look like open butterfly wings when viewed from the opposite side of the valley. *Come on, not far to go.* Dread filled his stomach like a heap of coal being tipped into a tram.

A shout went up and he noticed half a dozen boys gambolling down the hill. He knew them all, most of them younger brothers of mining colleagues.

'Hey, Idris,' shouted one. 'You home on leave, then?'

It was Evan, Gwilym's younger brother, his tanned skin darker still with mud. Idris didn't want to speak to anyone, but ignoring them would cause more attention. 'What are you scallywags up to? Shouldn't you be at school?'

A boy called Cyril came up behind Evan, his red thatch of hair sticking out at all angles. 'Finished early today, didn't it? And we're not up to anything, Idris, mun. We're collecting sticks for a Guy Fawkes Night fire.'

Were people still bothered about a man who'd tried to blow up a selfish king and a few MPs three hundred years ago, when there were good men being blown up all over the world right now? A simmering anger gnawed at his guts. He pushed it away. 'Bonfires aren't allowed now. Nor fireworks. Defence of the Realm Act, isn't it.'

'Oh, give over, Idris,' Evan said. 'We'll only make a small one, away from the village.'

'Well I don't want to know about it.'

'You're in the 2nd Rhondda Battalion aren't you?' Cyril asked. 'You killed anyone yet?'

'They haven't gone anywhere yet,' Evan said. 'Mrs Vaughan's Percy told her and she told my mam. And they're the 114th Brigade of the 38th Division now. They're still training at Winchester.'

Percy Vaughan. He was fit and ready to march off to foreign lands next month. As were Charlie, Henry, Maurice, Robert and the rest of them. Not like him.

Cyril screwed up his eyes. 'That right, Idris?'

'That's right.'

'I wish I was old enough to enlist. I'd kill them boche, I would.' Cyril dropped all the sticks, apart from a large one. He pointed it at each of his pals in turn. 'Pow, pow, pow, p-pow. You're all dead!'

Each boy clutched his chest and made a variety of noises, two of them falling to the ground.

The innocent charade made Idris uncomfortable. 'You boys better get those sticks away before someone else sees you with them, like Harries the Police.'

Cyril gathered his sticks together and the group continued to hurtle across the hill calling, 'Bye Idris,' and, 'See ya!'

The first drops of drizzle moistened his face as the clouds darkened and swallowed the overconfident sun.

Finally at his own back garden, he undid the gate catch, carrying his backpack awkwardly to the door. Taking a deep breath, he opened it with caution. The scent of soap was mingled with a vague whiff of meat stock, welcoming him home. The familiarity briefly gladdened his heart, in the way seeing Anwen used to. Still did. Except he didn't want it to.

'Hello?' he called.

There was singing coming from the kitchen beyond. His mother's voice. He tramped through to see the fire burning brightly in the range, on top of it a steaming kettle, in front a tin bath. Everything was as it would have been any other Friday afternoon he'd lived here.

'Mam?'

Meg Hughes twisted round. 'Oh my goodness, Idris!'

He stepped forward and threw his arms around her. 'Hello Mam.'

'Good heavens, *bach*, you scared the daylights out of me.' She clung onto him, her head barely reaching his shoulder. 'You didn't send word to say you were on leave.'

'No, I'm—'

He was unable to get out any explanation before Meg launched into the latest village news. When she went back to the scullery to fetch more water to heat, there was a faint knock on the front door. He ignored it, glad of his decision when he spied Florrie Harris pass by.

When Meg returned, Idris said, 'Da not in yet?'

'No. He probably went to pick up some baccy from Mr Davies and must've got chatting there.'

'Mam, I—'

'Jenkin will be so pleased to see you. He's got involved with the scouts and that keeps him and his friends occupied.'

As she finished saying this, they heard the back door open and a voice call, 'Hello? Whose is this rucksack?' Isaiah tramped in, grinning broadly, still sooty from his shift. 'We didn't know you were due home on leave, *bach*.'

This was the moment. He took a deep breath. 'I'm not on leave.'

'What is it then, desertion?' Isaiah laughed heartily.

Idris glanced from his father to his mother. His head ached with the pressure of his news.

Isaiah stood in front of the bath, concealing the range with his solid frame. 'What's up, lad?'

Idris pulled out a chair from the table, sitting heavily. 'I've been discharged. On medical grounds.'

His mother's hands flew to her cheeks as she exclaimed, 'Oh *bach*, what's wrong?'

'My heart beats a bit too fast, that's all. Not good for soldiering apparently.'

'But you managed to hew coal for five of your ten years down the mine.'

'Aye, I did. But we don't get examined by the doctor at the mine, do we?'

Isaiah shook his head solemnly. 'No lad, we don't.' He released a full throaty wheeze of a cough. 'Well, *bach*, you'll be wanting your old job back, or are you not fit for that anymore either?'

Idris stood up from the chair, stretching to his full height. 'I can cope with it fine. I could have coped with the war. But they've got rules.'

'Why don't you have a rest for a few weeks?' his mother suggested. 'Till after Christmas. You look all done in.'

The back door slammed shut. He'd better say what he had to quickly.

'No, Mam. I can't live off you and Da. I'll go down Monday, see if they've got work.'

'Oh they'll have work all right,' said Isaiah. 'We've had a few newcomers replace those who've enlisted, and they're about as much use as a straw pick.'

Fifteen-year-old Jenkin appeared in the doorway. 'You're not going off to war, then?'

'No, your brother's staying, thanks be to the Lord,' said Meg. 'His heart beats a bit too fast for the army's liking, but he's perfectly fine otherwise.'

Jenkin ran to Idris, throwing his arms around his chest. 'I'm proud of you, Idris, for being willing to fight for what's right, even if you can't fight now. It's nice to have you home though.'

Idris enfolded his little brother in his arms, so touched by the show of respect and affection that he felt a lump form in his throat. 'Thank you, *bach*.' Despite Jenkin's words, he couldn't help but feel he'd let him down.

'Now Jenkin, scrub your father's back for him,' said Meg. 'I want to heat up yesterday's soup for dinner.'

'But Mam, I want to meet up with my friends.'

'Don't argue with your mother,' said Isaiah. 'The quicker you get it done, the quicker you'll get out.' Talking to his wife now he said, 'Did you manage to get any meat for supper?' His eyes crinkled in hope.

'Yes, the butcher had a few rabbits in today so I bought one. The scrawny pigeons weren't worth the money.'

Idris sat, watching the ritual he'd grown up with. His father shed soiled clothes onto the stone floor before he stepped into the bath. He lathered up the bar of Lifebuoy soap, washing his front then handing it to Jenkin, who had the scrubbing brush at the ready. An inky layer of dust floated on the surface of the bath water.

As they continued with the task, Idris's mind wandered to his pals still at Winchester, getting ready for the off. When his mother finally tapped him on the shoulder, the bath had been cleared and the table laid.

'You look fit for bed already,' she said, placing a bowl of vegetable soup in front of him. He leaned in, taking a deep breath. 'That smells wonderful, Mam. You put some of your dried wild herbs in here?'

'One of the things you can still find in abundance. You should invite Anwen over one supper-time. You can discuss the wedding now. You were meant to get married summer just gone.'

Idris pointed his fork at Jenkin. 'I don't want everyone knowing the reason for my discharge.'

'If you give me a coupla coppers…'

'You do as you're told,' said Isaiah. 'If I find you've opened your gob I'll tan your backside, you hear?'

'Such a lovely girl is Anwen,' Meg persisted. 'You won't find a finer girl in the whole of the Rhymney Valley.'

He couldn't argue, because that was the problem. Instead he kept quiet and ate his food.

–

Sara appeared in the small scullery as Anwen poured steaming water from the kettle into the sink. She watched as Anwen scraped flakes of Sunlight soap into the water before adding soda crystals and swishing the water around.

'Mam's fallen asleep already. She seems even more exhausted than normal today.' Sara leaned against the dark wood draining board.

'Meg's visit yesterday tired her out.'

'Has Da gone?'

'Yes. Said he'd have supper when he got back.'

'The McKenzie Arms isn't closing any earlier since the Defence of the Realm Act,' said Sara.

'So it would seem.' They both knew the public house would benefit from their father's wages tonight, as it did most nights.

'Anwen, do you think Mam will ever get up again? I mean walk. Not just because Uncle Hywel has carried her down.'

Sara frowned and Anwen knew why. Da had kicked up a fuss six months back when he'd come home to find Mam tucked up on the chaise longue downstairs. When he'd shouted at Hywel that it would kill her, Mam had burst into tears. Yet before Da had arrived she'd been the chirpiest they'd seen her in a long while. Uncle Hywel had carried her tiny frame back up and promptly left. He only came round now when he knew Da wouldn't be there.

'I dunno, Sara. The hospital said she's recovered from the fall as far as they could tell.'

'But they don't know everything. What about Jane Probert next door but one? They sent her home saying she was all right, and next day she was – *dead*.' The last word was whispered. 'And her with a new baby.'

'The post mortem said it was a growth in her stomach. They can't always know that, doctors. Especially as she was pregnant just before.' Anwen's sinuses stung recalling the sad demise of Jane, only two years older than her.

Sara, in the middle of wiping a plate, halted. 'I'm scared.'

Anwen dropped the wire wool into the water before wiping her hands on the pinny. She wound her arms around Sara's petite body, a full three inches shorter than her own. She rested her sister's head on her shoulder.

'What are you scared of, *fach*? Mam's doing fine. Her brain's not been affected by the fall. She enjoys reading the books I get from the Institute library.'

Sara gazed up at Anwen. 'It's not a life, though. And her brain must be affected. She can't remember falling.'

Anwen sighed. 'I know. But the doctor did say it wasn't cause for concern.'

'I wish Da would get the doctor back, especially since it doesn't cost anything.'

'Apart from the subs the workers pay towards the hospital each week, but yes, I understand what you mean. I'm not sure the doctor can do anything else.'

Sara stepped back from her sister's embrace, studying the four walls of the kitchen in turn. 'Death is all around us,' she whimpered.

'The Bible says, *In the midst of life we are in death*. It's always been so.'

Sara's gaze was unfocused. 'Sometimes I think I can feel it, Death, like Jack Frost, moving through the village, through our house, breathing on me in the night.'

A tremor cut through Anwen to her core. She was unsure how to bring this conversation to an end. Sara, for all her love of musicals, books and flowers, for all her kindness to wildlife and other people, had always been a child of sorrows. She felt losses and distresses most keenly, from a dead bird in the woods to a drooping flower, from a lost friendship to a cruel word from one person to another, she took them all to heart.

'There's been so much death in the village, so many of them children. Four on our street alone in the last year. And six miners in the last eighteen months.'

Anwen was relieved when Sara omitted all the deaths from consumption, mainly women. And the old men, and not so old men, coughing their life blood away with years breathing in the black dust.

Anwen squared her shoulders. 'We've much to be thankful for, Sara. Mam's family worked the fields in Cardiganshire for less money, in pouring rain, summer blaze and freezing wind. The houses here are new. A *model* village they called it, when they opened the Workmen's Institute and hospital five years back. So enough of this talk. Let's get finished up and get ready to go to the Institute.'

Sara's face brightened. 'I'm *so* excited about seeing *The Bohemian Girl*. Mrs Brace at the grocer's said she saw it on Wednesday and lovely, it was. Said Mrs Jones from Owain

Street is playing the Gipsy Queen. Beautiful voice, she has.' Sara slumped, a frown taking over once more. 'I only wish Mam could come with us.'

Anwen rubbed her sister's back. 'You can tell her all about it when we get back.'

Regaining the smile, Sara said, 'Yes, I'll do that.'

–

Between the top of Jubilee Green and the Workmen's Institute, people were gathering in large numbers when Anwen and Sara arrived. The moonless night was illuminated by the Institute's lights. Arm in arm, the sisters were wrapped in coats and gloves, their mother's old hats perched atop their neatly pinned hair.

Anwen surveyed the line of people. Idris was unlikely to be here. A painful anxiety coursed through her as she recalled his haggard appearance and how cold he'd been towards her. She'd been able to gauge his mood since they were nippers, both recently arrived in the new village. The cheeky smile and wayward black curls of the nine-year-old Idris, three years her senior, had attracted her from the beginning. She'd seen through the cavalier, joking lad to the kind heart beneath. He'd always defended the smaller, weaker children against bullies, gaining him a grudging respect over the years from the more aggressive boys. They weren't keen to cross him, tall and sturdy as he was.

'You're smiling,' Sara said, knocking her arm gently.

'Just glad my sweetheart's back, even if for a short time. Come on, let's join the queue.'

Sara huddled closer to her. 'Can you smell that? It's like a bonfire.'

'Whoever that is will get into trouble if Sergeant Harries catches them.'

'I love bonfires,' Sara said. 'They remind me of being a little girl. Do you remember how Da used to burn the twigs and autumn leaves at the bottom of our garden? We'd all help him collect them. You and me. Tomos and Geraint.' She spoke the latter names faintly. 'He used to keep the garden tidy back then.'

He did, thought Anwen, in those days before their brothers passed on. They'd loved the physical work of the garden, digging alongside Da. Sometimes they'd sing a rousing chorus or two, one or other of them adding a harmony. She'd be tending the flowers with Sara and Mam, or hoeing and pruning. If they'd done a good bit of work, Da would get Mam to make some sandwiches so they could picnic on the hill behind the garden. It was so far away from their lives now, it was like a dream.

Their uncle's landlady, Winnie Price, joined the queue behind them, flanked by Florrie Harris, a neighbour of Idris's. 'I hear your intended's on leave, Anwen. Florrie says she saw him go through his garden earlier.'

'Aye, I saw him,' the older woman said, her threadbare coat obvious even in the dim light. 'Why isn't my Robert back then?' Her face displayed a mixture of worry and annoyance.

'I'm afraid I don't know, Mrs Harris. I've only seen Idris briefly.'

'I knocked on the door to ask, but no one answered. I just keep praying the war will end and my Robert will never have to set foot on foreign soil. Why did he enlist when he didn't have to? And him with seven babbies to support.'

'There'll come a time when they'll all have to enlist, you mark my words,' Mrs Price said. 'What do you think the Derby Scheme's all about, getting the men to agree that they'll join the forces in the future? They'll pour ever more of our lads' blood onto foreign soil.'

Sara's grip on Anwen's arm tightened.

'Give over, woman,' came another voice. It was Edgar Williams, the under-manager at the pit, complete with bowler hat. He'd arrived with his wife and younger son. 'So, our hero's back on leave, is he?'

'There's no need to mock, Edgar Williams,' Mrs Harris said. 'Just trying to do right by their country and Mr Lloyd George they are.'

'Lloyd bloody George,' the under-manager said. 'Him and his pretty speeches. All very well for other men to go and fight, but he's robbing *me* of good miners. It's our quality steam coal'll help our navy win this war. What are we going to do, get the *women* to dig the coal out?' He spat on the ground.

A young man ran across the road, calling, 'There you are.' It was Edgar's older son Daniel, smiling as profusely as his father was scowling.

'Just talking to the ladies, son,' he said lightly, as if they'd been discussing a concert at the chapel.

Daniel chewed at his top lip before saying, 'Hello, Anwen. It's been a while since I've seen you.'

She noticed the smart tie and his shirt with a fold-down collar. 'It is.'

'Ah, there are the Merediths at the front of the queue,' Edgar said. 'Come along. We will join *them*.' He took his wife's and younger son's arms and the three of them hurried off, pushing in to join the mine manager and his wife.

'Sorry,' Daniel said. 'I'd better go. Perhaps we'll talk after the performance?'

Anwen shrugged. 'Perhaps.'

His smile lingered a few seconds before he ran off to join his parents.

'That's it, run after Mama and Papa,' Sara said after he'd gone, injecting her accent with a heavy dose of posh English, copying the phoney inflection of Daniel's mother, Esther Williams.

'Sara, don't. He's a nice boy. At least, he was at school.'

'Never mind him.' Mrs Harris said, leaning between them. 'The queue's moving, so shift along.'

–

22

'That was wonderful,' Sara shouted over the enthusiastic clapping, after the last triumphant chorus of 'Oh, What a Full Delight' ended the opera.

Anwen tilted her head towards Sara's ear. 'My favourite was "I Dreamt I Dwelt in Marble Halls".'

'Oh yes, that was beautiful.'

The clapping went on for a full two minutes. After the performers, choir and orchestra accepted the audience's appreciation, the conductor took his bow. Anwen and Sara shuffled along the chairs, only to be faced with Daniel Williams in the aisle.

'Hello again.'

'Hello.' Anwen searched her mind for something else to say, as he only grinned. 'How are you finding the bank in Tredegar?'

'Fine. What are you doing? Helping at home?'

'Screening. At the mine.'

'I see. You should have stayed at school. You were the cleverest in the class.'

His ignorance grated on her. 'Some of us need to earn as early as possible, to help our families.'

She hadn't meant to be cruel, but he didn't inhabit the same world as her, even though he only lived around the corner on Jubilee Green.

'I suppose so,' he conceded, holding her gaze.

'We don't see you or your family at chapel anymore.'

'We go to St Peter's now.' He leant forward a little to whisper with a grin, 'Mama thinks it's more posh.'

It was her turn to say, 'I see.'

'Daniel!' Esther Williams called over from several rows ahead.

'Coming, Mama.' His gaze swivelled back towards Anwen. 'I'd better go and join them.'

Anwen said quickly, 'We have concerts at the chapel that everyone's welcome to.'

He stopped in the middle of moving away, his eyes examining hers. 'Will you be singing?'

'Sometimes, yes.'

He nodded and left. When he was out of earshot, Sara said, 'Does he know you're spoken for?'

Anwen frowned. 'What difference does that make?'

'Daniel Williams likes you. You were encouraging him.'

Anwen let go of Sara's arm. 'I was not. I was being friendly to an old school chum. No harm in that.'

'I do hope you're right. I'd hate for you to end up with Mr Williams as a father-in-law. Or worse, Esther Williams as a mother-in-law!'

Anwen was about to exclaim her horror at the idea when she spotted Sara's grin.

'Sara, that is not funny!'

'Yes it is.'

Anwen laughed. 'All right, it is. And ludicrous.'

They started down the steps, weaving through the crowd, towards the exit.

'What a shame Mam's not able to join us on these nights out anymore,' said Sara. 'She did love the musical performances so.'

'Do you remember that operetta we came to about six years back, *The Merry Milkmaids*?'

'Oh yes!' Sara clapped her hands together. 'It took a lot of pleading to get Mam to let me stay up for that.'

'I recall Mam singing some of the songs on the way home, even though it was gone ten o'clock. Old Mr Hughes at number ten leant out of his bedroom window to tell her to shut up, as I recall.'

'Oh yes. And because he was always rude to everybody, she sang all the louder! And we joined in too.'

Both girls giggled so hard they couldn't stop.

When Anwen managed to get her breath back, she said, 'Come on, let's get home, see if Mam's awake so we can tell her about tonight.'

Idris hadn't wanted to come to chapel, not this soon, but he hadn't the heart to upset his mother. If he sat with his head low enough, as if in prayer, people might not realise it was him. The three-piece suit, purchased for Sundays and special occasions from a near neighbour when her son died, was now too big for him.

People were entering in a steady stream, filling the simple wooden pews of the Ainon Baptist Chapel. He had the misfortune to look up as Anwen passed with her sister and uncle. He couldn't bring himself to return her smile, even though the sight of her lightened his heart.

The service passed slowly, Idris thinking his own thoughts while the minister held forth with much enthusiasm. He spent the time imagining his trip to the pit tomorrow, to ask for his job back, the many scenarios that might unfold, his stomach squirming as he pictured each in turn. Having exhausted all the possibilities, he planned how he'd affect a quick escape from the service.

But the latter was not to be. As he followed his mother out of the pew she grabbed his arm.

'Let's get a cup of tea, *bach*,' she said, pointing to one side of the chapel, to a room where people were beginning to congregate. Jenkin had already raced outside with some of his friends.

'I don't think—' he began.

'No point running away, lad,' said his father. 'You've got to face people eventually. No shame in being discharged on health grounds.'

He followed his parents, not acknowledging the smiles or curious glances in his direction. Before he reached the door of the side room, Anwen appeared suddenly in front of him.

'Idris.'

'Anwen.'

'I've seen nothing of you since you arrived. When are you due back to camp?'

Idris's mouth opened to answer, but he didn't know what to say. When he did speak he said, 'Can we take a walk outside, to talk?'

'Of course. I'll go and tell Sara and Uncle Hywel.'

His mother was only feet away, regarding him. 'Making plans, that's good.'

When Anwen returned, she and Idris wound their way through the crowds, exiting down the steps onto Gabriel Street.

'Let's go along to Mafeking Terrace.' His heart thumped against his ribcage and he found it hard to swallow.

They set off to the right. She took his arm, making him uncomfortable. Maybe he should have written, given her some clue. But that was the coward's way, not his way.

The street before them was still damp from an earlier downpour that had come and gone within five minutes. The reflection of the low winter sun in the puddles appeared like circles of gold.

As they passed the last house on the terrace, the valley opened up before them with the mountains beyond. The forest green of the low vegetation, the lighter, lush grass and the earthy browns of the bare trees were picked out in turn. In the floor of the valley stood a separate group of buildings: Dyffryn Gwyrdd Farm.

'So, how long have you got?' Anwen took no notice of the scene, looking instead along the road that led to Rhymney.

'I've been discharged. Health's not good at the moment.' It came out in a rush.

She stopped, unlinking her arm from his, her brow furrowed. 'Oh Idris, what's wrong with you?'

'It's nothing. Just, my heart beats too fast.'

'Tachycardia?' Her voice was breathy.

She was so clever. Too clever for this small place. 'Yes, that's what the doctor called it.'

'Oh Idris. I read about it in a medical book I found in Schenck's bookshop. Thought it might help me find out what's wrong with Mam.' She took hold of his arm, caressing it with her thumb. 'What are you going to do about it?'

'Nothing. It's just the army fussing. I'm returning to the mine.' He twisted left to look back at the colliery. A few men were doing Sunday shifts now, according to his father. So even on a day of rest he couldn't escape the audible reminder of his fate.

'You're going back to the pit with tachycardia?' There was something approaching panic in her voice.

He huffed through his nose, a feigned impatience. But it was a fair question. 'It's only a fast heartbeat. The doctor didn't even mention it at the initial examination. They let me go through the training. Probably just an infection.'

'So, you're home for good?' She couldn't hide the relief in her voice.

'I am. But – Anwen, I don't want to get married now. Not with the war. Not with everything unsure.'

Her face fell. 'Surely that's a *good* reason to get married. When *do* you want to do it, then?'

It's for her good, if not yours. Just do it. 'Never, Anwen. I'm sorry.' He couldn't say anything that suggested he'd change his mind in the future. He had to give her the chance to find someone else, someone who wouldn't die prematurely and leave her with little children.

Tears formed in the corners of her eyes as she squeezed them shut momentarily. 'You mean, you don't love me anymore?'

He hesitated. 'No.'

She gasped as more tears fell. Turning on her heels, she hurried away as quickly as her skirt and petticoat would allow.

Idris groaned quietly. This was the worst thing he'd ever had to do, even worse than carrying Tommy Morgan's body from the mine to his family home, three years back. He peered down the long road in the opposite direction to where Anwen had fled. A walk to Rhymney would be best now, to work off this terrible guilt and sadness.

He hadn't gone many steps when he found himself rubbing the bridge of his nose. There was a handkerchief in his pocket, which he pulled out, pretending to himself that he was starting a cold and it was irritating his eyes. He wiped at them and blew his nose, but couldn't stop the briny drops from trickling down his face.

–

Anwen ran back to Gabriel Street, past the chapel, ignoring her friends Violet and Gwen, who called hello as they stood by the gate. She could barely see for the tears stinging her eyes. She didn't want anyone seeing her like this.

Twisting left, she hurried up the hill, past the fancier houses of the traders and under-manager on Jubilee Green, with their bits of front garden and railings. She crossed the road, ran past the communal gardens, finally taking a right past the Workmen's Institute and onto Edward Street. She hurried down the road until she reached her own home.

Rushing into the kitchen, she noticed the fire was almost out in the grate. She'd need to build it up again, keep the house warm for Sara. These trivial thoughts she used to divert her mind from the cold reality of Idris's words. The hurtful truth wrung any joy she'd had from seeing him today.

She dragged out a chair, before collapsing into it. Alone in the room, she allowed the sobs full reign.

Idris had told her once that he would adore her until the day one of them left this earth, and then beyond that too.

Anwen had been the happiest she'd ever been that day. Idris had scooped her behind a tree and kissed her. What happened after was the most wonderful moment of her life: he'd got down on one knee and proposed. She'd only been sixteen, and he nineteen, but she'd known all along he'd be the only one for her.

Had the army training changed him that much? Or was it his condition? But it did happen; people did fall out of love.

Anwen raised her head, fancying she heard a sound. Not their father, please. Maybe Sara wondering where she'd got to? No, it was a distant voice calling, 'Hello?'

It was Mam.

Yes, it was her mother she needed now.

Chapter Three

Anwen examined the fancy front door. It was dark green with a large pane of glass. In the semi-circular window above the door was written 'McKenzie House'. She tapped the knocker and awaited a reply. There'd be lost wages for taking a morning off from the pit, but there was nothing else for it. She wanted this job even more now there was no prospect of marrying Idris. A wave of nausea passed through her.

As she waited, her hands were clammy. She'd seen Mrs Meredith, the mine manager's wife, around the village. She was a polite woman, but haughty.

The door was opened by Miss Meredith, who she'd seen at chapel, though her parents attended St Peter's, the parish church on Gabriel Street, a few yards along on the other side of the road from the chapel. The young woman smiled as she said, 'It's Anwen Rhys, isn't it? *Bore da.*'

Anwen was thrown initially by the use of her first language to say good morning. Not many of the elite used it. Perhaps Miss Meredith knew a little and was trying to make her feel welcome. 'Yes. *Bore da.* I'm here about the housemaid's job.'

'Of course. Come in.'

Miss Meredith appeared a few years older than her, around twenty-five perhaps. Her skirt was short, showing half her calf. Her own father would have belted her from this village to the next if she'd dared to expose so much of her legs. On the young woman's feet were shoes with a buckle and a heel. Her blouse was white with lace and embroidery. Anwen felt shabby beside her, with her worn-out boots and long skirt that had been her grandmother's.

'Mother is in the dining room. It's this way.' Miss Meredith went ahead along the wide hallway, with its terracotta and green floor tiles. At the end she opened a door, allowing Anwen to enter first.

Margaret Meredith was sitting at a heavy oak table with papers in front of her. Her hair was expertly pinned up. Close up, Anwen could see that her skin was good for her likely age.

'Mother, this is Anwen Rhys, about the housemaid's job.'

'Of course. Sit down here opposite me.' Her accent was only faintly Welsh, in comparison to her daughter's. 'Elizabeth, it would be a good idea for you to stay. You'll need to hire staff when you *eventually* marry. Take a seat.' She pointed at the end of the highly polished table.

There was amusement on Elizabeth's face. 'Yes Mama.'

'So, Miss Rhys, what experience do you have for this post?'

'Well, I've never worked as a maid before, but I've helped my mam keep house for these last seven years. The last year I've run the house myself, as she's ill, though my sister helps now she's left school.' She was yapping on, as her father would say. This woman didn't want to know her family history. 'I've also worked for seven years at the pit, screening coal. I know that's not housework but...'

'I suppose it shows you're strong,' Mrs Meredith concluded. 'A job and keeping house. That cannot be easy.'

'No, but I manage to keep up with it all. And now, with the war, we women all have to do our bit.'

'Quite so, quite so. Are you not tempted, therefore, to work at the munitions factory at Ebbw Vale, like some of the other girls?'

Gwen had started there a few months back. The money was likely better than here. 'With my mother unwell, I don't want to take extra time travelling to Ebbw Vale, or get lodgings away.'

'Very commendable, Miss Rhys, that you value your family.' She shuffled some papers in front of her, though why was not obvious. 'Why do you want to change jobs? Your current one is in the village already.'

'Screening is not very… well it's not—'

Elizabeth came to her rescue. 'It's not a nice job, is it Anwen? It's dirty and hard.'

'But necessary,' said Mrs Meredith. She placed on her nose a small pair of spectacles, regarding one of the sheets of paper in front of her. 'Your duties would start at six a.m., cleaning grates, setting the fires downstairs, before serving us breakfast.'

She nodded, showing she understood.

'You wouldn't be cooking, of course. We have Rose for that. After serving breakfast, you would dust and sweep every room. The bathroom is also cleaned every day.'

They had a proper bathroom?

'Each day, one or two rooms are given a proper clean. The kitchen and scullery, however, are Rose's responsibility. Mondays and Tuesdays, Onner arrives to wash and iron the clothes. Come, I will show you around the house and tell you what each room requires in detail.' She kept her back straight as she stood, running her hands down her skirt to neaten it. 'Elizabeth, you may accompany us.'

'Yes Mama.'

Anwen felt a flutter of excitement. She had long desired to explore this house.

The two older women led the way back into the hall, opening another door to enter a larger room. As the tour began, Mrs Meredith gave her the specifics of her job. Anwen concentrated hard in order to remember the details so she wouldn't need to ask too many times.

The room Mrs Meredith referred to as the *drawing room*, possessed yellow wallpaper with embossed flowers. At the windows the curtains, luxuriously draped, were a plain yellow. There were two settees, both cream velvet Chesterfields, plus a leather, buttoned, winged armchair. There were paintings on the walls and photographs on the mantelpiece and occasional table.

On the ground floor there was also Mr Meredith's study, with a sturdy oak desk and bookshelves filled with many volumes. The bedrooms all contained beds with honey-coloured inlaid wooden headboards and deep, silk quilts, along with well-polished dressing tables and solid wardrobes. Her own house possessed only chests of drawers, handed down through several generations. The rugs all over McKenzie House were colourful and thick on the gleaming wooden floors.

Having peered briefly into the master bedroom, Miss Meredith's room and the guest room, they came to a fourth door. Mrs Meredith knocked on it.

'Yes?' a male voice within called.

'I'm coming in, Tom, to show the possible new housemaid.'

'All right.'

Mrs Meredith opened the door to reveal a handsome man, around Anwen's age, propped up on the bed, a book in hand. His hair was a rich, dark auburn, as was his short moustache.

'Come in.' Tom beamed widely at Anwen as she followed his mother inside, his blue eyes twinkling. 'So this young lady might be replacing Jenny?' His accent betrayed no evidence of his Welsh roots.

Mrs Meredith didn't reply, saying instead: 'You may find this room a little more of a challenge than the others.' She frowned at Tom.

The floor was strewn with clothes while the bedside cabinet, dresser and drawer top were covered with books, papers, cufflinks and other odds and ends.

'Mother, you know that we creative people are untidy,' he said, following it with a chuckle. 'What's your name?'

'Anwen Rhys, sir.'

'Welcome to McKenzie House, Anwen Rhys.'

'She hasn't got the position yet,' said Mrs Meredith.

'Of course she has. No one else is going to come forward. Too busy doing more essential work, which is better paid.'

'Tom!' said Elizabeth.

'You know it's true, Lizzie.'

His mother tutted, gesturing for them to leave. 'Please clear up before Jenny reaches your room to clean.'

'Yes, Mother.' Tom leapt from the bed, stretching. She didn't see what he did next as Mrs Meredith shut the door.

Where was Jenny? It was she who'd mentioned at the chapel that there was a position going. They were the same age and had gone through school together, though she'd never been as good a friend as Violet and Gwen. She was marrying the minister's son, Joseph. Lucky her.

Just before they reached the stairs, Jenny emerged from the door they hadn't yet entered. The water closet was a proper one with a wooden seat, not like the one her family had in the garden.

'All finished in the bathroom?'

'Yes, madam.' Jenny dipped her knee a little.

'Good. Then you can explain to Miss Rhys what needs to be done in there.'

—

Back in the dining room once more, Mrs Meredith sat down. Anwen stood opposite her, having not been invited to take a seat this time.

'During the morning cleaning you would have a short break,' Mrs Meredith began. 'There will be half an hour for lunch, before you start on the afternoon duties.'

Lunch. What she called dinner.

'In the afternoons, there will be outdoor cleaning and seasonal jobs. Often you will change into a black dress I will provide, and put on an apron. You will then be tidy to run errands for me and answer the door when people call.'

That didn't sound so bad. It all depended now on what wage would be offered. If it really was what Jenny had indicated, it would keep her father happy and provide her with enough money.

34

'Your wage per week would be...' She glanced at the sheet. 'Um, thirteen shillings—'

Anwen's heart sank.

'Eighteen, Mama. Father said we'd have to compete with the wage for screening coal.'

The older woman put her spectacles on. 'Oh, yes, eighteen shillings per week.'

Eighteen shillings! She was getting sixteen from the mine. Her father surely couldn't object now.

'If you wish to take the position, of course,' Mrs Meredith added. 'Initially on a month's trial.'

She wanted to exclaim her excitement, but suppressed the outburst. She wanted to appear calm and refined. 'Yes please.'

'I require you to begin next Monday, as Jenny is getting married on Saturday. Very inconvenient, as she has been an excellent maid and I don't suppose I'll find better this side of the war.'

'I'm sure we should give Miss Rhys a chance to prove otherwise before we make such statements, Mama,' Elizabeth said.

Those small words of encouragement transformed a moment of disheartenment for Anwen into a determination to show how good she could be. Yes, she'd be even better than Jenny. 'I will do my very best, Mrs Meredith. Thank you.'

Mrs Meredith glanced up at Anwen, lips pursed. 'I will require you to refer to me as *madam*, and to Mr Meredith as *sir*.'

'Yes, madam.' She gave a little curtsy, as she'd seen Jenny do.

'I have a meeting now with the other ladies of the Prisoners of War Fund committee. We're arranging a concert with a *first* class programme of music recitals. Lady Felicity Rees-Thomas is our chairwoman you know, a personal friend, of course.'

Anwen nodded and smiled, for she was sure the name was meant to impress her.

Margaret finished by saying, 'That will be all. My daughter will show you out.'

Elizabeth led her down the hall to the front door. She opened it and waited for Anwen to catch up. 'Welcome to McKenzie House.'

'Thank you, Miss Meredith.' She dipped a knee again.

'Elizabeth. And you don't need to curtsy to me. I know Mother won't approve so call me Miss Elizabeth when she's around, but otherwise… Honestly, you're only a bit younger than me so it's ridiculous.' She took Anwen's hand and shook it. 'It's nice to meet you. I've seen you at chapel, of course. I hope you'll be happy working here.'

'Thank you – Elizabeth.' She remembered something she had meant to ask Mrs Meredith. 'I was wondering. Are there any other jobs going here at the moment? Scullery maid or some such?'

'I'm afraid not. We keep only one housemaid, a cook and the washer-woman. Do you know someone in need of a job?'

'It's my sister, Sara. She's fifteen. Left school in the summer.'

'If I hear of anything, I will let you know.'

Outside once more, Anwen surveyed the view. A gust of wind blew the loose strands of her hair around her face. From the front path she observed the pit to the right, Dyffryn Gwyrdd Farm in the middle and the terraced houses of the workers on the far hill. They looked grim in the dim light of the leaden sky, like a symbol of the bleak lives of their inhabitants. She turned instead to view the valley, the green patchwork of the slopes and dips, the evergreen woods beyond the path. Places she'd walked with Idris. They'd been a salve to the grime of the pit. Now it was simply a place of remembrance and regret.

As she started off on the path that rounded the pit on its way to the houses, her wayward tears soon turned to choking sobs.

–

Idris passed the Workmen's Institute, coming around the top of Jubilee Green next to the greengrocer's and onto the road that led down to the pit's entrance. The sky was still pitch black and would be for another couple of hours. His way was lit by the electric light from the houses, provided by the pit, as people started their long day. It was a five-minute trek from his door to the colliery, one he hadn't expected to take again for a long while. Rather, he'd thought he'd soon be hidden underground in a trench in France, wearing an army uniform. Instead he was back in his old moleskin trousers, singlet, flannel shirt, the worn waistcoat and jacket, his oldest cap and a shabby scarf – a uniform of sorts.

From this vantage point he examined the dark valley, with only pinpricks of light visible from the buildings of the pit. He sighed, each step of his bulky boots stomping on his self-esteem.

From behind there came an unexpected voice. 'Hey, Idris, is that you, *bach*?'

Idris twisted round, ripped from his self-indulgent musings. Running towards him was Gwilym, his loose jacket flying out behind him. His best friend, before Idris had signed up. Gwilym fell into an easy step next to him, like Idris had never been away. Coming up quickly behind were the other men of the morning shift, their tin boxes and bottles rattling as they marched. Gwilym had called him an idiot for signing up, for jumping into the fray. *A bloody fool's war, you mark my words.* A hot shame engulfed Idris as he recalled his reply: *You're a coward, Gwilym Owen.*

The other men remained several paces behind. Further back still came the women, chatting in muted voices, their shawls wrapped tightly round their heads and shoulders.

'Haven't seen you since you got back,' said Gwilym, hands in pockets, his tins tucked under his arm.

'Only been back four days.'

They passed the book shop, continuing down past the McKenzie Arms onto Station Road, with its scant five houses. Men joined their procession as they went, from James Street, Owain Street and West Road. On they marched, like soldiers on parade, the others chatting, him and Gwilym silent.

They'd entered the yard before Gwilym said, 'How are you, then?'

Idris had no idea how to condense a complex answer into a short reply and as luck, or bad fortune, would have it, he didn't need to. There, leaning against his office door was the under-manager, Edgar Williams. His thin lips were drawn into a smug smile under a ginger moustache that contrasted with his pale brown hair. His suit was too new for the job, given that he spent time underground at some point every day.

'Well, if it isn't our very own hero, Idris Hughes, back at Number One pit. What, beaten the Hun already, have you, boyo?'

Idris came to a halt five yards from him, Gwilym dropping in by his side. 'Don't rise to it, Idris,' he whispered.

'No?' said Williams, the word climbing the scale. 'So you've come crawling back, tail between your legs.'

Idris carried on towards the lamp room, catching Williams' right arm with his own as he passed.

'Here, watch it! I'll be getting reports from the deputies and checking up on your work. I've got my eye on you, Hughes.'

--

There was silence as the eight miners were lowered down in the cramped, wooden cage. Idris hunched his shoulders, dreading the descent, the eight hours of hewing coal ahead of him. Yet ten years ago he'd gladly taken a position here, behind his mother's back. She'd been furious, but her arguments about him getting a clerical job had not swayed him. His friends would be working and he'd wanted to be like them. He'd started as a trapper, opening and shutting a small door for ventilation. Later he'd been a putter, placing the trams for the pit ponies. At nineteen he'd become a hewer, earlier than boys normally did, on account of his height and broad shoulders. As time had passed he'd started to struggle a little, but always managed to fill a good number of trams. He'd wanted to prove he was as good as any of them.

The cage rattled to a halt. Idris got out in front of the others. Already, the oppression of the dusty air and surrounding mass of rock pressed down on him. His lamp was checked by the deputy, who nodded and returned it to him, locked. He retrieved a pickaxe, following Cornishman Jory Damerell, the man he'd work next to and who would be his butty. The roof lowered as he went along. Idris bent his back, crouching, his lamp held out in front of him. After around two hundred yards he reached his spot, hanging the lamp on a hook in the wooden prop. He undressed, folding his jacket, waistcoat, shirt and vest on the ground. In the tunnel ahead he could see the odd dot of light from the lamps. Beyond them was an abyss.

He took a deep breath, which did nothing to still his nerves. At least there'd have been fresh air in the trenches, not this sooty stench. As he dug the point of the pickaxe into the coal he grunted his frustration. What would his friends in the 114th Brigade think of him, back in the relative safety of the village?

Not only had the army discharged him, they'd written a final humiliating sentence on his record that he'd told no one about.

Not likely to become an efficient soldier.

Chapter Four

It wasn't until they were eating their supper that night, leftover potatoes, bacon and rabbit with a bit of winter green, that Idris's family gathered together. Isaiah entered the kitchen and picked up the cup of tea Meg served him, drinking it down in one.

'Ah, that's better. Why didn't you wait for me this morning, son?'

Idris shrugged. 'Just wanted to get it over with, going back in there.'

'You're not still upset at having to leave the army, are you?' said Meg.

He raised his eyes briefly, saying nothing.

She put down the cutlery she'd just lifted. 'Why would anyone want to risk getting killed, when they already have a job contributing to the war, along with a lovely wife-to-be?'

His mother had conveniently left out the deaths on their doorstep, like those sixteen men killed in the explosion of 1902. People still talked about it now.

'I've broken it off with Anwen.' There. He'd said it.

'You've done what?' said his father. 'You don't know when you're well off.'

'Yes,' said Jenkin. 'Anwen's pretty and lots of the men like her.'

'Hush your noise now, Jenkin,' said Meg. 'This is grown-up talk.'

'I don't want to talk about it,' said Idris.

'It's not going away just because you don't want to talk about it,' said Isaiah. 'Do you think Anwen will consider you less a man because of being discharged?'

Idris was rapidly losing his appetite. 'It's got nothing to do with that.' Yet it had everything to do with it. Anwen would surely prefer a fit husband, a hero, like Owain Glyndwr or Llewelyn the Great, fighting for what was right.

'You're a good catch, son,' said Meg. 'You could get a clerical job, not dirtying your hands…'

It was a well-worn lecture he'd stopped listening to years ago.

'… and if you're unfit for military duty, well that's just—'

Idris bolted up, knocking his chair over. 'That's enough, Mam.'

Isaiah rose from the chair slowly. 'Sit down, boy, and don't you talk to your mother like that.'

'I'm not a boy anymore. None of you understand!' He picked up his coat and made for the scullery.

'Sit down, boy!'

He ignored his father's command, striding to the back door and into the garden. He immediately regretted his rudeness to his parents, but it was done now. Better to sneak off to the park on Jubilee Green, sit among the trees and just… think.

–

It was dark when Idris got back to the house. His mother was sitting at the table in the kitchen, darning a sock. His escape had done nothing to alleviate the ache inside his head.

'We could do with more coal for the fire.' Meg's gaze remained on the needle.

'I'll get it.' He collected the scuttle from the fireplace. 'Then I'm going to bed.'

She didn't respond.

When Idris arrived at work next day it was still raining, a dismal grey shawl over the dreary outbuildings. Ahead of him was Gwilym, on his way to the lamp room, the artificial light glinting off the reddish curls. He was about to follow on when he found Edgar Williams standing in his way.

'I hear you weren't up to soldiering, Hughes.'

Idris tried to dodge him but Williams blocked his way.

'Excuse me sir, I need to get my lamp.'

'I've been told you have a bad heart.'

'It just beats a little faster than it should. It's nothing.'

'I was thinking, maybe we should give you an easier job, with the women, screening the coal.' He treated Idris to a lop-sided smirk.

Idris clenched his hands behind his back. He'd be paid a lot less as a screener. The only other men who worked sorting the coal were the old ones. 'I can do the job.' He managed to skirt past Williams, on his way to the lamp room.

Behind, Edgar's voice called, 'We'll see.'

'What was that all about?' said Gwilym as Idris came up beside him.

'Oh, you know, Williams shouting his mouth off as usual.'

'Will you walk up the hill with me after the shift today? Not skulk behind.'

Idris didn't want to have the inevitable conversation with Gwilym, yet he couldn't avoid him forever. 'Of course.'

Gwilym collected his lamp first. 'My da's off to a memorial this afternoon, second cousin's boy, killed at the Dardanelles, only twenty-six. They'll be a band playing and rifles firing and all that. Quite a send-off, poor bloody sod.'

Idris said nothing as he stepped up next to collect his lamp, glad he was soon to be swallowed up by the inky chasm.

It had, after all, been a pleasant stroll home with Gwilym when their shift had finished, with them parting company as they reached the crossroads separating their streets. Their exchange had not touched on their quarrel or the war. Instead, they'd talked of the nationalisation of the coal mines and of the strike back in July that had secured some concessions for the miners. By the time Idris reached his back door a small chink of his anxiety had been chipped away.

That was, until he opened the door and saw his mother's friend, Rhonwen Evans, sitting at the kitchen table, her two-year-old granddaughter leaning against her knees. Her son-in-law, Maurice, was another who'd joined the Rhondda Pals at the same time as him and Charlie Jones.

'Hello Idris,' said Rhonwen enthusiastically. 'I'm sorry to hear you're not so well.'

So his mother had already started telling people.

'Your mam's gone to find some old books for little Lily here.' She waved a piece of paper in front of him. 'Now you're here I can read you Maurice's letter.'

All he wanted was to get the soot off his skin and have something to eat. Rhonwen read the whole letter, all about the training, the food, and the fact they were going to be shipped overseas soon.

'I 'ope the war finishes before they get that far.' Rhonwen placed the letter in her coat pocket.

'We all hope that,' said Meg, strolling in from the hall. 'These books should keep the young'un occupied for a while.'

'Thank you, *cariad*. It'll help fill the long hours while her mother makes up the money in the munitions factory,' said Rhonwen.

Idris nodded slightly, waiting till she and her granddaughter left before exhaling noisily.

'She read you the letter, then?' asked Meg.

'Didn't even occur to her I might not want to hear it?'

'You're going to have to get used to that, Idris. People aren't going to stop talking about the war because you've been discharged.'

She went to him, folding her petite body around his broad one, despite the dirt on him. 'What's to be done with you, Idris *bach*?'

He clung onto her, grateful of the comfort. 'I'll be all right, Mam. Don't you worry.' This was said with conviction, despite being convinced he'd never be all right again.

'And I heard in the grocer's that Mr Churchill's resigned from the Cabinet over the Dardanelles expedition. Not that I understand any of that, but others seem to think it's a bad step.'

'Who knows?' He was too tired to offer an opinion.

She let him go. 'Come on now, I'm all behind with Rhonwen coming round. I need to get the bath ready. The water's on the boil.' He heard the clunk of the bath as she tipped it up to drag it into the kitchen.

He'd wash the dirt off fine. He just wished he could wash the shame away with it.

–

Anwen pulled open the threadbare curtain in the kitchen, staring into the blank garden. She rubbed her arms as she went towards the fireplace. It gleamed with the scrubbing Sara had given it yesterday. She'd worked too hard, her exhausted limp last night the proof of this. Anwen kneeled to light the fire. She needed the room warm, the kettle boiled, before Da stepped into it.

She still felt disorientated from the dream she'd had that morning. In it, she and Idris had been in Cardiff, strolling through the arcades with their high glass ceilings and elegant hanging lamps. Idris's hand had been soft in hers, his laugh warm. They had visited the arcades on a number of occasions before the war, picking what they'd have in their own home if they could ever afford it. What they talked about in the dream she couldn't recall, probably nonsense that wouldn't make sense in the light of day. But it had been so vivid, so real, that she'd experienced the gnawing ache of loss as she awoke and realised it was mere fantasy, full of beautiful goods she'd never own and a man who would never be her husband.

Madog appeared in the doorway forty minutes later in baggy long johns, his hair bedraggled. He stretched and scratched, producing a yawn that was punctuated with a belch. 'Where's my bloody breakfast?'

'The eggs and bacon are cooking, Da.'

'I don't want the eggs hard. Get on with it. I'm 'ungry.'

She scurried back to the stove, relieved to see the eggs were not overcooked. He left the room, returning shortly with his baccy tin to lean on the doorway.

'Where's your sister? She should be starting the other chores.'

'She had a bit of a cough in the night. Thought I'd give her an hour more.'

He took two stomping paces into the kitchen, throwing the tin onto the table. His hands, gripped into fists, were jammed against his hips. 'I'll give her a bloody hour. I'll give her a bloody hand across the arse.'

Anwen scooped up the eggs and bacon, placing them on the warmed plate. 'I haven't done the fried bread yet.'

'Give it here.' He snatched the plate from her. 'I'll start on this.'

Several minutes of quiet were interrupted only by the sizzling pan and Madog's chewing. When it was ready, Anwen brought the fried bread and an extra egg to him.

'Have you organised that job for your sister?'

Anwen had dreaded this moment, envisaging Sara in the cold and damp, the coal dust irritating her lungs. 'Isn't she more use here, in Mam's place, like—?'

He thumped the table, making Anwen jump. 'She has to pay her way else she's no use here. That's the trouble with having only daughters. Not like sons, bringing in a good wage.'

'Da, I've got a new job with a better wage at the House, eighteen shillings instead of sixteen. I start Monday.'

'What house?'

'The Big House, working for the manager's wife.'

'You're bloody Lady Muck now, are you?'

'It's two shillings more a week, Da. I thought, with the extra, Sara wouldn't need a job and she could do Mam's work here.'

'Are you stupid or just dozy? Two shilling extra a week don't make up for another wage, do it? You do your fancy job, but your sister's going to screen coal. If you don't bloody sort it out, I will.'

'But Da—'

His hand went out, connecting with her cheek and knocking her off her feet. She landed on the floor, her shoulder hitting a chair as she went down.

The door from the hall flew open. 'What's all the noise?' Sara ran in, stopping short of the table when she saw Anwen sprawled on the floor. She bent down to help her up.

'Your sister tripped. Bloody clumsy, she is.'

'Your face is red,' Sara said, taking Anwen's arm. It was her way of showing she knew that to be a lie. But if she went too far their father would start on her next.

'I knocked my face on the edge of the chair as I went down.'

'She's getting you a job at the mine today,' said Madog, dipping the fried bread into the soft yoke. 'You'll start Monday. But I still expect the washing, cooking and tidying done, you hear?'

Sara said nothing.

-

Anwen spent her whole shift mulling over what she could do to prevent Sara working at the colliery. Her sister had been tiny as a newborn and consequently delicate all her life. She'd rarely joined in with the sports and vigorous activities many of her friends enjoyed. These thoughts brought Anwen always back to the same conclusion. It would be tough, but it was the only solution she could think of.

At the end of her shift, Anwen headed down the gritty path to the pit entrance. The men of the morning shift were emerging too, dusty black but laughing and chatting, happy, no doubt, to be above ground. Two youths passed by, their dark brown hair, a little too long, reminding her of Tomos and Geraint. How old would they have been now? Twenty-three and eighteen. For a moment she imagined it was them, alive and healthy, heading home for some dinner. Mealtimes had been a riot of discussion and sometimes argument, but always good-natured. Da had appreciated a good debate in those days. Now he tolerated no opinion but his own. Sara was waiting for her at the top of the path out of the colliery.

'I haven't seen Da come out yet,' said Sara.

'I saw him in Mr Williams' office as I passed. You need to get along home to get his dinner ready.'

'It's all done. And I've given Mam hers. I wanted to tell you that I asked at the shops about jobs, but they're making do because there's less to sell these days and—' Sara stopped, directing her eyes behind Anwen, then rolling them as if alerting her to something.

It was Idris, passing by with Gwilym. He glanced only briefly in their direction.

'Hello,' said Gwilym, ambling over to them. 'I heard from someone whose sister works on the screens that you're leaving the pit.' He peered back at Idris. 'Aren't you coming over, mun?'

'Got to get home quickly,' said Idris.

'Have you?' He regarded Anwen again. 'So, are you leaving in preparation for the wedding?'

Hadn't Idris told his best friend? Everyone who knew them must assume they were still intending to marry. 'I'm not sure if I am leaving yet.'

'But—' Sara started.

'I think you ought to ask Idris about the wedding,' said Anwen, clenching her jaw to prevent her chin wobbling. 'Sara and I need to get on.'

'Of course.' Gwilym frowned as he joined Idris once more.

Anwen waited until they'd got a good few steps away before saying, 'Let's get home. Hopefully I can get washed up before Da gets back.' The queue of men leaving the early shift had dwindled to nothing. 'Then I've got an errand to run.'

It would be a heart-breaking errand, but she'd run out of options.

Chapter Five

A light drizzle was falling when Anwen lifted the knocker on the door of McKenzie House and tapped it twice. This was a foolhardy errand, likely to get her fired before she'd even started, but she had to try.

Anwen was about to knock again when Elizabeth opened the door, grinning at her.

'Good afternoon, Anwen. How can I help you?'

'Good afternoon, Miss Elizabeth. I was wondering if it would be possible to speak to Mrs Meredith.'

'I'm afraid she's out. Is there something I can help you with?'

Anwen slumped a little. 'I need to speak to her urgently about the housemaid's job.'

'Oh dear.' Elizabeth's face was full of concern. 'If there's a problem that needs sorting out, I can try and help?'

Anwen detected a kindred spirit in this young woman, despite their class differences. 'All right.'

'Come into the dining room where it's warm.'

Once in the room, Elizabeth pulled out a chair from the table and gestured to Anwen to sit down.

'What's the problem?'

Could she be entirely honest with this woman? 'My father, who is rather a strict man, has insisted that my sister, Sara, get a job. He has asked me to get her work screening the coal, but she's only fifteen and has a tendency to chestiness.'

'I'm sorry to hear that. I have seen your sister with you at chapel. She is small for fifteen.'

'She's a good little worker all the same, but would be much better with an indoor job. She helps with all the things that need doing at home now Mam's sick. It's just... the cold and the dust. I worry.'

'So, you're proposing that your sister takes the job here, and you continue at the mine?'

'Do you think your mother would allow that? I could bring Sara up tomorrow afternoon to meet her.'

'I'll put forward your case when she returns. Will you be at chapel tomorrow?'

'We're always at chapel on a Sunday. Sara and me, anyway. Mam's not well enough and Da, well, he's not a religious man.' Not since Tomos and Geraint's demise. Angry with God, he was, convinced the Almighty was picking on him personally.

'If my mother is agreeable, you can bring Sara along to meet her after lunch.'

'Thank you, Miss Elizabeth. That is very kind of you.'

'I assume if she doesn't want to employ Sara that you'll still take the post?'

Anwen nodded as she rose. 'I have taken up enough of your time.'

Heading back to the front door, they heard a clattering down the stairs.

'Goodness Tom, could you make any more noise?'

Young Mr Meredith stood on the bottom step sporting a smart three-piece suit, a shirt with a rounded collar and a striped tie. He held four books in his hands. 'I'm sure I could if I tried. Ah Miss Rhys. Nice to see you again.'

Anwen was disturbed by the way he gazed at her. She guessed this was just how young men of his class acted.

'Mr Meredith.' She bowed her head slightly.

'Good God. Tom, please. Mr Meredith is my father.' He laughed long and stridently. 'Having another recce before you begin work on Monday?'

'We were just clarifying a few points,' said Elizabeth, saving Anwen from an awkward explanation.

'Are you going back through the village, Miss Rhys? I'm off to Schenck's to sell and buy some books.'

'Yes I am, sir.'

'Wonderful! Give me a moment to fetch my coat and I'll accompany you.' He ran off towards the understairs cupboard.

'Is that permitted?' she mouthed to Elizabeth.

'It's getting towards sunset, so I think it would be a good idea for him to escort you down the road to the village, don't you?'

When Tom returned, there was amusement on his face. 'Absolutely the gentlemanly thing to do. Come, let us away.'

Anwen couldn't help but laugh. He opened the door, bowing with particular emphasis.

Her elevated mood lasted until they reached the gate, when regret set in. Such a shame she may not be working here after all.

Anwen needn't have worried about what to say to Tom. He was full of chat, about the books he'd read and how he often visited Mr Schenck's bookshop. They took the road that curved round the colliery, coming out at James Street where her friend Gwen lived.

'Do you enjoy reading, Miss Rhys?'

'I do. I often go to the library in the Workmen's Institute. Many of the people here are keen to learn, even if they left school early.'

'I'm supposed to be at Reading University, but there's not much point going at the moment. Not with most students in the forces now.'

'They don't have to go.'

He went slightly in front, walking backwards to face her. 'No, they don't. They just volunteered. But soon I think they'll have to.'

'You haven't gone, though?'

'No. I was sent home in October. Bout of influenza. Got a bit weak.'

'I'm sorry to hear that. You look well.' She realised immediately it sounded like a criticism. It wasn't her business, after all.

'Why thank you. That's a nice change to being told all the time by my mother that I look pale. Still got a bit of chest pain, but I'm better than I was. So, what do you like to read?'

'Novels. Edith Nepean, Gwyneth Vaughan, the Brontës, Jane Austen, EM Forster. And poetry.' She picked English poets rather than Welsh ones she liked. 'Byron. Wordsworth. Coleridge.'

'What good taste you have.'

It was at this point they reached the bookshop on the corner. On the pavement diagonally opposite, several men stumbled out onto the pavement from the McKenzie Arms Hotel.

'Oh dear, they're the worse for wear,' said Tom.

They watched as the men wove their way up Gabriel Street. A version of '*Ar Lan y Môr*' was battling with 'Hello, Hello, Who's Your Lady Friend?'

Anwen, smiling at their good-natured high spirits, turned back to wish Tom farewell. As she was about to speak she saw a familiar figure ambling down Jubilee Green towards them. Idris, carrying a parcel, glanced from her to Tom, and back again as he passed, his expression stern.

'I'll wish you a good evening then, Miss Rhys,' said Tom, about to open the bookshop door. 'And I'll see you on Monday.'

She hadn't told him en route that Sara might take the job instead. 'Good evening, Mr Meredith.'

She hurried away up the road, glancing back only once to see Idris peering up at her. He twisted round to continue on down Station Street.

–

The morning was sunny as Anwen and Sara made their way to chapel. The cheerful light did not improve Anwen's mood. Today she'd find out whether Sara had the housemaid's position, in which case she would be asking for a job back that she detested. If not, Sara was condemned to the filthy, back-breaking work at the pit. She was thankful her sister had enough colour in her cheeks today to suggest she was healthy enough to take on the job.

A golden hue inhabited the chapel, lit as it was by the sun's rays through its top windows. Elizabeth was by their side no sooner had they stepped through the door. It was three quarters full in there, with the seats on the balcony almost entirely occupied.

'I thought you'd want to know without any delay that my mother has agreed to your request. And she doesn't require a meeting with Sara this afternoon.'

An equal amount of relief and disappointment flooded Anwen. 'Thank you, Miss Elizabeth.'

'What's this about?' said Sara.

'You haven't told her?' said Elizabeth.

'I wanted to know for sure,' said Anwen. 'Sara, the house-maid's job at McKenzie House is yours. You don't have to work at the pit.'

Sara beamed. 'They had two jobs?'

'No. I'm continuing with my old one.'

'No! Oh Anwen, don't give up the job for me. You wanted it so much.'

'It's a lovely house and you'll like it there.'

'*Please* Anwen—'

'Shh now. Get our seats for us, and for Uncle Hywel, as near the front as you can.'

'Would you mind if I joined you?' Elizabeth asked hesitantly.

'Of course not,' said Anwen, delighted that she should want to do so. 'Get a seat for Miss Meredith too.'

Sara wandered down the aisle, stopping four rows from the front and shuffling sideways into the pew there.

'I admire you,' said Elizabeth, watching Sara take a seat. 'Sacrificing something for the good of someone else.'

'It's what we're all doing in the war, isn't it?'

'If only.' Elizabeth massaged her temples. Recovering, she added, 'Did you read that a passenger ship, the *Ancona*, was blown up near Sardinia by the Austrians? Men, women and children screaming and drowning in the water.'

'That's horrible.' She tried not to picture the scene, but the screams filled her brain, like those made by some of the women in the village when their husbands or sons were killed in the pit.

'You giving up the job for Sara isn't about the war. Not everything is. There are many things to be protected, or fought for, besides peace.'

Like better wages for workers, thought Anwen, not daring to voice that sentiment to the manager's daughter.

'Have you heard of the Suffragettes?' said Elizabeth.

'I've read about them in the papers. Like Emily Davison throwing herself under a horse a couple of years back at the Derby.'

Elizabeth sighed, removing her gloves and placing them in one hand. 'Most upsetting, for there are other things we can do. Have you ever been to a meeting?'

She could imagine what her father would have to say about that. She wasn't sure what to make of the Suffragettes, or Suffragists, herself. Or indeed, what the difference was between them. 'I didn't know they met around here.'

'They used to. They're involved in war work now, for which some have moved away.' She looked regretful.

Idris's mother entered the chapel, his father in tow. '*Bore da*, Anwen. Good morning, Miss Meredith.'

Behind Isaiah were Idris and Jenkin. Anwen stiffened her body with determination. '*Bore da*,' she intoned, the same time as Elizabeth.

'And a lovely one it is, too,' said Meg.

Lovely for some. But it wasn't Meg's fault Anwen felt the way she did. She smiled to make up for the uncharitable thought.

'I'll join Sara,' said Elizabeth. She set off elegantly down the aisle in a blue velvet skirt with white buttons down the sides. Above the skirt was a thigh-length matching jacket.

Meg watched Miss Meredith too, continuing the conversation only after she'd sat down. 'I was just saying to our Idris, there's a concert here soon and I believe you're singing in it.'

'That's right.'

'Such a lovely voice you have.' She patted Anwen's arm, her mouth smiling but her eyes sad.

'We'll sit down,' said Isaiah, taking Jenkin with him.

Meg followed on. Idris didn't move for some moments. Anwen wanted to get away from this uncomfortable situation, but was rooted to the spot.

Finally Idris said, 'I see you've already found other male company.'

He must be referring to Tom Meredith, she realised. A fury smouldered within her. He was twisting this around, as if his breaking off the engagement had somehow been *her* fault. As much as it broke her heart, it took all her willpower not to shout at Idris. How dare he! She was about to tell him that young Mr Meredith had simply been accompanying her back to the village, and about the housemaid's position, but what came out in an exasperated tone was, 'Well, Idris Hughes, it's nothing to do with you anymore, is it?'

With that she proceeded down the aisle, back straight and neck stretched, trying to emulate Miss Elizabeth's demeanour.

–

After chapel, Anwen made an early dinner of bits of cheap ham with some slightly dry bread. She and Sara ate it sitting around Mam's dressing table. A combination of Madog's absence and the bright winter sun brought Anwen to a decision. Sending Sara downstairs with the empty plates, she waited until she was out of earshot before confiding in her mother.

'I was thinking, today might be a good one to get that new dress for Sara.'

'Her old Sunday best is looking a little worn and frayed,' Enid admitted. 'You're a good girl, going without your own fripperies to save up a bit.'

It hadn't been easy, knowing how her father snooped round for money all the time. Keeping it in a little pouch she'd sewn on the inside of her skirt had been her only option. 'It will only be second-hand at best, but Mrs Bowen assured me she had a couple of dresses that might fit her small frame.'

Enid shifted her hips back and forth, trying to get comfortable. 'I wish I was in a position to make her something, or at least adjust an old dress, but sitting in bed doesn't make that easy.'

'Don't worry about it, Mam. I wish I had the time, but at the moment...'

'And sorry I am to the heart of me for that. When I think the clothes I used to make when you were younger. It were your *mamgu*, Cadi, what taught me.'

'And lovely clothes you made, Mam.' She didn't want her mother to dwell on this, so changed the subject. 'And I thought, we could walk up to Rhymney afterwards, have a trip out, if you don't mind being left for the afternoon. It's ages since we went out of the village. I think I have enough for that.'

Enid smiled. 'It would be a splendid thing to lift Sara's spirits, for she does seem even sadder than usual. Meg and Rachael said they'd visit today, so if I have any needs, they'll help me.'

Sara came back up the stairs and entered the bedroom. 'What are you two whispering about?'

'We weren't whispering, *cariad*,' said Enid. 'Anwen's got a surprise for you.'

The younger girl clapped her hands together. 'What is it?'

Anwen directed her towards the stairs once more. 'Get your coat on and wait and see. *Hwyl fawr*, Mam.'

'Bye bye, *cariadon*.'

Walking down Edward Street to Jubilee Green, Sara had tried to guess what they might be doing, but it wasn't until they neared number eleven that she cried out, 'Oh, Mrs Bowen's! Is it clothes we're looking at?'

'A new Sunday dress for you.' Anwen knocked on the door.

It wasn't long before Mrs Bowen's daughter, Amelia, answered and invited them inside.

Mrs Bowen was in the front room. Two rails of clothes dominated the space.

'Come in, come in,' said the seamstress, waving her arms. 'I'm glad to see you could make it. Now, I've had a look, and I have three dresses in Sara's size that might be... suitable.'

Anwen knew she meant *that you can afford*, having already told her what her budget was.

Mrs Bowen hung the dresses sideways on the rail to display them. Sara examined each in turn, her eyes wide. She spent most time on the peach dress, with the high neckline, nipped in waist and long, flowing skirt. It was a few years out of date, but still pretty.

'Can I try them all on?' she asked.

'Of course you can. Amelia, show Miss Rhys up to the dressing room.'

Anwen looked through the rails as she and Mrs Bowen chatted.

'It's not easy for Amelia, of course,' said the older woman. 'Being left by her fiancé has taken its toll, poor girl.'

Anwen guessed that her hostess hadn't heard of her own unfortunate circumstances.

When Sara appeared once more, she was carrying the peach dress. 'I like this one best. And I was lucky that it did fit the best, too.'

'I'd say it's just the right shape for you. Let me wrap it up, *fach*.'

She went to take the frock from Sara, only for Anwen to intervene. 'If you don't mind, Mrs Bowen, Sara will wear it, so could you wrap the dress she has on instead?'

'Of course. I see it could do with a bit of mending. I'll buy it off you if you like. I'm sure I could make something from it. It won't fetch much, but it's better than nothing.'

'Yes, we'll do that, thank you.' It would help towards the treat, especially if her father didn't give her any more than the pittance he'd already offered for next week's food.

On their way again, Sara started back up the hill.

'No, we're going this way.' Anwen indicated downhill with her head. 'Taking a walk to Rhymney, if you're up to it.'

'Oh yes. We haven't been in a while. But what are we going to do there?'

'It's a surprise and a treat.'

'Another one?'

'Life's been short enough of them recently.' Anwen tried to look bright, but her expression must have given away her feelings.

Sara took hold of her arm and hugged it. 'You could do with a treat too. It is very sad, what's happened. About Idris, I mean.'

Anwen removed her arm in order to link it through Sara's properly. 'Let's forget all our worries for now. Today's going to be just for us.'

'Yes, just for us,' Sara repeated.

–

'That's a film I'd like to see.' Sara pointed at the billboard as they passed the Imperial Cinema on Rhymney's High Street.

Anwen turned to inspect the poster for *Solambo*. 'It's a shame the pictures don't open on a Sunday. I read that it's set in Carthage, two hundred years BC, when they were fighting the Romans.'

'The Romans used to be in our country.'

Anwen chuckled. 'That was a long time ago too, *fach*. I think they left about sixteen hundred years ago.'

'I know that, but they've discovered lots of villas belonging to them recently. Like that one at Caerwent, and the one in

Merthyr at Penydarren Park.' She walked backwards to face Anwen, almost bouncing as she went along. 'And that pavement they found in Gloucester last year. I so loved reading about their progress in the newspapers.'

'Maybe we'll try and come in next week, in the evening, to see the film,' said Anwen. 'For now, we've just got to keep walking down the High Street a bit.'

'Where are we going? There aren't any shops open.'

'Apart from one.' They walked for a couple of minutes more. 'Here we are.' Anwen pointed across the road.

'Perilli Bros Refreshment House,' Sara read, excited once more. 'I've never been in there before.' She examined the sign which read, *Confectioner and Tobacconist. Ice Creams.* 'Don't they get fined for opening on a Sunday?'

'They do, regularly, according to Gwen. But she said the Italian cafés just pay up and stay open.' She started to cross, then looked back over her shoulder. 'Are you coming, then?'

A horse and cart came clattering down the road, causing Anwen to run to the other side.

Sara crossed over, grinning.

Anwen laughed. 'Come on, I've been looking forward to this.'

Sara peered at the windows either side of the door. They were chockablock with jars of sweets, boxes and packets of chocolate, cigars and cigarettes.

When Anwen pushed the door open, her sister followed her in. The aroma of tobacco filled the air. To the right was a further room. It contained several tables with white cloths, condiments and small vases of greenery.

A middle-aged gentleman with tanned skin and salt-and-pepper hair came from behind the counter. Around his waist he wore a long white apron. He bowed slightly.

'*Signorine*, how may I 'elp you?'

'We'd like a table for two, please,' said Anwen.

'*Certo*. My daughter, Angelina, will show you to one.'

A young woman came forward. She had on a smart black dress with a white collar and cuffs, a short pinny with a small, nipped-in bib and a frilly white cap that covered just the front of her head. Her dark hair was pulled into a bun.

The sisters were seated near the back of the café, close to another counter. The waitress handed them each a menu.

'We've got pressed beef and ox tongue on special today.' Unlike her father, her accent was the same as theirs.

'We're just having tea and cake today, thank you,' said Anwen.

'The desserts are listed on the back. Can I get you some tea while you're choosing?'

'Ooh, yes please. I'm gasping,' said Sara.

The waitress beamed at her. 'Right away, madam.'

When she was out of earshot, Sara said, 'Madam! I've never been called that before.' She turned the menu over and read it. 'I think I'm going to have some ice cream. Italians are meant to be very good at making it.'

'I will too. It will be a little odd with tea, but never mind. Perhaps we should have had a soda fountain drink.'

'Next time,' said Sara. 'Now I'm going to be working, I will save up some money so I can treat you.' She returned her attention to the menu. 'I'll have a peach melba.'

Anwen looked at the choices. 'Yes, that sounds nice. I'll have that too.'

Sara took her hand and stroked it. 'This is the best thing that's happened to me all year.'

'I'm glad you're enjoying it.' Anwen was sad to think her sister's world had shrunk so much that this was the highlight, but she was happy to see her so cheerful for a change.

―

Anwen stirred the pot on the stove, content with the meal she'd been able to put together for supper. In the pot alongside the rabbit was the winter kale she'd found growing wild beyond the garden. On the hillside she'd picked chickweed, then found the bronzy-yellow velvet shank mushrooms in the small woods at the top. From Mr James the greengrocer she'd purchased two carrots, past their best but welcome all the same.

At twenty past six Anwen heard the front door close. By how quietly it was pushed to she guessed it was Sara.

'Mm, that smells wonderful,' said Sara, sniffing in deeply as she entered the kitchen. 'Like Mam used to make before the war.'

'How was your first day, *cariad*?'

Sara removed her coat, placing it over the chaise longue and taking a seat at the table. Her skin was pasty. 'Tiring. I can't have a rest when I need it, like here. I wish I could have worked in an office, typing. Lucy Ahern does that, in Merthyr. You can sit down all day doing that. Oh, I'm so sorry, Anwen. I know how much you wanted that job. You must think me so ungrateful.'

'No, I quite understand. It's not ideal. Maybe we could save up, a tiny bit each week, so when you're older, you can go to college to learn. When the unions secure a decent wage for the miners and work's more secure. When maybe women can do more jobs too, with better pay. If the Suffragettes get their way.'

'Da said those women who go marching are off their nuts and are trying to overthrow the men.'

'Do you believe that? Is it any different to the miners going on strike, like they did in July, during a war? They're all fighting for what they're entitled to.'

'I suppose. I wish no one had to march or go on strike, that everyone was just treated with respect.' Sara put her hands on the table, laying her face on them. 'What would you like help with?'

'Nothing. You rest. I've been in hours and got most things done.' Maybe not most, but Sara didn't need to worry.

'Was Ma all right on her own?'

'Violet popped in at dinner time to give her what I prepared this morning. Just bread and dripping, like the rest of us. This rabbit stew should fill a gap.'

Sara brightened at the mention of food. 'I had some lovely tender ham with bread and butter at dinner time. What they call *lunch*. I feel bad about that.'

'It's good that you had it. Eat as much as you're offered. With good food you'll soon get bigger and healthier.'

'Young Mr Meredith is very jolly, isn't he?'

'He is.' The mention of his name gave a little lift to Anwen's spirit. Idris used to be like that, before he enlisted.

'I'll go and see Mam,' said Sara.

'In that case, take her some food.' She placed a ladleful of the bubbling stew into a large bowl.

'It smells wonderful. Like childhood.'

The front door slammed, causing Sara to jump and drop the bowl on the floor. It shattered, spraying meat, vegetables and stock around a wide area.

'Oh no.' Sara panicked, trying to retrieve the pieces of crockery first.

'Leave it. Go to the scullery. I'll clear it up.'

'No!' Sara's face was defiant. 'You've done enough for me.'

Madog shoved the hall door open so fiercely it crashed against the wall.

'What's all the bloody noise?' He strode in, swaying enough to have to grab a chair. He had a flour-sack bag in his hands, which he placed under the table. 'What's all this wasted food on the floor? Who bloody did this?'

'I'm sorry—' Anwen began.

'It was me, Da,' Sara interrupted. 'It was hot and then the door made me jump—'

'Clumsy bloody cow.'

His hand shot out, knocking Sara's hair out of place as it came down with a resounding slap across her scalp. She screamed, falling towards the table, catching herself. Lifting his hand once more, he went in for a second time. Sara cowered over the table, covering her head with her hands.

Anwen was filled with fury. Her heart pounded as she lifted the small but heavy pan that lay to one side of the stove. With a brief shriek, she swung it with all her might towards her father, who had his back to her. The pan glanced off the side of his scalp, but it was enough to take him down.

She lowered the pan. Sara straightened herself. They both gaped at the prone figure of their father.

'Oh Anwen, what have you done?'

Chapter Six

'Is he dead?' said Sara, a tremble in her voice. She leant over Madog, peering at his head.

'No, I didn't hit him hard enough.' The stiffness in her voice covered her uncertainty. *Oh God, what would happen to them if the police decided she'd murdered him?*

'He's not moving.'

'Here, let me see.' Anwen bent down, putting two fingers to his neck. She'd seen the doctor do it once at the pit, when they'd brought out a man involved in a rock fall. The doctor hadn't found a pulse then, but there was a definite one here as she squeezed the sagging skin under her father's ear. 'He isn't dead.'

A small voice in her brain followed on with *more's the pity*. She was awash with shame. However awful he was, he was their father, and he had been a better man once.

'When he wakes up, he'll remember what you did and he might really hurt you, Anwen.'

'How often does he wake in the morning not even remembering how he got home?'

'But if he wakes up on the floor like this, with a sore head, he might.'

Anwen pondered the problem for some moments. 'Take some stew up to Mam. If she's heard the noise and asks about it, tell her Da came in drunk, fell over and broke a bowl.'

'Then what are we going to do?'

'You stay upstairs with Mam. I'll run down and fetch Uncle Hywel.' She went to the stove, ladling stew into a second bowl, giving it to Sara with another tea towel and a spoon. 'Go on, quickly. Stay with Mam and keep quiet. I'll be as quick as I can.'

Out of the house, Anwen ran to Lloyd Street, a road parallel to her own. Knocking quite loudly on number five soon brought Mrs Price to the door.

'Hello Anwen, what can I do for you, *fach*?'

'Is my uncle in, Mrs Price?'

'Hy-wel!' she called. 'Hold on.' She was going towards the kitchen door when he appeared.

'What's up, Anwen? Is it Enid?' He rushed to the door.

'No, it's Da. We need your help.'

Hywel's face darkened. 'What's he been up to now?' he whispered, then said louder, 'I'm going out, Mrs Price, I'll be back later.'

'All right, *bach*.'

As they hurried up to Anwen's house, she told him the truth, adding the story of the jobs and how Da had insisted Sara get work.

'Enid should have kicked him out years ago. When your brothers died, Enid indulged his grief while trying to cope with her own. The drink's got to him.' His step became quicker, as if his body was fuelled by anger.

'We couldn't cope without him now, with Mam laid up.'

'Perhaps she wouldn't be laid up if he'd not been there.'

'What do you mean?' He'd overtaken her now and she was having difficulty keeping up.

'Nothing… He made her do too much. She probably fell trying to do it all. If she'd kicked him out, I'd have come to live there and made sure you were all fine for money, you know that.'

'I asked him about you boarding with us, but he wouldn't have it.'

'I doubt it would be a good idea anyway, him and me in the same space.'

Back at the house now she ran to the kitchen, relieved to see her father hadn't moved. Hywel bent down to examine him.

'There you are,' said Sara, hurrying into the room. 'Should we go and fetch the doctor?'

'No,' said Hywel, rising. 'He's fine, breathing away. Anwen, if you could help me, we'll put him in a chair, a bit of food in front of him like he was eating and fell asleep. He's got a bump formed already, so he'll want to know where it came from. Tell him he came in and fell, banging his head, but seemed all right. When he sat to eat he fell asleep and you didn't want to disturb him.'

'We never do,' said Sara. 'It's more than our lives are worth.'

'You shouldn't be living with this. Anwen, are you and Idris coming here when you marry? I don't like the idea of my sister and Sara being left alone with him. And maybe Idris being here—'

'I'm not marrying Idris.'

His frown lines deepened. 'Why?'

'Not now.'

'No, all right… Let's get things sorted out here. Sara, you go and sit with your Mam, read to her or something.'

Sara nodded. She scurried back to the hall, stopping in the doorway to emit a chesty cough. She was soon off again, but still wheezing.

'Has she been coughing again recently?' asked Hywel.

'A bit. But she's been much perkier, with more colour in her cheeks, in the last few weeks.'

'What's that over there?' He went to the flour-sack bag Madog had dumped by the other side of the table. Hywel opened it, pulling out a bottle. There were several in the bag.

'What the devil are these?'

'It says *whisky*.'

'I can see that. Did Madog bring them in?' Hywel regarded his brother-in-law with resentment.

'Yes. He often brings stuff home, puts it in the larder at the bottom and tells us to mind our own business.'

'Does he now? Buying off those profiteers, is he?'

'We'd better leave it where it was, otherwise he'll kick up merry hell.'

He put the bag down. 'Come on, let's get this cleared up and your father shifted.'

—

'So what happened the next morning, then?' Violet leant forward in her old wooden armchair, cradling her sleeping toddler, Benjamin. His sister, three-year-old Clarice, was at the table with a small metal paintbox, a brush and a jar of water.

On the other side of the fire sat Anwen, swaying slightly in the rocking chair. Already the burden of Monday night was easing with confiding in her good friends. On a dining chair twisted round from the table sat Gwen, pushing back the blonde tendrils from her face in an effort to tidy her hair. She had another new blouse on today, making Anwen feel quite dowdy. That was the advantage of working at the munitions factory, earning four pounds a week. Not like Anwen's sixteen shillings for sorting coal. She didn't resent Gwen her money; she'd heard terrible stories of women dying in agony, their throats burnt by the black powder of the shells in the munitions. She and Violet had tried to persuade her not to work there, six months ago when she'd started, but she wouldn't be swayed.

'Da woke up when I came down in the morning to do the grate and start the fire. Like Uncle Hywel predicted, he didn't remember a thing. Said it was our fault, of course, that we must have left a chair out for him to trip over.'

'Hywel is right, though,' said Gwen. 'You shouldn't have to put up with his nonsense. I certainly wouldn't. Couldn't you report him to the police?'

'What are they going to do?' Anwen said. 'They'll just say it's a family matter. Then Da'll be even worse. And with Mam being—' The swift growing fullness behind her eyes sprang abruptly as tears down her face.

Gwen got up immediately, enfolding Anwen in her arms. 'There, there. I know it's hard for you. When your mam was well she could handle your father's nonsense.'

'I'm glad Idris is back,' said Violet, rocking Benjamin gently. 'The quicker you two get up that aisle, the better.'

That was the problem with keeping your sorrow buried. She'd been too distressed to tell them when it first happened.

'What's up, *cariad*?' said Gwen, stepping back.

'Last – last Sunday, after chapel, I went for a walk with Idris.'

'Yes, we saw you. You came running back past the chapel and ignored Violet and me.'

'I'm sorry, but it was with good reason.'

'You're not in the family way, are you?' Violet said.

Anwen's head flew up. 'Of course not!'

'He was on leave in July, so it wouldn't be impossible,' said Violet. 'Not everyone shows by four months.'

'Idris doesn't want to marry me anymore!'

'Get away with you!' said Gwen. 'He's been following you around like a lost puppy ever since you were knee-high to a mangle.'

Anwen's insides squirmed. Several images from over the years passed through her mind. They'd started courting unofficially when he was eighteen and she was fifteen but hadn't admitted it to their families until a year later. If they'd had their own way they'd probably have married there and then. Their families had said they weren't old enough, that they had to save and wait until her majority at twenty-one. She'd reached that last April – three weeks after Idris enlisted. Not that she'd done any saving.

'He's changed since he signed up. He's very… grim, and well, not hisself.'

'It'll be this illness, whatever it is,' said Violet. 'He'll recover and realise he's made a mistake.'

'No, I don't think that's it. He told me that he didn't—' more tears sprang from her eyes and the words choked her '—*doesn't* love me anymore.'

Gwen took hold of her once more. 'Oh *cariad*, I'm so sorry. There there, now.'

She kept hold of Anwen as the moan softened into a series of strangled sobs.

'What am I going to do without him?' she wailed.

She wept on for another couple of minutes, during which time she heard Clarice's little voice pipe up, 'What wrong with Aunty Anwen? She got tummy ache like I did yesterday?'

'That was last week, lovey,' said Violet. 'Aunty Anwen doesn't feel well, that's all.'

'Poor Aunty Anwen. I draw a pit-cher of her. And Aunty Gwenny.'

Anwen, all out of sobs for now, straightened herself and blew her nose. 'Right, that's enough of my self-pity. Sit yourself down, Gwen.' It was time to rebury the hurt until she was alone. 'Have you heard from Charlie, Violet?'

'A short letter two weeks back. He's never been much of a writer. Thinks he'll be off soon.' She rocked Benjamin again, although he hadn't stirred. 'Don't really know why Charlie signed up. Off he went to enlist, not a word to me first. At least Idris told you.'

'Did he?' Gwen looked at Anwen. 'My brother didn't say a word before he went to the recruitment office.'

'Yes, he told me.' Anwen had heard this complaint from Violet before. 'Not that I had any more choice in the end. He called in one Saturday evening to announce it, all pleased with hisself. I asked him not to go, to wait and see if they got called up. But he'd made up his mind.'

'They all had,' said Gwen. 'Henry was impressed by Mr Lloyd George's speech, about putting a Welsh army in the field, and how they should be helping to defend the small nations like Belgium and Serbia, and other *little five-feet-five nations*.'

'I'm afraid I laughed when Idris told me that,' said Anwen. 'What with him nearing six foot.'

'Indeed,' said Gwen. 'It's bad enough that Henry's gone.' Her mouth turned down at the corners. 'I do miss him. Never thought I would, the way he always used to tease me.'

Violet rose gently, carrying Benjamin over to the chaise longue and lying him down on it, covering him with the small blanket that had been draped over a dining chair. 'Another cup of tea?' She went to the teapot keeping warm on the stove, topping it up with hot water from the kettle.

Anwen nodded. 'I read in Da's paper this morning that there's been another ship sunk. The *Anglia*, a hospital ship. Just off Dover.'

'I can't even begin to imagine what that must be like for the families,' said Gwen. 'Do you think the Germans'll get round here, to Wales?'

'What for?' said Violet. 'What's here?'

'What's here?' Gwen's eyes widened in disbelief. 'Why, the ports at Newport, Cardiff and Swansea, the munitions where I work, the mines. And they got to Ireland to sink the *Lusitania* last May, didn't they?'

Violet handed them a cup each. 'Doesn't matter if you don't go to the war, it comes to you, one way or another. I wonder how many of our men will come back to Dorcalon?'

'Don't Violet, please,' said Gwen. Violet had been in this dark frame of mind for a few weeks and it wasn't the first time their friend had sought to silence her.

'How are you coping on your own?' said Anwen.

'The separation allowance doesn't give as much money as Charlie was bringing home from the mine, but at least I get to keep it all. Charlie can't hold back what he called his "spending money", for the public house and the football.'

'It's a shame there's less to buy with it then,' said Anwen, who suspected some of Charlie's money went on gambling.

Gwen fished in her handbag and fetched out a pot of geranium stain for her lips. 'And there'll be less still if our navy doesn't get rid of them U-Boats prowling round our shores.'

'Don't know what'll happen when Clarice and Benjamin need bigger clothes again. Growing like weeds, they are.'

'Mrs Bowen buys second-hand clothes as well as selling them,' Gwen said. 'You could take the babbies' clothes and get a bit for them, then put it towards bigger clothes.'

'What if I need little clothes in the future?'

'You're not going to need them any time soon, with Charlie being away. Unless you know something you haven't told us.'

'No. And that's one blessing at least,' Violet said quietly.

'What I was thinking,' said Anwen, 'was that Uncle Hywel will need new lodgings soon. Da won't have him with us. You could take him in, Violet, get rent. And Uncle Hywel is handy round the place.'

'I dunno. Charlie might not approve. And people might talk.'

'Get away with you!' said Gwen. 'Hywel's almost old enough to be your da. And loads of people have lodgers. Mrs White was widowed two year back, and she has four lodgers. You don't think she's playing around with all four of them, do you?' She giggled, almost spilling her tea.

'Gweneth Austin!' said Violet. 'Don't be so naughty. Mind, it would be useful to have extra money. I'll think about it.'

'I finish the pit-chers.' Clarice hopped down from the chair to bring them over. 'That's for you, Aunty Anwen.'

Anwen took the offered piece of newspaper, the picture of her in bold brush strokes just visible over the print. Her face was a wonky light bronze circle, reflecting her olive complexion, the brown hair sticking out at angles.

'Thank you, Clarice. You are a clever girl.'

Clarice beamed, showing two rows of tiny milk teeth. She took the other sheet to Gwen, presenting it proudly. Gwen was silent for a few seconds, finally saying, 'Goodness, Clarice, you could be an artist.'

Something about her expression made Anwen lean over to inspect the drawing. She'd given Gwen yellow skin. Anwen glanced at her friend's hands, holding the picture up. They'd got used to her changing complexion, but Anwen was reminded how unnatural it was, persuading her further that the munitions was an unhealthy place to work.

'Now why don't you draw a nice picture of your baby brother?' said Violet.

'It's Clarice's fourth birthday on December first, isn't it?' asked Anwen.

'That's right,' said Violet.

'I've seen some painting books in Mr Schenck's shop.' She'd scrape together a few pennies to buy one for her.

'The pity is, I've been saving a bit of money during the year for their birthdays and Christmas,' said Violet, leaning her head on her hand, 'and now there are hardly any toys left to buy.'

There was a strident knock at the door and Violet went to answer it. Anwen heard her thanking someone, before she came back to the kitchen with a letter.

'It was Mrs White next door. Said she found this on her door mat but it's for me.' Violet stared at the letter, unblinking.

Anwen joined her and viewed the address. It was Charlie's writing. 'Aren't you going to open it?' When letters had arrived to her from Idris, she'd almost torn the envelopes apart in her eagerness to hear his news.

Violet lifted the flap open slowly. Anwen sat back down, not wanting to pry. Violet pulled out the letter, her eyes moving quickly as she read the lines.

Placing the note on the table, Violet said, 'Has your family had a letter from Henry today, Gwen?'

'I dunno.'

'Only they're coming home tomorrow, on leave for thirty-six hours, all of them, according to Charlie. Before they... you know.'

Gwen's hand gripped the front of her blouse. 'Go to war.' The three words hung in the air like a fatal verdict. She sprang up, hurrying to the door. 'I'm going to see if we've had a letter,' she said, before disappearing into the hall.

Chapter Seven

Idris had been leaving chapel on Sunday, spilling out with the rest of the congregation, when he'd spotted them: healthy young men in uniform, straight-backed and rhythmic of step, striding out as if with their battalion.

On the chapel steps people stopped and pointed up Gabriel Street. Even from that distance he spotted Charlie Jones and Henry Austin. Someone alerted Violet and Gwen as they appeared through the door. The two of them lifted their skirts a little to run off down the road, leaving Anwen staring after them. When she peered down at him their eyes locked for a moment. Her expression could have been of pity or shame.

His split-second urge to bolt up the back alleys to his house two streets up was checked by his mother, clutching hold of his arm. 'Come on, *bach*, let's stroll down and wave to your friends. For who knows when we'll see them again?'

Some of his old Rhondda Pals – the 114th Brigade of the 38th Division, as Evan Owen had rightly pointed out they'd become – greeted him in turn. The handshakes and good-natured slaps on the back, the pointless greetings were endless. Time and again he was asked how he was and responded, *Fine, fine*. Nothing of any substance was uttered.

When the last one waved a farewell, Idris's legs had almost buckled with relief.

–

For two days Idris had gone over the scene, his friends' high spirits, even laughter. Had it been the prospect of seeing their loved ones, or excitement to get stuck in to the war? He'd skirted around the edge of the village to get home after work yesterday and today to avoid them.

Now, sitting at the kitchen table, trying to escape into a novel, real life caught up with him. At the front door he heard the murmur of voices, then his mother inviting people in. Idris put the book down on its open pages. It was late afternoon, getting dark.

'Look who's come to visit you, *bach*?'

Idris rose to see Charlie Jones, Percy Vaughan, Robert Harris and Maurice Coombes. They were all in uniform, causing a knot of envy to form in his belly. 'Well, mun, I didn't expect you lot to put aside any time for me.'

'Don't be daft. We wanted to see how you were,' said Charlie.

'I'll be in the scullery,' said Meg, closing the door behind her.

Idris pointed to the seats at the table and sat down. Charlie's dark brown hair was shorter than it had been, neatly parted on one side.

Jenkin came rushing into the room, maybe alerted by the voices. 'Oh, mun, you all look smart in your uniforms. And look at that.' He pointed to Henry's shoulder badge, a red dragon, indicating they were in the 38th (Welsh) Division.

'Yes, we finally got our proper ones,' said Henry, 'instead of those bits and pieces of uniforms they rigged us out in for training. One poor so-and-so even had on a scarlet jacket from the Boer War.'

'I bet you're a crack fighting force now though, with all your training.' Jenkin's face glowed with excitement as he spun round to take them all in.

'I wouldn't say that,' Maurice laughed.

'What exercises do you do? We've been doing military exercises at scouts. I wonder if they're the same.'

Idris looked down at the floor, feeling inadequate in the company of these men, all fit for action. Despite Jenkin's words about being proud of him for enlisting, he knew he'd let his little brother down.

'I hope not,' said Maurice. 'Well, not the stuff we did at Kinmel Park, anyway. Limbering up on telegraph poles mounted on bus tyres, long route marches, gun training with broomsticks and dummy rifles... and that was after we'd scrubbed the floors and latrines.'

Jenkin looked disappointed until Henry added, 'It got better once we got to Winchester. Did some proper training there.'

The young lad was engaged once more, asking for more details. As Maurice and Henry provided them, Idris noticed Charlie had gone quiet, sitting furthest away. Idris moved along to sit next to him.

'So, when are you off to the Front, or wherever you're going?' Idris had no inclination to know, but it was a better avenue of conversation than his discharge and how he was doing.

'Thursday. France. Can't say where.'

'I wouldn't ask... Looking forward to it?'

Charlie opened his mouth to speak but faltered. His forehead puckered. 'Only a madman would look forward to it,' he muttered, perhaps so the others didn't hear.

'But you were the one most up for—'

'Giving the Hun a bloody nose? I've talked since then to men on leave. Bloody carnage, it is. People said it'd be home from home for us hewers, being used to being underground. But although we know there could be an explosion or rock fall here, how often does it happen?'

'Not often is still too often,' said Idris.

'But in the freezing, diseased mud in a field in France, thousands are killed. Every minute could be your last. And sometimes soldiers wish it would be.'

Charlie must have been quoting someone else, for he'd never been an eloquent man. Plain-speaking, with a bit of a temper, not maudlin, that was Charlie Jones.

'See this here, in last week's *Herald*, for instance.' Charlie picked up the paper on the table, opening it and folding back the pages. 'Casualties for the 6th Welsh. Missing. Wounded. Killed. How long before it's the 38th Welsh?'

'I read the newspapers,' said Idris. 'I know it's not a party.'

'Aye, but the papers don't tell the half of it. And then there are the pieces about how ready we trainees are for the off, how proud, how we're keen to recruit others. You're well out of it.'

Idris wanted to fling himself out of the chair and through the door. What did Charlie know of being labelled *Not likely to become an efficient soldier*? 'I'd still rather be doing my bit.'

'Aye, you're a good man, Idris Hughes, always after doing the right thing. You just keep on digging out that *good steam coal*, as Edgar Williams is always at pains to tell us.'

'D'you hear that, Idris?' Jenkin's eyes were wide with wonder. 'They'll be going on a ship, overseas.'

Maurice laughed heartily. 'Well how else would you expect us to get abroad, *bach*? Fly?'

'The Royal Flying Corps would.'

'Yes, but I don't think they'd fit us all in those small planes.'

The door from the scullery opened tentatively. Meg peeped round. 'Would you like a cup of tea, lads?'

Charlie spoke for them all. 'No thank you, Mrs Hughes. We'll be going shortly.'

She nodded, disappearing back into the scullery. The tension in Idris's muscles eased.

'In fact, we were going to ask if you'd come out to the McKenzie Arms,' said Maurice. 'So many offers of pints we've had, reckon we could stand you a few too.'

Idris's brain worked quickly. 'Not tonight, I'm afraid. Said I'd help Gwilym fix a chest of drawers at his house. His mam wants it done quick, like.' Although it was true, they'd made no plans to do it this evening. 'And I thought buying drinks for others was banned now.'

'You know Reg Moss. He keeps his own rules, and Harries the Police turns a blind eye,' said Charlie. 'Anyway, it's your choice, mun. But we're off tomorrow and I've no idea when we'll see you again. Reckon we'll make an evening of it, if you fancy coming down later.'

'Don't you want to be with Violet and the kiddies?'

'I've spent time enough with family. Reckon I can be allowed out for some fun. Condemned man and all that.' The laugh that followed was without humour.

'I'll come with you,' said Jenkin, looking hopeful.

Henry stood and ruffled his hair. 'When you're a few years older, *bach*.'

Jenkin followed Henry and Maurice into the hall, still chatting about army life.

Charlie got up from the chair and moved towards the door. Before he reached it, he spun round. 'I'm not ashamed to tell you, I'm scared to bloody death, mun.'

Idris had no words of comfort. How could you tell someone in his situation it would be all right? 'Take care,' was his only response.

'You too.' Charlie entered the hall and soon Idris heard the front door shut. He picked his book back up.

Jenkin came back to the kitchen. 'I bet you're glad they popped in. I'll have something to tell Evan and the others, especially at scouts, when Mr Beadle gets us exercising.'

Idris put the book back down, accepting it might be a while before he got back to it.

–

'Come in,' Violet's voice called before Anwen had even reached the open back door.

'I gather they've all gone.' Anwen stopped by the sink where Violet was washing up. 'Here, I'll give you a hand with drying.'

'Charlie left about an hour ago.'

Anwen assessed Violet's face. She looked like a woman who'd caught her husband with another woman, her lips pressed into a pink slash. Her hands worked too quickly as they brushed the frying pan in the sink.

'It must have been nice having him home, even for such a short time.'

'Short time is right.'

'I guess the army is needing to get them off—'

Violet stopped her brushing suddenly. 'Thirty-six hours, and half of that was spent at his parents in Bargoed and at the McKenzie Arms. I don't resent him seeing his family, and I could understand him having a couple of hours to catch up with pals. But—' She yelped in frustration. 'And he made a fuss about Hywel being here.'

That would explain why her uncle had spent time at theirs and slept on the chaise longue at Gwilym's house for two nights. 'I think Uncle Hywel was happy to give you time to yourselves.'

'Which would have been fine if Charlie hadn't been rude to him. He doesn't appreciate that we're short of money since he enlisted. And then not to even be here half the time. At least Hywel helps out.' Violet lifted her hands from the water and shook them. 'I'll put the kettle on. You go and sit down in the kitchen.'

Anwen felt there was more to this than their conversation suggested. Or it could be that her friend was simply frightened for her husband, but didn't want to cry.

'Violet.'

'Yes?'

'Are things all right? Apart from Charlie going off to war...'

Violet paused drying her hands. After a short while she smiled. 'As all right as it is for anyone. Oh, don't mind me. I'm tired. Charlie was tired. The war puts a stress on everyone.'

'It does that, *cariad*. Now you sit down and *I'll* put the kettle on. Go on with you now.'

Violet beamed. 'Yes, madam, whatever you say.'

The service at the chapel was over, a particularly depressing occasion, with news of soldiers from the surrounding villages of Rhymney and Tredegar having died. They were men who'd signed up early in the war and had already been dispatched abroad. Anwen pondered, as Sara and Hywel led the way to the smaller room for tea, how long it would be before news of fatalities from their village started to filter through.

Hywel veered off to another part of the chapel to talk to a friend of his. Sara stopped to cough, pulling a handkerchief from her coat pocket to cover her mouth. She'd been doing that a lot the last few days. Anwen caught up, putting her arm through Sara's free one.

'Shall we go home?'

Sara was taken aback. 'No. I like being here, talking to people.' *Better than being home where Da will be waking up and complaining*, were the unspoken words.

Sara coughed once more. 'I'm sorry.'

'What for?'

Gwen, by the door to the tearoom, waved and came over. 'That's a nasty cough, *fach*. My mam swears by the Lightening Cough Cure. That'll sort you out.'

'I'll be fine,' Sara said defensively. 'Nothing a bit of honey and pepper tea won't sort out.' She carried on to where the minister's three daughters were serving the drinks.

'Is she all right?' asked Gwen, looking concerned. 'I didn't mean to offend her, poor lamb.'

'She's been coughing more since starting work at the House. But it has been colder and damper recently.'

'Yes, that's what it might be, then. But – well, I'd get her checked by the doctor, just in case.' She placed a hand on Anwen's shoulder and squeezed gently. 'I'm parched. Coming to get a cup of tea?'

'In a moment.' She'd spotted Elizabeth Meredith and decided to approach her. She hadn't sat with them this week, being a little late and taking a pew at the back. 'Hello Miss Mere— Elizabeth. I'm glad I've seen you. I was wondering how Sara is getting on at the House.' What she really wanted to know was whether she'd been coughing a lot there, too.

'She's very thorough.' Elizabeth hesitated. 'Maybe not as quick as my mother would like, but her excellent attention to detail is most satisfying.'

Anwen's heart sank a little at the polite criticism. 'I'm sorry she's been slower than you'd like. She's had a chesty cold recently that won't be helping.' She remembered Gwen's initial words. 'There are a lot of colds going around.'

'There certainly are. Tom has been in bed a couple of days with one. Mother doesn't want him getting ill again when he hasn't fully recovered from the influenza.'

At the mention of the illness, Anwen remembered how they had all thought her brother Tomos had contracted influenza. Her heart was heavy with the memory. 'I'm sorry to hear that.'

'He'll recover, don't you worry. I am a little more concerned about Sara. Has she been to the doctor? She is always cheerful but I do wonder if she is hiding things so people don't get concerned.'

It was a show Sara had long performed. She didn't like people to label her as 'ill'.

'Anwen, Miss Meredith.' Mrs Price, Hywel's former land-lady, touched Anwen's arm. 'Isn't it terrible? I've just heard that little Irene Marks on Owain Street died early this morning. The consumption again. Third little babby this month.' She sniffed into a handkerchief. 'What's to be done? And the diphtheria took so many last year.'

Anwen was surprised to see Elizabeth remove a handkerchief from her own bag, patting at the corner of each eye where tears had appeared.

'I'm so very sorry to hear that,' said Elizabeth. 'There's so much that could be done, if only...' She tailed off, not expanding on what those things might be.

'This war certainly isn't going to improve things,' said Mrs Price. 'Food shortages don't help our poor children get healthier.'

'No, they don't,' said Elizabeth.

The minister's wife, Agnes Richards, who'd been standing behind them, must have overheard. 'At least the Rent Restriction Act should help. The landlords won't be able to keep putting up the rents and leaving little money for anything else.'

'Quite so,' said Elizabeth. 'But if there is no food to buy, having more money will do little good.'

'Perhaps we should grow our own, on the spare land around the village,' said Anwen, immediately regretting talking out of turn in a conversation between the manager's daughter and the minister's wife.

Elizabeth considered her with surprising admiration. 'Have you ever grown your own vegetables?'

'We used to,' Anwen replied, remembering the long rectangle of produce that had once graced their garden. September three years ago, after her brother Geraint died in the night, her father stormed into the garden, kicking and chopping at the vegetables growing there. He'd blamed Geraint's death on those vegetables, saying their old next door neighbour had poisoned them after he'd had a quarrel with him. The doctor had diagnosed consumption, but Madog wouldn't have it. 'We haven't grown them for years,' she said as an afterthought.

'I must go to the Marks family after I've finished here, to offer comfort,' said Mrs Richards. 'The Lord giveth and the Lord taketh away,' she concluded, moving on to talk to someone else.

'The Lord giveth and maybe it's beholden of us to make the very best of what he gives,' said Elizabeth. 'There's too much complacency.'

'I don't know about that, Miss Meredith. What can we do?' said Mrs Price.

'What indeed?' said Elizabeth, as if in a dream. 'It's certainly about time I did something. Good day, ladies; I must take my leave of you.'

Elizabeth wove through the crowds and was soon out of view.

How Anwen wished she had Elizabeth's position and connections, or at least, her confidence, then maybe she *could* do something.

–

The Workmen's Institute was the last place Idris wanted to be of an evening, listening to the union man rambling on about rights and wages and conscription, but his father had almost dragged him from the house.

He'd been glad to be a part of it all once, the union, the committees for arranging funds to build the hospital and Institute. Both had been completed five years ago. He'd been proud to contribute his penny per week. Penny ha'penny, it was now.

Their union representative was a skinny blond man called Philip Hubbard, a fireman in the mine. He'd rambled on about the South Wales Miners' Federation's disapproval of conscription, and how they were going to make their opposition clear to Asquith's government.

Isaiah and Gwilym were sitting either side of Idris in the main hall. As people stood, interrupting each other and arguing, the pair of them shouted, 'Hear hear,' and several variations of, 'Sit down and shut up,' according to who was talking, like many men in the room.

A small man with dark olive skin, known to everyone as Twm Bach, jumped up to shout, 'If our army gets short of men, don't you think it's beholden of us to go and fight alongside our countrymen?'

'*Short* of men is what you are,' shouted a voice. 'You wouldn't reach anywhere near the minimum height, Twm Bach!' People laughed.

'It's not Britain's problem as I see it,' bellowed Idris's butty, Jory Damerell, who'd moved up from Cornwall two years before. 'Let those who started it sort it out. What's it got to do with us?'

Twm Bach started, 'Lloyd George says—'

'Lloyd George! Let him go and fight then,' said Jory, causing more shouts of support and derision.

At this point another figure stood, yelling, 'Quiet!' It was Edgar Williams, the under-manager. 'Of course we must help our fellow human beings against the evil of the Germans and Austro-Hungarians, that is not in question, is it?' He glared at Jory Damerell, daring him to answer back. 'But, comrades,' he said, adopting Hubbard's language, 'we *are* doing our bit, digging the coal for our good navy to blast the U-Boats out of the water.' He caught Idris's eye, fixing his gaze on him. 'And any miner who goes running off thinking he can do any better sitting in a godforsaken trench is a fool.'

There was further quarrelling for and against his words.

'As for Britain not fighting in the war, only an idiot would think like that,' Hubbard continued, shouting above the din. 'Consider how miners' wages have gone up since the trouble started. Let's face it, war is excellent for business, and not just ours. The steel industry, munitions. It's all good for the economy.'

'You sound like Lloyd George,' called Samuel Bevan, a timberman in the mine.

'Nothing wrong with Lloyd George,' said Twm Bach. 'He should be prime minister, not Asquith. About time we had a Welshman as prime minister, if you ask me.' There were more cries of *hear hear.*

Beside him, Gwilym got to his feet. Idris pulled on his jacket for him to sit down, but he resisted.

'War is excellent for business, is it Williams?' Gwilym snapped. 'The only people who'll profit in the end are the bosses. You wait and see. Come the end of the war, we'll be on the march for decent pay again.'

There was a murmur of assent from some quarters of the hall.

'In the meantime,' said Jory, 'we've got Christmas coming up and nothing in the shops to buy for our children, despite this so-called wonderful pay increase. And food's not exactly flowing either.'

'That is not the subject of this meeting,' said Hubbard, 'but rather whether we should go out on strike if the government insists on—'

'Then it should be the subject! That's what we're all concerned about.'

From then on the meeting broke into factions, discussing various topics. Isaiah and Gwilym attached themselves to the nearest group. They talked of the shortage of meat at the butcher's, despite the recent influx of rabbit, pigeon and the occasional mutton and chicken.

So absorbed was Idris in catching snatches of these conversations that he didn't hear someone creep up behind him, until Edgar Williams's low voice said, 'So you weren't man enough to speak up against me yourself. You had to get your friend to do it.'

Idris kept his gaze ahead as he replied, 'Gwilym says what he wants. It's got nothing to do with me.'

'Like hell it hasn't, Hughes. Watch your step – and your back.' Williams made his way to the door, upright and brash, pushing through the men and not apologising.

'What was that about?' said Gwilym, joining Idris once more.

'Williams was blaming me for *your* big mouth.' He leapt up. 'I'm off home.'

'Idris, mun, don't be—'

Idris left, not hearing what Gwilym had to say, following in Edgar Williams's footsteps. He didn't see the under-manager until he was outside, hanging back at the top of the double steps. There was someone waiting for Williams at the bottom.

Madog Rhys, Anwen's father. Idris stepped quietly to the top of the steps, watching as Madog and Williams disappeared into the dark of Jubilee Green. Now there was a strange pairing.

Chapter Eight

Anwen gazed around the bookshop, wondering where to begin. She was the only one there, other than the owner, Mr Schenck, who was sorting through a box of books on the counter. The shop had opened around twelve years back. It had always been a place of fascination and peace for her, with its high dark wood shelves of books and the constant aroma of beeswax and paper. A couple of small, square tables were placed in the centre, one of which always held a selection of the latest volumes. Anwen spied DH Lawrence's *The Rainbow* and Virginia Woolf's *The Voyage Out* among them. On the other table she spotted *The Railway Children*, picking it up and peeping inside. She'd had a copy of that as a twelve-year-old, bought for her by Mamgu Llewellyn, her maternal grandmother. One day it had disappeared into the fire, like most of the other books they'd owned. Now Anwen mostly borrowed from the library, knowing her father wouldn't dare harm those.

She was about to sit down with the book when the shop bell rang. She readied her smile for whoever the new patron might be, a smile that got stuck halfway when she saw it was Idris.

He glanced briefly at her before making his way to the second room, where they kept the history books he loved. Anwen placed *The Railway Children* back where she'd found it. She couldn't afford the book and it wasn't what she'd come for. Outside, the sky darkened further with incoming slate clouds. Mr Schenck put on the lights.

Inspecting the second-hand shelves, always neatly in author alphabetical order, Anwen quickly found *Peter and Wendy*. Sara had borrowed it from the library at the Workmen's Institute several times so Anwen was sure she'd love her own copy. She ran her fingers over the green cover with its beautiful gold illustrations.

'Can I help you with anything?' said Mr Schenck, his Dutch accent still evident, though his English was very precise and accurate – probably more so than many in the village. He wore a suit with a waistcoat, his fob watch tucked into the pocket, and a round-collared, high-necked shirt.

'Thank you, Mr Schenck, but I believe I've found what I'm looking for.'

He peered down at the title. 'The boy who never grew up. A book of wishful thinking maybe, from Mr Barrie.'

Anwen often wished she'd never grown up. Maybe that was the appeal of the book to Sara. 'It's a Christmas present for my sister.'

'The first of December already. Where has the year gone? Shall I take that for you?'

She handed him the book. 'Thank you, though I'd like to browse for a little longer.'

'Of course.'

Anwen moved from the novels, to a section labelled 'Travel', wondering what lands she could visit via a book. As she was taking down one about Scotland, the door opened swiftly, clanging against the door stop. Esther Williams, the under-manager's wife, stormed in. Following her were a group of half-a-dozen women, each with a furled umbrella looped over an arm.

'Can I help you, Mrs Williams, ladies?' Mr Schenck moved away from the counter to greet the group.

'I have to say,' started Mrs Williams in imitation of Mrs Meredith's accent, 'that I am *most* surprised to find you still trading in time of war. When there are so many shortages, how can you justify selling such – fripperies?' She dismissed the shop with a flick of her hand.

Anwen watched as the woman's minions nodded in agreement.

'I am now a Guardian, which means that I have the authority to check on the morality and behaviour of the village.'

Anwen had read about this new type of Guardian, who were different to the Poor Law Guardians who oversaw the running of the workhouses. Instead, they were primarily tasked with looking after the women's virtue, making sure they didn't run amok while the men were away, and weren't seduced by the soldiers in their dashing uniforms. It made her angry that women were taken for such weak, silly creatures. That Esther Williams should have been put in a position to keep an eye on them all was worrying indeed.

'My first concern, Mr Schenck, is foreigners in the village. Now, you claim to be Dutch, but your name sounds very *German.*'

'The two languages are similar, having a common root, that is true, madam.'

One of Mrs Williams's acolytes stepped forward, a pinch-faced woman from West Street, called Mrs Watkins. 'It's all the same though, isn't it? You Dutch aren't fighting the Hun, you've just stepped back to let them get on with it.'

This was awful. Anwen had read how the Germans in some British towns had suffered their shop windows being smashed, and nasty things written on their homes, even though they were guilty of nothing.

Mr Schenck spoke calmly as he said, 'I do not know the answer to that, as I am not privy to the actions of the Dutch government. I am but a humble bookseller who left the land of his birth seventeen years ago. I agree it is regrettable that they have decided on this stance, but some good has come of it, I believe. There is, as a consequence, neutral ground across which soldiers from both sides can be treated and where prisoners of war may be swapped.'

There was no sign of Idris. Perhaps he was absorbed and couldn't hear what was going on. Or maybe he was hiding because he didn't want to get involved. Either way, it was up to her to come to Mr Schenck's defence. She stepped forward. 'What is it exactly you are accusing Mr Schenck of, because you seem to be accusing him of something?' She placed her quivering hands behind her back.

'And who are *you* to question a Guardian?'

'I didn't think the duties of a Guardian were to question innocent people about their nationality,' said Anwen.

'Our powers are far-reaching. And one of my duties is to make sure the women in this village remain virtuous, not loose, so you'd better watch your step. What is your name?'

Mr Schenck put his hand up. 'You've no need to tell her.'

'That's Anwen Rhys, that is,' said one of the group. 'She lives down Edward Street. Her father's Madog Rhys.'

'Anwen Rhys,' repeated Mrs Williams. 'I shall make a note of that. As for you, Mr Schenck, you might show more solidarity with our brave soldiers and the miners here if you closed the bookshop for the duration of the war and concentrated on making a better contribution to the war effort. You're still relatively young – in your forties, is it? Why not work at the mine or in munitions?'

There was the plod of heavy boots on the wood floor, getting louder as their wearer got nearer. Idris appeared from around a bookshelf, standing defiant, his jaw set firm. 'Mr Schenck is offering an excellent service here, lifting our spirits with a little escapism. And his nephew, Noah, works at the mine, so this family *is* doing its bit. I don't see your son Daniel down a mine, or in the army, Mrs Williams.'

The old spirited Idris was so evident, Anwen was for a moment back in the past.

'Well really! I know who *you* are. Idris Hughes, who wasn't good enough for the army. Probably not good enough for the mine either. Edgar's keeping an eye on you, and now I am, too.'

If Idris had fallen foul of the under-manager it was very brave of him to stand up to his wife, thought Anwen. A smidgeon of admiration crept in among the resentment and hurt.

'Now, now,' said Mr Schenck. 'I like to think my shop is a place of peace and thoughtful contemplation, a whole world of discovery in two rooms. Would you not like to explore, ladies, find a book for a loved one for Christmas?'

'Fripperies and nonsense!' proclaimed Mrs Williams.

'Quite so, quite so,' murmured some of her entourage. A couple of them shuffled awkwardly.

'These miners shouldn't be able to afford such things when times are hard.'

'My understanding is that they are earning more since the war,' said Mr Schenck.

'That has *nothing* to do with it. Now ladies, we will depart and spend no more time in this… this den of sin!'

With that, she ushered her group out of the door, some of them chattering at once in condemning tones. The rain was falling faster now and for some moments they huddled in the doorway.

Mr Schenck considered his two customers. 'My goodness, *a den of sin*! That is indeed an extraordinary claim. Thank you for coming to my defence. I don't think it will make any difference to the illustrious Mrs Williams, who is always waging her own war.'

Outside, Esther Williams and her ladies were putting up umbrellas. After, they crossed the road to the McKenzie Arms.

'Can it be true that she's been appointed a Guardian? I thought only the larger towns had them.' Anwen said this as much to get Idris's attention as to make a point.

Idris stared out of the window, not replying.

'Who knows?' said Mr Schenck, lifting his shoulders and lowering them. 'But I see much trouble resulting from it.'

Idris disappeared back round the bookshelf without another word.

'I will pay for that book now,' said Anwen, going to the counter in the middle of the room.

'I hope your sister will enjoy it,' said Mr Schenck.

She would if it was hidden well, and Da didn't throw it on the fire.

–

Anwen congratulated herself as she sprinted up the stairs. Mam would be pleased with the two Jane Austen novels she'd found in the library today.

She knocked on Mam's door briefly. Plunging into the room, she came to an abrupt stop. Her mother was sitting on the side of the bed, facing the window.

'Mam, what are you doing?' Anwen ran to her, dropping the books on her father's side of the bed.

Her mother gaped at her, as if frightened of something. 'I – I don't know. I don't know how I got here.'

'Can you get any further? I mean, if you've managed to shuffle around and get your legs over the bed, you might be able to do more.'

'No. Help me back, please.' Her mother's chest was rising and falling rapidly.

Anwen took her mother's legs, manoeuvring them onto the bed. Taking her by the arms, she struggled to pull her back up to the pillows. She straightened the sheet and blankets, covering her mother and tucking the bedclothes under her arms.

'I didn't hear you come in.' Enid looked over at the books on the bed. 'You've managed to get me some Jane Austen! Wonderful.'

Anwen leant over to retrieve the books, handing them to her mother before sitting on the edge of the bed.

'Thank you.' She opened *Mansfield Park*, reading a little of the first page before closing it and laying it on her knees. 'Anwen, do you think Sara is ailing a little more than usual? That cough hasn't got better and she is often pallid.'

'I know, Mam. I did suggest we get the doctor in, but she got quite cross. She says she's just tired from the work and that the winter cold is making it worse. I wonder if I did the right thing giving up the job to Sara. It's longer hours than sorting the coal.'

'But much better conditions.' Enid patted her daughter's arm. 'You did the right thing and I'm proud of you.'

'I wish Da hadn't insisted that she work. I couldn't dissuade him.'

'I tried, too, goodness knows I did. But I'm not in a good bargaining position these days. Your father's still out, is he?'

'Yes, but I don't know where.'

'He is giving you money for the bills and food though, isn't he?'

'He is.' Though barely enough. Her wages paid for a good deal of what his should have paid for, and even then he sometimes snatched money from her. And now from Sara. She wasn't going to tell Mam this, though. 'I'd better go and start on supper.'

'You're good girls, both of you. I don't know what I'd have done without you.'

'Mam, shall I tell the doctor you moved to the edge of the bed? He might examine you again and see if—'

'No. I'm sure it was a fluke, done in my sleep maybe.'

'But if you can do it in your sleep—'

'I said *no*. And don't tell your father.'

Anwen left her to it, taking the stairs down with a heavier heart than when she'd gone up.

–

Sara arrived back on Monday evening as the clock on the dresser chimed half past six. Despite the day of rest yesterday, she was drooping like someone who'd already done six long days.

'I'll just get my coat off and I'll give you a hand.'

'No, you sit down. I've done supper. I managed to get a piece of salted bacon in the butcher's so I've made a cawl of sorts.'

'I'm not hungry tonight. I'll go and see Mam.'

'Hold on a moment. Shut the door.'

Sara did as she was told, resting her coat over a chair.

'Is the job too much for you? If so, I'll get the doctor up and he can tell Da you're not up to it.'

'Don't you dare!' said Sara, her voice louder than normal. 'I like it at the House. I don't get out otherwise. I don't see any of my old school friends now. I think it's because I've been unwell so much that they get fed up with me.'

She slumped onto the chair and burst into tears. Anwen flew to her, cradling her in her arms.

'Oh Sara, I hadn't realised.' But when she thought about it, her sister hadn't mentioned friends recently.

Sara's sobs got louder before they turned into a cough. It carried on while Anwen found her a clean hankie, handing it to her as she rubbed her back. It was a good five minutes later before the rasping cough ceased.

'I'm going to get the doctor, Sara. That's more than a cold.'

'No it's not! I just have a weak chest. I need some herbs, that's all. Have we got any Cough Cure in the house?'

'I think we've run out.' Not that it ever did much good when Sara was having one of her spells. 'There is a little bit of honey in the cupboard, if you'd like that in a cup of tea.'

'I'll go and see Mam now and have it when I come down.'

'And then we'll have our supper.'

Sara nodded. No appetite and a rasping cough. A sense of helplessness overwhelmed Anwen for a few seconds before she told herself it wouldn't help. What would she do if her sister came down with a bout of influenza? She'd have to insist on her giving up the job, even if she had to tie her to the bed. And take the consequences when Da found out.

Back from her shift, washed and cleanly clothed, Anwen considered tackling the housework downstairs, the sweeping, dusting and polishing. It was already Thursday. She examined the kitchen forlornly. Barely any of what was usually achieved by this time had been done. It was hard keeping up now that Sara was working too.

Her father hadn't returned yet. As they'd left work, she'd seen him traipse off in the opposite direction, despite being unwashed and in his dirty pit clothes.

First and foremost, the front step needed a good scour. She put some cold water into a bucket and took it with the scrubbing brush and soap to the front door. As she opened it, she jumped, jolting the bucket so that the water went over her skirts.

Elizabeth was on the edge of the pavement, holding Sara up. Behind them was the Meredith family's motorcar, a black Morris Oxford. Her sister's skin had a grey tinge. Anwen put down the bucket and ran to her. Several neighbours were outside, watching with curiosity.

'My goodness, what's wrong?' said Anwen.

Sara coughed, lifting a handkerchief to her mouth.

'Perhaps we could step inside?' said Elizabeth.

'Of course.' Anwen went back to pick up the discarded items and put them to one side in the hall.

Elizabeth held Sara's arm as she helped her in. Anwen cringed with shame for her inadequate house, before the anxiety for her sister weighed her down once more. She led them to the kitchen. Although not as tidy as the front room, where she would in other circumstances have taken Elizabeth, it was warmer.

'Could I have some water, please?' Sara was having difficulty breathing.

Anwen ran to the scullery to fetch it, bringing the cup back as Elizabeth helped Sara into one of the wooden armchairs by the fire.

'Could I talk to you in the other room?' Elizabeth whispered, nodding towards the scullery.

Anwen led her through, closing the door after her.

'How long has Sara been like this?' Elizabeth asked.

'Always. She's never been strong. Every cold goes to her chest.'

'But bad like this. She coughed up a little blood earlier.'

A tingling dread crept across Anwen's body, causing her to wrap her arms around herself tightly. Geraint and Tomos had coughed up blood. But it wasn't necessarily bad, was it? 'I haven't seen any blood before. She's been coughing more, recently, but she insisted she was all right. I bought her some cough mixture and she said it had helped.'

'Why is she working at all? I know you said your father insisted, but can't he see she's ill?'

Anwen crumpled into the one chair in the room. 'Our father is not a patient man.'

'He will have to see sense now. You must fetch the doctor. You should have done so long ago.'

Anwen closed her eyes momentarily. 'I told her the other evening I would, but she got agitated, said she loved working at the House and didn't want to give it up. I think it's been a refuge.'

'Is your father a violent man?'

'He likes things done his own way. Since Mam fell down the stairs, we have to do the best we can. She could handle him better than we can.'

'Is your mother not getting any better?'

'The doctor and hospital couldn't find any reason why she couldn't walk, yet she can't. And the more she stays in that bed, the more I fear she never will.'

'I see there is more going on here than your sister's condition, and it is all probably contributing to her poor health. I'm afraid my mother insists that Sara is not to come back to work at the house, and I agree with her. She is simply not well enough.'

'I understand.' At least the manager's wife saying it might hold some sway with Da. It all depended on his mood.

They heard a distant door slam, then another, closer.

'My father,' Anwen said in explanation, jumping up to sprint into the kitchen.

He was standing erect, cleaner than when she'd seen him last, scowling at Sara reproachfully. 'What's all this then, the manager's motorcar outside my house? Have you brought disgrace to my family, Sara Rhys?' He lifted a hand above her and she cowered.

'Please Mr Rhys!' said Elizabeth sharply, stepping into the room. 'I have brought Sara home because she is unwell. She is not fit to work. The girl needs care and attention.'

Madog lowered the hand, stumbling back slightly. 'Not fit to work? She only has a bit of a cold.'

'You must fetch the doctor. I'm afraid we won't be taking her back at the house. And she must not work anywhere else... Sara, I will bring your wages on Friday. Take care now. I bid you all farewell.'

She reached the front door before Anwen could get there to open it for her. Madog stood in the kitchen doorway, a grimace marring his countenance.

With one leg out into the street, Elizabeth halted as Madog murmured in Welsh, 'Laughing stock I'll be, my daughter fetched home in a motorcar, not even fit enough to flick a duster.'

Elizabeth looked back at him to reply in the same language, 'It's more than a laughing stock you'll be if I hear you've raised your hand to your daughter again. She's ill, Mr Rhys, not a malingerer.'

His mouth opened in surprise.

Anwen stepped out to speak to Elizabeth, only to see Idris and Gwilym, no doubt on the way to Gwilym's house at the end of the terrace.

'What's going on?' Idris regarded Anwen.

Madog was at the door by this time. 'It comes to something when a man can't be master in his own house. Since when did management get to be boss of my hearth too?'

Elizabeth rounded on him. 'This is nothing to do with the pit, or my father being manager; it's common decency that a woman shouldn't fear she will be thrashed for being ill, or any other perceived misconduct.'

'He hit Sara?' Idris's voice rasped in incredulity.

'I only raised my bloody fist, that's all.'

'You want to be careful, talking to Miss Meredith like that,' said Gwilym. 'Find yourself without a job, and a house, you will.'

Idris stepped forward. 'You want to watch yourself, Madog Rhys, that it's not you gets a fist raised to them, for one of these days you will go too far.'

Anwen was trembling from her shoulders to her knees. Doorways were filling up with curious spectators, leaning out to watch the show. She was aware of Mam's faint voice from upstairs calling, 'What's going on? What's happening?'

Madog's features twisted in hatred. A stream of profanities gushed forth, aimed at Idris. It was an intolerable situation, especially with neighbours listening in. Anwen held back the pressing tears.

His vitriol spent, Madog stood defiant in the doorway.

'I think I had better fetch the doctor now,' said Elizabeth, unfazed by the vulgar language. She patted Anwen's shoulder. 'I won't be long.' She went to the motorcar, taking a crank from inside it, going to the front and winding it until the engine started. She got back in and set off.

Idris glared at Anwen's father. 'You are a sick man, Madog Rhys. You need to watch your step.' He and Gwilym tramped on to the end of the terrace.

Madog spat on the ground then disappeared inside. Anwen followed quickly, afraid he'd hurt Sara, despite the warnings.

Sara was still sitting on the chair, bent over, handkerchief to her mouth. Madog went to the scullery, returning with wet hands.

'You'd better get your sister to bed. Quicker she's well, the quicker she'll be earning again. I'm going out.'

'But you haven't washed.'

He ignored her, leaving through the back door.

Sara went ahead of Anwen to the hall. She took the stairs slowly, Anwen standing just behind her to catch her should she falter.

In the bedroom, she helped her sister undress and get into bed, propping her into a half sitting position on her pillows to make it better for her chest. 'I'll bring you some food.'

'I don't want any.'

'You've got to eat something. I'll get you some of the broth left from last night. Elizabeth is fetching the doctor.'

Back on the landing again, Anwen heard her mother call, wanting to know what was going on. She'd have to play it down, say Sara had a bad cold; that Da got annoyed and shouted at the nosy neighbours to mind their own business.

Mam didn't need any more to worry about.

–

Dr Roberts took off his coat, shaking it and hanging it on the hatstand in the hall. 'Where is Sara?'

'In her bedroom,' said Anwen as she hurried to the stairs. 'I'll show you the way.'

Sara was sitting up with a book when Anwen and the doctor reached her room, her skin grey and damp with sweat.

'I'll examine her alone, if you don't mind,' said Dr Roberts when Anwen sat on the bottom of the bed. 'I'll come and speak to you afterwards.'

'Oh. Right. I'll be in the kitchen.' She left, wondering whether she should go and talk to her mother first. She hadn't called, so she must be sleeping.

When Anwen entered the kitchen, Elizabeth was placing the kettle on the stove.

'You didn't have to do that.'

'It's no bother,' said Elizabeth. 'I do know how to do things in a kitchen.' She offered a tiny smile.

Anwen went to the dresser for three cups and saucers, bringing them back to the table and sitting down. Elizabeth joined her. They sat in silence until steam issued forth from the kettle's spout. Elizabeth jumped up.

'No, it's fine,' said Anwen, going to the dresser. 'I know where everything is.' She took the tea tin down and went to the stove, placing four spoonfuls in the pot. As she filled it with water, she hummed a tune.

'"*Calon Lân*",' said Elizabeth. 'A beautiful song.'

'We sing it in the choir sometimes.'

They chatted in muted tones about chapel, and the concerts and talks held in the village in the last few months, keeping the mood hovering only a tiny bit above the gloom of the situation.

Dr Roberts returned to the kitchen ten minutes later.

'A cup of tea for you, Doctor?' asked Anwen.

'Thank you.' He took the offered cup and sat on one of the armchairs.

'So, what is the prognosis?' said Elizabeth.

'I've taken a sample of her expectorate and it will be tested, but it will take quite a while to get the results.'

He was avoiding an answer. Whatever it was, Anwen needed to know. 'Do you think it's consumption?'

'Almost certainly, yes.'

Anwen leant over, clutching her stomach, her face creased in pain. Dr Roberts jumped up, putting his tea on the table. He was just in time to catch her as she stumbled out of her chair, taking her to the armchair he'd just vacated. She'd known in her heart of hearts that Sara was seriously ill, but hearing it confirmed was agonising. Tomos, Geraint, and now Sara. How could they bear another loss? But not everyone died from consumption. Some survived, in the right circumstances. A few, too few.

'I'm sorry,' she said to Elizabeth.

'Why?'

'Because if it is consumption, I've put your family in danger by bringing Sara to you.'

'It's not quite as simple as that,' said the doctor. 'Though I would advise sterilising things she may have come in contact with.'

'Will she have caught it from Geraint?' asked Anwen.

'I don't know. He died, what, four years ago?'

'Three.'

'You had a brother die of it?' Elizabeth's question was faint, breathy.

'Two,' said Anwen. 'Tomos died eight years ago.'

'It can lay dormant for a long time,' said the doctor. 'The advice I just gave Miss Meredith, you must take too. Also boil the clothes she's worn, and her sheets. Don't use them for anyone else. Any handkerchiefs she uses must be burned. She's to stay at home but must get fresh air, take a turn in the garden every day, even in the cold. And she needs feeding up.' He leaned down to open his bag, from which he took a sheet of paper. 'Here, this will tell you what you need to know about containing it. Would you like me to find out about a place in a sanatorium?'

'I don't suppose that's covered by the subs we pay.'

'I'm afraid not.'

'Then no, we can't afford that.'

'I'm sorry… Now, while I'm here, I might as well examine your mother.' He tipped the cup up to finish the tea. Picking up the bag, he headed for the door.

Now the initial shock was over, Anwen's head was flooded with a kind of blankness. There was too much to do, too much to think about. She had to be the strong one of the family.

Chapter Nine

Anwen hadn't seen her father since he'd gone out yesterday, after Elizabeth's initial visit. She'd allayed her mother's worries with a reassurance that he'd stayed with a drinking pal, but she really had no idea where he was.

As she stood in the scullery now, leaning over the washing copper, the back door flew open and banged against the draining board. Madog stomped in from his shift, heading straight to the kitchen.

'Where's my bloody dinner? Nothing's out, nothing's cooking.'

'Is it that time already? I'm sorry.'

'You'll be sorry on the other side of your face. And what's all this?' He pointed at the copper and the clothes on the dryer. 'It's Friday, not bloody Monday.'

She wiped her hands on the wraparound apron. 'The doctor came yesterday. He said I was to do it.'

'Your sister's only got a cough. I'm not paying for more soap to—'

'Da! Sara's very ill. Dr Roberts thinks it might be, well, he's pretty sure it's… the consumption.'

Madog became dead still. 'No. Weak chest, she has. She always has.'

'We've been fooling ourselves, Da, thinking it couldn't happen again like with Tomos and Geraint.'

Even with his swarthy colouring, Madog went pale. He plonked himself into an armchair, placing his arms on his knees and lowering his head. 'My boys, oh my boys. Why were they taken from me? Better to lose daughters than sons, for what do they bring to a house but little bits of money and a lot of lip?' He started rocking, moaning low, 'My boys, my boys.'

He went through this performance every now and then. She thought of it as such since he showed no sad emotion for anyone else in the world. Here was Sara, ill, and he could only think of his sons, already passed on.

He lifted his head, apparently recovered. 'I'm not paying out for another coffin,' was all he said before he propelled himself out of the chair and marched away to the kitchen. A few seconds later, the front door slammed. He'd gone out unfed, yet again. There was no checking on Sara for him, no asking how Mam was taking it. He had stopped worrying about anyone but himself long ago.

She and the doctor had decided not to tell Mam just yet. He was worried about her too, unable to fathom why she wasn't on her feet by this time, reiterating that the x-rays had shown nothing amiss. It was a worry, but now not at the top of her long list. Getting Sara better was her prime concern.

–

Idris was traipsing down to the grocer's shop, the sun hurting his eyes as it sat low on the mountains. The air was so cold it burnt his nostrils as he breathed in.

Every day now Mam had sent him out for something after he'd had his bath and dinner. Bread, meat, vegetables and margarine had been the most common requests, despite the first two being rare at this time of the day. Today she'd asked for lard. He'd realised quite quickly it was her way of getting him outdoors and not allowing him to stay brooding in the house.

Coming out of Alexandra Street and onto the top of Jubilee Green, he spotted Dr Roberts heading towards Edward Street. He hoped Sara hadn't taken a turn for the worse, poor girl. He felt sick with worry for his dear, dear Anwen, having to cope with yet more illness in her family.

Skirting past the Institute, he decided to go through the gardens on Jubilee Green, despite their winter nakedness. You were less likely to come across people in there this time of the year.

This reasoning was disproved halfway down when he saw Polly Coombes sauntering through the gate at the opposite end. Dark blonde, she was, and tall for a woman. Her clothes were always a little brighter in colour than those of others. She was the youngest sister of Maurice Coombes, one of his fellow Rhondda Pals. The family had come from London when Polly was an eleven-year-old and she'd been at school at the same time as Idris. He recalled that Anwen had never taken to her, said she was 'false', but he'd never witnessed it himself. Despite that, he had no wish to get drawn into a conversation with her right now.

She waved, quickening her step. 'I thought that was you, Idris. Been wondering when I'd come across you. Been back a while now, haven't you?' Her London twang had been softened a little by the valleys.

He slowed his step, not wishing to appear rude. 'About five weeks.'

'My mum heard it from your mum. And you're not going back to the army, neither?' She looked infinitely happier about it than he felt. 'And I hear you and Anwen Rhys have called off the engagement. She never was good enough for you.'

Anwen not good enough for him! Imagine. If only there was some way to get rid of Polly politely.

'You're still dressmaking with Mrs Bowen, are you?'

'Indeed. People still need clothes despite the war, them that can't sew theirselves or can't be bothered and have the money to spare.' She trilled a laugh, like a bird tweeting. 'The well-to-do always want clothes and we've a good reputation. We're making blouses for Mrs and Miss Meredith at present, and shirts for the young and older Mr Merediths. Both handsome men. I went there to help measure them. Such a modern house; it's wonderful to visit.'

Why had he asked? He'd expected a yes or no. He nodded respectfully.

They reached the gate. 'Where are you off to?' he asked. He had no interest in the answer except to make sure he went in the opposite direction, even if it meant going the long way around to the grocer's.

'To my sister's on Islwyn Street.'

The detour would not be necessary. 'Good evening to you, then.' He raised his cap.

'And to you, Idris. I hope I'll be seeing you again *very* soon.' She lowered her face, looking up through her eyelashes in mock coyness.

He walked away, aware of her lingering a while. When he reached the pavement diagonally opposite the grocer's, he glanced around quickly. She'd only just set off from the gate.

'Lard,' he muttered as he crossed the road. That was something at least they wouldn't be short of.

—

'It's only me – Cadi. Mamgu.'

Anwen heard the voice call from the hall as she sat at the table in the kitchen, preparing dough in a bowl. Beside her sat Sara, cutting an old newspaper into stars, happy as a child. She'd begged to come downstairs today, to join in.

Both the girls got to their feet. Anwen experienced an equal measure of delight and relief at her grandmother's cheerful voice. The yoke of work and sadness was lifted, if only temporarily.

Cadi got to the kitchen before the girls got to the hall. She placed the three overloaded sack bags down, hurrying to her granddaughters to fling her arms around them.

'How are my darlings? Looking forward to Christmas?'

Sara beamed. 'I'm so excited, Mamgu.' Her voice was weak.

Cadi held her tighter, flashing a questioning glance at Anwen.

'What have you brought?' Sara let Cadi go, peering into the bags her grandmother had put on the floor.

'Hey, don't peek in that one now.' Cadi pointed to the bag on the left. 'Otherwise there'll be no surprises. This bag is food. You can take that. The other one's my clothes.'

Sara tried lifting the food bag, but despite her grim determination to complete the task, all her effort produced was a small cough. Anwen relieved her of the bag without a fuss, placing it on the table. 'You empty that out, Sara. I'll take Mamgu up to my room.'

'What are you doing, *cariad*?' Cadi asked Sara, noticing the paper shapes and scissors on the table.

'Before the war Anwen and I saw some lovely star decorations in a shop in the arcades in Cardiff. We couldn't afford them so I'm making my own.'

'I'm sure they'll be just as beautiful.' She followed Anwen out of the room.

'It's very kind of you to share your bed with me,' said Cadi. 'Are you sure it's not an inconvenience?'

'We can top and tail. It'll be fine. It's what we used to do as children…' She trailed off, recalling the days when Tomos and Geraint were still around.

Cadi climbed the last step, her face sad. 'Of course.'

'It's very kind of you to come and help us with Christmas. It's been a difficult month.'

'No need to thank me. There's nowhere else I'd rather be than with you. How has Sara been the last few days?'

'Not good. She's found it hard to get out of bed even for her brief time in the garden for fresh air. She's been coughing more and is exhausted all the time. She insisted on coming down for Christmas Eve preparations, but I don't know how long she'll last before she needs to go to bed again.'

'We could make her a bed up on the chaise, then she can join in.'

'Perhaps.'

Anwen led the way into her bedroom, pointing to the space at the left side of the bed, next to the small window overlooking the garden. 'You can put your bag over there.'

'I'll go and have a word with your mam, then come down to help. Have you got the dinner on for when your da gets in?'

'Not yet. I'm just preparing some bakestones. I managed to find some flour at the back of the larder. I saved some margarine and currants and a couple of eggs, and there's a bit of milk left.' Or rather, this was what she'd managed to hide from her father. She was wary of telling his mother that, unsure of how she'd react.

'What a lovely treat for Christmas Eve. I'm looking forward to having my family around me.'

Anwen smiled, all the time wondering whether her father would stick around for the evening. He usually behaved better when his mother was here. Cadi was planning on staying a few days so it would be interesting to see if he could keep it up.

Downstairs again and having put a kettle of water on the stove, Anwen went back to the bowl, placing her hands in to knead the as yet rough dough. She hoped the bakestones would come out even half as good as Mam's.

Sara had piled up the few items of food Cadi had brought, including biscuits. 'I'm so glad Mamgu's come. It'll be different with her here. Maybe she could persuade Da to let Mam come down. Uncle Hywel could fetch her like he did before, when he comes for his dinner tomorrow.'

'Maybe.' She feared even Mamgu could only push Da so far.

'I wish we could have a Christmas tree. Mrs Meredith was talking about getting one for the Big House.'

'They're expensive and where would we put it?'

Sara scanned the room. 'It doesn't matter. This will be the best Christmas *ever*.'

Anwen worked the dough silently, thinking back on many childhood Christmases it would be difficult to beat. That wasn't what Sara needed to hear. 'Of course it will, *cariad*, of course it will.'

—

Anwen opened one eye, then the other, surprised to spy the first hint of Christmas morning light through her thin curtains. It wasn't like her to sleep much beyond the time she'd normally get up for work. It must be about half past seven now. Changing position, Anwen realised Mamgu was already awake, sitting up, peering across at her.

'*Nadolig Llawen, cariad.*'

Anwen heaved herself up, walked on her knees to the other side of the bed and kissed her grandmother's cheek. '*Nadolig Llawen*, Mamgu.' She shivered and rubbed her arms. 'And it will be a happy Christmas once I get the fire going. I want to make everything ready and nice.'

'I'll come down and help you.'

The two of them got out of bed, turning their backs on each other to get dressed. Anwen slipped on an old frock. She'd put on her Sunday best later, after all the preparations had been done.

'Sara was coughing in the night,' said Cadi. 'I went in to her, but she said she was all right and not to fuss. I fell asleep and didn't hear her again.'

'I must have been fast asleep. I didn't hear anything.'

Cadi opened the bedroom door. 'You get the fires going. I'll start preparing the food for later. It's lucky Madog managed to get hold of a chicken, isn't it? Fancy someone managing to get two and wanting to sell one.'

Anwen smiled but didn't comment. She wasn't convinced by her father's explanation, imagining it had been given only because his mother was there. More likely he'd acquired it in a less than honest manner.

Dressed now and in the kitchen, Anwen swept out the grate. Cadi was in the scullery, washing the few vegetables they'd managed to get hold of. After finishing with the fire and washing her hands, Anwen went to a drawer in the dresser, pulling out the one tablecloth her family owned, white cotton with a crocheted lace trim. The lace had been made by Anwen's other grandmother.

Cadi entered the kitchen. 'I'll take cups of tea to Enid and Sara. Then I'll pluck that chicken.'

'Thank you. I'd like to have it all ready by the time we leave for chapel. The chicken can cook while we're out.'

Cadi made the tea, commenting as she poured, 'Don't suppose Madog will be bothered just yet. He never was an early riser when he didn't need to be. That's why I was surprised when he changed shifts to the morning one in the spring. Night owl, he is.' She lifted the two cups and saucers. 'Sara won't want to miss too much of Christmas day. Like a child she is still, bless her.' Cadi left the room to deliver the tea.

Anwen went to the drawer to fetch the cutlery for breakfast. As she was about to lay the knives and forks on the table, a piercing scream came from upstairs. Her body jerked with fright, her hands dropping the cutlery.

Almost tripping on her skirt, she rushed up the stairs. The door to Sara's room was open. Slumped against the bed, was Mamgu, sobbing. There was broken china around her. Enid's voice from the other room was shouting, 'What's happened?'

Anwen stepped slowly in, an icy chill climbing up from her toes, making her legs weak. The metallic smell caught at the back of her throat. She gasped. Even in the dim light of the room she could see Sara was lying on her back, head flopped to one side. Her skin was pale, her eyes staring up, her lips apart. On the sheets and her nightie were copious amounts of blood, both brown and red. Anwen's hand flew to her mouth, all breath sucked from her lungs. Her parents' bedroom door creaked. Anwen was aware of her father's form in the doorway. Mamgu began a rhythmic lament on a low note.

'What's bloody going on here?'

Anwen turned to her father, the tears flowing down her cheeks. He looked from her to his mother, who was now rocking back and forth.

'What, what is it?' he asked quietly.

A voice from the next room called, 'What's happened? Please tell me.'

'Da, Sara's gone,' Anwen sobbed, seconds before the intense buzzing stress in her head rendered her unconscious.

Chapter Ten

The pony-drawn cart reached the cemetery gates and the small coffin was retrieved from the back of it by Idris, Isaiah, Hywel and Gwilym. Anwen was being clutched by Mamgu as they watched. For several days before there had been sleet, but today the sun was shining as if Sara in her heavenly home had ordered it.

Earlier, there'd been a short service led by Pastor Richards in their home, attended only by her family and Idris's. When they'd left the house, the street had been lined with villagers. Anwen and her family had followed the cart as it was drawn away, beginning the three-mile slog to Rhymney cemetery.

The villagers had fallen in step behind, singing four verses of 'Guide Me, O Thou Great Jehovah', after which they'd fallen silent.

Now at the gate of Rhymney cemetery, they entered the grounds, Madog marching ahead of them.

Anwen peeked behind. There were still plenty of people following. Idris, Isaiah and Jenkin were close behind in their Sunday suits, walking parallel with Gwen and Violet. Elizabeth was walking behind them with some other ladies from the chapel. She had offered the motorcar for their journey, though they'd turned it down. Anwen recognised a couple of girls who'd once been school friends of Sara's, who'd drifted away when she'd become poorly. The group of ladies who cleaned the chapel made a solemn group. Her mother had once been part of them, many of them had been her friends as a young mother in the village. Everyone else she spotted had played some part in her and Sara's lives, however small.

They trudged down a path past two fields of headstones, turning left to tramp across the grass to an open grave. She recognised the spot; she'd been here several times before to visit her brothers. Da was mean with many things, but for the burial of his family he always had enough money to do a 'decent job', as he put it, despite his threat not to buy another coffin.

The immediate family gathered round the grave, everyone else standing at a discreet distance. The coffin was lowered as the minister spoke solemn words. Anwen was barely listening, concentrating more on not being sick. She crossed the large lapels of her coat one over the other, gripping them with one hand. *When will this be over?*

Another grief lurked behind her one for Sara. For all the comfort given by Uncle Hywel and Mamgu, how much more solace would she have received from Idris's loving arms? She wanted to look round for him, gather at least a tiny piece of comfort by his presence, but she didn't allow herself to raise her eyes from the grave.

The minister finished. Madog picked up the first clod of earth, throwing it onto the coffin. Anwen went next. She ungloved her hand, bending to pick up the soil. It scalded her with its deathly chill. In it went, the last contact between her and her beloved sister. Cadi went next, then Uncle Hywel. The minister said a few more words.

It was all over, people parting to let them through, when her father broke into the Welsh lullaby, 'Suo Gân'. *Slumber child, upon my breast, It is snug and warm…* She had not heard him sing for many years and was surprised at how clear and melodic his voice was.

As one the crowd stopped, facing the grave once more, slowly but surely joining in. It touched her soul while at the same time extending her anxiety. How long before she could leave this place of the departed? Idris was behind his father, his face sombre, singing with the others. Willing herself to look away, she focused on the bare trees.

Finally the singing finished and people departed once more.

Cadi took her arm. 'We must get to the gate to speak to people as they go through.'

'Can't we just go home?' said Anwen. Her body was as weary as her spirit. All she wanted was to hurry to the warmth of her house. She yearned to sit with those she knew best.

'People have taken the time to come. They'll want to give their condolences.'

Anwen nodded, submitting to the necessary tradition.

They walked together as a family to the gates, her father slightly ahead.

Madog set himself up opposite the three of them at the gate. They were the only family. Mamgu's sister, Great Aunty Maggie, had told her she couldn't spare time for the funeral when Mamgu returned to Abergavenny briefly to impart the news. Enid's family in Cardiganshire had conveyed in a letter that it was too far to come.

People drifted by them, shaking hands and mumbling awkward words of comfort. Even Polly Coombes, a classmate at school and a shallow creature if ever she'd known one, took her hands and squeezed them. The shop keepers were represented by Mrs Moss, the landlady of the McKenzie Arms, and Mrs Prosser, the butcher's wife. Gwen, Violet and Elizabeth were just behind them.

When will this end, please, when will it end? Anwen couldn't bring herself to reply any more than a murmured thank you, the repetition of which made her want to scream. She imagined herself doing so, running from the cemetery, throwing herself in front of a cart, or a train, to rid herself of this all-enveloping ache.

So much in a world of her own was she, that Idris went unnoticed until he was in front of her. She almost jumped, working hard to keep her face devoid of any kind of reaction.

'I'm so sorry for your loss, Anwen,' he said. 'She was a lovely girl, full of affection for everyone.'

His heartfelt words made her want to throw her arms around him and sob, to hold onto him forever. This was the first day she'd seen Idris since Sara's death, even though Meg and Isaiah had been round with offers of sympathy and help.

'Thank you for your kind words, Idris.'

He gave a brief nod, moving on to Cadi and Hywel, only shaking their hands, adding nothing. Isaiah came next, close to tears himself, only patting her shoulder but not speaking.

When will this end?

–

Anwen heaved a sigh of relief as she entered her home with Cadi after the three-mile trek back.

Meg Hughes appeared in the hall. 'You must be frozen with this chill. I've lit a fire in the front room and there's a kettle on the boil.'

'Thank you for stepping in to do this,' said Cadi. 'How's Enid?'

'As well as can be expected.'

Anwen was almost in the kitchen when she heard others at the front door. Isaiah entered with Idris, though Jenkin was not there. She had difficulty swallowing, anticipating the awkwardness. Still, the day was not about her, but about Sara. That's who they would speak of, reliving happy memories, if other such teas were anything to go by.

'Jenkin's decided to go home,' said Isaiah. 'I think another old school pal dying has got to him. He lost Bertie Smalls a few months back.'

Anwen remembered this sad death. A fourteen-year-old boy, down the mine, caught in a rock fall. She entered the front room. The place that had so recently housed her sister's coffin was now laid up for tea, the table covered with their only cloth. Mamgu had managed to persuade the butcher to keep them a pig's head from which Meg had prepared brawn to put in the sandwiches. Next to them sat a small pot of mustard. There were even some bakestones with a pot of Mam's homemade apple jelly. On the upright piano a framed photograph of Sara had been given pride of place. Anwen switched on the light before stepping back into the kitchen, where Meg was placing a kettle on the stove.

'Where's Da?'

Meg looked round. 'Isn't he with you?'

'He went ahead. I thought he'd be here.'

'No, *cariad*, he hasn't arrived yet.'

Hywel appeared in the front room doorway, his face serious. 'I'm going to fetch your mam down. It's not right she's in that bedroom day in, day out. This is her daughter's funeral. Your father can't object on a day like this. If he shows up.' The last sentence was delivered with some venom.

'She's dressed and presentable,' called Meg. 'She insisted on putting on her Sunday best.'

'I'll get Idris to give me a hand.'

Anwen helped Meg take milk jugs and cups into the front room, placing them on the table.

'About time Enid joined the land of the living again,' said Isaiah.

Cadi clucked her tongue. 'I'll have to speak to Madog about this again. Dr Roberts didn't think there was any reason for her lying in bed forever more.'

Anwen wanted to curtail this conversation. 'Is there anything else I can do, Mrs Hughes?'

'Dear me, no, *cariad*, you sit and rest after your long spell in the cold, get yourself warm. And what's all this *Mrs Hughes* business? You've called me "Meg" since you were sixteen.'

She did as she was bid, relieved to be given permission to sit. Meg left the room with Cadi and Isaiah. Soon there were sounds of a confused conversation and something being dragged. Cadi came in, moving chairs along, ahead of Isaiah and

Meg who were struggling with the chaise. Once in position, Hywel carried his sister in. Idris came up behind with two folded blankets, handing them to Cadi to tuck around Enid.

'Thank you,' said Enid, her tone sad. Her eyes were red and puffy. 'I cannot stand being locked away from everyone when my daughter has just been buried.'

Locked away. It made her sound like a prisoner. Was that how her mother felt?

Cadi pointed to the food on the table. 'Come on now, everyone, we're all ready for something to eat, I'll be bound. Meg's done us proud and I'm very appreciative that she offered to do this.'

'Hear hear,' said Enid. 'She is a true friend.'

Meg was framed by the doorway, rubbing her hands on her apron, her face neutral. 'I'm just doing my bit.'

'Take the apron off and come and join us now.' Enid indicated the seat next to the chaise.

Idris sat on a seat away from the fire. It was also as far from Anwen as he could get. Despite not being at all hungry, Anwen went to the table to show her appreciation. Two quarters of a sandwich and a tiny piece of mustard was all she took. She'd got back to her seat before Idris got up to help himself, the last of them to do so.

'Are you comfortable, Enid?' said Cadi.

'Very much so. It's more relaxing in some ways than sitting in bed.'

'Then we must bring you down more often.'

'We'll see.'

Anwen's intense frustration almost surpassed her distress. She wished she were a man, able to handle her father. Or that Geraint and Tomos were still around to do so. None of her siblings had got past fifteen. She squeezed her eyes tight as the grief of the loss of all three of them collided into a massive sorrow.

'Are you all right, *fach*?' said Cadi next to her, touching her arm.

'Yes, Mamgu. Just remembering them all.'

Cadi nodded. 'So many to remember.' She had suffered her own lost children and siblings, having many more to recall than Anwen.

Meg rose. 'The kettle must have boiled now. I'm sure a cup of tea will be welcome to everyone.'

Idris jumped up. 'I'll help you, Mam.'

'A good lad you've got there,' said Enid. She displayed no bitterness at what had occurred with regards the engagement. She had said at the time, *sometimes things are just not meant to be.* It had served as no comfort to Anwen.

'And you've got a great girl.' Isaiah smiled sadly at Anwen, giving her the impression he regretted her loss to his family.

Everyone fell silent for a while until Enid said, 'Isaiah, would you be kind enough to get the photo album down from the bookshelf?'

'Of course.' He heaved his body up with some difficulty. He was older than Meg and this showed in his stiff limbs. How he still managed in the mine, Anwen wasn't sure.

The bookcase – an old mahogany piece her mother had acquired from a neighbour who'd moved away – held no books. It contained instead odd pieces of china, a wooden musical box and two dolls that had belonged to Anwen and Sara as children. The photo album contained a few official photographs that they'd had taken with a local photographer, along with older, faded photos from the generation before.

Meg and Idris returned with two teapots, placing them with the cups and jugs on the table.

Idris faced the room, saying haltingly, 'I'll be getting back and leaving you to it. I'm truly sorry about Sara. Truly sorry about everything.' He left the room.

'He's not been hisself since he was discharged,' Meg said, as if by way of explanation. 'Let's all have a drink and look at your album, Enid.'

The rest of the group gathered around the chaise longue. Anwen gratefully took the tea offered her by Meg, but remained in her seat by the fire, staring into the flames.

—

Idris followed his mother into the Rhys's kitchen, glad for a reason to escape the close proximity to Anwen. It was killing him inside, not being able to put a loving arm around her in her distress.

He heard Enid's words, 'A good lad you've got there,' fade as he moved away from the door. He didn't deserve her good opinion, especially as she had no idea why he'd broken up with her daughter.

If only he could think of a way to make it up to her. Perhaps give her some of the money he'd saved for their future? Maybe he'd leave it until a time she might be most in need of it.

'I'll fetch the two teapots down and you get the tea from the larder,' said Meg.

He did as he was told, all the time wishing he could escape. What use was he here, if he couldn't be a comfort to his beautiful Anwen? No, not *his* Anwen anymore. That was his own doing, but the reality of it was agony, nonetheless.

When Meg had filled the teapots up and put the woollen cosies on, they carried one each back to the front room. Those there were gathered around Enid, looking at a photo album. There was a snap in there of him and Anwen, taken by a photographer at Barry Island, the day before war was declared. He didn't want to see it.

He hesitated before saying, 'I'll be getting back and leaving you to it. I'm truly sorry about Sara. Truly sorry about everything.'

Out in the street the icy rain of yesterday had returned. Where could he go? It was one of those rare occasions he felt like going for a pint, to drown his sorrows. The McKenzie Arms wasn't open this time of day anymore, which would probably save him from a sore head and a shaft-load of regret.

He turned onto Bryn Road, heading towards the pit. His head was already swimming with the torment of the choice he'd made. Life without Anwen. Or rather, life with her always there on the edge, struggling with her family, and he unable to do a thing. And maybe, one day, she'd be happy with a new love.

The tears sprang from his eyes before he had time to stall them. He blessed the rain for disguising them, although there was no one else around. He couldn't go home in this state and upset Jenkin. He took a left onto James Street. A good long walk, past the Big House and into the forest, that's what he needed. A forest that he and Anwen had loved to visit. But everywhere was filled with her. He'd have to live with that.

Chapter Eleven

The service at chapel had gone by slowly, the minister's voice only a remote sound as Anwen's mind wandered into another realm. The one thing that got her attention in the sermon was the line: 'In the midst of life we are in death.' She'd quoted that very line to Sara not two months back. Sara had said she could feel death breathing on her in the night. It was like she'd predicted her own passing. Anwen clutched a fist to her chest, pushing at the chasm left by Sara's extinction.

Uncle Hywel tapped her arm and she came to.

'The service is over, *fach*. Are you staying for a cup of tea?'

'I don't know if I can.' It had been only two days since the funeral. Could she stand another half-hour of people's sombre nods?

'You don't have to. I'll walk you home if you like.'

Home wasn't a welcoming place, though, either. Mam had developed a cold since the funeral and was asleep most of the day. At least her father would be out, who knew where by now.

'I think maybe I'll stay. Would you like to come back for some dinner? It won't be much, just stew left over from what Cadi made yesterday, before she left.'

Da had made it clear that his mother had served her purpose and it was time for her to 'bugger off back to Abergavenny'. What he didn't know was that she was returning permanently with all her things, by the end of the week. How that would go down with her father time would tell. The possibility filled her with optimism, that's all she knew.

'That's kind, but Violet is cooking me dinner. I'm paying for meals, you see.'

Disappointment weighed heavily on Anwen. 'I wish Da had agreed to you lodging with us.'

'You know I'm always there when you need me.'

They wove through the chatting congregation. Just before they reached the door to the smaller room, the minister's wife, Mrs Richards, waylaid her. Hywel carried on.

'I'm so sorry to hear about Sara. I would have called in but have had many people to visit. How sad it is for you to have such a reduced family group here in the chapel. I see your grandmother is not present either.'

'She's gone back to Abergavenny.'

'Slowly you have dwindled and now there are only—'

'Anwen, I am glad to see you here.' Elizabeth came up next to them. 'Could I speak to you alone, please? That is, if Mrs Richards has finished with you?'

'Well, yes, of course Miss Meredith.' Mrs Richards took her leave of them.

'My goodness, she's not much good at comforting the bereaved, is she?' said Elizabeth. 'How upsetting for you.'

'Thank you for rescuing me.'

'I would genuinely like to talk to you. We were wondering, my family... oh goodness, is this too soon?'

'What might be too soon?'

'Would you be able to take up the position of housemaid? In your own time, of course.'

'I – I don't know.' It hadn't even occurred to her that the position would still be open. 'Thank you for offering it to me, but I will need to think about it.'

'Of course. Let's get some tea.'

Having collected their cups, they fell into conversation with Gwen and Violet, little Clarice clinging to her mother's legs as Violet rocked Benjamin. Anwen's two friends seemed a little nervous talking to the manager's daughter at first, but soon relaxed as Elizabeth chatted in Welsh to them.

'I heard recently that there are two million more women being employed in Britain now than last year,' said Elizabeth.

'That many?' said Gwen. 'That's wonderful to hear. I've been working in the munitions at Ebbw Vale for the last year and there are a few of us there, I can tell you.'

Elizabeth asked Gwen questions about the factory, listening with rapt concentration to the answers, while Anwen considered Elizabeth's job offer. Her father had made no fuss, so far, about her lack of wages. He almost certainly would soon. Even if he didn't, did she want to spend all day in the house, even if it was a full time job in itself?

No. And if Cadi did come back, her father might be more inclined to accept her staying if Anwen was earning and out all day.

They'd finished talking about munitions and Elizabeth had moved on to admiring baby Benjamin when Anwen said, 'Yes please.'

'Yes please to what?' said Gwen.

'To the job at McKenzie House.'

'I'm so glad.' Elizabeth was smiling.

'That will be good for you,' said Violet. 'Get you out and about. Well, I need to get these two littl'uns home for their dinner.'

'And I need to find my parents. They'll both be chatting nineteen to the dozen with people,' said Gwen.

The two women drifted away.

'When would you prefer to start?' asked Elizabeth.

'I will have to wait for Mamgu to get back, as my mother needs someone there to help her, particularly now she's so downhearted after Sara's passing. Hopefully by the end of the week.'

'Come to the house and let us know when would be best for you. I should get away too. Are you staying?'

'I will come too, but I must tell Uncle Hywel first.'

Anwen slipped sideways past several groups, excusing herself, until she spotted Hywel. Now she had a new purpose in life, returning home was less daunting. She could tell Mam her news, then make sure she had clean clothes for the job.

'Uncle, I'm going now.'

'All right, *fach*. I'll call round tomorrow after my shift, see if you need anything.'

'Thank you.' She kissed his cheek and left.

Outside the front door of the chapel, a smart figure was waiting on the steps. It was Tom Meredith in a stylish, knee-length coat and Derby hat.

'How fortunate am I,' he said, spotting Anwen leaving with Elizabeth. 'I've come to accompany my sister home, and I'm lucky enough to be able to escort another young lady also.' He bowed slightly.

'I'm going in the opposite direction, Mr Meredith, up to Edward Street, so you don't have to worry about me.'

'How disappointing. So, what is the verdict?'

'Verdict? Sorry, sir, I don't understand.'

'He means, have you agreed to take the position of housemaid,' said Elizabeth. 'And the answer is yes, Tom. Though I believe Miss Rhys has more pressing matters at this moment in time?'

'Oh, yes, of course.' The smile evaporated. 'I was so very sorry to hear of Sara's passing.'

'Thank you, sir.'

'Good day to you, Miss Rhys.' Tom lifted the hat briefly. 'I look forward to seeing you when you begin the job.'

'Thank you once again, sir.'

She and Elizabeth exchanged farewells. Nothing could replace Sara, but at least now she had a reason for getting up in the mornings.

Anwen had finished the morning's cleaning, though it took longer than it might have done had there been a maid in attendance the last month. A half-hearted attempt had been made to keep things clean and tidy, but the dusting and polishing had clearly been inadequate. Elizabeth had told her that the cook, Rose, had filled in the best she could.

In the kitchen now for her half-hour dinner break, Anwen was faced with the cook. Her curly blonde hair was pulled into a bun on which was perched a starched cap, the odd coil of hair escaping round her ears. She was grim-faced, fists on hips, glaring at her. 'I hope you don't think you're having dinner now. It's gone two. I've put it all away.'

'I'm sorry, Rose, but I had to do the cleaning for longer than normal, to catch up with things.'

'It's not my fault if you're a bit slow. No better than that sister of yours. You can thank Miss Elizabeth for speaking up for her that she stayed as long as she did.'

Anwen was taken aback. 'My sister died on Christmas Day.'

'I heard. Sorry about that.'

'And I've been slow because things have been neglected.' This girl had no authority over her and she wasn't going to be blamed for things that weren't her fault.

Rose puckered her lips. 'Are you suggesting I wasn't up to the job?'

'I'm sure you would have been if you hadn't already had so much to do.' She'd better make some concession otherwise she'd never get her dinner.

'I have: like doing dinner after it's over.'

'Rose, would you be so kind as to fetch Anwen some lunch.' Elizabeth was in the doorway, standing tall. 'There's plenty of chicken, vegetables and potatoes left over. I'm sure it will warm up in no time over a saucepan of boiling water. She's worked very hard this morning trying to catch up with things.'

'Yes Miss, of course, Miss.' Rose curtsied then hurried to the pantry.

Where were families of the Merediths' class getting plenty of food when it wasn't available in the shops? Under the counter, maybe, for greatly inflated prices. A little voice in her brain said, *It isn't fair.* She waved the thought away. Even if the Merediths had shared their extra food around the village, it wouldn't have gone far.

'How are you finding things?' Elizabeth came further into the kitchen.

'Fine, Miss Meredith. It's all very straightforward.'

'It's all looking so much better. Thank you. Now, after lunch you can change into the uniform provided for you. My mother would like you to run some errands for her in the village. I believe my brother also has an errand for you while you're there.'

Tom. A spark of cheer lit a corner of her mind. Such an entertaining and polite young man. 'Very well, Miss.' She curtsied, emulating Rose.

Elizabeth grinned, appearing to be amused by the exchange. 'Thank you. I will see you later on, no doubt.' She left the room.

Rose emerged from the pantry, thumping the leftovers on the table. '*It's all looking so much better!*' she imitated Elizabeth's middle-class voice, raising the pitch. 'Who's the new pet then? It was bad enough when that soppy Jenny was around. And I hear you've been seen out with Miss Meredith. Stepping over the boundary, that is.'

'Miss Meredith was kind enough to visit my sister when she was ill, and attend the funeral. There's nothing wrong with that, is there?'

Rose opened her mouth in shock. 'Nothing wrong with it? Are you cracked? They are *them* and we are *us*. You should keep in your place.'

Anwen wanted to say that maybe Elizabeth should keep in her place then, but she couldn't be bothered to argue with Rose.

'Suppose I'd better get this *lunch* ready. If you want a cuppa tea you can get it yourself.' She pointed at the stove.

Anwen picked up the kettle, taking it to the scullery to fill it up. She certainly did need it, but she'd be glad when dinner was over and she could get back to her duties.

–

The grandmother clock struck six in the hall of McKenzie House. Anwen had just been dismissed by Mrs Meredith after her first, long day. She returned to the kitchen to change from the uniform and retrieve her coat and hat from the servants' hatstand. Rose was at the table, chopping carrots.

'Off home, are you?'

No doubt Rose would be resentful about that as well, but she could be pleasant even if the cook couldn't. 'That's right.'

'I've got another hour. Make dinner, serve it. Home. Can't say I'll be sorry today. My feet are killing me.'

There was no awkward attitude in her voice. Anwen could have been listening to Mam or Violet. 'Do you live in the village?'

'Mafeking Terrace. Moved in there with Mam and Da four year back. We were up at Merthyr before then. I was under cook to a family there. They had more functions and bigger ones, but it was easier because there was more staff, though that was before the war. Could do with an under cook myself.'

Anwen wondered how cooking three meals a day for just one family could be so hard, but she guessed Rose had other duties that under other circumstances might have been given to a scullery maid.

'I can see that would be useful.'

Rose stopped chopping and regarded Anwen. 'Sorry about earlier. I like to keep things tidy and do things in order. The Merediths do put upon me sometimes. You'll find that yourself, no doubt.'

Anwen's sympathy went out to her. She'd heard before of middle class families taking advantage of the staff. 'I'll see you tomorrow, Rose. Have a good evening.'

'Thank you. And you.'

Anwen left through the scullery door, as she'd been instructed by Mrs Meredith. Outside the air was frosty. The sky was lit by a full moon, still fairly low in the sky behind McKenzie House. She'd left home in the dark and she'd return in the dark. This would be her fate until winter transformed itself into spring and the light stretched into the evening.

It was twenty-five past six by the time she got in, remembering with relief that Mamgu was coming back today.

She called, 'Hello?' in the hall as she removed her coat. The only reply was a faint one from upstairs. Mam.

Pushing open her mother's bedroom door she saw her sitting up in bed, a blanket round her shoulders as she read the *Monmouth Guardian*. Enid put the paper down, her face brightening only a little from the melancholic expression that had tainted her face since Sara's loss. '*Cariad*, how was your first day at the Big House?'

'It was fine. Hard work, but warm and not too dirty at least.'

'I am so glad that you were able to take that job on. I know it was too much for my poor Sara.'

Guilt stole over Anwen like a plague, threatening to annihilate her.

'Don't look like that, *cariad*. This world was too much for her... Would you help me with the pot, please? I've been bursting to go for hours.'

'Has Mamgu not arrived yet?'

'She came this morning, got me some dinner and this paper. Meg came and went. Then I heard some kind of argument between Mamgu and your father when he got in. She came up to see if I needed anything, then said she'd be back later. She's so kind to up sticks to help us out.'

An argument. That didn't bode well. She helped her mother with her needs, going afterwards to Sara's room, which was to become Mamgu's. It contained none of her grandmother's possessions. What was going on? Anwen went down to the kitchen to find the fire in the grate almost out and nothing even prepared for supper. She gave a deep sigh. There wasn't much food in the house. Whatever was in the larder she'd have to cobble together and make the best of it.

She'd opened the larder door and was peering in when the back door opened and was knocked shut. Da. He'd clearly washed and changed after his shift, yet he was still somewhat dishevelled. He paused by the scullery table, a sack bag in one hand, in the other a dead chicken, intact and retaining its feathers. He dropped it on the table, the head drooping to one side, its eyes blank.

'See what you can make of that. Struck lucky I did. Bit old but it's better than nothing. Not become squeamish, have you?' He was standing straight, his speech coherent.

'No, Da. I'll put it with the leeks and the couple of potatoes we've got in the pantry.'

'Haven't you been to the shops? I need more than that for my supper.'

'I've only a bit of money left. I'm not being paid till Friday next. Besides, the shops were a bit bare yesterday and I've been at work since six this morning.' She didn't like to mention it was his payday and he needed to provide some money for the week.

He dug his hand in his pocket, pulling out a few coins and tossing them on the table next to the chicken. There was a florin, a half crown, a threepenny piece and a few coppers. 'There'll be more before Monday, if you're lucky.'

'Thank you, Da.' She swept up the coins, placing them in her skirt pocket before he changed his mind. 'Do you know where Mamgu is? She should have been here.'

His expression darkened as he regarded her. 'Reckoned she was going to live here, daft old bat. I told her straight, she can come and help with the house and with your mother, but there's no room for her.'

'What about Sara's roo—'

He lurched towards her, causing her to back against the larder shelves. 'There's no bloody room, you understand?'

'Yes, Da.'

'I'm sleeping in the little bedroom.'

'How will she help us from Abergavenny?' She knew she was pushing her luck, but she needed to know what the situation was. If Mamgu could only come to help sometimes, it would make her job at the Big House nigh on impossible.

'She's gone to find lodgings. She'll explain. I've got to go out again. Just make sure you have that stew ready for when I get back.'

'Yes, Da.'

He left the scullery, still holding the bag with its mystery contents. She heard him clomp upstairs.

A minute later he was downstairs again. The front door opened and closed. He was gone.

–

There was a knock on the back door just after nine. Cadi stepped in before Anwen got there, removing her hat and hatpin, placing them on the dresser.

'You didn't have to knock.'

'I didn't want to give you a shock, that's all. I'm guessing your da is out.'

'Yes. Where have you been? Da said you were finding lodgings.'

Cadi sat down heavily on the scullery chair. 'You wouldn't be so kind as to fetch me a cuppa tea, would you? I'm parched.'

'Where are your things?'

'In Alexandra Street with Florrie Harris, widow, as she was keen to point out on several occasions, as if it were something unusual. I pointed out I was one too, but she wasn't impressed with that. Anyway, one of her daughters has moved to Aberdare, and she wanted a lodger.'

'How are you going to pay the rent?'

'Same way I paid my sister. By taking sewing in. Dab hand I am, very neat.'

'I know you are.'

Mamgu had made lovely clothes for her and her siblings when they were babies. They were still in a trunk under Mam's bed, ready for the next generation. There wasn't much prospect they'd be used any time soon.

'I can do it here, in between doing jobs, while I keep your Mam company. She must get lonely in the day.'

'I'm sure she does, though she never complains.'

'Not her way. I thought that the first time Madog brought her home. Quiet thing she was, a thinker. She was the heart of this home.' Mamgu was talking about Enid as if she'd passed on, but in a way she had. 'Reckon we could get her downstairs more, what do you think? Then when I'm cooking and doing cleaning, I'll be company for her. And her for me.'

Anwen flung her arms around Cadi's shoulders. She leant her face on her soft, salt-and-pepper hair.

'What's all this, then? Are you going to get an old lady a cuppa tea, or stifle her?'

'I'm so glad you're going to be nearby. I've been so lonely since we lost Sara, and, and...'

'Since Idris broke your betrothal?'

'Yes. Why is life so hard?'

'Don't ask me, *fach*, if I had the answer I'd have had a better life myself.'

Anwen got up. 'Come to the kitchen. I'll fetch you that tea and a nice bowl of chicken stew.'

'Chicken, is it? Lead the way.'

Chapter Twelve

Idris didn't want to be here, at the Workmen's Institute, yet again. He'd had enough at the meeting before Christmas, with all the pointless arguments. He was still a paid-up member of the South Wales Miners' Federation though, and what they decided affected him, as Da, sitting next to him, had reminded him countless times in the last few days.

The hall was so full there weren't enough chairs for all the men to sit on. Their union representative, Philip Hubbard, had already recapped the big meeting for them, one he'd attended on their behalf.

Edgar Williams was currently standing, his thumbs wedged in his waistcoat pockets. 'So, what you're saying is, the union voted unanimously against miners being conscripted.'

Hubbard stretched his head upwards, puffing out his chest. 'They voted against the idea of *anyone* being conscripted.'

Williams addressed the audience. 'So there you have it, men: it's come down from the powers that be that we're better to stay put than sign up. We're doing essential work.'

Idris longed to shout *hypocrite*. Williams had always made barbed comments about the union. Now, when it suited him, he agreed with them.

Someone in the crowd stood. It was Gwilym, not sitting with him and Isaiah on this occasion. 'That's all very well, the union voting against it, but it's not up to them. If the government passes a law to bring in conscription, we'll have to go anyway.'

A small piece of Idris admired his friend for speaking his mind, though he was no doubt building up to some anti-war sentiment.

'The union has a lot of influence with the government,' said Hubbard. 'You mark my words. They'll sort it out.'

Isaiah pulled himself up with the help of the seat in front. 'But what does the union mean when it says it doesn't want conscription? Hubbard said, "not for anyone". Mr Williams, you're implying they just mean essential workers. I'm confused now, see.'

Idris doubted his father was confused. More likely he'd also spotted Williams's slant and was using it to stir up a bit of contention.

'Well, I believe—' Hubbard hesitated.

'And if it applies to all necessary workers, what if they *want* to enlist? Does that mean they won't be allowed to?'

'Early days, early days,' Williams interrupted as Hubbard managed one word in reply. 'It's all to be worked out.'

Isaiah pointed a finger in his direction. 'In that case, why have you called this meeting at all? Call one when there's something concrete to tell us, like whether the government's actually voted one way or the other.'

Edgar Williams glared at Idris before settling his beady eyes on Isaiah. 'If I had my way, it would be *illegal* for essential workers to enlist.'

'Aye, we all know what you think,' said Isaiah. 'But you're not the government, are you?'

Williams's glare of pure loathing came to rest on Idris once more, even though he had not spoken once. Of course the under-manager would blame him again, for inciting his father and friend. If he was going to take the blame anyway, he might as well speak up against this hypocrite. He got to his feet slowly.

'So what do you expect the country to do, then? Sit around while we're all slowly picked off? Because that's already started to happen, what with air raids on Kent and eastern coasts of England.'

'Pish!' Williams flicked his hand, dismissing Idris's statement as if it were a fly. 'Just on the edge of Britain, and not much harm done.'

'Don't you read the papers, Mr Williams?' Twm Bach's voice rang out. 'What about the Zeppelin raid on Staffordshire and Loughborough a couple of weeks back?'

'That's right,' said Idris. 'Over sixty killed, and more injured. Those places are not on the edge of Britain. And they're not so very far from here, either.'

Isaiah patted Idris on the back. 'Well said, lad.'

Twm Bach had warmed to the theme. 'And they say the kaiser hisself has decided to direct the next attack on the Franco-British Front. And who knows when they'll be marching *our* way?'

The whispers already evident among the men turned to mutterings. Heads were bobbing, fingers were wagging and faces creased with debate.

Idris raised his voice to be heard over the throng. 'So don't talk to us in that complacent manner about how men shouldn't enlist!'

'This meeting has achieved as much as it can this evening,' said Williams. 'I don't know about you men, but I have a home to go to.'

Hubbard seemed about to object when he was knocked by someone passing him. He looked on helplessly as men started to vacate the room.

'Wasting our time again they are, Williams and Hubbard,' said Isaiah, waiting until several people had passed him before he made for the door.

Idris was about to follow him when he was faced with Gwilym, tapping his shoulder. 'Good to hear you speaking up, at last. More like your old self.'

Idris grunted. 'Just can't stand his self-serving rhetoric anymore.'

'I'm not sure what that means, but you're probably right... I was wondering if you'd like to go for a hike up to Carn Stwpa on Sunday. You know, like we used to.'

The complete change of subject threw Idris, but it was not unwelcome. His head was pounding and he was more than happy to consider something less stressful. They'd enjoyed a lot of walks up on the mountains in the past, him and Gwilym, getting fresh air into their lungs, their legs stretched and moving instead of cramped and immobile in the pit. 'I suppose I could.'

Gwilym grinned. 'That's great, Idris, great. I'll call for you after dinner. Are you heading back now?'

'Yes. Better catch Da up.'

'I'll come with you.'

—

It was a sunny day, after several days of rain and squalls. Anwen was pleased that the weather had chosen to bless her day off with an unseasonal mildness. She was holding little Clarice's downy hand as they strolled through the gardens. Gwen was carrying Benjamin. In the middle of them was Violet, free of any children for a change.

Gwen regarded Violet. 'Have you heard from Charlie since he was sent abroad? We've had a few letters from Henry.'

'Two letters. They're part of a reserve division at the moment. He asked for some warm socks to be sent. They're not supposed to tell us much.' Violet spoke abruptly, unsmiling.

'Henry doesn't tell us anything much either. Censored, they are.'

Violet added nothing to the topic, saying instead, 'Let's sit on the bench here.'

They squeezed on together, Clarice sitting on Anwen's lap and Benjamin on Gwen's. The gate on the lower side of the garden squeaked. The three women looked round.

'Oh no,' Gwen whispered. 'Not Esther Williams and her cronies. She's been making trouble round the village again.'

'Let's talk quietly among ourselves,' said Violet. 'Maybe they'll pass by and not interrupt.' She leant towards them, commenting on the minister's sermon that morning. The other two listened intently.

'I'm so glad I saw you three,' came a strident voice. 'In my capacity as Guardian, I am duty bound to have a word with you about your efforts for the war.' Her little group of followers gathered behind her, nodding approvingly.

'We three have been working hard all week, Mrs Williams,' said Gwen. 'We're now enjoying a well-earned rest on the Lord's day. In your capacity as a hardworking *Guardian* I should think you would like a day in which to gather your energies for the coming week.'

'In my capacity as Guardian I am never allowed to rest, Miss Austin. Our Lord would quite understand that I need to keep vigilant against idleness, which is one of the seven deadly sins. You, for instance, Mrs Jones.' She gave Violet a hard stare. 'I notice that you are not working at all towards victory for our country. The mine is always in need of coal screeners and the munitions factory needs workers. Consider Miss Austin here.' She pointed to Gwen. 'She has sacrificed her once fair skin in order to do her bit in munitions.'

Gwen quickly tucked her hands away under her coat sleeves.

'I'm sorry that you think my contribution is not up to your standards, Mrs Williams,' said Violet, 'but I have children to care for. Should I leave them at home to fend for themselves?'

'You have a mother, I hear tell, down in New Tredegar. She could care for them while you work.'

'I don't know where you've heard tell of that, but clearly you have not also heard that she is poorly. My father, who still works, struggles to care for the pair of them.'

'Then maybe, Mrs Jones, you should have them living with you, so they do not struggle.' Mrs Williams stood her ground, a smile of triumph on her face.

Violet said nothing in reply, though Anwen knew she had suggested this to her parents, who were adamant they were fine and did not need looking after.

'As for you, Miss Rhys. I hear you are working up at McKenzie House.'

'Yes, that's right. Six in the morning till six in the evening.'

'Being a maid is hardly essential war work. I advise you to go back to coal screening. And now you have your grandmother close by I see no reason for you to be wasting your time, as your sister did before you.'

A boiling outrage bubbled up inside Anwen. How could she say such a cruel thing about Sara? Behind Esther Williams, the women took an almost imperceptible step back.

Anwen got to her feet. She pushed down the most excessive of her thoughts. 'My sister has just died, Mrs Williams. And I would thank you to show her a little more respect. She would not have lasted a day sorting the coal in the cold, dirty air. It's a wonder to me more of us aren't suffering because of it.' *Stop.* She was going to go too far, criticising management and the owners.

'How *dare* you speak to me like that, yet again! Goodness gracious, it's no wonder your intended cast you aside, with such an opinionated mouth.'

The deep hot fury, trapped beneath the indignation, was about to spew forth, when she noticed Mrs Williams looking with abundant satisfaction down the path. Anwen followed her gaze. Idris and Gwilym were tramping up towards them.

'Such a fortuitous coincidence. And here's another one who talks out of turn to his betters.'

'I think you have the wrong end of the stick, Mrs Williams,' said Idris, coming to a standstill with Gwilym. 'It was Anwen who broke off our betrothal. Not that it is anyone's business.'

'I can't help thinking the pair of you are made for each other. Well, you were no use to the army, and probably no use to Miss Rhys either, don't you think, ladies?' She let out a brief, mirthless laugh, which was copied by her followers hesitantly.

Gwen stood up and ploughed in with, 'What about your son, Daniel, Mrs Williams? He must be twenty-one now, since he was at school with us. Why hasn't he enlisted?'

Esther Williams blinked several times. 'Because the bank is essential work, of course! If nobody looks after the money, how will the country pay for the war?'

Gwen tutted. 'Not the level Daniel works at. See, you expect us all to do war work, but think your son should be an exception. And why don't *you* work sorting the coal on the screens, instead of telling everyone else what to do.'

'Don't you argue with me! Ladies, it's time for us to take our leave.'

Mrs Williams's cronies spared no time moving away from Anwen and her friends, Esther hurrying after them, her nose in the air.

Violet got up to relieve Gwen of Benjamin. 'Well, what a card she is! She could pick a fight with an angel, that one.'

Gwilym drew nearer to the women. 'You've got that right – hey, where are you going, mun?'

Idris had started to move off. 'It was a hike we were going on, wasn't it? Better get going before the sun starts to set.'

'I guess we had. Good afternoon, ladies. I hope you won't be bothered by Mrs *Guardian* again. Who made her that, I'd like to know?' He lifted his cap in farewell, running after Idris who had already reached the top gate.

The three women sat back down with the children. Anwen tilted her head slightly, so it was not obvious she was staring in Idris's direction. Gwilym had caught him up, but there was someone else there too, a woman.

Polly Coombes. Idris and Gwilym set off once more, in the direction of James Street. Polly followed, taking Idris's arm.

Anwen flicked her glance away. It felt like she'd been kicked in the stomach. Tears nipped at the corners of her eyes. And right under her nose like that, it was so cruel.

'Are you all right?' Gwen looked down on her, her brow creased.

Anwen stiffened her posture. So much for gallant Idris, claiming she'd broken off the betrothal. Resentment was useful when you wanted to stave off sentiment. But Polly Coombes? Well, if that was the kind of woman he liked now, they were welcome to each other.

Anwen joined in the nursery rhyme Gwen had started singing. She sang louder, getting up to dance with Clarice.

To hell with you, Idris Hughes.

–

Another Monday morning. It was almost like he'd never been away from the mine, so routine had the work become. Over two months he'd been back now. He was nearing the bottom of Station Road, the dim illumination of the pit buildings in front of him drawing him on against his will. He wanted to stride into the light, not the shadows. Anwen had been his light, yet he'd abandoned her. He didn't want to become her darkness, for her to resent him in years to come. The men passed through the gate like a battalion advancing to war.

'What's wrong with you, Idris, *bach*?' said his father beside him.

'Monday morning,' he muttered.

'Aye, Monday morning,' his father agreed.

As they passed the under-manager's office, Edgar Williams stepped out.

'Been waiting for you, Idris Hughes.'

Idris stopped, as did Isaiah.

'I'll see you later, Da,' he said. He didn't want to get his father involved in whatever gripe Williams had with him today.

Isaiah hesitated before saying, 'See you later, son.'

Williams waited until Isaiah was out of earshot before snapping, 'Come inside.'

The desk in the office was piled with papers, as was the filing cabinet. Williams leant his slight weight against the edge of the desk.

'I hear you were harassing my wife yesterday, Hughes.'

Of course. 'I would say it was more a case of her harassing the young ladies in the gardens, telling them what they should be doing, in her capacity as *Guardian*.'

He frowned. 'You're confused. She was apparently advising them to support the war effort. No harm in that.'

'Almost shouting at them, she was. I could hear her clearly from outside the gardens.'

'The young women were insolent. They deserved a good talking to.'

'From what I could hear, they were being polite and respectful, considering they had been set upon.'

'Are you questioning my wife's version of the events? Anyway, the main reason I've called you in is because you haven't been filling as many trams as you should. Not as many as you did before you enlisted. I've checked the paperwork.'

Idris was aware of his shortfall, though he'd been surprised when he'd collected his last pay. He thought he'd been improving each week, yet his pay told him he'd slipped back a little. As he glanced around he spotted, through the murky window, several men gathered outside. His spirit shrank.

Williams carried on. 'I have men here in their fifties able to shift more coal than you. That Rhys girl you were to marry left her job at the screens. It seems to me, Hughes, that you should take her place, with the women and the old men.' He released a rapid cackle of a laugh, like a machine gun in full flow.

Idris calmed himself, clasping his hands loosely behind his back. 'I've not got into my stride yet. Being away seven months means I'm out of practice. But I'll be up to speed soon.'

'I think you've had chance enough—'

The door was pushed open and there stood Gwilym, a group of around six men behind him. Idris groaned inside.

'Reckon there could have been a clerical error, Mr Williams.' There were voices of assent behind Gwilym.

Williams considered the gathering. 'Get to your stalls, men.'

'Leave Idris alone,' called Twm Bach, his sing-song voice recognisable though his height rendered him unseen.

'Watch your mouth, Twm Bach,' shouted Williams, 'else you'll find your tram number decreasing too. And maybe you'll work with the women: they're more your size.'

There was a 'boo' from one man, alongside the muttering of the rest of them. Was Williams admitting he'd fiddled the figures for the number of trams he'd filled, Idris wondered, or was it merely an idle threat?

He had no time to ponder this before Williams yelled, 'Now get to work, all of you! Our navy's waiting for that coal.'

Idris wasted no time vacating the office, making straight for the lamp room with Gwilym and the other men.

There were long hours in the dark to consider what had been said.

–

Isaiah sat in one of the armchairs next to the fire, his arms stretched out as he perused the middle pages of last week's local paper. In the other armchair, Meg darned one of her husband's shirts. Idris sat at the table, a book in his hands. Isaiah folded the paper in half, holding it near to his face and squinting.

'You should get yourself a pair of spectacles, Da.'

Meg looked up from her sewing. 'I've told him that. When you even have difficulty seeing print in this wonderful electric light, it comes to something.'

'Don't see why I should waste my money on such things. I can read perfectly well when it's close up.'

Idris was about to start reading again when Isaiah said, 'That reminds me. Twm Bach told me Williams had a go at you at the beginning of the week, saying you weren't making the grade.'

'You didn't mention it.' Meg placed the shirt on her knees. 'You always used to tell us everything.'

That wasn't quite true, of course. He'd never told them about scrumping apples from McKenzie House's garden, nor of the many times he'd kissed Anwen secretly in the woods, before they were officially courting. A longing for those distant, innocent years assailed him.

But these things were not what she was talking about. He would chat about his day once upon a time. Now he spent the evenings almost silent, wrapped up in the books he borrowed from the Institute's library.

'What is there to tell, Mam? Williams has it in for me. He will for a while, until he finds some other poor soul to pick on.'

'Don't let him get to you,' said Meg.

'I gave as good as I got, without descending into rudeness like him.'

Isaiah humphed. 'Don't get too far on the wrong side of management. Doesn't matter for me at my age, but you've got years. Perhaps you could be under-manager one day.'

Idris tried to imagine wearing a fancy yet grubby suit every day, like Williams, telling men what to do. Perhaps you had to be that officious to get the job done, but it wasn't his way. 'I don't think so.'

The clatter of footsteps on the stairs was followed by Jenkin throwing open the door. He was wearing a khaki shirt and shorts and thick knee socks. On his head was a broad-brimmed campaign hat, a leather strap hanging down beneath his chin.

'For goodness sake, *bach*,' said Meg, 'Can't you do anything without breaking the house?'

'Sorry Mam. I'm going to be late for scouts if I don't hurry up. We're learning exercises to get fit.'

'You'll make a fine hewer with a fair bit of muscle on you,' said Isaiah.

Meg jumped up, dropping the shirt on the chair. 'He's not going into any mine. It's bad enough that Idris ended up there.'

'That's not my doing. He sneaked off and got hired.'

'It's not happening to our Jenkin. *He's* going into an office.'

'I'm not getting fit to go into an office, Mam! The war isn't ending any time soon. I'll be able to sign up in a couple of years, isn't it?'

Isaiah rose from his chair, standing next to Meg in unity. 'You're not going anywhere, *bach*. The war'll be over before you're old enough.'

'That's not what the scout master said. I'll be eighteen in two years and four months. He reckons it could be going for a while yet, like that Hundred Years War in England back in the Middle Ages.'

Meg picked her sewing up once more and slumped into her seat. 'God help us. Who knows how many we'll lose if that's the case.'

Jenkin crossed his arms. 'You didn't stop our Idris going. Isn't that right, Idris?'

'I was over twenty-one, *bach*.' The very idea of Jenkin signing up made his head throb. Was that how his parents had felt when he'd left?

–

It would be the first time Idris had stepped into the public house since coming home. He wasn't sure of the wisdom of it as they trod carefully down the sloping street of Jubilee Green, trying not to slip on the recently fallen snow.

'This is a bit of a celebration, isn't it?' said Gwilym next to him, clapping his gloved hands together once before rubbing them. 'Your first trip to the McKenzie Arms since you came back from the army.'

'I'll not stay long. I'm not much of a drinker.'

'Come on, cheer up. You can't hide away forever. Here, maybe we'll see that Polly Coombes down here again, eh?'

'Let's hope not.'

Gwilym laughed. 'Mun, I thought we were going to be stuck with her for the whole hike, yacking on about frocks and lace. Her face was a picture when you told her we were walking all the way to Carn Stwpa.'

'Not that we did in the end.'

'No. When we've got some good long evenings, we'll have a go. Mind, she's a good-looking girl, Polly,' Gwilym said.

'You'd better snap her up then, before someone else does.'

Gwilym chuckled. 'Not me, mun. Not my type.'

'Then who is?' Idris immediately wished he hadn't asked.

'I'll know when I meet her. Here we are.' Gwilym led the way across the road to the McKenzie Arms Hotel.

They entered the front door, peeling off to the larger of two bars. It was already busy with men recently washed, the pervading scent of soap in the air.

'I'll get these in,' Gwilym said. 'Look, there's a coupla seats at that table by there.'

Idris did as he was bid, not noticing Philip Hubbard until he started to remove his coat.

'Now there's a fine bit of clothing. You didn't pick that up in Dorcalon, I'll be bound.'

'No. An officer gave it me,' said Idris. 'At Winchester. It was old to him.'

'Old! I bet it was. Toff, was he?'

It was a redundant question: all the officers had been, at the very least, middle class.

'Yes, course he was,' Hubbard continued. 'There's them, disregarding good clothes with plenty of life in them and here we are, patching the patches on ours.'

Idris considered Hubbard's clothing. He'd seen worse on the streets of Dorcalon.

'Ah, here he is, the old Janus.'

Idris followed Hubbard's gaze. Edgar Williams had entered the bar, thumbs in his waistcoat pockets, standing in the doorway as if he owned the hotel.

'Janus?'

Hubbard leant forward. 'Two-faced, isn't it? Acts like he's on our side when he's with us, then sucks up to those above.'

Williams strolled through the throng of men. He stopped at the bar, hailing the barman, despite several other people waiting.

Hubbard clucked loudly. 'Upstart. Thinks he's the manager, that one. Truth be told, Herbert Meredith's got more manners than he has, and I'm no admirer of Meredith's class, believe me.'

Hubbard picked up his glass and took a long swig, giving Idris a moment's respite from the monologue. 'At least there's good news for everyone here. Especially Williams, though it pains me that anything pleases him.'

Idris had no time to ask what the news might be before Gwilym returned with his beer and Edgar Williams's clamorous voice boomed over the loud chatter in the bar.

'Silence! *Silence!*' The voices in the bar diminished over a few seconds to nothing. 'Our esteemed comrade, Philip Hubbard, has some news for us.'

Hubbard vacated his seat, clutching the lapels of his jacket, his chin jutting out. He coughed. 'I thank my respected colleague, Edgar Williams, and am honoured to bring the latest news from London. I have heard, today, that the Military Service Act has been passed by Parliament—'

Conversation began again, positive responses interjected with negative ones.

'*Let him finish!*' Williams yelled once more.

'Conscription has been imposed on single men aged eighteen to forty-one—'

'Shame!' a voice called.

'Someone has to fight the bloody Hun!' called another.

'*But* – exemptions have been made for men in essential war work. That includes us miners.'

'Does that mean our boys who've volunteered will be sent back?' Idris couldn't see the speaker, but he knew the voice of Freddie Vaughan, the father of Percy.

'No, I'm afraid it doesn't,' Hubbard said. 'There are also exceptions for religious leaders and those who are medically unfit.'

'The ministers here are all too old to fight anyway,' said one wag. There was a ripple of laughter.

'So you're exempted on two counts, Idris Hughes,' Williams called over.

The laughter stopped dead and there was a brief silence, followed by murmuring at the bar.

'At least I won't need to have the old men and the women digging out the coal. What's wrong with you all? You should be celebrating! Come on, you can get back to your drinking now.' Williams made his way towards Idris's table. Was he coming over to administer another of his threats?

As it happened, Williams ignored him and Gwilym completely, saying to Hubbard instead, 'I'll see you in an hour.'

'Aye, I'll be there.'

Williams wove his way back across the room, twisting to regard the men there when he reached the door. 'And I want no sore heads in work tomorrow morning.'

'Thinks he owns the bloody place, that one,' said Hubbard.

Gwilym slapped him on the back good-naturedly. 'Cheer up. You got what you wanted with regards conscription, didn't you, *bach*?'

'Aye. At least, for us lot, I suppose.'

Idris put down the glass he was about to drink from. 'I'm sure all the men would like their jobs exempt from conscription.'

'Ooh, don't go on, mun,' said Hubbard. 'There's work to be done here. And if we do it well, perhaps we'll keep the good rates we're earning now after the war.'

Idris had hold of his glass again but didn't lift it. 'And that's what it's all about, isn't it? What about the pay of those conscripted? How are they going to get any better?'

Hubbard shrugged his shoulders. 'I don't know, mun. Not my concern.'

'No, of course it bloody isn't.'

Philip Hubbard stood, picking up his glass. 'Excuse me.' He joined a group two tables away.

'Not like you to swear,' Gwilym said.

'Well, I've had enough of his rubbish. The better pay hasn't put any more food on the table.'

'Not sure what any of us can do about that. Lot of it comes from abroad. Can't get the ships in past the Germans.'

Idris was tempted to leave his drink and abandon this attempt at socialising. Until his butty, Jory Damerell, turned up, beaming widely, obviously keen to join them. He'd have to sit this out and hope the time went quickly.

Chapter Thirteen

Anwen was always self-conscious cleaning in a room where there was a member of the family present. Today, as Anwen polished the drawing room, Herbert Meredith was sitting in the winged armchair with the *Telegraph*. Margaret Meredith was seated on one of the cream velvet Chesterfields, reading a small green volume. Next to her was Elizabeth, a huge book upon her knees that she was studying intently. Anwen scooped out a small portion of wax from the tin, rubbing it onto the shelves from which she'd removed the ornaments. She breathed in deeply. Lavender, one of her favourite scents.

Mr Meredith tutted, shaking his head. 'The *Arethusa*'s been sunk in the North Sea. Another ship gone. A mine was responsible. Sea's filled with them, I reckon.'

Elizabeth looked up. 'And all because of the greedy ambitions of old men. And ordinary folk suffer.'

'Do not speak of things you do not understand,' her mother said.

'What, because I'm a poor, feeble woman who doesn't have the intelligence to understand anything beyond dresses and running a house?'

Herbert Meredith peered over his spectacles. 'Now Lizzie, don't be rude to your mother. I'm sure your opinion is as informed as that of most men on the street. However, let's leave it to the politicians.'

'Listen to your father,' said Mrs Meredith. 'You don't want to be considered unladylike or unnatural, like some of those Suffragettes. Politics is not for ladies.'

'Nor is helping out in the war effort, apparently.'

'Not at the munitions or screens, for pity's sake, as you were proposing. That's not for *our* class.' Mrs Meredith removed a lacy handkerchief from her pocket and patted her nose.

Anwen wondered at Elizabeth proposing to work in those places. Maybe it was easy to suggest such things when you knew your family would prevent it from ever happening.

Elizabeth returned to the book, her lips pulled into a thin line as she examined it.

The clock on the mantelpiece struck ten. Elizabeth got up, placing her tome on the table. 'I believe that signals it's time for morning coffee. I will go to the kitchen to hurry it along.'

That meant it would soon be time for a sit-down and a cup of tea for her too. Anwen was relieved as today she was more tired than usual. Mam had woken in the night, crying out. Anwen had read to her for half an hour before she'd dropped off again.

Elizabeth, beside her now, said, 'You have done an excellent job, Anwen. Come along. I'll help you take the dusters and so forth back to the scullery.' She winked, picking up the tin box of cleaning items, leaving Anwen with only the duster and polish.

Rose already had the treats on a tray ready to go when Anwen and Elizabeth entered the kitchen.

'There you go, Miss Elizabeth. I've put four cups on there in case Mr Thomas decides to join you. And there's some of my bakestones and lemon biscuits. I've baked a nice Victoria sponge for your afternoon tea later.'

Anwen accepted that this was how the middle classes lived, but wondered again where were the ingredients coming from, before they got under counters for privileged customers.

'That is kind of you, Rose. However, I will be taking my morning coffee here, in the kitchen. It's warmer than the sitting room.'

Rose raised her eyebrows. 'Very well, Miss. Let me take a cup and saucer off the tray, and a couple of cakes and biscuits.' She transferred them to the plate already on the table.

'I'll take the tray,' said Elizabeth. 'Then I can talk to Tom on my way back.'

Anwen went to grab it. 'Oh, but I should do that.'

Elizabeth was too quick for her. 'Nonsense. I'm not helpless. Get some coffee for me while I'm gone, please, and your own refreshment.'

By the time Elizabeth returned, Anwen had a pot of coffee plus a pot of tea for her and Rose arranged on the table, along with milk and sugar.

Rose poured tea for herself. 'I'll take mine to the scullery. I want to get on with vegetable preparation. There's pea soup and a mutton hash for dinner, not to mention lunch to be doing.'

Elizabeth sat herself down. 'Goodness, you need a break.'

'Don't you worry about me, Miss. I'd rather get on.'

Rose seldom stopped to take the morning or afternoon breaks with Anwen, who shared the time only with Onner, the washer woman, on Monday and Tuesday mornings.

The cook disappeared, closing the door behind her.

Elizabeth sat elegantly sipping at her coffee, her hair pinned neatly into a bun above a crisp, white blouse with a lace yoke. She also wore a black skirt that, like the others she'd worn, showed some of her calf.

'You being here has done wonders for Rose. She's a good cook but has always been a bit on the lazy side. You work even harder than Jenny did and it appears to have rubbed off on Rose. I've never known her make so much effort. How are you finding it here, Anwen?'

'Much better than working on the screens. Though I do feel guilty. They need people to do the screening for the coal, which is essential for the navy.'

'I know. I was threatened with eviction from the family home if I went to get such work.' She shook her head impatiently.

'That's terrible.' Anwen put her hand over her mouth. 'Sorry, Miss Elizabeth.'

'No, you're right. But there are other ways to help the war effort, you know. For instance, what you said in chapel about growing food.'

The door from the hall opened wide. Tom strode in, shirt sleeves rolled up, no collar on and the top button of his shirt undone. It gave him a roguish appearance, with his dark red hair wild and a little too long.

'Tom, do you always have to make such an entrance everywhere?'

'Sorry, decided to come down for those cakes and biscuits after all. And a strong cup of coffee.'

'There are coffee and cakes for you in the drawing room,' said Elizabeth.

'But it's cosier in here, sis. It reminds me of sitting in our old kitchen with Mamgu Powell as a child. Do you remember?'

'Of course I do.'

Tom sat at the table. Anwen wondered if she should leave them and join Rose. It seemed impolite to intrude on the family. 'I'll take my tea to the scullery.'

'You will not on my account,' Tom said.

'Absolutely not,' Elizabeth concurred. 'Now sit and enjoy a bakestone and a biscuit.'

Anwen did as she was told, really quite thrilled to be spending time with two such interesting people. They spoke of the end of the Gallipoli campaign in the Ottoman Empire, the recent train crash at Dowlais and the talk the following week at the Institute.

Tom brought his full attention to Anwen. 'So what do you do in your spare time, apart from read and attend talks?'

She pointed to herself. 'Me? I don't really have much time to do anything else. Except singing with the choir from time to time.'

'Do you play an instrument at all?'

'Tom! Some people can't afford instruments.'

'Oh, on the contrary, Elizabeth, we do have a pianoforte in our front room. Mam used to teach me and Sara and my brothers a bit. I don't often get time to play now, though.'

'Your brothers?' said Tom. 'Have they left home?'

'No.' She looked down.

'Oh. I see. I'm sorry. Life can be hell. That's why we've got to make the most of what we have.'

A retort lay on her lips: *that's easy for you to say*. But she didn't think what he'd said came from a selfish place. Just one that considered the reality of the situation. Make the most of it or sink.

'We had a brother who died,' he continued. 'Eight days old. Lizzie was eight and I was four. Remember it as if it were yesterday. Poor little mite. Edward.'

'I'm sorry to hear that.'

Elizabeth leant over to help herself to more coffee. 'Enough of this talk now. I saw a snowdrop this morning, peeping through what's left of the snow. A portent, I hope, for something better around the corner. Like spring.'

'I do hope so,' Anwen said. 'I'm tired of gloomy winter.' The way her life had gone recently, winter was likely to follow her into spring and summer.

The grandmother clock in the hall struck the half hour.

'That's my tea break over.' It was time to begin on the cleaning upstairs. 'May I start in your room, Mr Meredith, since you are down here and it's due a full clean today?'

He pulled a face. 'It would be better if you left me till last. Give me time to have a clear-up.'

'Start in my room, Anwen,' Elizabeth said. 'Honestly Tom, what else do you have to do all day? I think it's about time I involved you in a project.'

He held up his hands as if in surrender. 'Please, not one of your *projects*.'

Anwen left them to their conversation, taking her crockery to the scullery to wash up.

Rose was crouched partly under the table when she entered. She quickly got up, a carrot in her hand. 'Put that on the table by here. I'll wash it up in a minute. I'm still peeling veg at the moment.'

'All right. I'm going to start upstairs.'

'I guess you won't be back down until lunchtime.'

Anwen collected the tin box with the necessary cleaning items and left the room. She smiled at Rose as she departed, since the girl was staring at her. Rose half smiled in return and went back to scrubbing vegetables.

–

The audience was clapping what had been a fascinating talk by John Evans, a writer of travel books. That Anwen had been vaguely aware the whole time of Idris, six rows in front of her, sitting with Gwilym and Twm Bach on one side, his father and mother on the other, had distracted her a little. At least Polly Coombes wasn't with him tonight.

The last time John Evans had been here she'd sat with Idris. They'd held hands, him caressing her fingers, whispering to each other when something Mr Evans said appealed to them. The all too brief memory vanished, leaving her winded. If only she could block those memories out. He didn't love her anymore, a fact that cut to the core of her being, but what could she do?

Over on the other side of the room she could see Elizabeth with Tom. It was unlikely she'd have had the nerve to join them had she been on her own, as she'd thought she would be. It was all very well them joining her for tea in the kitchen, talking to her as if she were their equal, but out here people would say she was hobnobbing above her station.

Uncle Hywel touched her arm. 'That was a good talk on the Lake District, wasn't it?'

'Very entertaining. I would so like to visit there, but I don't suppose there's much chance of that.'

'Too expensive for the likes of us. Still, it's nice to dream. I like the talks about other parts of the country because we can escape there for a while. It's a bit like having a holiday.'

The nearest thing Anwen had ever had to a break was taking the train on a few bank holidays to Barry Island. She smiled at the recollection of tiptoeing over slimy seaweed on the way to paddle in the cool water as a child. 'I'd be quite happy with a day at the seaside.'

'Not much prospect of that at the moment. Do you mind if I go and talk to John Evans? I'd like to thank him personal, like.'

'Of course not.'

'I won't be long.'

People were starting to gather in groups, raking over the details of the talk. She was wondering if there was anyone she could join when there was a tap on her shoulder. It was Meg Hughes.

'Hello, *cariad*, here on your own, are you?'

Anwen was about to reply when the double doors into the top tier of the lecture theatre were thrown open. A figure came up to the rail, laying one hand on it. It was Samuel Lloyd from Dyffryn Gwyrdd Farm. His countenance suggested he was not there for a social call, an impression supported by the presence of a rifle in the crook of his arm. The chatter decreased.

'I thought I'd find a big crowd of you here. Good. I want as many of you as possible to hear this warning and take heed.'

The room was now deadly silent, every single person peering up at Lloyd. He glowered at the crowd. Taking the gun from his arm he placed it upright, holding the barrel.

'People have been trespassing on my land, look you. First, some of my chickens went missing. Thought it was the foxes, but no sign of blood. Then a sheep went. A fox can take down a lamb, but it's damned hard for it to take a sheep. Then another went missing, then more chickens. Them hens do be for our personal use, see, and my wife knows them all.'

'Are you blaming us, Lloyd?' Isaiah said.

'I'm not blaming you personal, like, Isaiah Hughes, but it's got to be people from round here, hasn't it?'

'Might be. Might not be.'

Lloyd continued his rant. 'I've also found a coupla pigeons dead on the field with bullet holes. Then a rabbit in a trap, not one of mine. I reckon there's been a bit of illegal activity on my land, see, and I don't like it.'

Reginald Moss, the manager of the McKenzie Arms, stepped into the space in the middle of the room. 'You don't own the pigeons and rabbits, Lloyd, they can roam at will. And pests they are, so who cares if they're pilfered? Do you begrudge people food to survive? We're not after starving now, especially when we've a war to help win.'

The farmer lifted the gun a little, causing some to gasp and step back. All he did was bang the butt on the ground. 'I may not own those animals, but I do own the land, see, and people are trespassing to get to the vermin. And you have to watch you don't shoot a homing pigeon 'cos that's illegal. Moss, I don't see your hotel going without meat. My wife tells me there's not only been a glut of rabbit and pigeon for sale in Iolo Prosser's butcher's shop, but recently some mutton. Now where has that suddenly sprung from, eh? And I'm thinking that people aren't after feeding themselves, but making a profit from my loss, and I'm not bloody 'aving it, see!'

Another figure joined Moss in the middle of the room, the large, bald crown of Iolo Prosser, his thick, dark eyebrows at odds with the lack of hair. 'You accusing me of poaching, Samuel Lloyd?'

'Where'd you get the rabbits, pigeons and mutton from then, Iolo, tell me that?'

'From my usual sources. I don't agree with Mr Moss, though. We're hardly in the realms of starvation. I think, Mr Lloyd, that you need to be sure of your facts before you go around casting aspersions.'

'And who's to say your *usual* sources are bona fide? You wouldn't want to be in trouble for receiving stolen goods, would you? I've already contributed plenty to this war with wool for soldiers' clothes, have two sons in the trenches and one of my two daughters at the munitions. Short of workers now, am I, and spring coming up with new lambs. I'll be losing those to the foxes next with lack of shepherds.' He paused, lifting his hand to point a finger towards the room below him, sweeping it around to include everyone. 'Sheep theft is a serious business, see, and you can be sure I'll get the police involved. I notice that Harries the Police is here, off duty like, but I 'ope he's taking notes.'

A tall, thin, swarthy man, greying at the temples, stepped forward, hands linked behind his back. 'I am that, Mr Lloyd. Come and see me tomorrow when I'm on duty and give me more details, if you will.'

'I'd be glad to, Sergeant. But be sure, I will shoot anyone I find trespassing.'

'I don't recommend that,' the Sergeant began, faltering to a halt when he saw Lloyd head away.

Slowly the chatter began once more.

'Well, there's a to-do,' Meg Hughes said, reminding Anwen of her presence. 'I did wonder about all the extra meat in the butcher's recently.'

'It might be perfectly lawful,' Anwen said, aware that both Isaiah and Elizabeth were heading their way.

'And I'm Lillian Gish the film star. You're a nice girl, Anwen, and too willing to see the good in people. No, something's not right.'

A nice girl, but not nice enough for Meg's son. Or pretty enough. Or clever enough. Or – who knew what exactly? *Oh, Idris.*

Isaiah puffed up the last steps towards them. 'Are you ready, Meg? I'm wanting my bed and so is Idris. It's early we've got to be up tomorrow.'

'And I haven't?' Meg retorted. 'Bye bye, love. I'll pop in to see Enid next week, would you tell her?' She took Anwen's hands, squeezing them with affection.

'Of course. And thank you for coming regular. She enjoys the company.'

Meg was no sooner taking the first step down than Elizabeth was taking the last step up. She too was out of breath but it appeared to be more down to excitement than exhaustion.

'Anwen, dear, what do you think all that was about?'

'Mr Lloyd? He's been put out and who can blame him?'

'And clearly in need of some help, by the sounds of it. You told me a while back you used to grow vegetables. Do you know about cultivating them?'

'A bit.' She'd been an eager helper to her father in the days he used to dig and plant.

'I don't suppose you ever kept chickens, did you?'

'No. My mother's parents do, in Cardiganshire. I used to visit when I was a child and help on the farm a bit. But I don't really know much about them.'

'No matter, it's something that can be learned.'

'Are you wanting to grow veg and keep chickens at McKenzie House?'

'Something like that. If I leant you a book about growing vegetables, would you read it?'

Anwen laughed. 'I'd read almost anything. Sometimes I fear the world could run out of books for me to read.'

'Excellent. I must go and find Tom. It would be typical of him to forget about me and walk home alone.'

Elizabeth gambolled lightly back down the steps. Anwen scanned the room for Tom. It wasn't long before she spotted him, waiting at the bottom of the steps for his sister. Elizabeth waved at her, and so did her brother. She waved back. Her eyes strayed to the door where Meg and Isaiah were leaving with Idris. He was now eyeing Tom, approaching the same door. Idris's gaze lifted to settle on her, his face oozing disappointment. She swallowed hard, imagining what he might be thinking. *The maid, no better than she should be, giving in to the wills of the master.* A similar storyline had made up a subplot of a novel she'd read recently.

Idris followed his parents out, not holding the door open for Tom and Elizabeth behind him. What was the matter with him? *He* gave *her* up.

But even as the resentment against him simmered, part of her hoped he was beginning to regret breaking off with her.

–

Reaching the entrance hall of the Institute, Idris's conscience was bothering him. He should have held the door open for the Merediths. It was all down to Tom Meredith's proximity to Anwen, the way he smiled at her. Anwen had never been a silly girl, but it wasn't unusual for young women to be taken in by men with money and position. Then ending up in the family way. They soon found out that such men wanted them for one thing. If only he could warn Anwen. But she would never believe he was simply looking out for her. And maybe he was fooling himself too. The green-eyed monster had him in his clutches.

Elizabeth and Tom Meredith overtook them hastily in the entrance hall and soon exited into the night.

Meg tapped his arm. 'What's wrong with you, *bach*? You're like a bear with a sore head.'

'You know what one of those is like, do you?'

Isaiah pushed open the door. 'I'm not surprised he looks like that. I feel like that too after Lloyd throwing his weight around, trying to spoil Mr Evans's talk.'

Outside at the top of the steps, lit only by lights from the Institute windows, Idris welcomed the chilly breeze. Somewhere in the dark he detected voices, arguing, one of them shouting louder than the other.

'Who's that?' Meg said, peering over the wall, next to Idris. 'Can't see a thing on the streets late at night since they started turning the lamps off at ten o'clock.'

'You stay here Meg, we'll find out what's going on.' Isaiah indicated that Idris should follow him down the steps.

Why couldn't they just go home? It was nothing to do with them. He trailed behind his father, trudging through grimy slush.

'I'm just telling you, like I told them in there.' Samuel Lloyd was pointing at the Institute.

'I was taking a stroll along here, minding my own business, so why involve me?' It was Madog Rhys. He'd been here that night of the union meeting as well, when Idris had followed Edgar Williams out.

'I'm not involving you. I'm just warning you like I warned the others.'

Madog lifted his hand, screwing it up into a fist. 'That sounds like a threat to me.'

'Don't be daft, Madog mun,' Isaiah shouted. 'He's got a shot gun, you fool.' He tramped over to them, reluctantly followed by Idris.

'Don't call me a fool, old man,' Madog growled.

Isaiah stood his ground in front of the pair of them, arms crossed. 'No need for that.'

Madog spat on the ground. 'Don't you talk to me, Isaiah Hughes, with your lump of a useless son next to you. He's not worth a hundredth what my daughter's worth.'

Idris was astounded to hear him pay her a compliment. It had been years since he'd shown any signs of respect for any member of his family.

'If you want *that* conversation, it's for another time,' Isaiah said. 'Right now you two need to go your separate ways before you wake up the whole village.'

'Mind your own bloody business.' Madog stumbled in their direction, the worse for drink. 'Need sorting out you do, Idris bloody Hughes. Insult my family, would you?'

As he drew nearer, Idris detected the stench of stale whisky and tobacco on his breath.

'Are you daft, mun?' Isaiah said. 'Look at the size of my son compared to you. Insult your family? At least he doesn't knock them around, like you do.'

Madog was not deterred. He reached Idris, getting too close, staring up into the face of a man who was a good five inches taller.

'Stop right there, Rhys.' Samuel Lloyd had his rifle at chest level, pointing it towards Madog. 'Woman-beater now, is it? I've no time for men like you.'

Madog staggered backwards. 'A bit of a slap don't hurt them, just shows who's boss.' He pointed a stubby, yellow forefinger at Idris. 'You let my girl down.'

Other people started to vacate the building, peering over the wall at the top of the double steps to see what was occurring. Anwen was among them. Idris wondered how long she'd been there.

Isaiah noticed them too. He lowered his voice. 'I think you should go home. And don't let me hear you've taken any of this conversation out on Enid or Anwen.'

'Enid?' Madog laughed. 'She's not in a position to get out of hand, is she?' He wobbled, then lurched away in the direction of Edward Street. Those at the top of the steps ventured down.

'Shame Harries the Police isn't here,' said the farmer. 'Must still be inside.'

Hywel was now next to them, Anwen coming up behind.

'What's he been doing now?' Hywel's voice was sharp. He watched Madog's retreating back with narrowed eyes.

'Sounding off just because I told him what I told you lot in the hall. Is that his daughter there?' Lloyd pointed at Anwen, half hidden from him.

She stepped forward. 'Yes, it's me, Mr Lloyd.'

'I was sorry to hear about Sara, *cariad*.' His manner softened completely. It could have been a different man to thirty seconds ago.

'Thank you, Mr Lloyd.'

Idris recalled his and Anwen's childhood, playing with the Lloyd children on the farm, only a short distance out of the village. Like Samuel had said in the hall, his sons had enlisted, two of the twenty-nine who'd gone together to join up.

'It's just you and your mother now in the house with him, is it, Anwen?'

'Yes, that's right, Mr Lloyd. Though Mamgu's there in the daytime.'

Idris had the urge to wind his arm around her, tell her it would all be all right with him there. Hold her in close and keep her safe.

'I'm going to come and sleep in Sara's room for tonight,' Hywel said. 'I don't trust the man.'

Anwen's sad face tore at Idris's heart. Madog might be a brute, but he was her father and this whole incident, out in the open, would be humiliating for her. If only he could protect her from such crushing shame.

'He... he sleeps in Sara's room now, Uncle Hywel,' she said.

'Then I will sleep on the chaise longue. I'll leave before he gets up tomorrow.'

'Thank you, Uncle Hywel.'

'I'm glad someone will be there for her,' Isaiah said.

Idris wanted to say the same, but he'd forfeited the right to have any opinion on her life. His head thumped at the thought of this reality.

Chapter Fourteen

'How glorious it is, to get out in the fresh air.' Gwen took a deep breath as she, Anwen and Violet left the houses of James Street behind and took the path round the pit. She went ahead with little Clarice, singing as they skipped along.

Violet and Anwen were clutching Benjamin's hand, helping him as he tottered along.

They caught Gwen and Clarice up, on the road below the first terrace of McKenzie Cottages. Leaning over the verge of the path together, they marvelled at the yellow coltsfoot they found, peeping up through the grass.

'Spring's on its way!' There was relief in Gwen's voice. 'Longer days and some light left when we get home from work. How I do miss the daylight working in the factory!'

'At last,' Anwen said, yet she couldn't feel the eager anticipation she normally experienced this time of the year. 'It would be nice to reach the forest, have a little walk through there.' Nostalgia mingled with regret. 'It seems ages since we did so. It used to be one of my favourite places when we were young.'

The sun peeping weakly from behind the white fluffy clouds several times this morning had prompted her to suggest the walk. It wasn't mild, but it was certainly not as cold as it had been. That their destination would be so entangled with memories of her and Idris had only vaguely lit the edge of her mind.

'I've never understood why you favoured it so much,' Violet said. 'The walk over the hill behind yours to the woods was always prettier in my opinion.'

'But the pine forest is more... mysterious,' she said. Summer or winter, the forest was always dark with leaf cover. On their walks through, she and Idris used to make up far-fetched stories. She didn't know anyone with an imagination like his. How they'd enjoyed each other's tales, absorbed some minutes, laughing the next!

'You and your imagination!' said Gwen.

Indeed. It worked too much all the time, leaving her longing for what she dreamt of.

Gwen peered up the road. 'Oh look. I do believe that's Miss Meredith.'

She was right: Elizabeth, dressed in her coat and hat, a handbag on her arm, was rushing towards them from the direction of McKenzie House.

The three women came to a halt. 'Maybe there's an emergency,' suggested Anwen. 'Let's walk up.'

It wasn't long before Elizabeth reached them, breathing heavily. 'Hello, ladies.'

Elizabeth studied the children, smiling at each of them. 'Clarice and Benjamin are growing so quickly... Anwen, I'm so glad I've seen you. I was about to call at your home. I'm sorry to curtail your jaunt, but my mother wishes to speak to you.'

'She wants to see me now?'

'Yes, it's rather urgent.' Elizabeth glanced at the other women. 'It's something of a delicate nature.'

'I see.' Anwen searched her brain for possibilities, even as she said, 'You two carry on. I'll catch you up if I can, or I'll see you later at Gwen's.'

'Of course, you can't miss my special tea!'

Mrs Austin had invited them on account of it being Gwen's twenty-first birthday next Wednesday, St David's Day.

'Don't worry, I'll make sure she's as quick as she can be.' Elizabeth swung round and hurried off in the direction of her house.

Anwen followed, wondering what could be this important. Then she remembered: last week it had said in the newspaper that well-off families were being asked to give up their servants so they could do war work. She'd feared it would come to this at some point.

Elizabeth opened the gate and entered the garden. Anwen's chest tightened.

Having not quite reached the front door, Elizabeth spun round to face her. 'Before we go in, I have to tell you I don't believe a word of it. But I promised my mother I wouldn't mention the precise nature of the matter to you. I'm sorry.' Elizabeth unlocked the door. 'Come, let's get this over and done with.'

This was sounding more daunting by the second.

Sprinting down the stairs was Tom, properly dressed on this occasion, with a collar and jacket added to his usual indoor ensemble. A smile lit his face, a detail that today didn't lift the burden of her current concern. 'Good afternoon, Anwen. And to what do we owe this pleasure?'

Elizabeth placed her bag on a small table. 'If you'd been up earlier Tom, you might already have some idea. I'll tell you later. Excuse us.'

'Oh dear. Sounds serious. I'm going out for a while.'

'Don't be late for dinner.' Elizabeth continued to the drawing room, not even removing her coat or inviting Anwen to do so.

The door opened before they got to it, Mr Meredith appearing in the doorway. 'That was quick, Lizzie. I'm leaving your mother to deal with this. I'm going over to the colliery. There are men doing overtime and I need to speak to Mr Williams.'

In the room, Mrs Meredith put down some needlework, a grave expression marring her otherwise attractive face. 'I won't beat about the bush, Miss Rhys.'

Miss Rhys. Not 'Anwen' anymore. That did not bode well.

'Food has gone missing from the pantry and Rose believes that you have taken it.'

A searing heat stole across her cheeks, an occurrence that would surely suggest she was guilty. 'No, Mrs Meredith, I have taken no food from the pantry. Rose won't even let me near it. And I'd never steal anyway.' She realised as she said it that it was no defence.

'I went in the pantry yesterday after receiving a box of vegetables from the greengrocer. I noticed there were fewer eggs than there should be, and one fewer tins of cocoa. Rose then informed me that certain other items had vanished but she wasn't sure if someone in the family had simply removed them. Flour, eggs, chicken, bread, butter and two tins of cocoa have disappeared, that we know of. What have you to say for yourself?'

'I have no means to take them from the house without someone seeing. I don't bring a basket or a bag with me.'

'Rose says she noticed your pockets were bulging one day when you left, but she assumed at the time it was your gloves.'

Why was Rose pointing the finger at her? After a shaky start to their relationship they'd been getting on well. 'Yes, I have put them in my pockets several times. But I promise you, Mrs Meredith, that I have not taken anything from this house that I was not supposed to.'

'How do you explain Rose seeing you with a bag of biscuits a few weeks ago?' Anwen's employer folded her hands in her lap and pinched her lips in.

'Rose has a very poor memory for someone who is only twenty-three,' Elizabeth interrupted. 'For she was present when I gave those biscuits to Anwen, ostensibly for her mother, who is bedridden. I did the same for Rose when her father was unwell.'

Anwen had forgotten about the biscuits, given a couple of weeks after she began work at the house.

Mrs Meredith slumped a little in her chair. 'This clearly needs further investigation. I really don't know what to think.' She composed herself, flattening down non-existent creases in her skirt. 'For now I will retain your services, but if I find you are responsible for the missing food, you will be dismissed.'

'I understand,' said Anwen, who wasn't sure she did, given that she had done nothing wrong.

'Now, you may return to your family, or whatever it was you were doing when my daughter fetched you.' She picked up her needlework and continued sewing.

Elizabeth rushed to the door, opening it for Anwen, who charged through. It was tempting to march straight to the kitchen to have words with Rose. Then she remembered it was Sunday and she went home after lunch.

Elizabeth caught her up at the door. 'Do you mind if I walk a little way with you?'

Anwen was tempted to say she did, that she'd had enough of the Meredith family today, but the glimmer of contrition and hope in the other woman's eyes stalled her pettiness. 'Of course not. I'm going to catch up with my friends, since I haven't been too long away.'

'I won't take up much of your time. I can imagine how much you value your day off from here.'

Imagine would be all she could do as it was unlikely, in her position, she'd ever fully understand.

They'd reached the path before Elizabeth said, 'I am truly sorry about all this. I did tell my mother that I didn't believe you would do such a thing.'

'Thank you.' Anwen opened the gate and hurried up the footpath, in the direction she'd been going when she'd been waylaid.

Elizabeth matched her quick pace. 'The shortage of groceries puts everyone under suspicion. Look at Farmer Lloyd and his outburst at the talk. Food is going to become scarcer before this war is over. The farmer is short of help to produce what he already has. I wonder...'

'What do you wonder?'

'If we could offer help. But also, we could grow vegetables, together, as a kind of co-operative.' There was more than a little excitement in Elizabeth's voice.

'What do you mean by "we", exactly?'

'Whoever wants to join. There's common land between Lloyd Street and Edward Street, between Alexandra Street and Islwyn Street, and also behind the first terrace of McKenzie Cottages.' She took Anwen's hands in hers. 'You seem a very resourceful woman. Would you help me organise people?'

The pleasure Anwen derived from the compliment fought with the terror of being responsible for something so big. 'I don't know. I've got work, and home. And choir practice. I'm not sure I could fit it in.'

Her conscience poked her, whispering, *go on; you wanted to do something useful for the war effort.* Sara was gone, Mamgu was nearby, more than willing to help with Mam. It was getting lighter so there would be more hours to do things outdoors. What would Da think? He was out more and more these days, so let him think what he liked. And there was no Idris to spend any time with, no prospect of caring for him and their babbies. And she was *needed*, to help her country in time of war.

'Yes! I will help you with it.'

Elizabeth could barely contain her excitement, bouncing on her heels and clapping the knuckles of her curled hands together. 'Thank you, Anwen. I am going to speak to Mama about this. Maybe some of your time at work could be spent on this project.'

A touch of reality burst Anwen's newly swelled bubble of enthusiasm. The business of the stolen food might be hanging over her for a while, apart from other practical considerations. 'Where will we get the gardening tools? What about seeds and bulbs? How will we recruit people to help?'

'I have several ideas, but I need to speak to a few people first. As for volunteers, I've booked a room at the Institute for Monday week for a meeting. I'll need help advertising it. Tomorrow afternoon I have an appointment to see Farmer Lloyd. If it's all right with my mother, I will take you with me. *And* if it's all right with you, of course. Two of us putting the case forward might do better.'

A lot seemed to depend on it being all right with Mrs Meredith. Given the mood she was currently in, Anwen didn't hold out much hope. Still, that was for Elizabeth to worry about.

'Yes, that would be fine by me. I used to know Mr Lloyd quite well, being friends with his children. What case do you want to put forward?'

'I'll tell you all about it tomorrow. You being more acquainted with him might be very useful.'

They spotted Gwen and Violet on the path, about to enter the forest, dawdling with the children.

'I will bid you good day, Anwen, and hope your afternoon with your friends goes well.' Elizabeth took Anwen's hands once more, giving them a quick squeeze. Throwing a wave to the others, she did an about turn and marched back towards the house, almost breaking into a run.

–

The chapel was full this evening, on the ground floor and up in the gallery, as Idris would have expected on St David's Day. The chapel was particularly welcoming tonight, warm and scented with both linseed oil from the wood and the soapy aroma of newly laundered clothes. For the first time, Idris had been keen to venture out of the safety of the house. The memory of past concerts on this festival filled him with a sense of being home.

His father leaned across Jenkin to speak to him. 'Why haven't you rejoined the choir, Idris, *bach*? It's a good tenor voice you've got.'

'I want to get back into the way of work and everything else first.' It was vague, but they accepted his explanation.

How could he do something that would bring him so close to Anwen? She was in the choir loft in the gallery behind him right now, for he'd spied her there as they'd come in.

The pastor, Mr Richards, arrived at the pulpit. Some of the congregation shushed their neighbours and conversation ceased. He spoke in Welsh, with some concession to those whose first language was English.

'Tonight, we have a treat in store for you to celebrate this day of our most honoured saint, David. Mr Henry, the headmaster of Upper Rhymney School, will give a talk on The Indomitable Spirit of the Welsh Patriots. Miss Maddox will be treating us to a rendition of several tunes on her harp and our own choir will be singing a number of our old favourites. To start the programme, the choir will begin with "A Delyn Aur".'

The congregation regarded the choir in their lofty position. Anwen was on the front row. The cherubic smile he'd so grown to love over the years was on full display as the familiar song progressed. They followed up the song with three others, after which it was the turn of Miss Maddox's harp.

Mr Henry was on next. Idris had been looking forward to the talk, his former headmaster being an eloquent speaker. It started well, as he told the stories of the country's past heroes. But as he shifted to the pluck and bravery of the current *Sons of Wales*, who were *upholding the honour of the Principality on the battlefields of France*, Idris shrivelled within. He wondered what poor, frightened Charlie would make of the sentiment now he'd been there over two months.

His mind wandered to distant days, until at long last the talk was over. *Please let it be the choir next.* But Idris was disappointed when Miss Maddox started up for another two tunes, melodic as they were.

His wait was finally rewarded with the next song, 'Dafydd Y Garreg Wen', 'David of the White Rock'. Anwen was singing a solo along to a low, rhythmic hum from the rest of the choir. Her pure voice rang out, pleasing his ear as much as her physical presence delighted his eye. *Last night an angel called*, Anwen sang in their native language. She'd been *his* angel for so long it was inconceivable she no longer was. Yet it had been his choice. For her. He'd done it for her.

After three other songs, the choir sang 'Hen Wlad fy Nhadau', a song so popular that the congregation couldn't help but join in. There was a rousing final chorus, their voices dimming only slightly for the last song of the evening, the national anthem, 'God Bless the Prince of Wales'.

Pastor Richards gave a final address, wishing all a good night. He'd barely finished when the congregation began rising, chatting with warmth and good humour. Despite Mr Henry's talk, Idris's heart had risen to the rafters during Anwen's solo and had not yet come down to earth.

'Well, there's a rare treat,' said Meg. 'A smile on your face, Idris, *bach*.'

'A good sing always lifts the soul, don't you think, Mam?'

'It does that. Wasn't Anwen in fine voice this evening?'

'Yes, she sang well.' He struggled to keep all emotion from his voice, speaking as if she'd been referring to any other young woman in the village.

'He doesn't care, Mam, do you Idris?' Jenkin said. 'Anyway, I've seen her with that Tom Meredith, the manager's son. Got money he has, so she's better off with him anyway.'

Meg gave him a light clip across the ear, making him duck and shout, 'Ow! What was that for?'

'For talking out of turn,' Meg said. 'Anwen's long been a friend of this family and if I want to mention her I will. If others don't see her worth that's their lookout.'

Idris's soul deflated, sinking down from the ceiling and settling itself back in his chest, brooding. The carefree sensation had been good while it lasted. In the meantime, Anwen had disappeared from the gallery and emerged on the ground floor.

'There she is,' said Meg. 'Let's tell her how wonderful she was.'

Meg pushed through the crowd in her direction. Before she reached her, Daniel Williams appeared in front of Anwen, telling her something that put a smile on her face. He was blushing, awkward, eyes sparkling. Jenkin had said she was admired by the men. She would never be short of a suitor.

It would never again be him, thought Idris.

Anwen marvelled at the scene before her as she took her place on the front row of chairs in the small meeting room of the Institute. There were already around twenty women gathered there, with five minutes still to go until the meeting commenced. Elizabeth, placing some papers on the table, had a wide grin on her face.

It had been a busy few days, putting up and handing out leaflets, going to visit Mr Lloyd, in between the other hectic aspects of her life. A visit to Mr James the greengrocer had not been an overwhelming success, but he was at least willing to consider their proposals. Mrs Brace the grocer had thought it a splendid idea. Prosser the Meat had intoned cheerfully, 'Well, you've got to have some veggies to eat with my meat.'

Elizabeth gestured Anwen over. 'Come, you must sit at the table with me.'

'Oh no, I couldn't put myself forward like that.'

'Nonsense. You have been instrumental in getting this whole project going. Farmer Lloyd reacted well to our proposals because you were there.'

'But you came up with the idea, I'm only helping.'

'Oh, my dear, it was you saying at chapel that we should grow our own vegetables that sparked the idea. It's obvious really, but it's amazing how we've all concentrated on what we can do to help our soldiers, forgetting that we need to keep healthy in order to do that.'

'Look.' Anwen pointed to a group of women coming in from the back. 'There must be at least half a dozen there.' At the rear of the group was Gwen. She sprinted down to the front.

'I told you I'd get some of my fellow munitionettes interested, didn't I? There are quite a few of us in the village now. Reckon a few more veggies wouldn't hurt us.'

'That is excellent,' said Elizabeth. 'Thank you.'

'I'll see you after,' Gwen told Anwen. 'Good luck!'

She was going to need it. She offered up a short prayer for strength.

Another couple of women entered the room. Anwen counted them. Nearly thirty! She was wallowing in the satisfaction when a further group entered. Her insides shrank. It was Esther Williams and her band. They took seats at the back, unusually for Mrs Williams, who always managed to make herself the centre of attention.

Anwen tapped Elizabeth's arm. 'I don't suppose they're here to help.'

'Ah. The illustrious Esther Williams. She'll have an opinion on this as she does everything else.'

'It doesn't help that she was recently appointed a Guardian. It's given an official stamp to her interference.'

'A Guardian? Really?' Elizabeth screwed up her eyes as she regarded Mrs Williams. 'I'd heard some had been appointed in the area, though I wasn't aware Mrs Williams was one of them.'

At eight o'clock precisely, Elizabeth coughed and said in a loud, authoritative voice, 'Good evening, everybody, and thank you for attending this meeting.'

The audience took a few seconds to settle, not noticing Mr Lloyd coming through the door. He remained at the back.

When the room was quiet, Elizabeth continued. 'I would like to start with a prayer, for all those killed and injured in the Zeppelin raid on the northeast coast of England last night.'

Several declarations of horror were heard from the audience. One woman lamented, 'And those poor babbies too.'

After the prayer, Elizabeth remained standing. 'As you are all aware, we are facing shortages of all kinds of food. The German ships are preventing supplies coming from abroad. Much of our food is provided by other countries, eighty percent of our wheat and forty percent of our meat, for example. There has also been a large increase in the price of food.'

Anwen was impressed by Elizabeth's composure, her clear speech and the fact that she had done some research. She had the attention of the listeners.

'Food production has fallen. Farm workers have left to enlist or go to the factories. Much of our livestock is sent to the Front. It could be that eventually our government will have to implement rationing, limiting the amount of food any one person can buy.' There were a couple of gasps. 'But it seems to me – to many of us – that in an unofficial way, there already is rationing.'

As Anwen considered her fellow villagers, she wondered whether Elizabeth was in fact the best person to talk about food shortages or rationing. The Merediths might have less food than they usually did, but they certainly were not short of it.

In the pause Elizabeth left, maybe to let what she'd said sink in, Anwen stood before the sensible bit of her brain told her not to. 'We've all experienced the lack of food first hand. The queue at the butcher's is down the street now, and you can't be guaranteed to get anything, even a scrawny pigeon.' She glanced at Elizabeth, hoping she wasn't too cross at the interruption, but her grin said the opposite.

Anwen was on the verge of losing her nerve, so plunged on before that could happen. 'The greengrocer's isn't much better. We're often palmed off with vegetables more than past their best. The grocer's shelves have half of what they used to have on them while the baker runs out of bread by ten o'clock. We've been in conversation with Mr Lloyd, who you all know as the owner of Dyffryn Gwyrdd Farm.'

The farmer leaned up from his position against the wall, taking Anwen's announcement as his cue to come forward. Soon he was standing by Anwen and Elizabeth's table. 'Yes, I've spoken to Miss Rhys and Miss Meredith here, and I think we have come to an arrangement that will suit us all.'

'Farmer Lloyd is short of workers,' said Elizabeth. 'If we could provide say, maybe four or more to work on a rota, he said that, in return, he'll provide us with some tools and seeds to plant our own vegetables, on the common land round about.'

'Aye, I will that. We grow our own, and I'm sure some of you do too, but not enough. If we could harness some of the

172

unused land you could grow more, make up for the shortfall in the village.'

'With all due respect,' came a voice from the back. Esther Williams rose from her seat. 'Won't that put Mr James, a green-grocer here for many years, out of business?'

'The prices I've heard he's charging for inferior stock, he deserves to go out of business,' the farmer said. 'Keeping the best stuff to sell on at inflated prices, I'm told.'

Mrs Williams sniffed. 'I'm sure he'll be pleased to hear you've said that behind his back.'

'I'd be quite happy to say it to his face, though I daresay you'll tell him before I get a chance.'

'Well! This whole scheme sounds unworkable. I'm sorry, Miss Meredith, but I shall be speaking to your parents about this.'

'Please do, Mrs Williams. I have talked to them about it extensively. They are fully in support of it. As is the coal company, who've given permission to use the land.'

'As for Mr James,' said Anwen, 'we have talked with him already, and will do so again. We intend to include him in our plans. We will be negotiating a rate at which he can sell the vegetables, so neither he, nor we, lose out.'

Esther blinked rapidly, pursing and unpursing her lips. 'I shall be informing my husband when he gets in from his very important meeting, how women are being spirited away from attending the needs of their menfolk, who need support so they can get on with producing the coal to power our ships. In my capacity as… that is, in my opinion, I say it's not proper for these women to be neglecting their duties.'

Gwen, sitting in the middle of the throng, faced the back to say, 'First you tell us we should be doing our bit for the war, then apparently we'll be neglecting our duties if we do. I work at the munitions and I'm still willing to do a bit more.' There was a murmur of *hear hear*. 'You should help out: you'd be able to keep an eye on us poor, vulnerable women then.'

There was laughter from young and old alike.

Esther's face reddened. 'You have not heard the last of this! Come along, ladies. We're leaving.'

The group with her, six women of various ages, looked at each other. The one furthest from Esther stood, waiting for the others to do the same. One by one, they gradually complied.

'Come on, chop chop,' Mrs Williams demanded.

Only the person next to her remained seated, a petite young woman with sun-browned skin. 'If it's all the same to you, Esther, I'd like to stay. I'm sick of spongy carrots and limp cabbage.'

'Oh *do* get up, Mary Jones.'

'No. I'm staying.'

'Please yourself. Come along, the rest of you.'

Mary pressed her knees to one side, allowing the other women to shuffle past her. They followed their leader like duck-lings swimming after the mother duck. Mrs Williams threw the door open with a clatter and exited. The last of the group shut it quietly after her.

'Thank you,' said Anwen to the remaining woman. 'So, you're Mary Jones?'

'That's right. Number thirty-three James Street.'

'Thank you for staying Mary.'

Elizabeth lifted a sheet from the table. 'Right, let us continue.'

–

Anwen removed her hat and coat, placing them on the stand in the hall. She wondered if Edgar Williams had returned from his 'very important meeting' and whether his wife had tattled on the poor wives and daughters of Dorcalon. What could the silly woman do? Maybe raise the men against their own womenfolk, if she told a twisted enough tale, and she wasn't beyond doing that.

All those remaining at the hall were eager to help. Elizabeth had taken their names, plus details of the times they could spare. Tomorrow they were going to draw up a rota and a more detailed plan.

Right now, she needed to see if Mam was still awake and needing a cup of tea. She'd want to hear how the meeting had gone. About to ascend the stairs, she was stopped by the opening of the kitchen door.

'There you bloody are.' Her father had a face on him like a wet Monday, as Mamgu often said. 'Come in here. Where have you been? Your mother said you were at the chapel doing a choir rehearsal, but I went there an hour ago and it were all closed up.'

No sooner had she asked herself why Mam had lied than the answer became obvious. Imagine if he'd come to the Institute, making a fuss! She didn't want him knowing yet what she was up to.

'It finished early so I went to see Uncle Hywel at Violet's.'

'The washing up wants doing and the kitchen floor needs a scrub where I spilt my supper. Helped myself to more of that cawl.'

'Oh Da, that was tomorrow's lunch too.'

'Lunch! Bloody *lunch* now, is it? Dinner not a good enough word, or is that what you call supper now? You're talking like the manager's daughter. I'll give you la-di-da, ideas above your bloody station.'

When he raised his hand she thought he was going to hit her, but instead he slammed his fist on the table. 'Fortunate for you I'm in a good mood. Been my lucky day, see. I'm going to bed now. I expect to see this tidy when I come down in the morning.' He staggered towards the door, something sticking out of the back pocket of his trousers. Money.

Though she'd seen few of them, she recognised the unmistakeable brown and pink of the new one pound and ten shilling notes, issued only since 1914. Where had he got them? It was tempting to creep up and remove one. It would be so easy. There were things she could buy, for Mam, for the project. But people would question how she'd got hold of paper money.

He closed the door after him, leaving her to scrub the table and floor where he'd spilt food. What a mess. His lucky day? He must have had a win on something. The horses, most likely. That people were still allowed to waste their money on such things while there was a war on appalled her.

She set to work. The sooner she cleaned this lot up, the sooner she could fall into bed.

Chapter Fifteen

The cloudless sky shone an intense azure as Anwen knelt to dig multiple holes with a trowel on the piece of land between Alexandra Street and Islwyn Street. There'd been a frost when she'd first ventured out this morning, and still the cold bit at her fingers.

Today, some of the women were spreading out the seedlings they'd sown last month. Gwen and Violet were sowing the next lot of seeds, for runner beans and marrows. Other women were digging trenches to plant a second round of seed potatoes.

Elizabeth arrived with a spade, slamming its blade into the ground. She was wearing trousers with a baggy shirt, a far more sensible idea than a skirt and blouse. Anwen wondered if she'd borrowed them from Tom. She had rather hoped he would come and join them in their digging, but so far he hadn't turned up, despite his sister's appeals.

'How are you doing, Anwen?'

'The soil's a bit harder here, but I'm making some progress.'

'I'll take over. Perhaps you'd like to organise the group thinning out the plants. Then you can pick a couple of them to transport the leftover seedlings to here.'

'Are you sure? I can carry on here if you want to organise the women.'

'No no. They respond well to you.'

Anwen pushed herself up, being careful not to stand on her skirt. 'Thank you again for the camellias you gave me for Mam. She was very touched. She really felt Sara's loss today. My sister always used to pick the columbines and wild pansies to make an arrangement in a jam jar for her on Mothering Sunday. I didn't have the heart to do it in her place.'

'I'm glad she liked them. Such simple things often bring the most pleasure to people.'

Like strolling hand in hand with the man you love, thought Anwen, spying a young couple on the pavement, going past Idris's house. *Idris*. She sighed long and deep, attempting to rid herself of the anguish that flowed around her bloodstream like a poison.

'I'm sorry, have you found it too much, the digging?' Elizabeth must have misinterpreted the sigh.

'No, I'm enjoying it. Just getting my breath.'

'We've made some progress,' Violet called out to Anwen as she approached the other group, working near the edge of the village.

'Wonderful. If two of you could take the seedlings to where Elizabeth is digging, you can start re-planting them.'

One of the volunteers was Esther Williams's former follower, Mary Jones, along with another of her cronies who had since abandoned her. They each picked up a wooden crate in which the seedlings had been carefully placed, carrying them across to where Elizabeth was now on her knees, digging.

A girl ran over from the potato planters, her hands and blouse muddy from her exertions. 'Anwen, is there anyone can come and help us? I'm not sure we'll get it finished today with just the two of us.'

Gwen straightened her back. 'I'll go. There's enough here to get this done.'

'Thank you,' Anwen said. 'I'll help here anyway, now Elizabeth's taken over from me.'

She stooped to begin digging up alternate seedlings, working along the row next to Violet. Clarice and Benjamin were running around in circles chasing each other. Clarice lifted the toddler up each time he tumbled onto the earth, as he did frequently, giggling at his soft landing. It was a joyful sound, making Anwen smile.

She'd been working a good half-hour when Violet coughed in a pointed way and indicated something with her head. Gwilym Owen and Idris were dawdling down Alexandra Street, hands in pockets, craning their necks to see what was going on.

Close by now, Gwilym called, 'Hello Anwen, Violet. You helping out with this allotment lark too?'

'That's right,' said Violet. 'Anwen and Miss Elizabeth had this brilliant idea to grow veg. We're helping Mr Lloyd at the same time and he's helping us.'

'What's all these, then?' Gwilym pointed at the plants in the crates.

Violet explained to him what they were doing, leading him over to study the seedlings. Idris stayed put on the sidelines, taking in the whole field.

Anwen was about to carry on when he piped up with, 'Mam said you were all making good progress out here and we should take a look.'

'I think we are.'

'I've noticed people working on the land opposite your house.'

'That's right. We're hoping to get some things planted up behind the cottages too.'

There was a pause. Anwen lifted her trowel to continue but he spoke again. 'What veg are you planting?'

'So far we've sown sprouting broad and runner beans, carrots, cabbages, cauliflowers, onions, peas, sprouts, turnips, leeks and parsnips.'

'That's good. And how is Mr Lloyd helping out, then?'

'He's provided tools and the seeds in exchange for some of the group to work on the farm on a rota. They're tending the sheep and learning about shearing for when the time comes.' She was warming to her theme, happy to have someone else to share her enthusiasm with. 'They've all been welcomed by Mrs Lloyd and Nellie and get good home-cooked food, what with them having their own vegetables and eggs.'

His mouth slowly stretched into the smile she had missed so much. 'It sounds like an excellent arrangement.'

'It is. And Mr Lloyd often comes down to see how we're getting on and to advise us.'

'You've all got a lot to do.'

'We could certainly do with more volunteers as spring and summer progresses, so spread the word.' A bit of mischief got into her, that she wasn't able to conquer before she blurted out, 'That Polly Coombes, for instance, she sits and sews all day. If she could spare some hours she'd get some exercise and fresh air.'

Idris's eyes widened. 'What's she got to do with me?'

'Sorry, I thought she was a friend of yours.'

'No. You could go to Mrs Bowen's to ask her. Anyway, it sounds like you're doing a wonderful job.'

'That's kind of you to say.' She bit the inside of her mouth, looking around at her colleagues, not knowing what else to do. Goodness, what a mess she must look in this old outfit, mud everywhere, her hair escaping from the pins.

'I had a letter from Charlie,' said Idris. 'Seems to be in the thick of it, in France, I think, though he doesn't exactly say. Not sure why he's writing to me about it. But I suppose Violet's told you.'

'The last I heard, he was supposed to be coming home on leave. But maybe things have got worse.'

'I dunno. Not mentioned it to me.'

Perhaps Charlie hadn't wanted to worry Violet. You'd think he'd have told her about cancelled leave, though.

'Well – Gwilym and I are going to kick a ball around with Jenkin and Evan now. Good luck with the allotments,' said Idris. 'I'll see you... around.'

'Thank you. Take care.' The last two words had slipped out without her thinking about it. She didn't want to sound like she was concerned for his welfare at all.

'You too.' He ambled back to Gwilym, who had just finished talking to Violet.

Mary, struggling back with one of the crates, watched Idris and Gwilym stroll away. 'It'd be good if some of the men would help.'

'They work hard enough as it is,' said Violet as she joined them.

This set Anwen thinking. 'What about some of the retired workers? Digging coal might have got too much for them, but they might manage to dig some soil.'

'You'd have to persuade them first,' laughed Violet.

It was food for thought. She'd speak to Elizabeth about it.

–

Jenkin was first on the field beyond the hospital and West Street Terrace. He dropped the football he'd been carrying and kicked it along the grass. Idris was soon running after it, tackling his brother and taking possession of the ball. Gwilym had suggested the activity at chapel, it being a nice clear day and not too chilly. Idris had missed the odd game of football with his mates, most of whom were now in the army. He wasn't sure he was in the mood for it, or fit enough, but he didn't want to disappoint his brother.

Gwilym and Evan were soon joining in, each playing for themselves.

As he was tackling Idris for the ball, Jenkin said, 'We haven't watched a match since you got back. I think the last time we went was Rhymney versus Merthyr Town.'

'That's right, Rhymney won two goals to nil.'

'They're still playing, you know, though Cyril told me some of the original team have had to join the army. Hey!'

Gwilym managed to get the ball away from Jenkin, who chased after him as he made for a bush on one side, which they always used for a goal. The other two caught them up and Idris got the ball off his friend, heading off to the bush in the other direction. As he reached it, Evan called for them to stop.

'We're all over the place, mun. We need some rules and to decide whose goal is where and who's playing who.'

Idris let out a huge sigh and bent forward. He already felt overwarm. 'Not done any running for a while.' He caught his breath and stood up. 'I've heard there are still matches on, though the newspapers don't seem to report them so much. Seems odd when the Welsh Rugby Union cancelled all the fixtures back in 1914 and encouraged all the players to enlist.'

'Yes, I remember that poster.' Jenkin coughed and quoted with gusto, '*Rugby Union Footballers are doing their duty. Over 90 percent have enlisted.* What did it say at the top?'

Idris squinted as he recalled it. '*This is not the time to play games.* Then something at the bottom about athletes following their example.'

'Aye, and they did.' Gwilym didn't sound impressed with that outcome.

'I wonder why they cancelled the rugby and not the football,' said Evan.

'Because the Football Association of Wales argued it was good for morale and the powers that be realised they could use the matches as recruitment rallies.'

'There's cynical,' said Idris, though he did recall speakers at one of the last matches he'd attended, appealing to the patriotic nature of those in the crowd.

Gwilym took his jacket off and threw it on the ground. He started running on the spot. 'You know I'm right.'

'Well I miss the rugby, anyway,' said Evan, 'for I always preferred it to football.'

Jenkin picked the ball up from under his foot, where he'd been keeping it steady. 'I think football's much more exciting. You agree, don't you Idris?'

'No, rugby's much better,' Evan countered. 'Gwilym agrees.'

Idris chuckled. It wouldn't be the first time the two pairs of brothers had ended up having this argument. 'We'll have to agree to disagree on that one, *bach.*'

'Come on then,' said Jenkin. 'Are we having a game or not? Me and Idris versus you two. This is our goal, that's yours.' He pointed to the bush on the other side.

'First team to get three goals is the winner,' said Idris. He was surprised at the little jolt of excitement he experienced. He was actually looking forward to it now, though he wasn't sure how long he'd be able to run around for. It took him back to before the war, to a simpler time.

Jenkin threw the ball towards the middle of the field, and they were off.

-

Rose was busy at the kitchen table when Anwen came in after her morning cleaning jobs. The cook was putting together a 'light lunch', as Mrs Meredith had called it when she'd given out instructions this morning. This entailed lettuce, tomatoes and a good quality ham, along with bread and butter.

'What are you skulking there for?' said Rose, frowning as she regarded her.

'I was just about to put the cleaning things away.' Anwen carried the tin box and broom to their place in the scullery, able to hear Rose muttering to herself about 'tasteless salad muck'.

When Anwen got back to the kitchen Rose moaned, 'Prefer a good hefty sandwich, I do. It fills a hole. And what's wrong with a nice hearty soup? I dunno, you get a bit of sun and people run away with theirselves thinking it's summer. And that Mr Tom's got his head in the clouds. He told me earlier he's having lunch *in the garden*. Imagine!'

'We shouldn't bite the hand that feeds us, Rose.'

'What's that supposed to mean? You and your fancy sayings. You're not one of them, you know. And you'd do well to remember it.'

'What I mean is, they pay us, and quite well too, so we don't really have cause to moan.'

'I know what you mean. I'm not stoopid.'

Rose was definitely in a contrary mood today, and had been since the episode with the stolen food. She'd apologised to Anwen for accusing her of the theft, though only because Elizabeth had insisted. She suspected the cook still thought she was responsible, especially as no food had disappeared since.

Remembering that the dustpan and brush were still near the front door, she left Rose to her slicing and mumbling. In the hall she bent to pick them up, but froze on hearing raised voices from the study. She knew she should move on, not eavesdrop, but recognising one of the voices as Tom's, she lingered.

'I don't have an endless pot of money, Thomas.' It was Mr Meredith. 'If you want to indulge in such extravagance, you will have to find work. Come to the mine. I could find you an examiner's job.'

'What about my degree?'

'You've missed this year now. Besides, most of your fellow students have enlisted, and some of the tutors too. There will be no completed degrees until after the war finishes.'

'Father, I would die of boredom. I'm not asking for much more than my allowance.'

'Your allowance is more than generous. I'm a mine manager, not Lord Aberconway.'

'You do well enough.'

Anwen considered the furnishings, even in the hallway. Yes, Mr Meredith was doing all right. However, she was indignant about Tom's attitude. Other able-bodied men had to enlist. He'd recovered from his influenza, surely.

'Work for the duration of the war,' said Mr Meredith. 'A job in the mine will be considered essential. You can avoid being called up, if that's what you want. The doctor's note's not going to last forever. You appear well enough now.'

'Are you all right, Anwen?'

She jumped. So eager was she to hear how Tom would defend himself, all the while bent in readiness to pick up the dustpan, that she hadn't heard Elizabeth coming down the stairs.

She straightened herself. 'Oh yes, Miss. I left the dustpan here and was just collecting it.'

'Good heavens, is that my father and brother arguing?'

'I'm not sure.'

'Anyway, I'm going out to meet one of my old school friends. Haven't seen her since the war began as she's with the Voluntary Aid Detachment. Has my mother left you any errands to run this afternoon?'

'She said to start on one of the rooms on tomorrow's list unless one of the family have something for me to do.'

'You could call on Farmer Lloyd if you have time. See how things are getting on there. He said he'd be getting hold of more seeds for us so you could fetch those back.'

'Yes, I'll do that.'

'Thank you. What would we do without you? I'll see you later.' She went to open the front door but turned back abruptly. 'Oh yes, another thing. I have three tickets for the Shakespeare tercentenary performance at the Institute on Saturday. An amateur troupe from Ebbw Vale who are supposed to be quite good. Only Tom and I are going, so there's a spare ticket. Would you like to join us?'

Anwen had asked Gwen, Violet and Uncle Hywel if they would like to go. Uncle Hywel was doing an extra shift at the mine and neither of the other two could make it. She'd asked Mamgu as a last resort, but her response, as she'd expected, was that she didn't understand that *funny oldey English*, and to *give her something in Welsh any day*. Anwen hadn't the heart to go on her own.

'Thank you, I would love to join you.'

'Wonderful. See you later on.'

Anwen picked up the items on the floor, preparing to move off when Tom appeared from the study, his father close behind.

'I'm going back to work,' Mr Meredith announced. 'You think about what I said, Tom.'

Anwen quickly lifted the bowler hat from the stand, hiding the dustpan behind her back as she handed the hat to her employer.

'Thank you, Anwen. Tell Rose I will not require lunch.'

'Yes, sir.'

He put the bowler hat on and left.

Tom regarded her with amusement, thumbs in his trouser pockets, shirt half untucked. 'I, on the contrary, am famished. I've already told Rose I'll be having my lunch in the back garden. It would be a crime to waste such a beautiful day.'

'Very well, sir.'

'And I assume it will be lunchtime for you too?'

'After I've served you, yes.'

'Please join me for lunch, stop me getting lonely.'

'I'm not sure—' His attitude toward his father still irked her.

'Go on.'

'Can Rose come too?'

He pulled a face. 'Is she likely to want to?'

He knew as well as she did that Rose mostly ate as she worked, picking at food. It was probably why she was so skinny. 'No.'

'What if I command you?' There was a twinkle in his eye that diminished her vexation with him.

She'd only heard part of his conversation with his father. She shouldn't jump to conclusions. '*Command* me?' She hoped the light-hearted question didn't come across as insolence.

He threw his head back and let out a 'Hah!' Grinning broadly he said, 'I'm not sure I'm capable of commanding anyone. Please, join me outside for your lunch break.'

His parents had gone out. Elizabeth too, though she wouldn't have cared: she was always crossing class lines. What if Rose told on her? What would there be to tell? Tom had instructed her.

'Yes sir. I will join you.'

They passed the first five minutes of lunch in silence. Anwen admired the flowers Mrs Meredith tended, now her gardener had enlisted. The cerise peonies with the bright yellow centres, the dusty plum hellebores and flushed tulips showed her employer had a preference for pink flowers.

Opposite her, Tom finished the first page of the newspaper he'd taken out with him. Folding the paper but holding it aloft, he said, 'What do you make of this rebellion in Ireland?'

'I'm not sure I'm in a position to make anything of it, sir. I only heard very vaguely about it this morning from one of the delivery men.'

'*A rebellion on Easter Monday, of all days*, my father said earlier. Not sure any other day would make it any better.' He folded the paper noisily and placed it to one side. 'Rebellions, demonstrations against the war in Germany – even those who aren't soldiers are fighting in their own way. The Russians rebelled ten years ago. Who's to say they won't again? The war doesn't seem to have given any party any proper gains, though the Germans have made advances. Gallipoli and the whole Dardanelles campaign was a travesty. It could go on a long time.'

'But I read in my father's paper that the Russians have taken Trebizond and the British troops are advancing on German lines in the trenches.'

'But only by a few hundred yards. The Germans have dispatched thirty thousand shells in forty days in Verdun. They've started on a fresh offensive in the Meuse. They've just torpedoed another ship that was only carrying passengers on a voyage, for pity's sake!' Tom slumped in his seat. 'Tell me, Anwen, what is your opinion on war poetry?'

'You mean Jessie Pope?'

Tom laughed drily. 'Miss Pope is maybe not the best for representing the war as it is. I was thinking more of Brooke, McCrae and Binyon's work.'

She hadn't heard of them but didn't want to admit it. 'I regret they have to write about it at all; that anyone should go to this silly war because some duke got killed. If we all went to war every time someone killed someone else, why, we'd always be at war.'

He finished his mouthful of food. 'It's not that simple, of course. I could explain some of it, but do you want to hear the history of different countries' power struggles over the last fifty years?'

'Not today. Recommend a book, or lend me one, and I'll read it.'

He raised his glass of water to her. 'I like you, Anwen Rhys. You've got spirit. I hope you have a sweetheart who appreciates your quick wit and intelligence.'

Her cheeks glowed with embarrassment. She'd never felt comfortable with compliments, unsure always if she deserved them. 'I have no sweetheart.' She was going to leave it at that, yet something compelled her to continue. 'I did have. We were engaged. Childhood sweethearts, wasn't it. He enlisted over a year ago: Rhondda Pals.'

'Oh, I am sorry. Has he been—'

'Killed? No. He was discharged in November. Ill health. But he came back changed. Didn't want to be betrothed anymore, see.' It was an effort to relay it without emotion. She pretended to herself that she was talking about someone else.

'I'm sorry to hear that.'

Why would he be? He didn't know her, not really. It was something to say.

He followed it up with, 'The man's a fool.'

'Thing is, he isn't. He's very clever.'

'You can be clever and be a fool. Believe me, I know.'

She enjoyed being imbued with some worth. Nevertheless, she was eager for lunch to be over so she could escape to her duties once more. She knew where she was with that. With this in mind, she finished up her lunch as quickly as was polite and shortly before he did.

Standing, she said, 'I'll take these plates now, sir. I need to get on.'

'So soon?'

'Miss Elizabeth asked me to call on Mr Lloyd with regards the vegetable patches and some seeds.'

'Very well. Let me take the glasses.' He picked them up, following her to the side of the house, to the doorway into the scullery.

An idea occurred to her. 'We can always do with extra help digging, hoeing, picking. If you're ever at a loose end.'

'Elizabeth has been on at me about this. I will give it serious thought. In the meantime, why don't you come out to the cinema with me one evening?'

'Oh, I don't know about—'

'There are a few good films showing at the moment. Do you like watching films?'

'Yes. I've been a few times, to the Cosy Cinema in Pont-lottyn and the Imperial in Rhymney. Not for a while, though.' Not since Idris had gone away. The pictures had been a favourite trip for them.

'About time you went again then.'

Should she? What was stopping her? Apart from the class difference, of course. 'Perhaps.'

'You decide when might be convenient for you, and I'll have a look in the newspapers to see what's on where.'

'Hello Tom.'

They both looked round. There, on the path outside the house, was Polly Coombes, bold as brass, her bright skirt and blouse topped with an open jacket. She gazed up from under her eyelashes and waggled her fingers in greeting.

'Polly,' Tom said, a smile on his face that did not convince Anwen, though Miss Coombes seemed satisfied.

'See you around soon, I hope.' Polly pouted in a most brazen manner.

'Probably.' He lifted his hand in a brief gesture.

Soon she was strutting back down the path the way she'd come. Tom ushered Anwen through the open door, into the scullery.

'My, you are certainly popular with the ladies of the village,' Anwen joked.

'Does that include you?' He wasn't teasing or smiling, but serious.

She didn't reply, saying instead, 'Has she been pestering you?'

His mood lightened. 'No. She's a funny little thing though, don't you agree? Not bright like you.'

Polly's appearance felt like fate had intervened for Anwen. It reminded her that Idris wasn't moping around after her. 'I will have a think about a time for going to the pictures,' she said.

'Good.'

'And you must think about helping with the vegetables.'

He waited for her to put the crockery on the draining board. 'You're persistent, aren't you?'

'When something is important, yes. It's getting so much lighter in the evenings now, so we could do with extra workers.'

He handed her the glasses. 'I can be persistent too, so don't take too long deciding on a date. Thank you for your company at lunch. I'll be out the rest of the afternoon. I've no doubt I'll see you tomorrow.'

He passed Rose in the doorway as she came into the scullery, hands firmly gripping her slight hips. She stared at Anwen for some seconds. 'Nice *lunch*, was it, with Mr Tom?'

'We were speaking about the vegetable-growing project.'

'It's alright for those what have time to dig vegetables. I've got my hands full cooking them.' She sniffed.

'But that's the problem, Rose. If we don't start growing our own there won't be any to cook. Food's getting short. And the government's asked for families like the Merediths to give up their servants for war work.'

'You can go do war work. I'm indinspendable.' She gave one firm nod of her head.

Anwen decided against correcting her last word. 'No one is, Rose.'

'As for a vegetable shortage, I don't know what Miss Elizabeth is thinking with her crazy project. She's not been subject to no vegetable shortage. Plenty of them here.'

'Elizabeth's aware that isn't the case for most people.' Yet it was a worrying aspect of this house that she tried to avoid thinking about too often. There was talk of profiteering. There were rumours of thefts in the area, from farms like Mr Lloyd's, from shops. A delivery cart had been set upon by masked men a couple of weeks back. Food came to McKenzie House variously by motor van or via Rose who shopped in the village, returning with items not seen by the rest of the villagers.

'It's there for people what's got the money,' Rose concluded, stomping away back to her kitchen.

Chapter Sixteen

Anwen's whole body had been abuzz with excitement for the last two hours. The Ebbw Vale Amateur Dramatic Society had portrayed some wonderful scenes from Shakespeare. Though the mood at the start of the evening had been sombre, with muted exchanges about the terrible events of Easter Monday in Ireland and martial law in Dublin, the audience were transported once the performance began.

Scenes had been re-enacted from seven of Shakespeare's plays, from the comedy of *The Merry Wives of Windsor*, through the whimsy of *A Midsummer Night's Dream* to the darkness of *Macbeth*. Some scenes had elicited laughs, others gasps, but all had produced effusive clapping at their finales.

The last scene to be played out was from *Much Ado about Nothing*. Anwen had read this play twice. How she now envied the love between Beatrice and Benedick.

The last line of *Much Ado* was delivered. The actors formed a line, bowing to rapturous applause from the audience.

Tom leaned towards her. 'They were good for amateurs.'

She inched a little closer. 'Yes, I've seen them before, doing other plays.'

'I've certainly seen worse, even in the West End.'

Was she supposed to know what that was? It was tempting to nod and pretend she did, but she was curious to find out. 'The west end of what? Cardiff?'

He emitted a small titter. 'No, Anwen, *the* West End. In London. Leicester Square, where the theatres are.'

'Oh yes. I see.' How stupid he must think her. She'd never been to London, knew little about it, except that the Houses of Parliament were there, and Buckingham Palace, where King George lived with Queen Mary.

'One day you should go. It's wonderful fun. You can get on a train from Newport straight into Paddington. Of course, I mostly went up from Reading with university friends.'

Increasingly out of her depth, she was relieved when the applause faded and people began to rise. They were halted by the librarian, Mr Pritchard, rushing on to the stage, which the actors had recently vacated.

'I'm sorry, but a moment more of your time, please,' he boomed in his rich voice. He would have done well on the stage. 'I have just been told some important news.' His expression told them it wasn't good.

Anwen's throat constricted; her breaths becoming laboured. Had the violence in Ireland escalated once more? Or had the Germans invaded, bringing ships from the Channel up the River Thames, or into Cardiff via the River Taff? The audience's excited post-performance chatter ceased. On the stage, Mr Pritchard scanned the crowd, like a nervous performer on his first night.

'I've been asked to convey to you all the sad news of the deaths of two of our finest, who enlisted into the Rhondda Pals Brigade last year.'

Anwen stared at the ceiling, offering up a silent, selfish prayer. *Not Charlie, please not Charlie. Or Henry.*

'Their families had word earlier of the deaths of Robert Harris and Percy Vaughan—'

Whatever else he'd been about to say was drowned out by exclamations of shock and disbelief. *Not sweet Percy – not dear Robert – Too young – Damned Hun! – all the Kaiser's fault – Oh God, poor Florrie, poor Annie. Poor Jane. And those babbies without a da.* The murmuring commentary continued.

Elizabeth leant across Tom. 'Did you know them, Anwen?'

'I knew Robert a little, and Percy was friends with my brother Tomos.' She gritted her teeth, trying to stave off the whining moan threatening to escape her throat.

'How old were they?'

'Robert was about thirty and Percy about twenty-five.' A tear ran down one side of her face before she buried her face in her hands.

'Oh dear, oh dear,' said Tom, stroking Anwen's arm gently. She was too upset to either appreciate or be embarrassed by it. 'There there. It's terrible. Simply appalling. Such a waste of young life. War always is.' He was almost echoing what she'd said in the garden.

Peeping up once more, trying to stem the flow of emotion, she saw that the audience was slow to move. There were women weeping. An old man held on to a seat for support, hanging his head low.

At long last one man sprang up, rushing along the row of people between his seat and the aisle. Having escaped, he ran for the exit, disappearing after flinging open the door.

'Good God, where's he going in such a hurry?' said Tom.

It was Idris Hughes.

–

No, it couldn't be. Not Percy and Robert. The room seemed devoid of air. He had to get out of here.

Idris left his chair, struggling to get by the people in his row. His mother was calling, 'Idris? Idris!' He needed to be on his own, in his house, his safe place, away from the shocked chatter of the people, most of whom hadn't known Percy and Robert as well as he had, hadn't spent the best part of twenty-four hours a day training, eating and sleeping with them. In those seven months at camp, closeted together, he'd got to know his bunk mates better than almost anyone else in his life.

Out of the door now he could breathe again. He had to get out of the building and down the street. He was glad of the cool air of the night, welcoming it as a friend to cool his emotion.

Percy. A keen rugby player, 'a fine figure of a man', as he'd heard Gwen once describe him. Robert had been in the choir at chapel, the finest baritone voice he'd ever heard, frequently featured in the annual Baptist Gymanfa. It was lost to the world forever.

He was finding it hard to make his breaths deep, catching as they did part way through, making him gulp in more air. He counted the front doors: thirty-one, thirty-two, thirty-three. Home. He almost fell into the hall, stumbling towards the open kitchen door, throwing his body into a dining chair. He should go to his room but he couldn't face the stairs just yet. Bending over the table, he covered his neck with his hands, pulling his head down more as the sobs began.

Percy and Robert. Percy and Robert. He was aware of the pulse in his ear, more than twice as fast as it should be. A vague nausea developed deep within his head. It was like the motion sickness he'd experienced once. His face and neck were sweating.

How long he sat there, frozen in that pose, he wasn't sure. He heard the front door close, tempting him to flee to the back garden. His limbs wouldn't comply with the appeal, heavy like a chunk of newly hewn coal. There were subdued voices, then footsteps on the stairs. Good; they'd decided to go straight to bed.

No such luck. The door opened and the light footsteps he recognised as his mother's tramped across the floor.

'Are you all right, *bach*?'

If he didn't reply she might go away, leave him to his sorrow. But of course, she wouldn't. It wasn't her way.

'Come on, out with it. It doesn't do no good keeping it in. This isn't like you. You were always too fond of letting others know how you felt, once upon a time.'

He lifted his head, regarding her with an expression that melted her indignation into sadness.

'Oh Idris, *bach*, it's a sorry picture you look.'

'I should have been with them, Mam. Maybe I could have helped them.'

'How? You don't even know how they were killed.'

The hard last word of her sentence shot through him. He hoped to God it had been over quickly, that they weren't even aware of what happened. A quick round of bullets to the chest. Over. Blown up in a split second. Finished. He'd read of the poison gas the Hun used, burning skin into blisters, or clogging lungs, a slow, painful death. His hands trembled. He clenched them, tucking them into his armpits.

'Look, Idris, I know it's an awful thing. Tears the heart from me, it does. But I believe there's a reason why things happen. You're here, Idris, and it must be because you have a purpose to fulfil.'

He wished he shared his mother's certainty that there was some kind of logic to the world. As far as he could see, there was no rhyme nor reason to anything. What was the point of a fourteen-year-old boy dying in a pit accident, for instance?

'Percy and Robert are not here to achieve anything anymore, but you are. What about the better conditions for miners you were so keen on before the war? What about raising a family – hope for the future when this war finishes?'

That particular ambition was not going to be realised with anyone. A dizziness overtook him briefly.

Meg pulled out a chair next to him, placing her hand on his shoulder. 'Idris, you may not consider this the time to mention it, but you will have to snap out of this self-pitying mood.'

'Self-pitying?' He sat upright.

'Yes, self-pitying.'

'Mam, I—' He was abruptly robbed of his ability to breathe, trying to catch his breath three times, before experiencing a coughing fit.

'Idris, are you all right?' She rubbed his back while touching his face with the back of her other hand.

He shook her off. 'I'm fine. Got that cold that's going round.' He didn't believe it and he could see by her expression that she didn't either.

'The doctor at Winchester discharged you for a reason, Idris. Isn't it about time we fetched Dr Roberts? You lost weight when you were away. I think you've lost more since you've been home.'

He had lost a little, he couldn't deny it, but he wouldn't make anything of it, either. 'I told you—'

'Yes, you told me. But you're not yourself, Idris Hughes, and I want to know why.'

'Digging coal's harder work than marching. I'm using more energy and food's not as plentiful here.'

'At least Anwyn and Miss Elizabeth are trying to do something about it. Why don't you help out some evenings? Get some fresh air. It might stop this self-absorbed nonsense.'

He glared at her. 'There aren't any men helping.'

'So? Doesn't mean there can't be. Have a think about it.' She went back to the hall, leaving him to his thoughts.

Chapter Seventeen

Having only just changed for her post-lunch duties, Anwen was already answering the door to the first of the callers who Mrs Meredith had invited to afternoon tea. Pulling the door open, ready with a greeting, she'd only got the word 'Good—' out when she realised she was facing two policemen, their metal jacket buttons gleaming.

'Sergeant Harries,' she finished instead.

'Good afternoon, Miss.' Harries lifted his helmet off and held it. 'We'd like to speak with Mrs Meredith, if you please.'

What was the etiquette for this? With delivery men, they were left waiting on the doorstep. The policemen might not appreciate that.

'Please, come in and wait in the hall while I inform Mrs Meredith of your visit.'

'Very well, Miss.'

They entered. An older policeman, PC Probert, who'd come out of retirement to replace PC Davies when he'd been conscripted, removed his helmet too. Anwen remembered him being the local constable when she was a child.

She went quickly to the drawing room, knocking but not entering until Mrs Meredith invited her to do so.

'Madam, the police wish to speak with you.'

'Goodness! Now, when my ladies are due? Very well, I will see them in the dining room. If any of the ladies arrive, please direct them here and inform them I have been slightly delayed and will be with them shortly.'

'Very well, madam.'

Anwen left, directing the policemen to the place specified. 'Mrs Meredith will be along shortly.'

She was about to leave when Margaret Meredith appeared. She entered the dining room, giving Anwen no thanks for holding the door open for her. Frown lines marred her forehead.

Anwen waited in the hall for the visitors to arrive. If Mrs Meredith was kept a while it might be an idea to bring them tea. She went to the large mirror, above the tall console table in the hall. After flicking imaginary dust from the bleached white apron, she straightened an already level cap. She hated being idle, wishing she'd secreted a small volume in her apron pocket, to read during such empty moments.

It wasn't long before Mrs Meredith appeared again, a tinge of red in her cheeks. 'Anwen, I am going to be indisposed this afternoon. There are six ladies in all due to call.' She named them. 'Would you please let them know that I have a headache so will be unable to receive them.'

'Of course, madam.'

'After that, fetch my daughter. I believe she's in the garden, digging.' Her puckered lips made it clear she was put out by this. Elizabeth had persuaded her to swap some of her flower beds for vegetable plots. 'And my son, who is… I'm not sure where he is.'

'He went out earlier, madam.'

'Of *course* he did.' She raised her eyes. 'I'd then like you to come down to the kitchen with Elizabeth.'

'Very well.'

Mrs Meredith's callers came two by two. Various degrees of regret were expressed by them, each sending wishes for a speedy recovery.

Anwen was about to close the door to the last pair of callers when Tom arrived back in the motorcar. A wind had recently whipped up, blowing his hair around his face. Anwen waited for him to come in, watching the last ladies return to their own motorcar. They greeted Tom as they reached the gate, holding onto their hats.

As Tom entered, Anwen said, 'The police have arrived, to talk to your mother.'

'Really, what's she been up to? Frightening Farmer Lloyd's sheep?' He laughed raucously, finding it much more amusing than Anwen did.

'When she thought you were in, she asked me to fetch you, along with Miss Elizabeth.'

'Good heavens, I can't be bothered with whatever that is now. Tell her I've a headache and I've gone to my room.' He took the stairs two at a time, not even removing his coat.

That Mrs Meredith had concocted the same excuse for the ladies Anwen did find perversely amusing, smiling wryly as she let herself out of the front door.

In the back garden she found Elizabeth, removing weeds from a patch of soil, unbothered by the wind that was causing Anwen to hold onto her skirt. She straightened up, waving as she spotted Anwen. 'Have you come to help? Don't think the black dress and clean apron is quite the outfit for this job.'

'Elizabeth, the police have arrived. Your mother is in the kitchen with them and wants the two of us to join them.'

'Goodness, how intriguing.' She brushed dry earth from her hands, following Anwen to the outside door into the scullery. Onner, the laundry woman, was removing sheets from the washing line, struggling against the billowing fabric.

A piercing voice could be clearly heard as they entered the house. Rose had taken umbrage at something. Entering the kitchen, they saw the table covered with food. Packets and tins, a roasted lamb joint, unskinned rabbits and three bottles of whisky were among the large array of provisions.

'I'm just saying, I do as I'm told. I didn't purchase the food. I collected it from the shop or delivery man and stored it away as I was instructed. I don't know where it came from before. Not my business to ask, is it?'

'What's going on?' said Elizabeth.

Mrs Meredith's face had drooped with weariness. 'Someone has reported our family for hoarding food.'

'Is it a crime now to store food away?' Elizabeth's question was aimed at Sergeant Harries.

'Not in itself, Miss, but there's been reports of people hoarding food and alcohol in order to sell it on at inflated prices.'

'I *bought* much of it at inflated prices!' Mrs Meredith said with exasperation, her Welsh accent more in evidence now. 'Aren't there worse things going on in Ireland the police should be sorting out?'

'There's not a lot we here can do about Ireland, Mrs Meredith,' said Sergeant Harries. 'And that's no excuse to turn a blind eye to what's going on in our own back yard.'

'Calm down, Mother. We will get this sorted out. Sergeant, who reported that we were hoarding in order to profit, which is what I presume you are in fact accusing us of?'

'We all know who the informant is,' Rose bellowed, pointing a stick finger at Anwen.

She knew it was only a matter of time until Rose accused her. 'It wasn't me. I didn't even know all this foodstuff was in the pantry. I'm not allowed in there.'

'Wouldn't stop you sneaking in, would it? And how'd you know it came from the pantry, eh?'

'Where else would it have been?'

'Funny how the food theft stopped when you were questioned about it.'

'Probably because the real thief realised they'd been found out.'

Rose got up close, pushing her face towards Anwen's. 'Things went missing on several occasions.'

'How do you know?' Anwen was aware of the policemen studying each of them as they spoke.

'Because I know my own pantry!'

'Enough!' Elizabeth currently displayed more authority than her mother, whose slumped posture was uncharacteristic. 'I thought this visit was about a report on profiteering, not about the apparent thefts.'

Rose piped up, 'They weren't *apparent*—'

'Please, Rose!'

'No one's said you've been profiteering, Miss Meredith,' Harries said. 'Only that you might be hoarding in order to do so in the future.'

'It amounts to the same thing.'

Another thought occurred to Anwen. 'If Mrs Meredith has bought these items from traders at increased prices, why aren't the traders being interviewed?'

'We're getting to that, Miss,' said Harries. 'But just because someone buys items at inflated prices, doesn't mean they're not going to sell them on at even bigger cost when food becomes really short.'

'Mama, where did these items come from? I was unaware there was quite as much as this in the pantry.'

'Only from the butcher and greengrocer. They called them "comestibles for their valued customers".'

'Some of them are groceries.'

'They were special items, they said, that Mrs Brace couldn't get.'

'For goodness' sake, Mother! This has trouble written all over it. And "valued customers" clearly means those who can afford it.' Elizabeth sounded like the parent. 'I've been telling you for a while we should learn to cope with less food before we are forced to. And is it fair to have so much when the villagers have increasingly less?'

Mrs Meredith stared hard at her daughter. 'Really Elizabeth, between that, your vegetable scheme and the Suffragettes, I swear you're becoming more of a socialist every day.'

Elizabeth ignored this. 'Sergeant Harries, are you making any kind of arrest?'

'Not at this juncture, Miss Meredith. Clearly quite a lot of investigation is going to have to take place. This is a starting point.'

'You must know who reported us.'

'As it happens, Miss, I don't. It was reported at Rhymney police, see. They contacted us as it's our patch.'

'How very strange.' Mrs Meredith took a handkerchief from her sleeve and dabbed at her nose.

'We'll leave you to it now, but we may well be back in touch.'

'Show them out, Rose.'

'But that's Anwen's job, not—'

'And I'm asking *you* to do it!' It wasn't clear if her employer was about to burst into tears or explode with rage. Rose didn't risk either, doing as she was bid.

As they left, Mrs Meredith told Anwen. 'I think it might be best if you went home for today.'

'But Mama, Anwen clearly didn't have anything to do with this.'

'I'm not saying she did. I just think it would be best for now. Come back tomorrow morning at ten. I'm going out.'

'Very well, Madam.' Anwen went to the scullery to change back into her own clothes, throwing the black dress and apron onto the table in a fit of pique. She was putting her coat on when Onner struggled through the door with a basket of sheets, thumping it down onto the table.

'Phew! You off now, love? Bit early for you. Was just going out to get the washing in when the police turned up. What's going on?'

Anwen didn't want to explain it all so simply said, 'Not entirely sure myself. Mrs Meredith has asked me to come back tomorrow morning at ten.'

Onner tutted. 'Trouble everywhere at the moment.'

'See you tomorrow, Onner.'

Onner nodded, getting on immediately with folding the sheets. Anwen left through the back door. She was soon wondering about the mystery informant. If she couldn't prove her innocence, it would certainly make it more awkward taking a trip out with Tom. But then, that was always going to be a delicate matter, and one they'd have to keep to themselves. It might prove impossible if Tom thought she was a thief.

–

When Anwen entered the scullery at the time requested the next morning, the laundry woman was there, busy ironing the items from the day before.

'Hello Onner. Bit less windy today, I'm glad to see.'

'Hello, love. Rose has been sounding off something rotten about you. She thought you'd been sacked when you didn't arrive this morning.'

Anwen was about to explain the situation to her when Rose came thundering through from the kitchen, a broom in her hand. 'What are you doing here? Off with you, sneaking in to steal more food, no doubt.' She thrust the broom at Anwen's legs.

'Stop that! Mrs Meredith asked me to come in.'

'Liar! She dismissed you.'

'No she didn't.'

'I don't think she did sack her, Rose,' Onner shouted over the clamour.

'Of course she did!' Rose lifted the broom and swung it, catching Anwen on the cheek.

'Here, stop that now, you mad woman,' Onner shrieked, grabbing the broom off the cook.

Rose was trying to snatch it back when Elizabeth rushed through the door and took the cook by her arms, pulling her away from Onner. 'What on *earth* do you think you're doing, Rose? My mother sent me down to accompany you and Anwen to the dining room. Onner, my mother would like to speak to you after she's dealt with this. I'll come and get you when she's ready.'

Onner leant the broom against the table. 'What's that all about, Miss?'

'She'll explain when she sees you.'

Elizabeth led the way out of the scullery, through the kitchen and into the hallway.

Rose pushed Anwen along, muttering for her ears only, 'This'll be the finish of you here, you wait and see. No more lunches with Mr Tom or gadding about like Lady Muck at performances with your betters.'

Elizabeth opened the dining room door, stepping back to let the two younger women in first, then came in after them, shutting the door. Mrs Meredith was sitting at the table.

'Ah, Anwen and Rose.' She pulled a piece of paper out from the stack on the table and placed it in front of her. 'Rose, could you tell me again why you think Anwen reported me to the police.'

Oh dear. This had not started well.

Rose smirked, her nose wrinkling. 'Well, like I said yesterday, Madam, the food thefts stopped when you challenged her about them. Reckon she thought she'd get her revenge.'

'That is very interesting, Rose.'

'Thank you, Madam.'

She was going to believe Rose on the strength of her opinion?

Mrs Meredith continued. 'Because I drove into Rhymney yesterday to talk to the police there, and the description they gave me of the informant did not fit Anwen at all. You picked on Anwen, but she is not the only one who works in the kitchen and scullery area, is she?'

Anwen's breath caught. There was someone else, of course. How had she not thought of it before? And Mrs Meredith was going to deal with her next.

Rose voiced Anwen's thoughts. 'You mean Onner, Madam?' The cook seemed pleased with her own deduction. 'I never did like the woman.'

'The description given to me was not that of an older woman, but of someone in their twenties – with curly blonde hair.'

Anwen's eyes widened as realisation dawned. She glared at Rose as the colour drained from the cook's already pale face.

'They – they wouldn't tell you that,' Rose blustered.

'Not normally, but I am good friends with Chief Constable Perryman's wife. We were at school together.'

'There are lots of people with blonde, curly hair!' Rose insisted.

'No, I don't believe there are that many, not around here, not people who know me and are in a position to tell the police what is in my pantry.'

Rose opened her mouth to speak but closed it without saying a word. She alternated squeezing and plumping her lips, maybe trying to think of something to convince them all she was innocent. Elizabeth, standing to one side of her mother, didn't look at all surprised.

Mrs Meredith continued. 'I took a chance on you when I employed you as a nineteen-year-old, with only six months' experience as an under cook. I believe you've been treated well here. Yes, I bought more food than we currently need because I was afraid of it becoming scarce. Now I have to ask myself, if you're capable of telling lies about being the informant, what else have you told lies about?'

Elizabeth took over at this point. 'You accused Anwen of informing when it was *you*. You insisted also that she was the one who stole the food, so we can only conclude that was you too. Presumably you either sold it or took it home to your family, and you've been trying to frame Anwen and get her fired.'

'Rose, you are dismissed,' Mrs Meredith pronounced.

'Well!' Rose stamped her foot. 'There's grateful for all the work I've done. I didn't like this job anyway. Too casual a household, what with housemaids being over-friendly with the family.' She gave Anwen a sideways glance as she sneered. 'Having favourites among the servants is not right at all.'

'You may go and collect your things.'

'I'd be glad to.'

'I will drive you home,' said Elizabeth. 'That will give me a chance to explain to your parents exactly why you've been dismissed.'

'Don't expect any sympathy from them.' Rose humphed, stomping off to the door, flinging it open.

'If you do any damage to my house, I can assure you I will deduct it from your wages,' Mrs Meredith called. She followed Rose, saying as she went, 'I had better make sure she doesn't take anything she shouldn't.'

Elizabeth waited till her mother was out of earshot. 'I'm so sorry that you got involved in all this, Anwen.'

'I assume I'm not being dismissed.'

'Good gosh, of course you aren't. I'll let you into a secret. Chief Constable Perryman wouldn't tell Mama who the informant was, but she'd long suspected the thefts were Rose. She wanted to see how far she'd go and whether she'd catch herself out if she went along with it. Mama took a chance today, saying the police had told her, but it paid off.'

So Mrs Meredith had never really suspected her? That was a comfort at least.

'I think we will all have to muck in together now, you, me *and* Mama. You may well look surprised,' Elizabeth laughed. 'I was when my mother suggested it. But she used to cook when Tom and I were little, when we lived in Georgetown and Father was a humble examiner.'

The confession was a revelation. Somehow Anwen had imagined this family had always held their current station. 'An examiner?'

'Why yes. Living in one of the terraces, rather like the ones on West Street. When my parents were first married, he was a hewer. They lived in a small house in Bedwellty then.' She came forward to peer out into the hall, making sure no one was about before shutting the door. 'You see, Anwen, we haven't always been middle class. But don't tell my mother you know that.' She grinned like a naughty schoolgirl.

Anwen experienced a new admiration for the Merediths. They'd worked to be in this lofty position, not been born into it, as she'd assumed.

'Why does your mother want to speak to Onner if she's not responsible for the trouble?'

'To offer her a few hours cleaning, so you can help with the meals.'

They had been busy, planning it all out.

'While you're here, I want to give you a magazine to read. Hold on.' Elizabeth left the room, soon returning with a copy of *Woman's Life*. 'This magazine has exercises for recovering invalids, to help them walk after a long period in bed. I wondered if they would help your mother. You did say the doctor could see no reason why she hadn't recovered.'

Anwen scanned the pages being held open. It was a splendid idea – in principle. 'My father thinks—'

'Yes, I am aware of what he thinks. He is not a medical man though, so he cannot possibly know. Please, take it. If it doesn't help, at least you have tried something.'

Anwen took the proffered magazine. 'Thank you, Elizabeth. I'll show Mam this evening.'

Then she'd have to hide it, for sure. Who knew what Da would do if he found it?

It was a dull evening. Anwen shivered a little as she went to her mam's bedroom window, noticing the volunteers busy working on the plot opposite her house. She must get ready soon and join them, before the light faded.

In bed, the covers thrown off, Mam was lifting and lowering each leg in turn, as detailed in the magazine. Anwen hadn't been able to find it in her room earlier. Perhaps Mamgu had borrowed it to study the next set of exercises, since she was helping Mam to practise during the day. The progress, being able to lift her legs a little higher each day, had given Anwen new hope.

Enid took a break, sitting back on the mountain of pillows. 'Such a shame about Jane Harris and her kiddies having to move in with Florrie. It can't be easy, having seven grandchildren living with her. She might be a bit of a card, but her heart's in the right place.'

'I guess the widow's pension doesn't go far with a big family. I heard Jane couldn't afford the rent. I saw her the other day, dragging herself along the pavement with her three youngest. Looked like the life had been sucked out of her, poor soul. She and Robert were childhood sweethearts.' A little like her and Idris, she thought.

'It's lucky Cadi managed to find new lodgings with Rhonwen Evans. At least she's a little less quarrelsome than Florrie.'

'That's true.'

'If you go into my bottom drawer, *cariad*, you'll find some old clothes I used to use in the garden years back. Blue serge skirt and a green linen blouse. Past patching but useful for gardening.'

'Thank you. I'll try not to ruin them further.'

'I wouldn't worry. I'll not use them again.'

Enid's head went down and she closed her eyes for a moment. She looked up towards the window, her eyes sad. 'I used to love being in the garden, growing the vegetables and the few flowers, being at one with the soil. Being at peace. When the four of you were all little and either helping out or running around the hillside where I could see you, laughing and playing, I felt the luckiest woman alive. Your father was different then. Always quick to temper, but there were still happy times. Then sometimes we'd have a picnic up on the hill, with sandwiches and the nettle pop I used to make. Your father would tell you all stories he'd made up. He was good at that.'

Anwen left the drawer open, going to her mother and taking her hand. 'Oh Mam. You're doing well with those exercises. I'm sure we could get you walking again. Then you could help on the allotments. It's certainly helped me take my mind off... things.' In fact they'd been a godsend, particularly coming not long after Sara's death. Her mother was right: there was something peaceful about being one with the soil. Sara had enjoyed doing little jobs in the garden, so would have loved helping on the allotments.

'Lifting legs is one thing. Putting weight on them's another.'

'These are only the first set of exercises. There are three more after. You've only been going a week.'

'I'm grateful to Miss Elizabeth. But Anwen, I don't want to raise hopes. And I don't want Mamgu getting into trouble from your da if he finds out she's been helping me.'

Sometimes Anwen wondered if Enid wanted to get better. Along with the use of her legs, she'd lost much of her ardent spirit for life, as if the fall downstairs had knocked it out of her. 'You shouldn't listen to Da. We can only try.'

'I was reading about the German air raid in the paper earlier. Got along the whole east coast from Scotland down to Norfolk, it said.'

'Are you trying to change the subject?'

'But this is serious. They dropped about a hundred bombs. The raids are getting worse. How long till they reach Wales?'

'There were few casualties this time, and most were dropped on unpopulated areas and over the sea. Don't worry about it, Mam.'

'Shouldn't you be on the allotment now?'

'I suppose I should.' Anwen went back to the bottom drawer, removing the clothes Mam had mentioned. 'Now, you will keep doing the exercises while I'm out, won't you?'

'Until I get tired. Or until your father makes an appearance. I suppose I'm lucky he's taken to sleeping in Sara's room as he rarely comes to see what I'm up to.'

It saddened Anwen that her father treated Mam as if she didn't exist, like she'd run out of usefulness for him.

'Well at least he doesn't bother me for his *needs*, as he used to call them.'

Anwen presumed she meant before the accident. But she didn't want to hear of her parents' intimate private lives.

'Didn't mind it before my fall, but when you're stuck on your back, unable to move much, it's like you're a – thing. And he was so rough, angry with me for not being what I was. Hurt me, he did.'

'Oh Mam, I wish you'd said before.'

'What good would it have done? You couldn't have challenged him without putting yourself at risk.'

'No, but I might have got the doctor involved, or Uncle Hywel.'

Enid made an effort to heave herself up from the pillows, surprising Anwen by sitting up straight. 'Don't you dare tell Uncle Hywel anything, you understand? I don't want him questioning your father. As for the doctor, it's none of his business. Anyway, it's over. Promise me you'll say nothing of this.'

'Mam, you're sitting up properly. That's marvellous.'

She slumped back on the bed. 'Promise me!'

'I promise.'

'Now go and tend to your veggies.'

Anwen left, heading to her room to get changed. It was distressing, what Mam had told her. Yet what overrode that was the fact Mam had pulled herself up. It was the second time, after that incident a few months back when she'd found her sitting on the edge of the bed. The two together gave her hope that recovery was possible.

As she was halfway down the stairs, her father came through the front door.

'Hello Da, I'm just going out to the allotments.' He'd never had a good word for her *waste of bloody time*, but he hadn't stopped her going, especially after Mamgu had been so enthusiastic about it.

'Not before I've had a word. Get in the bloody kitchen and stay there till I get down.'

She did as she was told, listening to him pounding his feet up the stairs, then a few seconds later, down again. Crashing into the kitchen in his usual manner, he threw something on the table. It was the magazine Elizabeth had given her.

'What's all this bloody nonsense? Where'd you get it from?'

'Miss Elizabeth thought I'd like to borrow the magazine as she knows I like to read about recipes and—'

'Bloody little liar. It was open at these exercises, for invalids. You had it hidden under your bed.'

He must have been searching for money again. Good job she always carried any she had about her person. 'It must have slipped off the bed when I fell asleep.' If only she hadn't left it open on that page, he might have ignored it.

'This is what I think of your exercises.' He picked the magazine back up, ripping it into shreds, tossing them into the air so the pieces settled all around the room.

She was so busy watching the snowfall of paper, she missed him lunging at her, catching her full in the face with his fist. While she lifted her hand to clutch her cheek, he went in for a second time.

'And don't you bloody dare put ideas into your mother's head. I told you: she'll never walk again. You understand?'

Anwen ran to the hall, grabbing her coat off the stand. From the kitchen she heard her father shout, 'And you can bloody clear this paper up too.'

Not now she wouldn't. She had to get out of the house. It had become a place of misery in the last ten years. Tomos, Geraint, Sara, her mother now bedridden... Would her father drink himself to death one day? Or would he, more likely, slap the living daylights out of her and see her off too? She needed to dig, take her frustration out on the earth.

Across the road, Mary Jones's smiled greeting changed to alarm when she saw Anwen close up. 'What have you done to your face, love? Your eye's all red and I think it's swelling.'

She should have looked in the mirror before she left the house. 'It's nothing, Mary. Something fell off the shelf in the larder and hit me in the eye.'

'You could do with some Zam-Buk balm on that. They sell it at Mrs Brace's.'

'I'll do it later. I'd rather just get on now.'

Anwen took herself to the other edge of the field to work apart. That would hopefully attract fewer comments about her eye. It was burning and her sight was slightly hindered by the swelling. If she could get a few good vegetables dug up it might help her forget about the pain.

She built up a rhythm to her work, *dig, dig, dig, pull – dig, dig, dig, pull*. She was concentrating so much on it she didn't notice anything until two shadows fell across her workspace, one near, one further back. She bolted upright when she saw who it was.

'Oh, Gwilym. And Idris.'

Almost at the same time, the two men exclaimed, 'What's wrong with your...' Gwilym went for 'eye', while Idris said, 'face.'

'Something fell off the larder shelf and hit me.' If she said it enough, she'd convince herself.

Idris glowered. 'Some*thing* hit you, or some*one*?'

She didn't dare tell them what really happened in case they went in search of her father and a fight broke out.

'Some*thing*. Is there anything else you wanted?' She injected a little iciness in her voice to keep them at a distance.

'Well,' Gwilym started, 'we were wondering if you needed any extra help, with your allotments.'

This she hadn't expected. 'I – I'm not sure. I should ask Elizabeth first. She's in charge.'

'Well, here's your chance.' Gwilym stepped back as Elizabeth approached. Beside her was Tom. His three-piece suit was at odds with his sister's makeshift outfit of old trousers and shirt.

'Hello Anwen,' Elizabeth started, before gasping.

Tom followed on with, 'Oh good gracious, what on earth has happened to—'

'Something fell off the larder shelf and hit me.' The lie was getting easier. 'Don't fuss, I'm fine. Gwilym and Idris want to know if they can help in the fields.'

Elizabeth clapped her hands together. 'That would be wonderful! There is plenty to do now and in the next few days, harvesting and replanting.'

Anwen wasn't sure she wanted Idris working close by, especially if Tom was going to be hanging around, but they did need all the help they could get and, who knew, he and Gwilym joining the teams might attract others.

'I'll show you what needs doing,' said Elizabeth. 'We have spare tools in the middle there. Anwen, are you sure you shouldn't be at home, resting that eye?'

'I'm fine, honestly.'

'Very well. Follow me, you two.'

Left with Tom, Anwen said, 'You've surely not come to help in that suit.'

He looked down at himself. 'Good Lord, no. Just came along with Elizabeth on the off-chance you'd be here. To ask you—'

'Yes, I know what you're going to ask me, but I won't be going anywhere while my eye's like this.'

'It does look painful. Have you seen the doctor?'

'Just needs a bit of Zam-Buk, that's all. Don't fuss. Let's wait till I'm a bit healed up, all right?'

He nodded. 'Of course. I quite understand. I'll leave you to it.' He took a few steps towards the road.

'Or you could get changed and join us?'

He turned back briefly to wave and smile, then kept going.

–

'You've got a face on you, Idris, *bach*.'

Idris rammed the spade into the ground, shoving his boot on the top of it to loosen the soil before dragging it up and tossing it to one side. His mother had nagged him about helping at the allotments, then had mentioned it to Gwilym. So he'd nagged him too. He was here to shut them up, but that wasn't what he was cross about. It wasn't even the brief appearance of Tom Meredith, though that was annoying enough.

'I'm not a violent man, Gwilym.'

'But?'

'But I swear I'll swing for Madog if I find out he hit Anwen.'

'You don't believe the story about something falling in the larder, then?'

Idris came to a halt. 'Do you?'

Gwilym balanced the tip of his spade on the ground and leant on the handle. 'No, can't say I do. Anwen's a strong girl, always been able to cope with life, but she needs people to look out for her, I reckon. And Madog...'

Idris stopped digging, straightening his back. 'What?'

'Oh, I dunno, mun.'

'He's up to something?'

Gwilym checked that no one else was nearby. 'You reached that conclusion too?'

'I've seen him creeping around, meeting people he wouldn't normally give the time of day to.' Idris told Gwilym about the night of the meeting, when he'd seen Madog with Edgar Williams.

'You see now, not natural bedfellows, is it?' said Gwilym. 'Is Anwen in some kind of danger, do you think?'

'Maybe. I warned Madog that I was watching him. Maybe I should. Or you could.'

Gwilym looked at him askance. 'Why me in particular?'

'Dunno. Just had an idea you admired her.'

'Admire her, yes. Want a romantic attachment with her, no. Perhaps we both should keep an eye on him.'

'You could be right.'

He returned to taking his frustration out on the soil, angry not only at Madog, but at his own body for letting him down so badly.

Gwilym dug more sedately beside him. They spoke no more of it for the moment.

Chapter Eighteen

Arriving home from work late one evening, Anwen was surprised to see her father still sitting in the kitchen. Normally he'd have gone out by now. His mother was at the opposite end of the table. There was an emptied plate in front of him, the whiff of meat suggesting Mamgu had made him supper.

'Here she is,' said Madog, sounding resentful about her absence.

'I told him you were going with Miss Meredith to pick up bits for the allotment.'

'Edgar Williams saw you go off in that motorcar. Doesn't like people hobnobbing above their station now, does he?'

Unless it's him doing the hobnobbing. It was a good job she hadn't been in the motorcar with Tom. They'd have to be extra careful not to be seen when they finally organised something. 'The allotment project is important—'

'Cut your yapping. I don't care about your bloody allotments. Doing good folk out of business, you'll be. Then see where it gets you. Now you're back, I'm going out.'

He left promptly, slamming the front door as always.

'Why was he waiting for me?' said Anwen.

'He had it in his head you were up to no good. He's developed an awful suspicious mind. Anyway, help yourself to the stew. Your father brought back some chicken and potatoes so I made them into a quick supper. I'll be going now. See you tomorrow.'

Anwen followed Cadi out to the hall. 'Thursday's meant to be a meatless day now.'

'It's only advisory. And try telling your da that, especially as he fetched it back.'

'Don't you wonder where he gets this food?'

'I try not to. Anyway, your mam's asleep, but you might want to peep in on her when you go up. Tired herself out with the knitting, but at least it's keeping her occupied. Meg and Florrie were round today too, so we've a little group of four making gloves for our boys in the trenches. It helps keep Florrie's mind off her loss.' There was a pause before Mamgu added, 'And the knitting group makes us all feel a little bit more useful.'

'Oh you *are* useful, Mamgu.'

She hugged her grandmother, grateful she'd brought a little bit of company to Enid with the group. Cadi had found some old, holey jumpers and vests at her sister's, bringing them with her to unravel and make useful once more. Since then, Meg and Florrie had found items in drawers in their own homes. Uncle Hywel had even brought Mam down to the chaise longue on a couple of occasions, so they could have the group in the comfort of the kitchen, instead of them all perching on the double bed.

'I'll peep in on Mam in a minute.' She opened the door, kissing her grandmother's cheek before the older woman stepped out.

An overwhelming urge to be close to Sara engulfed Anwen. She trudged up the stairs, gripping the handrail as she went. She had a brief chat with her mother, before going to what was now her father's room. His clothes lay in a neat pile on the chair, where Cadi had put them after laundry day. The drawers needed to be sorted out, and Sara's clothes given to someone who could use them. Her few knick-knacks still sat on top of the chest of drawers, shoved to one side, including the paper stars from Christmas. Anwen decided she would move them to her own room. The book she had bought for Sara at Christmas, *Peter and Wendy*, was still secreted beneath blouses in one of her own drawers.

She sat on the bed, unmade as it was, facing the window and the sunset, faded now almost to royal blue, just a hint of blood red on the outline of the hills. Eventually she pulled herself up, sighing. She switched the light on and went to the drawers, to start the sad task of clearing them out. Her attempt to pull one out was hampered, its unusual weight making it cumbersome. There was a dull clunking. She opened it enough to see that it was full of bottles, lots of them. The odd bottle or two was one thing. But this? The drawer above had tinned meat and fruit, along with packets of tea and coffee.

She closed that too, sinking to her knees. The wood was cool as she placed her head against it, clutching her arms around herself. Where were Sara's things? Under the bed? She drew herself round to peer underneath it. There were several sack bags, full of she knew not what.

Heaving herself up, she scanned the room. There was nowhere else they could be. The urge to cry over her sister's lost things was more overwhelming than the worry about where these new items had come from. She picked up Sara's remaining items from the top of the drawers and dragged her body to her room with them, sinking to the floor and giving in to the sorrow.

–

'So you think your father's buying stolen goods?'

Anwen sat in one of the fireside chairs, nursing the chipped cup Violet had given her, half filled with black tea. It had been a week since her discovery of the items in Sara's old bedroom and she'd not felt comfortable talking to anyone else about them.

'I don't know. I think he might have had a win on that race that replaced the Grand National, whenever that was. A couple of months back? I remember him muttering how he'd had a lucky break and I'd just read about the race. I can't report him to the police. What would that do to our family?'

'And you don't know if it's true.'

Anwen's whole body shrank inward, as if trying to disappear. 'Sometimes I just wish…' What did she wish? That it had been her father who'd gone, instead of her brothers and Sara? Or that he'd disappear, maybe run away with another woman? Much better if she could save him from the drink. She didn't anticipate that happening, but rather saw a grey future of fear and her father's dominance.

'I know, *fach*, I know,' said Violet. 'March. It was at Gatwick. The Racecourse Association Steeple Chase, the replacement for the Grand National. Vermouth. That was the name of the horse that won. I remember thinking Charlie used to like a bet on the National and I wondered if he was aware of it.'

'Have you heard from him lately?'

Violet jumped up, going to the door that led to the hall and listening. 'Sorry, thought I heard one of the babbies. No, I haven't had a letter for a few weeks.'

'I'm sorry about that. Reading the daily war summary in the newspaper it's clear the soldiers are very busy. Some Russian troops have now arrived in France to help, so maybe that will speed up the end. You must be missing Charlie terribly.'

Her friend sat down opposite her with a thump. 'Oh Anwen, I know it sounds terrible, but no, not really.' She let out a huge sigh. 'It's a relief, him being away. He'd become a bit domineering, to be honest, always wanting his own way. And those moods! Of course I want Charlie to come home, but I just wish he'd be different.'

Anwen's sympathy merged with the dread of depressing inevitability: did all marriages end up with the man dominating the household and the woman sinking into servility? Would Idris have become a tyrant too? Yet his father wasn't like that with Meg. Then again, who knew what went on behind closed doors?

'I'm sorry to hear that, Violet. Perhaps when he gets back from the war, he will appreciate what a lovely home you've kept for him.'

'Another cup of tea?'

'No, thank you, I'll be getting along now. Go and keep Mam company.'

When Anwen stepped back into the street, the pale blue sky was streaked with lilac clouds. She breathed in the cool evening air, a relief after Violet's stuffy kitchen. Setting off, she enjoyed the freedom of a walk on her own for around ten seconds, before she noticed Esther Williams walking down Bryn Street.

'You should get home,' Esther intoned when Anwen was still several paces away. 'Before it gets dark and people think you're a loose woman like Violet Jones, entertaining another man in her house. Murky goings-on indeed.'

Anwen stopped to survey Esther. 'What a vivid imagination you have, Mrs Williams. You clearly don't have enough to do as a Guardian, if you have time to go poking into other people's business.'

A pink tinge swept across Esther's face as she came to a standstill. Stabbing a forefinger into the air, she said, 'How *dare* you speak to me like that!'

'Oh I dare. Go on, report me to the police, or whoever it is you report to. I'll tell them you're a bully and unsuitable for the job.'

'You – you will regret this!'

Esther set off down the road, almost running. She was soon out of sight, whether on her way home or to harass some other poor soul. Anwen didn't much care either way. She'd had enough of Esther Williams. She'd had enough of the whole lot of them. Tomorrow she'd seek Tom out and say yes to a trip to the cinema. There had to be some fun among the boredom and torment.

–

The following evening, Anwen headed off through the village, her heart pumping hard, on her way to meet Tom. She hummed softly to herself, trying to contain her excitement and fear, as she met various villagers and wished them, '*Noswaith dda*.'

It was quite a story she'd concocted to her father and her mother, not wanting Mam to have to lie for her. She was going with Elizabeth to an allotment meeting in Bargoed, she'd told them, one where some people had started keeping chickens. She thought maybe they could start keeping a reasonable number of them in the village? Her father had recently moaned about the decreasing number of eggs available, liking an egg or two a day. He had, as she'd anticipated, been enthusiastic about the idea. She knew Elizabeth was staying in this evening, determined to read a book on keeping poultry she had purchased from Schenck's bookshop. That made the falsehood a little true. And if she was spotted with Tom in the motorcar and it got back to her father, she'd simply say Elizabeth had gone on ahead and young Mr Meredith had been tasked with fetching her. Perfect.

'*Noswaith dda*, Anwen,' said Rhonwen, approaching her on Gabriel Street, as she passed the Ainon chapel on one side and the school on the other. 'You look cheerful. Where are you off too on this lovely evening?'

She hadn't anticipated having to tell her fib to anyone outside her family. What if Rhonwen gossiped to others about it? It might get back to the Merediths, who'd know Elizabeth had done no such thing. Better to keep it simple.

'I'm heading off to a meeting. Allotments and so on.'

'Very nice. We do appreciate all your team's efforts. Have a good evening.'

'You too, Mrs Evans.'

She hadn't realised she was tensing her muscles until Rhonwen moved on and Anwen relaxed.

She was halfway down Mafeking Terrace by the time she heard the rumble of the Morris Oxford behind her. She turned as Tom pulled over and jumped out of the motorcar, the engine still running. He opened the passenger door for her and she ran round to get in.

'So you came then,' he said, once he'd got back in.

'Of course. I wouldn't have said I was if I'd no intention to.'

There was a crunching noise as Tom pushed the gear lever forward and they were off. 'You might have changed your mind.'

'Well I haven't.'

'You look very pretty in that dress. Makes a change to what you wear to our house.'

'Thank you.' She'd had a job explaining to Da why she had to wear her best dress, a green one she wore to occasions like weddings. She needed to look impressive for the councillors and JPs who might be at the meeting, she'd told him. It was the only point at which she thought she might fail in her deception. The dress was a little old-fashioned now, but the skirt fell in soft folds until the hemline where it flared out. The waistline was a little higher than her other dress and the sleeves were full at the top, narrowing around the cuffs. She'd never worn it to the picture house before, not even with Idris. But then, Idris didn't expect elegance.

In Bargoed, Tom parked the motorcar and they walked down to the Hanbury Electric Theatre, with its wide triangular roof. In the foyer, Tom bought the tickets – the best in the house – then led her to the front circle, a balcony overlooking the stalls. They sat in the third row back. It was the first time she'd been up here. She glanced at the people around them. They didn't look any different to her, making her feel at ease.

'The programme is starting with an episode of *The Exploits of Elaine*,' Tom said dismissively. 'I read in the paper that the main feature, *Circus of Death*, is quite spectacular. The performers have done all the tricks themselves so that there's no fakery. Taken enormous risks, apparently.'

'I do hope it won't be too frightening,' said Anwen, clutching the top of her dress.

'You've no need to worry. I'm here to hold your hand if you're scared.'

He raised his eyebrows, leaving Anwen unsure whether he was mocking her or serious. She felt uncomfortable at the idea of his hand in hers so soon.

The Exploits of Elaine came and went, being but a short part of a longer story and so not engaging Anwen much. It was maybe a little less silly than *The Perils of Pauline*, of which she'd seen a couple of episodes.

Circus of Death, on the other hand, was as dramatic as Tom had indicated, with a climax consisting of a female acrobat rescuing a baby from a monkey on a high chimney. The audience *oooohed* and *aaahhhed* their way through, with frequent gasps of shock and cries of, 'Look out!'. Anwen was quite exhausted by the time it had finished, partly due to the effort she'd made not to appear scared.

'That was jolly good fun, wasn't it?' Tom asked as they vacated their seats.

'It was very well done, though I can't believe there really weren't any tricks, for it would have been incredibly dangerous, especially for a baby.'

'I daresay you're right. Now, how about a cup of tea somewhere? I believe there's a café nearby.'

'No, I don't think so,' she said. 'I need my sleep, for I've got to get up early for work tomorrow, even if you don't.' She added a chuckle, realising as she was speaking that it sounded like a criticism.

'I guess you have. And what would we do without you at McKenzie House? Come along then, let's get you home.'

The drive home was pleasant, each of them relaying their favourite scenes of the film. The sun had disappeared, allowing the clear sky to show off its thousands of stars, like a twinkling carpet. Anwen looked out at them as she considered what a pleasant evening she'd spent, and what a gentleman Tom had been. It was then that he stopped the motorcar, on the road between Rhymney and Dorcalon. He switched off the engine and turned towards her.

'I've enjoyed your company,' he said. 'I'm so glad you finally agreed to come.'

'I enjoyed it too. The film was particularly good. Thank you for inviting me.'

She'd barely finished speaking when he lurched towards her, holding onto her arms as he attempted to kiss her. She shoved him away, yelling, 'Stop that now!'

She could just make out his pained expression in the dark.

'I'm so sorry. I don't know what came over me. It was just, you were just – so nice to me.'

'That's no excuse for dishonouring me. Why, Id— the man I was betrothed to, well, we were walking out a long time before he attempted to kiss me. And then he asked if it was all right to do so.'

'Yes, you're right. That's the decent thing to do. I'm sorry... sorry.'

He started the motorcar again. They proceeded in silence, until he reached the end of Gabriel Street, as instructed by her, where he stopped.

'Thank you for the trip out,' she said. '*Nos da.*'

'Good night,' he replied. 'No, wait.'

She halted, halfway through climbing out of the door. 'What?'

'I truly am sorry. I don't know what came over me. It was a most ungallant gesture. I promise, if you agree to come out with me again, that I won't repeat it.'

'I don't know, Tom. We'll see.'

She climbed out without another word and watched him drive away. She was angry with him, yes, but she also felt something else. Pity. Goodness knows what for, him being the golden boy, at university, with a glowing future away from the village. But she sensed that he was all at sea, like a lost little boy. Still, that was no excuse for being discourteous. She would be sure not to forgive him too quickly, otherwise he might try it again. Did that mean she was thinking of repeating the experience? She was too confused to make that decision now.

Idris had just finished filling his first tram of coal that morning, stopping for a drink of water from his tin bottle, mopping his brow with the shirt he'd now discarded. He felt hotter than normal. He'd have thrown the rest of the water over his head if it hadn't meant he'd be without a drink.

Today they were having a memorial service for Percy Vaughan and Robert Harris at the chapel. It was one of the few times he was glad to be hidden in the depths of the earth, hewing back to back with his butty, Jory. He would mourn their passing in the unholy blackness, in another type of trench to the one they'd met their end in.

From a distance he was aware of Edgar Williams's voice, echoing down the tunnel. He was somewhere close by, doing his inspections. He'd managed to avoid him the last few days, not missing the antagonistic glower he was usually treated to. He could hear fragments of the conversation Williams was currently having with someone – something about the air currents and whether there was sufficient for the safety of the men working there. He didn't usually hassle the hewers thankfully, only speaking to the deputies or firemen, reserving any discipline or opinion-spouting until they were above ground.

The under-manager's voice ceased. Idris lifted his pick, swinging it over his shoulder to start digging once more. He'd got in only three strikes when Williams called, 'Hey you, Hughes.'

Idris stopped mid-strike, lowering the pick, peering into the inky dark to ascertain the whereabouts of the under-manager. The rugged tunnels distorted sound down here, so it was sometimes difficult to tell where a noise was coming from. Jory kept on digging. Williams stepped into the dim light of Idris's lamp.

'Jones the fireman said you were here. Decided not to wait to give you the good news.' Half his face was in shadow, lending his features a menacing appearance. 'You're going to a higher place, Hughes.'

'Just say what you mean.' It was a wonder to Idris that a man with a less patient temperament than him hadn't knocked seven bells out of Williams long ago. Probably too afraid of losing their jobs.

'Above ground. Screening, like I promised you.'

Idris dropped the pick, placing both hands behind his back, one hand gripping the wrist of the other. *Don't rise to it.* 'But I've been producing more coal this last coupla weeks. I've kept a tally, see.'

'You're mistaken. Last week's was down on the week before.'

'It wasn't. Look at the numbers recorded.'

'I have. That's how I know.'

He'd fiddled the figure, he must have done. Idris knew for certain he'd sent out more trams of coal last week than the week before. 'I brought a piece of paper with me, and a pencil, in my pocket. Been marking off the trams.'

Williams's laugh was dry and brief. 'Couldn't care less. It don't prove nothing, does it?' He leant in so close their noses were almost touching. 'Now listen here. You can thank that silly bit of a girl you used to go with for your *promotion*. She was rude to my wife. Wouldn't say boo to a goose once, when she was on the screening. Now she can't keep her mouth shut. Encouraged by you, no doubt. And my poor wife's already distraught with Daniel being called up. But then, he is able-bodied.'

He'd been at school with Daniel Williams, a boy who went largely unnoticed. Not like his father at all. Idris had no pity in his heart for Mrs Williams, only a vague concern for their son.

'Take your change of job as a warning, Hughes. Tomorrow you'll be on the screens. And if my wife gets any more abuse from that one, or from you, you'll be out of a job altogether. You understand?' He pushed Idris away.

Oh yes, he understood. He imagined shoving Williams back, knowing he wouldn't. His reasoning was all an excuse. If it hadn't been this incident with Anwen, he'd have found some other reason to beat him down. Right at this moment, Idris had no fight left in him.

'One day that bastard will get his comeuppance,' said Jory, after Williams left. 'I'll be sorry not to be working with you anymore.'

'Aye, me too.' Idris retrieved the pick and was soon taking out his frustration on the coal wall.

–

Idris wasn't at chapel, despite his family being present. Next to Anwen, Uncle Hywel and Gwilym were talking of the new British Summer Time and how it would be light an hour later this evening. She'd vaguely thought about how useful it would be for working on the allotments, before slipping back to her preoccupation with Idris. She had a brief fantasy about him standing next to her, grinning warmly as his hand surreptitiously took hers.

Hywel spoiled the dream by leaning into her vision to say, 'Cup of tea? I can fetch you one.'

She caught the sigh of frustration in time, smiling instead. 'Oh, yes please.'

'Gwilym?'

'I'll be along in a moment. Just want a quick word with Anwen.'

When Gwilym didn't speak straight away, Anwen said, 'You're wearing a frown all of a sudden.'

'Edgar Williams demoted Idris to sorting on the screens on Friday. He said it was because you were rude to his wife.'

She had to think for a moment, the two episodes not linking at all in her mind. 'Oh, you mean when she was rude to *me*, on Wednesday?'

'I don't know no details. That's all Williams said. Reckoned you used to be a quiet thing but that mixing with Idris had made you "mouthy", as he put it, so it was his fault.'

The guilt trickling through her was brought to a halt by reason. 'Well that just doesn't make sense now, does it? I've known Idris since I was six years old, so whether I've become more *mouthy* recently has nothing to do with Idris.'

'I know it makes no sense. Williams has it in for Idris, that's for certain. He'd already threatened to put him on screening because he said his tram numbers were down. Reckon he'll use any excuse.'

'But to use my argument with his wife! It's inexcusable, especially when she picked on me.' She told him about the incident that occurred as she left Violet's house.

'Never been a happy woman, that one, even when she wasn't a Guardian.'

'Something's got to be done.' She stamped her foot on the wooden floor, before taking two steps away.

'Hey, where're you going?'

'I'm going to sort this out. Apologise to Uncle Hywel for me, would you?'

'You want some help?'

'No, I'll be fine.'

She carried on, darting sideways through the chattering throng. The sooner she spoke to Idris about this, the better. What on earth would he be thinking of her? Out of the chapel, she ran up the side road and across the field. Her firm knock on Idris's door quickly summoned him.

'Anwen?' He peered out as if he expected others to be with her.

'Idris, could I have a private word, please?'

He hesitated for a moment, before moving to one side. 'Go in the kitchen then, you know where it is.' His voice betrayed a little impatience.

In the kitchen a pan was bubbling on the stove, a tang of boiled vegetables pervading the air.

'Well, what is it?'

'There's no need to be so short with me, Idris Hughes. I know you must blame me for what happened.'

'I've never blamed you for what happened!' he interrupted. 'I know it's me who's changed.'

'What? No! I'm not talking about you breaking it off.' She pulled out a chair and sat down, suddenly drained. 'Gwilym told me what Edgar Williams said.'

'Ah.' Idris sat in one of the armchairs by the fire.

'I'm sorry, Idris. I never dreamed that you'd be punished for what I said to Mrs Williams. I got cross with her because she was implying Violet and Hywel were having a relationship behind Charlie's back. And that I was a fallen woman for being out on the street on a light May evening.'

'You're the very opposite of a fallen woman.' His expression was solemn.

Was it a criticism? Would he have preferred her to be a little more... flighty, like Polly Coombes?

'Don't be offended. It's a compliment. You're a good woman, better than many I know.'

'And you *know* many, do you?'

He frowned. 'I don't blame you for what's happened, Anwen. Williams has had it in for me a good while. I don't want you to worry about it. You've got your life, and I have mine.'

'But he shouldn't be allowed to get away with it.'

'There's nothing you can do, right? Just leave it be, Anwen.' He rose, giving the impression he was dismissing her.

'I'll be going, then.' In one swift movement she got up and left the room.

He followed her into the hall saying, 'Thank you for coming to explain.'

Many thoughts were tumbling around in her brain, all things she'd like to say to him. Instead she picked a simple, 'Farewell, Idris,' before opening the door and walking away.

He had his life and she had hers. And never the two were likely to meet again, he'd made that much clear. She shouldn't have bothered coming here.

Later that afternoon, the air warmer than it had been for a long time, Anwen was punishing the earth as she plunged the spade in to dig up the first of the turnips. The ample fabric of the wool skirt overheated her legs, while the long-sleeved top clung to her damp body, along with her chemise, petticoat, corset and drawers. It made her wish she could strip off a few layers in the way men did when labouring.

Gwen came strolling over, having just arrived on the field. 'I'm looking forward to trying this next lot of veggies.'

Anwen took a break. 'Me too. And starting tomorrow, we'll be selling some of them in the greengrocer's.'

'You managed to make an agreement with Mr James at last?'

'Elizabeth did. It includes a couple of our women on a rota to help out in the shop. Mr James makes a bit of money, and so does our little co-operative, to be used to further the project, of course.'

'So everyone's happy. Where would you like me today?'

'If you could help Mary and the others over there, they've got a few more rows to clear.'

'Where are Gwilym and Idris today?'

'They've started up behind McKenzie Cottages, sowing the next lot of vegetables. Sprouts, peas, beans and some more root veggies.'

'Another field. That's wonderful.' Gwen strolled away, singing.

Anwen had been grateful for the opportunity to place Idris as far away as she could. Her heart was tender after their encounter that morning and she didn't want to treat it to another battering.

'Hello there,' called Elizabeth, trudging across the ground, in trousers once again. 'Goodness, remind me never to get on the wrong side of you! You're spearing that poor earth as if you're trying to put it out of its misery.'

Anwen straightened her back. 'Sorry, it's been a frustrating day. Mrs Williams is up to her tricks again.'

'What's the silly woman done now?'

Anwen went through the events of her conversation with Esther and what she knew of what Edgar Williams had said to Idris.

'I'm sorry to hear that,' said Elizabeth. 'I can't stand either of them, the way they're always toadying up to my parents. Somebody needs to do something about the pair of them. Excuse me. I'll see you later.' She stomped back across the field and had soon disappeared down one of the roads that led to the centre of the village.

–

A few more women had joined Anwen and the others on the field during the afternoon, including Elizabeth, who strode back after an absence of half an hour or so. All were now harvesting the first of the beans, spring onions and spinach. They started singing as they cut away, dug out or pulled up the vegetables. Anwen's anxious stress of earlier was eased by the camaraderie of the women as they worked together in a common cause.

In the middle of a chorus, Elizabeth tapped her shoulder. Anwen's heart sank when she saw Idris there, on the edge of the field, with around eight of the older men of the village. Were they unhappy about the vegetable patches? A couple of them were chatting intently, pointing to parts of the field. She and Elizabeth went together to speak to them.

'How can we help you gentlemen?' said Elizabeth.

Idris glanced from Elizabeth to Anwen and back. 'These men came to see me up at the top field, wondering if there was something they could do to help. I said I would ask you, as you're in charge.'

'Aye,' said Abraham Owen, Gwilym's grandfather. 'We may be past digging for coal, but we're not past digging soil.' There was enthusiastic agreement from his colleagues.

Anwen considered them, scarred and haggard as they were, some stooped from years of bending in underground tunnels long before the colliery at Dorcalon was sunk. Most of them must be in their seventies. They were willing, and that was what counted.

'That would be splendid, wouldn't it, Anwen?' said Elizabeth.

'Yes, of course.'

'What do you think they could work on?' Elizabeth smiled at her and she knew she was being given the opportunity to make a decision.

'Well, Idris and Gwilym could do with some help behind the cottages, to really get that field going. And Idris, you know what the plan is for up there. Why don't you take charge and divide up the field for the next phase of sowing and planting, giving a section to each pair of men? You'll be able to get everything planted that much quicker now.'

'If you're sure.'

Elizabeth clapped her hands together. 'That's a splendid idea. Are you men willing to have a go at the top field, under Idris here?'

The men were delighted with the decision.

'We'll get going then,' said Idris. After a moment's hesitation, he set off with purpose, his new team following on and chatting eagerly.

'How marvellous,' said Elizabeth. 'Everything is slotting into place. And, oh my goodness, there's my mother!'

Striding across the field in navy skirt and cream blouse was Margaret Meredith, her hair pinned up neatly under a straw sun hat. All the women watched her progress until she caught up.

'It's such a nice day I thought I'd come and see how you're getting on.' Mrs Meredith's tone was matter of fact, as if her showing up was an everyday occurrence and not something to be marvelled at.

'Why don't you have a look round for yourself, Mother, have a word with the workers?'

'Splendid idea. Come on then, what are you all standing around for?'

Chapter Nineteen

It was Idris's sixth day as a screener, standing among the women and a couple of old men, picking out the stones and bits of rock, breaking up the bigger pieces of coal with a heavy hammer. All the waste products were dropped on the floor. Every ten minutes or so a couple of younger girls would bring wide shovels, clearing up the debris and sending it down a chute where it was crushed and disposed of.

Idris had settled into a rhythm as he sorted the coal. Constantly leaning over the belt may not be as back-breaking as bending in the mine, but it was still uncomfortable. At least the tedium allowed his mind to wander. Until the voice called out over the deafening clatter of rock.

'Hughes!'

Idris emitted a long breath of frustration. What now? It wasn't Edgar Williams's voice this time, but the screen foreman's.

'What is it, Floyd?'

The foreman came into view. 'The manager's asking for you. You're to go to Williams's office, straight away, like.'

His heart thumped uncomfortably in his chest. Had Williams reported him as being incompetent enough to be sacked? Idris needed this job, even at half the wage, to help his parents and brother out. Especially if they were serious about sending Jenkin off to work in an office. He'd need decent clothes, money for the train.

Idris brushed the dust from his hands and clothes, rubbing the back of his neck as he walked past the women in their once brightly coloured, but now grimy, shawls. He left meekly. No point in arguing.

From the screens building he walked across the yard, over the railway tracks, to the under-manager's office. There he knocked on the door, trying to see through the grimy window next to it.

'Come!'

Inside, Edgar was perched on his desk. His mouth lifted on one side in a sneer, implying he was indeed facing some kind of disciplinary action. Herbert Meredith was standing in the middle of the small space facing the door, his hands clasped behind his back.

'Mr Meredith has requested to see you, Hughes. What have you been up to now?'

Meredith swivelled swiftly towards him. 'I did not say Mr Hughes was in any kind of trouble, Mr Williams.'

'Oh. I assumed since you asked to see him…'

'One shouldn't ever assume anything, Mr Williams. Now, Mr Hughes.'

Edgar's brief confusion changed to a look of accusation as he glared at Idris.

'I hear you've been placed on the screens as your current health hasn't made it easy for you to dig the coal.'

'I was managing fine, Mr Meredith, but—'

'I found he was filling fewer trams than he used to.'

'I don't think—' Idris started.

'So I found him other work in the colliery to do, not wanting to make him unemployed. Got to look after your men, haven't you, Mr Meredith?' Edgar's ingratiating grin was for the manager's benefit.

The manager ignored the comment, turning his attention to Idris once more. 'I'm here because I've heard you're a good organiser, Mr Hughes, that you are able to manage men. I'm told the land behind the cottages has been planted in good time because of the way you handled your team, and that you were responsible for more volunteers coming forward.'

'The men were certainly keen, sir.'

Edgar coughed. 'I'm sure you, like I, sir, think that the men expending their energy in gardening can only rob them of energy for working in the pit. It would be an excellent idea for you to put an end to it.'

'On the contrary, Edgar, I think it's an excellent idea for the men to spend their time in the good fresh air while the evenings are light.'

'I see.'

'But that's not why I'm here. I understand you were a good worker before you enlisted, that you've hewed coal for five years, and before that you were a trapper and a putter.'

'That's right, sir,' said Idris.

'I can't help thinking you'll be wasted as a screener, with all that experience. You know the men well. They speak highly of you, the ones I've spoken to.'

Edgar pulled a face. Idris was certain those men didn't include him.

'We're short of an examiner underground,' Mr Meredith continued. 'Not quite as good a wage as the hewers, but a lot better than the screeners. And there are other jobs you can do training for, go up the ladder, so to speak. The job's yours, unless you'd prefer to stay on the screens?'

He'd reckoned to living out his working life with a pickaxe in his hands. Examiner. That might suit. Better than standing over the pieces of coal and debris all day long. 'Yes sir, reckon I could make a go of that.'

'Excellent. I'll take you straight away to Mr Matthews. He'll show you the ropes for the first few days.' He went towards the door, stopping before he opened it. 'We'll leave you to it, Edgar. I'm sure you have a round of inspections you need to be going on.'

'Quite so, quite so.'

Idris said nothing as he made for the door, the manager several paces ahead. Before he exited, he heard Edgar's muted voice behind him, halting a few seconds to take in his message.

'Think you're clever, do you, getting one over on me? We'll see. We'll see.'

––

'Amen.' Elizabeth pronounced the word in a low, breathy tone.

There were a few moments of silence in the large room at the Workmen's Institute. The thirty or so women and the few men at the allotments meeting kept their heads bowed in contemplation.

People began to straighten up and the murmur of voices became concerned discussion. Anwen, sitting next to Elizabeth at the front of the meeting, said to her, 'Lord Kitchener's death will be quite a blow to our soldiers, I should think.'

'That and the fourteen large British ships that were sunk in the Battle of Jutland last week, and goodness knows how many smaller ones. Thousands of men killed, I shouldn't wonder. Many of our soldiers are in the thick of their own battles, so I wonder if they'll even know.' Elizabeth brought up a sigh that sounded like it came from her boots. 'Such a waste of life. But still we must carry on. Would you open the meeting?'

'Me?'

'Yes. Here, you can read the statistics to them too.' She pushed the piece of paper across the small table in front of them.

'All – right.' Anwen stood hesitantly, at first waiting to see if people would stop talking of their own volition. Only Idris, at the back with Gwilym, sat up straight, waiting expectantly. On the second row, four men sat, even older than the ones who'd shown up at the field a couple of weeks back. She knew them vaguely, long-retired miners who lived with grown-up children.

Anwen coughed. 'I think it is time we started the meeting,' she announced in as authoritative a tone as she could muster.

The audience ceased their conversation, settling themselves down.

'Thank you for coming this evening. It's nice to see that so many of our volunteers are eager to hear how we're progressing.'

She read out the figures for the vegetables planted, of those harvested and what had been sold at Mr James's greengrocery.

'We couldn't have done any of this without you. In addition, Mr Lloyd is very pleased indeed with the help he's getting at the farm.' Anwen paused. 'What we need now is a concerted effort through the summer, and into autumn, so we can hopefully harvest at least some vegetables throughout winter, and store and preserve others. Are there any questions?'

One of the newcomers hauled his frame up – even with the help of a walking stick, he was still somewhat unsteady. 'Hello. First I'd like to say how I appreciate all your hard work. My daughter bought a cabbage of yours from James the Veg and a nice addition it was to the meal, I can tell you. Fresh, not old and tough. My friends and I,' he indicated the three gentlemen with him, 'wouldn't be much good at working the land. A bit past it we are.'

'You speak for yourself, Billy, *bach*,' called the swarthy old-timer next to him, his hair a thatch of white.

The audience laughed. Billy patted his friend on the shoulder, the veins on his hand matching his blue coal scars.

'We reckon we must still be good for something though, something to help the war effort, apart from sitting in our kitchens and reading about it in the papers.'

Anwen was stumped as to what to suggest, groping for ideas in her mind as she said, 'That is very commendable of you, Mr—'

'Thomas. Billy Thomas.'

'Of all of you. We will take your names down and maybe we will be able to find some sitting-down jobs.'

Idris stood at the back, putting his hand up as if he were in school.

'Yes, Idris?' Even now, her heart skipped as she said his name. There must be some way to rid herself of this affection for him. The anger and indignation of the break-up had almost melted away, leaving her with compassion for what he'd been through. No, it was more than that, if only she could admit it to herself.

'I know it's not to do with the allotments, but your mother and mine have been doing some knitting. Gloves isn't it, for the soldiers?'

'That's right. With Mrs Harris and my mamgu.'

'I'm sure there'll be others in the village could donate old items of knitted clothing, and maybe we could get a bigger group going, or two groups. I wondered, would Mr Thomas and his friends mind knitting gloves?'

'I'd be up for that,' said Billy. 'What about you lot? Could your knobbly old fingers manage that?' His companions regarded each other, nodding. 'Yes? Good. My legs and back might be weak, but my hands are as sprightly as ever.' He tousled the abundant hair of his neighbour, making it stick up on end.

'Hey, watch it!' said his friend, laughing, as did everyone else.

'I'll talk to you afterwards about it,' said Anwen. 'Now I believe we're going to hear some individual reports including the progress of the three fields.'

Mary Jones, now in charge of the allotment in front of Edward Street, rose to give the first of the reports.

An hour later, the attendees were enjoying after-meeting refreshments. Anwen had arranged a time for the four old gentlemen to come to her house to meet Cadi and her mother. Leaving them to chat together, she noticed Idris by himself, taking his empty teacup to the table. It was her opportunity to thank him, though she knew in her heart it was an excuse to be near him.

She clinked her cup down, next to his. 'That was a brilliant idea, about the knitting.'

'It was alright, I suppose. But thank you for saying.' He didn't smile – in fact, he appeared a little put-out. He'd likely have preferred to go back to Gwilym now, but she was not ready to part company with him.

'How is your job at the screens going? Not too tedious, I hope.'

He eyed her cautiously. 'I'm not on the screens anymore. I've been made an examiner, underground.'

'Have you? That's marvellous. Well, it's better, isn't it? You don't seem happy about it.'

'I'm surprised Miss Meredith hasn't mentioned it.' He crossed his arms, leaning lightly against the table.

'Why would she have done?'

'I had the impression you had something to do with it.'

He had her at a disadvantage. 'How could I? I have no influence with Edgar Williams.'

'It wasn't Williams what gave me the job. It was Mr Meredith. Seems he'd heard how well I was organising things on the allotment and thought I was wasted on the screens.'

'I've certainly not spoken to Mr Meredith about you.'

'But his daughter has. And I'm guessing she heard about my demotion from you. Am I right?'

She became a little flustered. It might be down to her, ultimately, but why was he so put-out about it? 'I did mention it to Elizabeth. I was so angry about it. The Merediths apparently don't like Mr and Mrs Williams much.' This was silly. Why did she have to justify an action that had yielded such a good outcome? Then she realised. 'Idris Hughes, is it too proud you are, to be helped by a woman?'

His cheeks reddened a little and he fiddled with his fingers. 'No, not by a woman in particular. By anyone.'

'Really, Idris, you are going to have to accept that there are people who have your best interests at heart. You put yourself forward to fight in the war, and it didn't work out. But it doesn't reflect badly on you, quite the opposite. Only nasty people like Edgar and Esther Williams are going to use it against you. You have to realise that.'

'Do I?' With that he propelled his body away from the table, striding past the neat rows of chairs until he reached Gwilym at the back, chatting to Gwen and Mary.

He said something briefly to his friend, then strode the rest of the way to the door, letting himself out without a backward glance.

'What on earth am I going to do with him?' she muttered to herself. *He's not your responsibility anymore, so you don't have to worry about it.* But I do, she thought, I do.

–

Anwen straightened up, as did her fellow workers, all standing on the field in front of the terraces of Alexandra Street. Coming ever closer they could hear a rendition of 'I'll Be a Sunbeam'. Down the road appeared a long line of marching children, singing their little hearts out, some voices in tune, some a little off-key.

The weather was not being kind to them this Whit Monday holiday, with its dark skies and intermittent rain, though the children didn't seem to care. Anwen recalled this day in her childhood, when she and her siblings took part in the Noncon-formist Sunday Schools' parade. Most of all, they had longed for the tea provided in the various church halls afterwards. How jolly these children were, their little faces scrubbed and their best clothes as clean as anyone could get them.

The street was a dead end, so the children's caterpillar curled round, bit by bit, its many legs finally making their way back towards the Institute. In this way, the parade would walk and curve and come back on itself, until every street had been covered. Only then would they go to the halls for their treats.

'I used to enjoy the parades as a youngster in Georgetown,' said a voice behind her.

She twisted round to see Tom there, his shirt collarless and undone, the sleeves rolled up.

'Sorry, didn't mean to startle you. I was sitting inside, getting bored, and I thought, why don't I go down and help Anwen with the allotments?'

'We're happy to have all the help we can get.'

'I thought of going to the field behind the cottages, as it's closest, but I can't help feeling the chap there in charge doesn't like me much. He always gives me queer looks when I pass by.'

Anwen leant back in surprise. 'Who, Idris? He's harmless.' Yet she knew he was not happy about her having any kind of association with a man of a higher class.

'In any case, why would I go there with all the old men, when I could spend time in your company here?'

Her stomach gave a little flutter before she admonished herself. Male attention, that's all it was. Starved of it, she was. She led him to a box of knives. 'Here. You can help cut the cauliflowers first. We've got a good lot of those.'

'So, here I am, helping out on the allotments, as you requested. Have you given any more thought to coming out with me again?'

She should have known there'd be a catch. 'Is that the only reason you're here?'

He shrugged. 'I appreciate the effort you're all putting in. But yes, I was hoping you'd see me in a new light. And forgive me for what I did.'

'I already have forgiven you, Tom.'

'I'm so glad. I know the weather's not as clement as it could be, but how about coming for a stroll by the river with me this evening? It's a nice walk, which I haven't done for a while. I fancy some company.'

'You're not going to give up, are you?'

He put his head to one side. 'No.'

'Let me see how you get on today and I'll decide later.'

'Ah, that's your game, is it?' he chuckled. 'Making sure I do a good job.' He took the proffered knife. 'I'll do my very best. Hey, who's that sprinting across the field?'

Gwilym was running up the hill towards them. When he reached them, he bent over, clutching his knees, coughing a little before gasping.

'What is it, Gwilym?' said Anwen. 'What's the hurry?'

He straightened up, blowing out a hefty breath. 'I've just come from the field behind the cottages. Idris and I got there to find it's been vandalised overnight. All the seedlings have been pulled out and ruined. Must have been more than one person, that's for sure.'

Anwen's breath hitched. All that work! What if they picked on the fields this side next? 'It was all for the benefit of the villagers. Who would do such a thing?'

Gwilym shrugged. 'No idea.'

Several people came to mind, all at once, jostling for first place as culprit: the men who were aggrieved by the women working, the shopkeepers who were resentful that food was being sold they had no part in, even though they didn't sell vegetables. The butcher, despite his words of encouragement, had been offering veg under the counter. And Mr Moss, the hotel landlord, had thought he'd get cheap vegetables and was angry when he was told the produce was only for the villagers. So many suspects, so much to do to make up for the loss. Her knees gave way, causing her to plonk in an unladylike fashion onto the ground. A number of the volunteers ran over.

'My dear, are you all right?' said Tom, taking her arm too late to stop her sinking.

'I'm fine.' She told the others what had happened as Tom helped her up, eliciting exclamations of anger.

'You carry on with the work here,' she told the women. 'I'm going with Gwilym to get Sergeant Harries, or at least to leave a message.'

'I'll come along too,' said Tom.

Anwen would rather he didn't, but equally had no wish to contradict her employer's son, even if they were friends now. It was like she had to be two different people with him. The men followed her across the field, cutting down an alley to Gabriel Street. The sergeant lived at number one, opposite St Peter's. Anwen knocked stridently on the front door, fuelled by exasperation. It wasn't long before the policeman opened it, not surprised, but curious maybe at the combination of people on his doorstep.

'Sergeant Harries, I'm sorry to disturb you,' said Anwen.

'It is my day off, and a Whit Monday to boot.'

'The thing is—' started Tom.

'The thing is,' Anwen interrupted, 'one of our fields of vegetables has been vandalised. So, I'd like to report a crime.'

'I see.' He looked towards Gwilym and then Tom, so obviously waiting for their confirmation. She seethed inwardly. Wasn't her word good enough?

'I've seen it,' said Gwilym. 'When I got there with Idris Hughes and the other men. Trashed, it's been. Not a plant left unharmed.'

'Well I haven't my uniform on right now, so if you leave it with me, I'll go up later.'

'Come on, my good man,' said Tom, taking on an air much like his parents'. 'I'm sure my father would not like to hear that a project he has endorsed has been ruined and that the police have taken no interest.'

Harries nodded. 'Hold on, I'll just make myself a bit more decent.'

He closed the door. A couple of minutes later he opened it again, doing up the belt on his blue jacket, his helmet already in place. 'Lead the way.'

They walked out of the main village, curving round to McKenzie Cottages. On the field behind, Idris and the band of older men were hoeing and digging, clearing away the spoilt burgeoning vegetables.

'Tut tut,' said the sergeant, standing between Anwen and Gwilym. 'That is quite a mess, isn't it? I'm not sure what I can do. I don't suppose they left a calling card.'

It was supposed to be funny, but none of them laughed. Idris, who was at the top of the field, walked down to meet them, his face contorted with fury. 'It's a wretched mess. If I ever catch who did this…'

'You and me both,' said Gwilym.

'I wouldn't be so hasty to admit that in front of me,' said Harries. 'And I doubt there's any way of finding out who it was. If there is, then the law will deal with it.'

'Like it's dealt with all the thefts and hijacking of carts and motor vans for the goods they're carrying?' said Idris. 'Haven't heard of any arrests there.'

'No, well, that's how it is much of the time,' said Harries. 'If there's no evidence…'

'What about fingerprinting?'

'There aren't going to be any fingerprints in the field, are there?'

'There might be on the motorcars, or the carts.'

'I don't see—'

'That's not our concern right now,' Anwen interrupted. 'Please, would you at least take down some details, Sergeant? Ask at the cottages if anyone heard anything. That's a thought. Tom, did you hear anything from your house?'

'No. But then I sleep through thunderstorms, so I'm not much of a witness.'

'I'll do what I can,' said Harries. 'But short of a witness coming forward, I don't know what else there is. Now if you'll excuse me, I'll go and knock on the cottage doors.' He tramped to the road, and soon disappeared.

'Is there anything I can do here?' Tom asked Anwen.

'The best help you could give is to pick those caulis for us, please. I'll be along a bit later, when I've had a look round here.' She didn't want his company right now. It was making it awkward with Idris.

'Of course. At your service.' He bowed low, springing off immediately afterwards towards the road, humming loudly.

As soon as he was out of earshot she asked Idris, 'Who do you think did this? I've thought of several people who are unhappy with our project. Could be any of them. Or none of them.'

'Or all of them,' he said, deadpan.

She nodded reluctantly. 'Would you like some help up here, clearing up?'

'No, there's enough of us.'

'I'll go and get on,' said Gwilym.

When he'd gone, Idris said, 'We'll clear it and get started again, digging the rows ready for the next attempt.'

'You're not giving up?'

'The hell we are! Sorry.'

'Don't be. I'm angry too, Idris. Thank you for your dedication. And thank the men for me. I'll leave you to it.'

Her departure was brought to a halt by Idris. 'Anwen?'

'Hm?'

'I know I've said this before, but be careful.'

Her head tilted to one side. 'In what way?'

'With "Tom", as you called him.'

Had she? Slip of the tongue.

'Don't get too close to a man of his class. They have a reputation.'

'*They* might do. Doesn't mean he has.'

'I'm just warning you.'

'*Warning* me?'

'I didn't mean it like that, like I'm threatening to do something if you don't do as I say. I'm not your father, you know.'

'I'm perfectly capable of looking after myself, Idris.'

'In that case, take care.'

The ease with which he strolled away belied his words of concern. She stared after him a while before she too went on her way.

What a cheek, thinking he had any say in her life now! She'd find Tom and tell him yes to a walk this evening. She hadn't been by the river for a while either, so she'd look forward to it.

–

Idris was more glad than usual to arrive home after his shift. The weather had warmed up a little today and the sky was blue. It didn't matter either way to Idris, who always felt too warm.

He placed his tin box and bottle on the table in the scullery, sitting on a chair there for a while to rest his bones. He'd better get a kettle and bucket of water on the boil. The quicker he got washed, the quicker he could have his dinner. Mam had said she'd leave him some bread and cheese as she was visiting Mamgu Price today in Rhymney. Da had stopped by for some baccy on the journey home, so he might be a while as he liked a gossip.

Idris was eager to get on with repairing the damage on the top allotment. It had become a matter of pride. They'd heard of no progress in finding the perpetrators in the three days since it had happened. He didn't expect they ever would. Instead, Miss Meredith had put wooden posts up on each allotment, with notes signed by her father, to the effect that should anyone be caught there'd be serious fines and possibly a spot of time in gaol.

Scraping the tin bath along the floor from under the table, Idris lumbered awkwardly with it into the kitchen, placing it with a clunk onto the floor. He yawned, squeezing his eyes tight shut and stretching. When he opened his eyes again, he noticed a piece of paper on the table. Perhaps Mam had left him some jobs to do.

Picking it up, he recognised Jenkin's precise schoolroom script. He must have left it before he went to school this morning. But as he read the note, his initial smile soon dipped down at the corners. A griping agony had him bent double, until his forehead touched the table.

Jenkin had run off with a group of his pals to enlist.

Chapter Twenty

Idris put the note in his pocket. How far would Jenkin have got? Which recruitment office would he have gone to? Pontlottyn? Rhymney? When he'd enlisted, Idris had gone with his pals to Bargoed in March of last year, but there was no need to go that far.

Forgoing the bath and making do with a cold wash, he was dressed within fifteen minutes. He left the bread and cheese, having lost his appetite. Jenkin had mentioned Gwilym's brother, Evan, so he decided to start at the Owen household. Where was Da? He was taking even longer than usual.

The question was answered as Idris stepped out of the back door.

'Where you off to in such a hurry, son?'

Idris pulled the note from his pocket. Isaiah took it, bringing it close to his face.

'Stupid rash fool! You know who'll be responsible.'

'Me, Da. He says he's replacing me in the army.' Idris leant against the door, the fear and guilt consuming him.

'No, *bach*, it's that Cadoc Beadle, the scout master. All these boys he mentions, Jenkin goes to scouts with. Always getting them to do army exercises, is Cadoc, filling their 'eads with tales of heroics.'

'I'm going to Gwilym's house now. Have your bath and I'll meet you back here, or at Gwilym's.'

'What are we going to do?'

'Find them, Da.' He took the note off his father, stuffing it back into his pocket.

'They might not look too closely at their ages, being desperate for men, like. I hear they gets a shilling for each poor bugger what signs up, so they're not so inclined to send any packing.'

That was what Idris was afraid of. He ran along the backs of the houses of Alexandra Street and Edward Street until he reached Gwilym's, right at the other end.

About to open Gwilym's back door, Rachael Owen beat him to it.

'Oh! Well hello there—'

'Mrs Owen, is Evan here?'

'Evan? Do you mean Gwilym?' She wiped wet hands on her apron, laughing.

'No, Evan!'

Her laughing stopped abruptly. 'No, he's at school, of course. Why have you a face on you?'

Gwilym appeared in the dark scullery, pulling a clean shirt on over his vest. 'What's up, mun?'

Idris handed the note to Rachael. She read it, her eyes darting quickly along the lines. Gwilym peered at it over her shoulder, his face slowly taking on the expression Idris's had done earlier.

'Evan left for school the same as always this morning,' Rachael said. 'We haven't found any notes. Perhaps he changed his mind. Perhaps they all did.' A smile, forced but determined, formed. 'Yes, I bet they're all sitting in school now, shame-faced at the thought of what they nearly did to their families.'

'Mam, we can't assume that,' said Gwilym. 'We need to be sure.'

Rachael twirled around with an impatient huff, vacating the scullery for some moments before returning with a shawl. 'I'll head down to the school and make sure all these boys are there, which I have no doubt the scallywags will be. Jenkin should get a tanned behind for putting us through such worry.' She ran off down the garden path.

'Come in,' said Gwilym. 'I'm about to have my dinner. I presume you've had yours.'

'No, I lost my appetite when I read that note.'

'No point getting all het up before we know what's what. Will you at least have a cup of tea while I have my bite to eat?'

Idris nodded, following his friend in and through to the kitchen where he saw Gwilym's grandfather, Abraham, eating at the table.

'What's all the to-do then, lad? Rachael dashed in and out again and didn't say a word. Not another field been wrecked, is it?'

'No Grancha.' Gwilym went quiet.

Idris sat opposite the old man, resigned to explaining yet again.

Twenty minutes later, Isaiah arrived at Gwilym's back door at the same time as Rachael. She gripped her shawl around herself against the unseasonably cool June day. In the kitchen she faced the men there present, waving Jenkin's letter in the air.

'They're not there, not any of them! Evan, Jenkin, George, Emlyn, Cyril and Christopher Williams. All absent. Their teacher thought maybe there was some new outbreak of something. I called at their houses on the way back. That snooty mother of Christopher's, Esther, said he was ill in bed. Almost pushed me out her gate, she did. The other three mothers reckon they're playing hooky. Always up to mischief, those three.'

'Then maybe that's it,' said Abraham, leaning over his empty plate. 'They'll be skulking somewhere, too ashamed to show their faces.'

'Did Evan take anything with him?' Isaiah asked.

'I watched him leave this morning,' said Rachael. 'He just had the bag containing his food tin and book. Couldn't get much else in there. Doesn't prove nothing, though.'

An idea struck Idris. 'Cadoc Beadle. You said he was always encouraging them to enlist. Maybe he knows which office they've headed to.'

'It's worth a try,' said Isaiah. 'Though I can't imagine him admitting he was behind it.'

Rachael wrung her hands together. 'Oh, you wait till his father gets in. He'll tan Evan's hide from this side of the village to the other. Aye, and Cadoc Beadle's if he's responsible.'

'Where is Earnest?' asked Isaiah. 'He should be back from the shift by now.'

'Doing a double, isn't he? Too much for a man his age. It'll be the death of him.'

'Mam!' Gwilym's embarrassment was edged with annoyance. 'Don't tempt fate.'

'Let's get going to Cadoc's.' Idris was aware they were taking up precious time, minutes that might make all the difference to finding the boys or not.

Gwilym lifted his jacket from one of the dining chairs. 'He lives on Islwyn Street, doesn't he?'

'Aye, the house at the end,' said Idris. 'He's a fitter on our shift, so he should be back now.'

The three men stepped out onto the street. Abraham hurried down the hallway, agile for his age, pulling his jacket on.

'Grancher, you don't need to come,' said Gwilym.

'I'm not going to Beadle's, look you, I'm off to the allotment. They'll wonder why we're all missing. I can tell them what's happened, maybe get a few people searching that way.'

'Good idea, Mr Owen,' said Idris.

–

Anwen reached the edge of the allotments behind McKenzie Cottages. Tom stood beside her as they observed the progress being made. A pile of slaughtered seedlings sat in one corner of the field, ready to make compost. The sadness that threatened to engulf her was lifted by the sight of the effort being made by the group of old men there, grown as it had since news of the calamity.

'They've done well in the short time, clearing and replanting,' said Anwen, feeling awkward that Tom was still standing there with her. He could have stayed helping in the bottom field opposite Alexandra Street, but no, he'd followed her round like some kind of deputy.

They'd had a pleasant walk by the Rhymney river on Whit Monday, the rain holding off as they'd passed across grass and under leafy trees, talking of their childhoods. His had not been so very different to hers. And, true to his word, he had not tried to kiss her. It was almost like having a stroll with Gwen. That's what she'd told her father she was doing. Almost like having a stroll with her – but not quite.

'They have done well,' he confirmed, glancing across the field. 'Where is that chap who normally leads here? The one with a chip on his shoulder.'

'Idris, you mean?' She'd never admitted to Tom that Idris was the man who'd jilted her. She scanned the field. Sure enough, he was missing, as was Gwilym. 'Probably got back late from their shifts.'

There was a pause before he said, 'What do you think about coming to see the film with me, then?'

'I beg your pardon?'

He tilted his head back and tutted. 'I swear you've not been listening to a word I've said the last ten minutes.'

'I was thinking about what we're growing and harvesting next. It's important.' She really could have done with walking around on her own to think these things through. 'What were you saying about the film?' She tried to concentrate as he replied, putting her new private queries about Idris's absence to one side for the moment.

'They're showing *Bella Donna* in Tredegar. It's set in Egypt, romance and intrigue and murder. Thought it might appeal to you.'

Her eyes were searching the path, wondering if Idris would arrive while they were there. 'I'm not sure I have time at the moment.'

'Maybe *The Exploits of Elaine* are more up your street. Damsel in distress and all that.' He laughed raucously at this thought.

'I found the one we saw a bit daft.' She spied a shock of white hair on the path below. 'It's Gwilym's grancher... Mr Owen!' she called, waving.

He had soon rounded the path and caught them up, sprightly for his age, but a little breathless. 'Anwen. Gwilym and Idris won't be coming today, not unless they locate Evan, Jenkin and the others.'

'Evan and Jenkin?'

'Aye. I'll explain to you all at the same time.' He called up to his fellow gardeners, beckoning them to come to the path. They tramped down, the younger men arriving more promptly than the older. When they had all gathered around, he explained what had happened.

Anwen was the first to comment. 'Oh my goodness, that's terrible. Do you think they really would have gone?'

'I dunno,' said Abraham. 'I can only hope they're playing silly beggars, but time will tell. If you could all keep an eye open we'd appreciate it. Now men, I believe we've got work to be getting on with.'

They trudged back to where they'd been working, Abraham following on.

Tom rubbed his hands together. 'In the absence of their usual leader, would you like me to take charge here?'

She hesitated. She didn't want to offend him, but neither did she want him thinking he could take over simply because of his class. 'No. Many of these men are retired and don't respond to the authority of bosses anymore.'

'I suppose that's fair enough.' His pouting bottom lip belied his statement.

Anwen called, 'Mr Owen!'

The older man returned down the slope. 'Is something wrong?'

'Not at all. I'd just like you to be in charge in Idris's absence, if that's all right with you.'

He scratched his head. 'Me in charge? That'll be a first. But I knows my veggies and how to grow them, so I guess I'm not a bad choice.'

'Thank you. I'm going back to the other field to get on with the work there,' she said. 'I'll let them know down there what's happened about the boys.'

She strode off, not waiting to see if Tom was following, though he soon caught her up. Her heart lay heavy, imagining the grief Idris must be experiencing over his missing brother. Tom had soon found other things to talk about. Anwen let him carry on uninterrupted.

–

Cadoc Beadle's house was the last one on Islwyn Street, at the end of the village and side on to the hill. Idris led the way, keen to question the scout master, at the same time trying to control the excesses of his aggression. Jenkin wasn't going to be dispatched on the first ship to the Front. There was training first, months of it. And they might have been sent away from the recruitment office. Better not to get too heavy handed. *Calm down.* It wasn't doing his heart rate any good as he experienced the familiar dizziness.

At number thirty-one Islwyn Street, despite his words of warning to himself, Idris banged furiously on the door. There was no reply.

Isaiah grabbed his arm as he was about to bestow a second volley of knocks. 'All right now, *bach*, I think the whole street would have heard the first time.'

Idris noticed the woman next door peeping round her door-frame. Next he heard a top window of the same house open and saw a man peering out.

'He's not in,' said Gwilym. 'Let's go.'

'No, wait a—' Idris started.

He hadn't finished before the door opened and Cadoc stood there, a tall, portly man in his forties, shirt sleeves rolled up. His hair, a slightly greying ebony and currently wet, was combed back. He put his round spectacles on to look at them. 'What's all this then? Can't you give a man time to get decent after a shift?'

'Where are they, Beadle?' Idris blurted out, pre-empting his father, who'd opened his mouth to speak but wasn't quick enough.

'Where's who?'

'Our boys,' Isaiah got in quickly. 'Jenkin and Evan. George, Emlyn and Cyril. We found a note to say they'd signed up. You're doing that is, filling their 'eads with heroic nonsense.'

Beadle stepped back a fraction. 'I – I don't know anything about them signing up. I've never encouraged that. Just thought it was an opportunity to get them fit, spur them on to be like our brave boys fighting in the trenches.'

Isaiah leant forward, nostrils flaring. 'Isn't it enough for them to be like our brave men working in the mines? Have you read the papers lately?' He lifted each finger in turn. 'German advances, Bulgarian invasions, a battle in the Tyrol, Ypres, East Africa, the Turks, Verdun still raging on? And that's the tip of the iceberg. Heroism? Bloody *mad*ness.'

Idris, with his own arguments planned, was stumped by his father's intense passion.

'I know that.' Cadoc considered the trio, panic in his blanched face.

Maybe he thought they were going to beat him up. Idris considered it an opportunity to take advantage of his fear, to make him spill the truth, if he really knew anything. 'Come on Beadle, what office did they go to?'

'I – I honestly don't know.' Cadoc's hand shook as he placed it on the door, maybe ready to close it. 'Whatever they've done, they've done it off their own bat.'

'We'd better not find out you're behind it then.' The hinted threat was a last attempt by Idris to extract information.

'I'm telling you, I know nothing!' Cadoc's voice ended on a squeak.

'Come on, let's go,' said Gwilym. 'We're getting nowhere here. Reckon we should go to the recruiting offices.'

'Very wise.' Cadoc closed the door immediately.

'It's all right, the show's over now,' Isaiah called to the inquisitive neighbours. When they'd disappeared he said, 'There are three of us, and three local recruitment offices. Reckon we should split up and go to one each.'

'The walks to Pontlottyn and Rhymney are easy,' said Idris. 'Tredgar'll take over an hour. I'll do that one.'

'Okay *bach*, if you're sure.'

'Come on. The quicker we set off the quicker we'll find them.'

—

'My goodness, how terrible for their families.' Elizabeth took a sip of her coffee, sitting at the kitchen table at McKenzie House with Anwen. 'If I'd known at the time, I'd have driven the men to the recruitment offices. So, they had no luck?'

'No,' said Anwen. 'A recruitment officer at Tredegar reckoned he'd seen some boys fitting the description, but a colleague had turned them away. Pontlottyn and Rhymney offices denied any knowledge.'

'Do you think they could be mistaken for eighteen-year-olds?'

'Not really, though Jenkin is tall for his age. Some eighteen-year-old boys look very young, so they might take that into consideration.'

The grandmother clock in the hall rang out half past the hour. 'That's my break done,' said Anwen. She gathered the empty cups and plates.

'There's no hurry. Have a longer break for a change. You've worked hard since Rose left.'

Something about Elizabeth's demeanour told Anwen there was more to this invitation. She'd been aware of someone arriving at the house just after they'd sat down. Elizabeth had been adamant at the time that someone else would answer the door to them.

Anwen put her crockery back on the table. 'All right.'

'Let's have another drink and we can discuss our project. Farmer Lloyd has several chickens he's rearing for us. We need to work out where we're keeping them and what we need, though Mr Lloyd is able to help with some of that too...'

And so the conversation drifted on until the clock finally struck eleven and Elizabeth said, 'I suppose we've had long enough. And it's time for me to think about lunch. I've enjoyed searching the recipe books and discovering new dishes. Cooking is quite an art.'

Anwen thought it probably was if you had a well-equipped kitchen and enough ingredients to use, but she wasn't about to crush Elizabeth's enthusiasm. She was impressed at how Elizabeth had risen to the challenge, along with Mrs Meredith.

'It's my parents' bedroom you concentrate on today, isn't it?'

'After I've finished in the hall.'

'Why don't you start on the bedrooms now? You can go back to finish the hall later if you have time – after all, it had its proper clean yesterday.'

She wasn't sure what Mrs Meredith would have to say about that, but Anwen didn't argue.

Back in the hall, she was halfway up the dark wood staircase, about to turn the corner, when she heard one of the downstairs doors open, either the dining room or the drawing room. She hunkered down and peered through the spindles, her curiosity overriding her sense of propriety.

'I hope this is the last we will hear of this matter,' came Mr Meredith's voice from down the corridor.

'Of course. I gave my word,' came a female voice, just before a figure appeared, her attire bright to the point of garish.

The woman leant round to pick up an unfurled umbrella from the stand by the door. Polly Coombes. Had she come for the cook's job? Polly straightened herself then leaned towards the mirror over the console table. She fiddled with her hat before doing up her lightweight jacket.

It was then Anwen noticed it. The small yet unmistakeable bump bulging through the blouse and skirt. Polly Coombes was pregnant.

She began to open the front door. Tom came into view, rushing to push it shut. He was properly attired, jacket and all.

'Hey!' she yelled. 'What are you doing?'

'You do promise not to mention this to anyone.'

'I've already told you and Mr Meredith, Tom. Even my parents haven't got the father's name from me.'

'Make sure you keep it that way.'

Anwen's stomach plummeted. Tom was the father? Of course he was. The way Polly had greeted him that day they'd been lunching in the garden, there'd been an intimacy about it. Idris had been right. Even Tom Meredith, a good-natured lad who cared little for class, could not be trusted. The whole affair was nauseating. Yet in many ways she couldn't care less. He'd acted true to type, as had Polly. Perhaps she'd hoped to marry into money but instead she'd been paid off. She didn't seem worried about it.

'Are you threatening me, Thomas Meredith?'

'You've got your money, and that should be the end of it.'

She pushed Tom's hand away and left abruptly. He leant his forehead against the closed door. Anwen took the opportunity to sneak the rest of the way upstairs, making sure the house-keeping box did not rattle. She had reached the top and was about to step onto the landing, when footsteps came galloping up behind her.

'Anwen?' Tom said, surprise in his voice.

'Sir?'

'What are you doing here?'

'About to clean your parents' bedroom, sir.'

'What's all this sir business?'

'I'm at work, sir, it's only proper.'

She carried on, stopping at the Merediths' bedroom door to open it. Tom was instantly behind her.

'I didn't hear you go through the hall while I was there. How did you get to the stairs without me seeing you?'

'When I went through you were leaning against the front door. You obviously didn't see me.'

'You were on the stairs already, weren't you?' The colour had drained from his face.

'I don't know what you mean. I came from the kitchen as you were leaning against the door.'

'You saw Polly, didn't you?'

Anwen didn't reply, instead opening the bedroom door and taking the housekeeping box in. She thought he would go off to his room, or back downstairs. But he followed her in.

'These things happen, Anwen. She made herself available. Men are simple creatures who have energies they need to release sometimes.'

An unwanted image invaded her mind, of him releasing his energy with Polly Coombes. She shuddered, banishing it immediately. 'If you don't mind sir, I need to get this room finished before lunch as I have other duties this afternoon.'

'Please, don't let it make any difference to our friendship. You have still to tell me if you will accompany me to see Bella Donna at the picture house.'

What was wrong with this man? How could he be so insensitive? 'No sir, it would not be seemly for me to accompany you.'

'But what's happened with Polly has nothing to do with me.'

'No, I suppose she got pregnant all by herself.'

'I mean—'

'Now, if you wouldn't mind...'

His shoulders drooped as resignation filled his face. 'I will leave you to your work.'

'Thank you, sir.'

259

So that was the end of that. Whatever *that* had been. You couldn't just be friends with a man, and certainly not when he was of a higher class than you, let alone anything else. She took the wax polish from the box, loading up the cloth before wiping it furiously across the top of the drawers.

Let that be a lesson to her, she thought to herself.

Chapter Twenty-One

'Come on now, Idris mun, losing yourself in the allotment will help you forget the problem for a while.' Gwilym sat opposite his pal at the kitchen table.

'That's what I've told him,' said Meg, lowering the clothes airer from the ceiling. Her manner was terse, as it often was when she was hiding her distress about something.

Idris wished he could absent himself upstairs but knew he would open himself up to yet more badgering.

'It's pouring with rain today and no one will be on the allotments, so why are you going on about it? I haven't got time, I've got to keep *searching*.' Idris slumped his body over the newspaper he'd been skimming when Gwilym had arrived, hoping it would give him some clues, yet not knowing how. He'd been using this excuse to avoid socialising since Jenkin went missing.

'But there's nowhere else to look,' Gwilym persisted. 'You've been to all the recruitment offices in the area, even Bargoed and Merthyr. You've scoured the countryside from here to Rhymney, Tredegar, Bedwellty and New Tredegar. What are you going to do now, investigate the training camps?'

Idris got to his feet. 'That's it! I'll go to the camps, take Jenkin's school record, prove he's not old enough. I could travel on the train to Kinmel Bay, he'll likely be there as that's where they're—'

'Oh *bach*, that's enough!' Meg's shrill voice made both the men jump. She dumped the shirt she'd removed from the airer over an empty chair. 'Enough. It's driving yourself nuts, you are, with this insistent mission to find the boys, and why? Because you think it's your fault Jenkin's gone?'

'Yes, but—'

'But nothing! Stop it now! Do you think I'm any the less upset? I'm his mother! I've lost two sons, one at birth and one still a babby. Do you think I relish losing Jenkin any more than you do?' Her cheeks and neck were crimson and moisture lined her eyes. 'We've informed the offices. We've informed the police. Sometimes all you have left is to sit and wait.'

'I can't just sit and wait.' Idris slammed his fist on the table, causing the cups and saucers there to rattle a complaint. He lifted his hands, aware that they were both shaking. He hid them behind his back, but soon his whole body was trembling. He had to get on the move, go somewhere, search, search, search. 'I'm going out.'

'Idris, wait!' said Meg. 'I was going to ask you to come to Enid's with me.'

'Why?' She was surely trying to divert his attention.

'Sometimes Madog is there. I'm not comfortable in his presence, especially if Cadi and Anwen are out. Couple of times I've let myself in only to be shouted out again by him.'

'He shouts at you?' Idris was aware she'd been successful in diverting him, but this was a worrying development his mother had not mentioned before.

'Increasingly drunker and crosser, he is.'

'He is that,' Gwilym confirmed.

He was desperate to find Jenkin, but he also needed to protect his mother. Perhaps, by the same action, he'd reinforce the warning he'd issued to Madog Rhys the day Miss Meredith brought Sara home, thereby protecting Anwen. But he would not let his mother think he came without effort.

'All right. I will come with you if I must. It's right that you still visit Enid, the condition she's in.'

'The only time I can guarantee Madog won't be there is when the knitting group comes around. Probably because there are a few older men in the group, and Hywel comes round to help. Reckon he doesn't fancy taking them all on.'

'When do you want to go?'

'When I've folded these. So drink up your tea while you're waiting.'

Idris caught a brief look shared between his mother and Gwilym, deciding to ignore the fact that they clearly felt they'd achieved some kind of victory. He picked the tea up, willing it to calm his nerves. His body was still shaking, though it was more a vibration within, now.

'I'll get going,' said Gwilym. He let himself out the back.

Having finished the folding, Meg gathered together some scrap wool into a sack bag she'd made a few days before. 'Enid likes to knit every day so I'm keeping her supplied. We've had such a good response to our plea for old wool garments.'

Meg wrapped her shawl around herself. Idris took only his cap, despite the downpour. They went out the front onto the drenched street, where the rain had eased to a drizzle. At Anwen's house they halted, glancing at each other before Meg tapped on the door.

'I find now it's better to knock first in case—'

She was unable to finish before the door was flung open by Madog, his face unshaven. He was chewing tobacco, but it didn't stop him saying, 'What d'you want?' He treated Idris to a sneer, ignoring his mother altogether.

'I've come for my daily visit to Enid,' said Meg.

'Have you now? Well, she's sleeping so don't need your company. And what's this? You brought a bodyguard?'

'I haven't been to see Mrs Rhys for a while and thought I'd pay a visit,' said Idris.

'You're not welcome in this house.' He poked a stubby, blackened finger towards Idris's face.

Meg held up the sack bag. 'I've brought some wool for Enid, so she can keep knitting.'

Madog took it, immediately throwing the bag into a puddle in the road.

Idris was about to protest when his mother pre-empted him with a shrieked, 'Was that necessary?'

'Enid's done with knitting for unknown people. If she's going to do any knitting, it'll be for *me*.' He slammed the door.

Idris retrieved the dripping bag from the puddle, gathering up a skein of wool that had fallen out.

They set off back towards their house, the pinched mouth of his mother telling him she was stewing inwardly. Her breathing had become so heavy she was almost blowing steam like an angry bull. Her next sentence burst out of her above the rain. 'I've never been convinced, you know, about Enid's accident.'

'What do you mean?'

'You know what I mean.'

Oh yes, he had a very good idea what she was getting at. He only hoped, for Enid's sake, and Anwen's, she was wrong.

When they'd passed the Workmen's Institute he said, 'I'm going for a walk, Mam.'

'In this weather, *bach*? It's getting worse again.'

'I need to stretch my legs.' What he needed was to go through things in his mind. He couldn't do that at home with his mother, and soon his father, talking at him.

'You're not going to hunt for Jenkin!'

'No, Mam. Just local. Fresh air, even if it is wet.'

'All right, *cariad*, but don't be too long, or else I'll be out looking for you.'

'An hour or so, that's all I need.'

'Make sure it is.'

He set off down to Gabriel Street, on the way to Mafeking Terrace. A walk to Rhymney and back would help clear his head a bit. He was unlikely to pass many people in this weather, allowing him to concentrate only on his thoughts.

–

Anwen approached the allotments behind the cottages, watching the air shimmering above the field. The men working there were distorted in the haze. She pulled her blouse away from her, longing to divest herself of at least her corset. That would be freedom indeed. The air was still cool after yesterday's rain, but she was overly warm from hurrying.

Gwilym came down to meet her, spade in hand, his identity becoming apparent only as he got closer. He lifted his other hand in greeting. 'Good afternoon, Anwen.'

'Gwilym, I wondered if Idris was working back in the field yet.'

'No. Went to see him yesterday. He's back in that cave of his since Jenkin ran away.'

Anwen grieved deep in her soul, her face passive in order to conceal this.

'What are we going to do with him?' Gwilym's face crinkled with concern.

'There's nothing I can do with him. He's made that clear. It's up to his family and friends.'

'Anwen, whatever's happened, you *are* his friend. You've known each other too long not to be.'

She knew this to be true. He was as much a part of her existence as these mountains and valleys, as the neat rows of terraces and the Baptist chapel. He was woven into the fabric of her life.

'And he still cares for you, I know. I've seen the frown when he's heard what your father's been up to.'

Anwen was immediately on the defence. 'What's my father done now?' She pictured the drawers full of bottles and other items in Sara's room.

'His temper, how he lashes out and threatens people.'

'Oh, that.' She hadn't meant to sound so dismissive, but she'd been anticipating him saying much worse.

Abraham Owen came shuffling down the incline almost sideways, in between two rows of sown seeds, causing Gwilym to whisper, 'We're looking out for you, remember.'

'You're getting on well here,' she called to Abraham, not wishing to discuss her family problems any further.

'Aye, *fach*, the men are doing a good job. But we could do with that daft blighter back. Idris, that is. What's he playing at? Can't you go round and talk some sense into him?'

'Mr Owen, Idris and I aren't—'

'Oh, I know, I know. But he clearly has more respect for you than he does most. Dunno why you gave him up; nice, decent lad, he is. And he thinks the world of you, you can see.'

Anwen glanced at Gwilym who shrugged slightly. Most people now believed she'd jilted him, after that strained conversation with Esther Williams in the gardens some months back.

'Grancher, let's show Anwen what we've planted—' he started, only to be struck dumb by something behind Anwen.

She followed his eye-line to see the very woman who'd just held her thoughts, ambling towards them with difficulty. She was sporting the kind of tight hemmed skirt that Margaret Meredith was still prone to wear, the fashion for which was now a year or two in the past. A 'hobble skirt', she believed it was called. Her employer managed the fashion with more elegance, besides which, her skirts were never quite this narrow. Mrs Williams had hitherto favoured the wider skirts from before the war.

She used a green parasol as a walking stick, aiding her advance. 'I see you've connived to take another two of my women from me.'

Anwen took three steps towards her. 'If you mean that two of the ladies you are friendly with decided, of their own accord, to join the allotment group, then you are right. But they are hardly *your* women.'

'You've been telling them lies about me. They'll barely even say hello to me now.'

'That's because you shout at them before they have a chance,' said Abraham. 'I've 'eard you.'

'I was not talking to *you*.' She didn't even bother to look at Gwilym's grandfather as she said it.

'No, but *I'm* talking to *you*. If your hands worked as much as your mouth and did something to help us, why, we'd have a field full of veggies in no time.'

'Grancher,' Gwilym warned in a low voice.

'Don't *Grancher* me. I know you're thinking that she could make trouble for you and your da. But if she tries that, I'll be reporting her to the manager, who sits over the likes of Edgar Williams.'

Esther chose to ignore the taunt, returning her attention to Anwen. 'As for *you*, setting yourself up as leader here, doing things above your station…'

'Elizabeth put me in this position,' Anwen countered.

'Elizabeth!' Esther pushed her face towards Anwen's. There were beads of sweat on her high forehead. 'It's "Miss Meredith" to the likes of you, you impertinent skivvy!'

On the hillside, the men had stopped to watch the performance below. Anwen stepped backwards from Esther's intrusive presence and the whiff of her cheap perfume. 'You know, Mrs Williams, for all your words about doing things for the war effort, you are doing nothing whatsoever.'

'I'm a Guardian!'

'With little to be guardian of, as far as I can see. You make up trouble so you can supposedly put it right. Perhaps you should use your *status* to do something about the scout master, make sure no other boys in his company go off to enlist. You're lucky your Christopher was ill and didn't go with the other boys.'

'*He* wouldn't have been so daft.'

'But his name was on the letter,' said Gwilym.

'That's what that foolish mother of yours said. It's rubbish.'

Gwilym threw his hands up. 'I saw the note.'

'And you forget, my poor Daniel has gone, and such a weight it is on a mother's heart.' She screwed up her face in pain, placing her hand on her chest.

Anwen might have had a little sympathy for her if she hadn't suspected Esther of play-acting to garner sympathy. 'Evan, Gwilym and the others are only fifteen and sixteen.'

'It's their families' fault,' Esther concluded with a firm nod of the head. 'In my household we have boundaries and we maintain discipline.'

'Is that so?' said Abraham. 'My pal Peter heard a right to-do coming from your house five days since. Said it sounded like the war had come to Dorcalon.'

Esther was silenced for some moments before snapping into a stretched pose, making her taller than the old man. 'Yes, I heard it too. It was next door. I have no idea what that was about.' With this, she popped up her parasol and tottered off back down the path, her body leaning forward so much that it was likely she would topple over at any moment.

When she was out of earshot, Abraham said, 'Like hell it was. Sorry, begging your pardon, Anwen.'

'Don't worry, Mr Owen. She'd make the pastor's wife swear, that one.'

'Whatever was going on at that house probably has no bearing on my brother and the other boys going missing,' said Gwilym.

But Anwen was not so sure.

–

Idris dragged his frame along West Street, carrying his jacket and waistcoat along with his food and drink tins. Today was the summer solstice, but summer still hadn't really got going. Fifty-four degrees, Twm Bach reckoned it said on his thermometer. Yet it might as well have been a heatwave as far as his body was concerned. He was heading home on a different route to his usual one, taking advantage of the alleyways that wove their way through Dorcalon, glad of their shelter from the rest of the world. His father had taken the normal route, announcing he was going to stop off for his usual baccy.

He'd got to the end of the alley between the terraces of Islwyn Street and was now faced with the field of vegetables and the labour force there, around half a dozen women. A couple of women spotted him from the middle and waved eagerly. He lifted his hand briefly in response, keeping his head down.

He skirted the field on the right, gathering speed along the soil path. It was too early for Anwen to be there, but he glanced around anyway. Violet was at the top of the field. Her children skipped around each other nearby, the younger of the two wobbling as he went. Violet waved and called but he didn't catch what she said.

Before he crossed the road, he spotted Miss Meredith beyond Violet. She shouted something to him, which again he failed to hear. Beside her, Anwen straightened herself, waving as the others had done, catching him off-guard. Joy filled every corner of him. It lasted several seconds before despair swallowed it up and he was possessed once more of his usual melancholy.

Why was he attracting so much attention? He didn't want to stop to find out.

He took the alley up to the back gardens. Relieved to hug the end house's shadow, he moved more slowly now. Rounding the corner he stopped, juggling his jacket, waistcoat and tins to enable him to reach his handkerchief in his pocket and mop his brow. His whole body was bathed in perspiration. A few more steps along he leant against the high fence of the nearest house for a brief respite. He was bone tired. Even the examiner's job wearied him beyond normal levels these days.

All seemed normal as he entered his back garden, yet he was ambivalent about moving forward, in the same way he had been six months back, on a cold, wet afternoon, newly arrived from the camp at Winchester.

Don't be so bloody daft, mun. Opening the back door released the sound of his mother singing in the kitchen beyond. It was the same song she'd been singing half a year ago. History was indeed repeating itself. He glanced behind, convinced he'd see the November rain and find he had imagined the intervening months.

Breathing deeply, he marched through the scullery, pulling open the ajar door to the kitchen. His mother, leaning over the range, straightened her back, beaming. 'Idris, *bach*, look who's back.'

His attention was drawn to the hunched figure at one end of the table.

'Jenkin!'

–

Anwen was working with more zeal now than she had been earlier. Even though Mrs Meredith's trip out that afternoon had given her and Elizabeth the opportunity to work on the allotment, a drop in her mood had initially robbed her of her usual enthusiasm. Jenkin's return had lifted her up, doubly so because she knew how happy it would make Idris, and now Isaiah, who they'd spoken to before he disappeared up the alley.

Tom's appearance on the field barely two minutes later made only a slight dent in her brighter frame of mind, though she had done her best to avoid him since the day of Polly Coombes's visit to the house.

'Elizabeth's over there,' she told Tom, without greeting him or waiting to see what he wanted.

'I've come to see you. Where can I help today?'

'There's work to be done on the allotment on Edward Street.'

'I'd much rather be here with you.'

Anwen didn't reply straight away. How rude could she be to Tom without overstepping the mark? 'If you want to be useful, it's the other field that needs more people.'

He put on his *little boy lost* expression, the bottom lip protruding. 'In that case, please say you'll accompany me to the theatre on Saturday night. I can borrow the motorcar so we can drive there in style and—'

'Did you take Polly to the theatre?'

He looked abashed, but also a little amused. 'Polly was a simple girl. She wouldn't have appreciated the culture.'

'You talk of her as if she's dead.'

'To us she is. She's gone to an aunt in Surrey, I believe.'

'So she's been paid off, pushed away to be forgotten about.'

Tom glanced nervously around. 'Do we have to speak of this? It's not your concern.'

She realised she was starting something that could get her into a great deal of trouble with her employers should Tom report it back. Yes, they'd consider this whole incident none of her concern, but she was riled enough not to care what they thought at this moment. 'You are unbelievable, Thomas Meredith. If you don't stop bothering me, I will tell your parents. I'm sure they wouldn't want to deal with another incident like that with Polly.'

'Please, Anwen, you don't understand.'

'Oh yes, I understand all right.' She noticed Violet move a little closer, so lowered her voice. 'All you're after is the latest shiny thing. You are spoilt and need to grow up and do something useful instead of pretending you're still ill.' Despite her determination, her hands were sweating with anxiety. Her mouth was dry, making the words difficult to say.

Tom chuckled, which irritated her even more. 'I'm used to women speaking their minds, and that's how it should be. My sister has certainly drilled that into me.'

How could he take it so lightly? 'This isn't funny.'

'No, you're right. But as for my illness, I'm not completely well.'

'Of course you are! Even fifteen-year-old boys are running off to enlist and do their bit. So what are *you* going to do, Thomas Meredith?'

'Who knows, perhaps I will enlist.'

'What, when it's all over? In the meantime, maybe you could help in the next field.'

The jocular grin had finally left his face. 'Yes, I can do that.' He marched swiftly in the direction of Edward Street.

That was the only way to deal with him, directly and with firmness. Perhaps he'd stop bothering her now.

Anwen's sense of relief was short-lived when she spied three figures striding up Alexandra Street. Even at a distance Anwen could recognise the tall, thin silhouette of Harries the Police. With him were PC Probert and an even older policeman. She watched with growing unease as they got closer.

–

Idris threw the clothes and tins down on a chair. 'You daft bugger, what the devil do you think you've been playing at?'

Jenkin ducked down, covering his head with his hands.

'Idris! Hush your cursing. Your brother's home and that's cause for celebration, not harsh words.'

Jenkin peeped through his arms. 'I'm sorry, Idris. Mam told me how you all searched for me, especially you.'

The heat fizzled out of Idris's anger. Jenkin was pale, thin in the face, as if he hadn't eaten for days. 'Where did you go?'

'We went to Tredegar first, to enlist, but got sent away. We spotted Pastor Richards there so went to the Ebbw Vale office, thinking it was less likely someone would recognise us. They turned us away too.'

Ebbw Vale: he hadn't thought to go there.

'You left six days ago. Where have you been staying?'

Jenkin pulled his arms round his body. He looked like a five-year-old again, who'd fallen over but was trying not to cry. Idris felt fiercely protective towards him.

'We used a bit of money we'd saved from doing jobs, bought a bit of bread, slept in the woods, but it wasn't that warm. When the money ran out we had a whole day without any food. Didn't want to come home for a telling off, see. Then Cyril ate some berries and was sick.'

'You fool, Jenkin, you fool.' Idris scooped his brother up from his seat and hugged him, covering him with a sooty film. 'Don't you ever do anything like that again, you hear, *bach*.'

The back door opened and a voice called, 'Hello!', before Isaiah ran into the kitchen, throwing his hands up with joy. 'Jenkin, you're home!'

Idris let his brother go seconds before he was scooped up once more, this time by his father.

'Anwen and Violet ran to tell me as I approached the Institute.'

That must have been what they were trying to convey to him, Idris realised.

Isaiah held onto Jenkin, unwilling to let him go. 'What's for tea, Meg?' he called out, clearly excited by his son's return.

'Mainly vegetable stew with just a little cheap ham, but at least the veggies will be good. Home grown in Dorcalon.'

'It'll have to do for a celebration. And I am mighty hungry, especially now.'

'The bucket of water's boiling for the bath. Now put the poor boy down before he needs another wash. He's already had one today.'

'I'll get the tub in,' said Idris. His step was lighter than it had been for months as he entered the scullery. Could he be coming out of the despair he'd been plunged into with his discharge? Jenkin disappearing had given him a new perspective on what was important in life.

There was a hefty knock at the front door that he heard from the scullery as he dragged the bath along the floor. It would be neighbours and friends, sharing their relief at Jenkin's arrival home.

He had the bath almost at the kitchen door when Isaiah entered, his face solemn. 'Leave that, *bach*, and come in here. Harries the Police wants to speak to you. Cadoc Beadle's been attacked.'

Chapter Twenty-Two

'But you don't deny you were at Mafeking Terrace two days ago.'

'No, I've told you that.' Idris shifted uncomfortably on the kitchen seat. Sergeant Harries was sitting opposite him, taking notes.

Constable Probert stood in front of the fireplace, bouncing awkwardly on his heels. Meg and Isaiah positioned themselves by the front room door, his arm around her shoulders. Jenkin had been sent to his bedroom.

'It was tipping it down on Monday. Where were you going?'

'Just to Rhymney and back. Needed to clear my head. My brother had gone missing—'

'Went to enlist, isn't it?'

'That's right. My search for them had got nowhere. I needed to be on my own.'

Harries sat back judging Idris with narrowed eyes. 'In the pouring rain, lad?'

'Why not in the pouring rain?' Meg interrupted with some vehemence.

'Mrs Hughes, if you can't keep quiet, I'll have to ask you to leave,' said Harries.

'This is my house!'

The sergeant ignored her. 'You could easily have made your way up the path between Mafeking Terrace and Gabriel Street, onto Islwyn Street, where Mr Beadle lives.'

'Did this mystery person who claims they saw me on Mafeking Terrace say I did this?'

'No, but the facts add up. You were seen threatening Mr Beadle six days ago, on Thursday fifteenth June. Do you deny it?'

'No. Though *threatening* would be overstating it.'

'His neighbours believed that was the case.'

'I was there as well,' said Isaiah. 'Are you going to question me too, and Gwilym Owen?'

'You weren't seen out by yourself two days ago.'

Isaiah let go of Meg and moved towards the table. 'You only found him this morning. How do you know he wasn't beaten up yesterday?'

'We don't know exactly when he was assaulted,' said Harries. 'I'm weighing up the evidence I have. Mr Beadle is still unconscious in Dorcalon Hospital so can't help us clarify the time. So, Idris, what were you doing before you went for this walk?'

'I went with my mother to visit Enid Rhys.'

Meg cut in with, 'Except that bully Madog wouldn't let us in. If Idris were going to beat anyone up, it'd be that good-for-nothing Madog Rhys!'

'Mam! I'm not about to beat *anyone* up. You're not helping.'

'Now there's a point,' said Meg. 'It's Madog who's capable of beating Cadoc Beadle up.'

Sergeant Harries surveyed her with interest. 'And what reason would he have for doing that?'

'Because he's a tyrant who hits his girls and terrorises his wife. Have you ever questioned him on how his wife fell down the stairs?'

'I'm here to investigate an assault on Cadoc Beadle, not Mrs Rhys.' He studied Idris once more. 'You blamed Beadle for encouraging the lads to sign up, according to the neighbours.'

'Yes, I think he was partly responsible. It's not something that would encourage me to assault him though.'

'What *would* encourage you to assault him?'

Idris tapped his fingers on the table in rhythm, biting his lip. He was tired of going over and over the same points.

'You had training to fight at the camp. Kinmel Bay then Winchester, wasn't it?' said Harries.

'Yes, but with guns, not bloody fisticuffs. And even the guns were props most of the time.' Idris got up and stood behind his chair.

'Mind your language, lad. And sit down.'

He leant over the table instead. 'You know what I was discharged from the army for? How did they put it? *Not likely to become an efficient soldier.* I have a rapid heartbeat and I tire easily.' He hated to admit it but at least he might use it now to his advantage.

'You're a coal hewer though, aren't you?'

'I was. I'm an examiner now. Mr Meredith found me a job that wasn't so arduous.'

'That was nice of him.' He didn't quite sound like he meant it. 'Was this because of your intended, who works for the Merediths?'

'She is *not* my intended anymore.' How did Harries even know these things?

'Calm down, lad. You've quite a temper on you, haven't you?'

'You'd be angry too if you were being accused of something you hadn't done, and after several days of worrying about your brother.'

'I think we've done as much as we can here,' concluded Harries. 'Probert?' He nodded to his colleague, who nodded back.

Idris breathed out a long sigh of relief. He couldn't take much more of this.

'Come along, then.' The constable was trying to take his arm.

Idris nudged it aside. 'What do you mean?'

Sergeant Harries brushed some dust off his uniform. 'We're taking you along to Rhymney for questioning.'

'But you've already questioned me.'

Meg surged forward, jabbing Harries in the chest. 'You can't take him. He's not done anything!'

'You can prove that, can you? And I wouldn't poke me again else I'll be taking you to the station for assaulting a policeman.'

'Some policeman you are! Can't even find the people who wrecked the allotments, or the people stealing from the grocery vans. You're a disgrace!'

Isaiah took her arm, leading her away to the edge of the room.

'Very wise, Mr Hughes,' said Harries. 'We wouldn't want any more trouble, would we?'

'Oh there'll be trouble all right, once Beadle wakes up and tells us who really assaulted him,' said Isaiah. 'Then we'll see who's in trouble.'

'Handcuff him, Probert. Then take him out.'

'There's no need for that, I'm not resisting,' said Idris.

'Do it anyway,' said Harries. 'Then join Pugh outside.'

Idris held up a hand and Probert cuffed it, placing the other cuff round his own wrist. A moment of panic engulfed him, causing a kind of claustrophobia born from there being no escape. But he couldn't let himself start thinking like that if he was going to keep his sanity in the next few hours.

Probert led him outside to meet another constable. Several neighbours had gathered on the street, along with a number of people who weren't neighbours. Idris started sweating once more as his heart pumped harder. Soon the whole village would know. He might even lose his job at the mine. Edgar Williams would have a field day. When Harries joined them, they set off on the journey to Rhymney police station. The gawkers, as he thought of them, pointed, whispered and tutted.

A shrill holler had everyone looking back at the house, agape. Idris and the policemen spun round to see Jenkin leap onto the street, face infused with blood, shouting, 'Leave my brother alone, you bastards!' in a voice that hadn't quite found its adult pitch.

Isaiah was quick on his heels, pulling him back into the house. Some in the crowds clucked their disapproval of Jenkin's language. *What do you expect? He's out of control, running away like that.* Others shouted variations on, *leave them be, hasn't the family suffered enough?*

The last person Idris noticed was Anwen, her expression filled with... what? Horror? Disgust? He looked away, not wanting to dwell on her reaction.

–

Anwen's first instinct was to run after Idris and the police, ask where they were taking him and why. Sense prevailed: it wouldn't help. She watched Isaiah, still trying to drag Jenkin indoors while answering people's questions. Meg spotted her and ran over.

'Anwen, I'm so glad I've seen you. *O Duw!* What's to become of my poor Idris?' She burst into tears.

Anwen placed her arms around Meg, clutching her small body to her own. 'Have they arrested him for Cadoc Beadle's assault?'

'Yes! Oh, my poor boy. Someone reported seeing Idris on Mafeking Terrace on his own two days ago, and now they're saying it must be him what did it.'

'What about the other boys' families?' said Twm Bach, coming up beside them. 'Have they questioned them? I bet they haven't. Just an easy target, is Idris.'

'You're right, Twm, you're right,' cried Meg.

Anwen led Meg, the woman who'd been for years her future mother-in-law, back to her front door, bestowing a series of comforting phrases in response to her repeated laments. As they were about to enter, they were approached by Elizabeth.

'Is there anything I can do to help? The motorcar is at your disposal.'

'That is so kind of you, Miss Meredith,' sobbed Meg. 'Anwen, please, would you go to Rhymney police station and find out what's happening? Be a character witness. Do *some*thing?'

'I'm not sure what I can do. I wasn't there when he was at Mafeking Terrace.'

'I wish I knew who'd told them that. Just troublemakers!'

'Perhaps we could find out,' Elizabeth suggested. 'I'll take Anwen in. We'll see what can be done.'

Meg grabbed her hand while still clinging to Anwen. 'Thank you, Miss Meredith.'

Isaiah came to the door to bring his wife in as she explained in a rapid babble Anwen and Elizabeth's mission.

Anwen considered her old skirt and blouse, spattered with soil. 'I'll have to change first, if that's all right?'

'So will I. I'll bring the motorcar to your house in around forty minutes. Or would you rather meet me on the main road?'

'The sooner we get to Rhymney, the better. So yes, bringing the motorcar to the house will be fine, thank you.'

-

At the police station in Rhymney they had to wait twenty minutes before Sergeant Harries appeared at the front desk.

'Jones, you didn't tell me it was Miss Meredith who had asked for me.'

The policeman on the desk looked up at the two women, apparently none the wiser as to who that was. That Anwen hadn't figured in Harries' statement didn't surprise her in the least.

'How can I help you, Miss Meredith?'

'*Miss Rhys* and I have come to find out what has become of Mr Idris Hughes, who you arrested this afternoon.'

The sergeant scratched his ear. 'Well Miss, it's not long ago we brought him in, so there's a good deal of questioning to do yet.'

'And I understand the only evidence you have is that one person saw him walking down Mafeking Terrace two days ago. Is that right?'

'Weren't any other people there, as far as we could tell.'

'Except the person who reported seeing Mr Hughes, of course.'

This hadn't occurred to Anwen. She was so glad Elizabeth had accompanied her as it was clear she was going to be much better at cross-examining the sergeant.

'It most certainly wouldn't have been them.'

'How can you be sure?' said Anwen.

When he failed to reply, Elizabeth said, 'Miss Rhys asked you a question.'

'Because... because they are an upstanding member of the community.'

'So is Idris Hughes,' said Anwen. 'He's never before been in trouble with the police.'

'He was seen threatening Cadoc Beadle. He's also been known to argue with Edgar Williams and threaten Madog Rhys.'

'Madog Rhys is my father, as I'm sure you are aware. And the only time Idris has used any threatening language towards him was when he suspected him of hitting me and my sister.'

'Idris Hughes hit you and your sister?'

'That is not what Miss Rhys said,' said Elizabeth, getting impatient. 'I was present at that incident, before Christmas. I saw Mr Rhys raise his hand to Sara, a sick girl. Mr Hughes came on the scene and rightly told Madog Rhys that there would be consequences if he raised his hand again.'

'I see.' Sergeant Harries pondered this for a while, rubbing his chin. 'Not good, hitting an ill child, and that's all Sara ever was, as I recall. But that doesn't have any bearing on what's happened here.'

'Have you interviewed the other families whose boys went missing?' said Elizabeth.

'They all have alibis for the whole period of time in which the attack could have happened. Idris Rhys is the only person without one for part of that time.'

Their reasoning was weak, but Anwen could see no point in carrying on the argument, Elizabeth, however, had other ideas. 'My understanding is that Mr Beadle lives on Islwyn Street. That isn't Mafeking Terrace.'

'It's only one street up from there, Miss, easy enough to divert off up the path.'

'And he was seen doing this?'

Manager's daughter or no manager's daughter, the sergeant's brief huff of breath made it obvious he'd had enough. 'I cannot discuss this with you anymore, Miss Meredith, as it's still under investigation by the police here. And I'm due back in Dorcalon.'

'Very well. I will have to speak to my father about this. It's difficult enough keeping men working in the mine to provide the coal needed, without them being arrested with no real evidence.' Elizabeth tapped her umbrella on the ground, bringing a full stop to the proceedings. She marched straight out.

Anwen glanced from Harries to Elizabeth's retreating back. Harries trudged away next, giving her no option but to follow Elizabeth out onto the High Street. It was busy, the Rhymney occupants bustling around the pavements, where it had started to rain.

'I'm sorry we've had a wasted journey,' said Anwen.

'On the contrary, I think it was very informative.'

'You do?' Anwen went over the conversation in her mind, not able to pull out anything of much use.

'It's regretful I had to bring my father into it, but sometimes using his position is useful in getting things sorted out. At least, I hope it will make the police more vigilant in their investigation. It worries me that Idris is simply a scapegoat.'

'I worry what being locked up will do to Idris. He's not well as it is, and terribly down with it.'

281

Elizabeth put her umbrella up, sharing it with Anwen. 'Don't worry my dear, I'm sure it won't be for long.'

However long or short, Anwen feared it would have a detrimental effect on Idris and pull him even further away from her.

Chapter Twenty-Three

Anwen stepped with relief from the rain into her warmer scullery. At work, Tom had been out all day, rescuing her from the awkward situation of having to ignore him, or worse, having to talk to him so as not to appear rude in front of the family. She had not seen Elizabeth either. Mrs Meredith had gone out just before noon, highly irritated.

Mamgu had not called from the kitchen as she normally did. She must be upstairs with Mam. She'd go up and keep them company for a while before having a bite to eat and getting ready for chapel this evening. The choir were practising for a forthcoming *gymanfa ganu*. She loved singing the sacred hymns in these festivals. Through all these thoughts was laced the worry over Idris. What if the scout master never woke up? What if he woke up and remembered nothing? Whatever the outcome, this was no time for faintheartedness.

When she reached the hall, two things happened at the same time. Someone knocked at the door and another person clattered downstairs. Her father, dressed in a smart shirt, waistcoat and jacket, with ironed trousers, stood by the newel post. That the whole ensemble was new was odd in itself. Where had he got it and where would he be going in it?

'Answer the bloody door, then. Don't stand there gawping at me.'

Anwen did as she was ordered, recognising Hywel's silhouette through the glass before unlatching the door.

'What the hell do you want?' Madog shouted.

'I've come to see my sister.' Hywel's retort was as barbed.

'I don't care anyway. I'm going out. You can do what the hell you like.' He picked up a cap from the hatstand and slapped it on his head.

Hywel squeezed his body against the wall to allow Madog's bulk to pass, yet he was still treated to an elbow in the stomach. He made a protest call of, 'Watch it!'

'Shut your yap,' was Madog's closing comment as he escaped through the door and banged it shut.

'His manners get worse,' said Hywel. He hung a worn-out jacket on the stand, revealing a collarless cream shirt tucked roughly into dark brown trousers patched at the knees. 'How are you then, *cariad*?'

'Better for seeing you. I was about to go up to Mam. Would you like a cup of tea?'

'Maybe later. I'll come up with you first. I heard about Idris. Terrible business. Don't think for a moment he did it.'

Enid was sitting up in bed, staring out of the window. She didn't move until Anwen said, 'Mam?'

Enid released a heavy sigh. 'I'm glad you're back. Oh, and Hywel. There's lovely.'

'Where's Mamgu?'

'Your father sent her packing. Came in here, he did, and told her to get out. She argued but he got aggressive, so she went.'

Anwen sat at the bottom of the bed. 'Has he been pestering you in any way?'

'Just going on and on about Idris beating up Cadoc Beadle and what a lucky escape you had.' Her chin drooped onto her chest.

'Idris didn't beat him up, I'm sure.'

'No. But your father was as pleased as Punch about it, saying it was fair retribution for jilting his daughter. *His* daughter, as if I played no part in your existence.'

Hywel stared out of the window. 'Talking of Cadoc Beadle and the scouts who tried to enlist, Isaiah told me that Christopher Williams's name was on that list in Jenkin's letter, but that he didn't go in the end.'

'No, Christopher's been ill, apparently,' said Anwen. 'Though Esther claims he was never going to go in the first place.'

'Ill, is it? Whatever he's had he must have passed it onto Edgar. Not been in work these past two days, he hasn't. Been so much better without him strutting around, harassing the men about filling more trams, as he has been recently. If he let them get on with it, maybe they would. Violet reckoned there was a hullabaloo coming from the house as she passed it earlier. Probably Esther fed up with having the old goat under her feet.'

'She's as much an old goat as he is,' said Enid.

Anwen took this information in, trying to recall something similar she'd heard recently. That was it! 'Abraham Owen said his friend heard a row going on there the day that the note was found. When he mentioned it to Esther, she claimed the row was next door.'

'Well, well,' said Enid, brighter now. 'So maybe she did discover that Christopher was planning on enlisting, and the row was about that.'

It all fitted. But how did it help Idris? 'If only he hadn't broken off our engagement, I could have helped him cope with things. Perhaps he wouldn't have been in this trouble now.' The whole situation became too much for her. She placed her forefinger and thumb around her nose, trying to stem the tears.

'Oh *cariad fach*,' said her mother. 'What could you have done when he was determined to finish it?'

'I should have persisted with him!' Even as she said it, she realised it was unlikely to have made a difference. Her desperation to have him back, to help him, had her floundering around to find a solution, any solution.

'We can try to help him now,' said Hywel. 'Though I'm not entirely sure how.'

Anwen lifted her skirt to wipe her eyes. Melting into a soppy, weeping maid was not going to help anybody. 'I'm going to change and go to choir practice.'

'It's a little early, *fach*,' said Enid. 'And you need something to eat.'

'I'll have it when I get back.' She got up from the bed and left them to their own conversation. She needed some time on her own to think things through. Later, she could talk to people at chapel about what happened two days ago, find out if anyone saw or heard anything. First she'd talk to anyone out on the allotments as she passed, see if they had any information.

Closing her front door, Anwen saw two women working on the field opposite, chatting together over crates of vegetables. She was about to join them when she saw Elizabeth advancing from the opposite side. Anwen carried on, meeting Miss Meredith in the middle of the allotment between the cauliflowers and onions.

'Good afternoon,' said Anwen. 'How are you?'

Elizabeth's expression was weary. 'I've had better days, as has my mother. And this so-called summer weather is so depressing. Do you have a few minutes to spare?'

'Yes. Choir practice doesn't begin until quarter to eight. What is it, Elizabeth?'

'When I told Tom I was driving to Tredegar this morning, he asked to accompany me, as he had some business there. When we arrived I left him to it, while I visited the shops and took coffee with Charlotte. When we met up again at twelve he told me he'd been to the recruitment office to enlist.' She swallowed hard. 'He said it was only a matter of time before the doctor discharged him and he'd have no medical exemption.'

Anwen's heart sank. 'Oh Elizabeth, I'm sorry. I'm afraid this may be my fault.'

'How so?'

'That day that Polly Coombes came to the house, I guessed he was paying her off for... well, you know. Tom asked me to the theatre. I refused to go, of course.' She omitted to mention their trip to the cinema and the walk by the river. 'A few days later he asked me again. I told him what I thought of him and suggested he was spoiled and needed to grow up, and said that perhaps he should enlist as he seemed well enough now. Especially as even fifteen-year-old boys were willing to fight for their country.'

Elizabeth lowered her voice even though the other women were too far away to hear. 'So you know the story of Polly Coombes. That is unfortunate.'

'I saw her condition. Tom realised I'd overheard them. He can't just go around putting girls in the family way, then move onto the next. Don't get me wrong, Elizabeth, I have no interest in a relationship with him, but that is not the point.' She wanted to make sure Elizabeth didn't suspect any romantic interest on her part. She shuddered at the thought. To think she'd once found him so charming.

'I see. You deduced that Tom was the father, then.' A little relief came into her face. She was perhaps thankful he wasn't telling all and sundry. 'I wouldn't blame yourself for him signing up. Tom does as he wants. And you were right. As much as I hate that so many are being sent to their deaths, he has idled for too long. He expects money and acts in an undignified fashion. I'm sure he'll pass the medical now. Our mother, of course, is distraught. So, here I am, escaping Mama's weeping and wailing, ready to lose myself in horticultural pursuits. I don't suppose there's any news about Idris.'

'No. He's still at Rhymney police station. And Mr Beadle still hasn't regained consciousness the last I heard.'

'Oh dear, what's to be done?'

'I thought I might talk to people here, and at the choir this evening. See if they heard or saw anything.'

'It can't hurt, can it? The police don't seem eager to find anyone else who might be responsible. Good luck, Anwen.'

'Thank you. And I am sorry about Tom.'

Both their smiles were strained as they parted company and went their separate ways.

While washing up after her morning break the next day, Anwen hit on an idea. Why didn't she visit Cadoc Beadle in hospital? She only had Sergeant Harries word for it that he hadn't woken up, repeated again when she'd come across him this morning on the way to the Big House.

All day she listened out for the chimes of the grandmother clock as she went about her business. She was thrilled when, at five-thirty, Mrs Meredith announced she could leave early. They were dining out with friends that evening, a 'last supper' as she put it. Tom was due to leave for training the next day.

By half past six she had arrived at the hospital and was speaking with Ellie Campbell, the staff nurse. Anwen had changed into her Sunday best, complete with her coat and a small, flat-brimmed hat she'd borrowed from her mother.

'You've come to visit Mr Beadle, is it?' said the nurse, retying the long white apron she wore over her blue dress. 'There's nice. He's only had two brief visits from the police so far. You're Anwen Rhys, aren't you, from the allotments? Are you a relative of Mr Beadle's?'

Anwen was afraid this might be a stumbling block. 'No, but my brothers were scouts in his troop. They had a great admiration for him and always said he treated the boys kindly. I want to repay the favour, knowing he has no family in Dorcalon.' She hoped this would satisfy Nurse Campbell.

'How very kind. He's this way.' She led Anwen down a corridor and into a room with six beds, three on each side, all occupied. The tang of carbolic and iodine caused Anwen to wrinkle her nose. Someone was snoring softly. At the end of one row Cadoc Beadle lay on his back, eyes closed, devoid of his usual round spectacles. One eye was tinted purple and green. The other had a cut across the eyebrow. There were other bruises to his face and a cut on his chin that had partly healed.

'He hasn't been very receptive so far, but talking to him might help. It often does.'

Anwen sat in the chair indicated by the nurse, who promptly left to attend to a man calling from the opposite side of the ward.

'Hello Mr Beadle. It's Anwen Rhys. My brothers, Geraint and Tomos, used to be in your scout troop. They used to enjoy their evenings in the hall.' On and on she went, talking of the activities she remembered them doing.

From the ward door, Nurse Campbell smiled encouragement at her before leaving. Anwen amazed herself with what she could find to say once she got started. At one point she stopped, sure she'd heard a soft grunt from Mr Beadle, carrying on when nothing further occurred. Half way through an account of Tomos getting caught up in knots when he tried practising the ones he'd been taught, there was a disturbance on the other side of the door. Anwen took no notice of the raised voices at first, convinced the scout master's eyes had twitched. As she leaned over to check at closer quarters for further movement, two figures burst through the door: the nurse and Esther Williams.

Mrs Williams, pushing the nurse away, hurried down the ward to Cadoc's bed.

'Why are you here comforting him, you stupid girl?'

Anwen sprang up, an urge to do battle strong after the rude interruption. 'I am here, Mrs Williams, because no one else is and someone should be, to hear what Mr Beadle has to say about his assailant when he awakes.'

'We all know it was Idris Hughes.'

'But it wasn't him.'

'I saw him myself, bold as brass, on Mafeking Terrace that Monday afternoon. Angry as the devil, he was.'

'So you're this so-called *upstanding member of the community* who reported him?' She should have known.

'My husband told me it was the right thing to do, to come forward.'

'Because he hates Idris. But Idris would never do this. And did you actually see him go up to Mr Beadle's house then?'

'I don't care about Cadoc Beadle and what happened to him or who did it! It serves him right, is what I say.' The genteel edge that normally coated Mrs Williams's accent was gone. In its place was a strong Valley's inflection which became increasingly high pitched. 'His stoopid posturing about patriotism and the war has driven my poor Christopher away. He went overnight. Yes, to enlist who knows where! You said his name was on Jenkin Hughes's letter, so it's his fault too. Of course, it would be him, brother of that detestable Idris.'

'That is enough, Mrs Williams,' said Nurse Campbell. 'I have patients here who need peace and quiet.'

'So you did know he intended to go before,' said Anwen.

'We found his note and stopped him. Locked him in his room, we did.'

That's what the *to-do*, as old Mr Owen had put it, had been about, and the argument Violet heard. 'So he wasn't ill.'

'I must insist you take this argument outside the hospital please.' Nurse Campbell's voice had become more insistent.

'Don't worry, I'm leaving,' said Esther. 'It's enough to see he's still unconscious. With any luck he'll *never* wake up.' She marched away, back down the ward.

Before she reached the door, a deep male voice from one of the beds called, 'That's it, bugger off you old bitch,' the last word descending into a hacking cough.

Esther halted by the door briefly before swinging it open and leaving.

'Really, Mr Jones!' said the nurse to the wayward patient. 'I'm sorry, Miss Rhys, but I'll have to ask you to leave. My patients have been disturbed enough today.'

'Of course, I quite understand.'

Nurse Campbell accompanied her back down the corridor. 'Such a bad business with the boys and Mr Beadle. I'm so glad there is someone who cares about finding out what really happened. I'm told the police have not made many enquiries.'

'No, because they've arrested an innocent man whose only crime was to be seen in a nearby street when it's possible Mr Beadle was attacked.'

'That's what I understood from my neighbours, who are friends with the Owens. I know they don't believe it either.'

At the reception Anwen said, 'Thank you for letting me see Mr Beadle.'

'You're welcome. Good luck, Miss Rhys. And if I can, I'll let you know when Mr Beadle wakes up.'

'Would you? Thank you so much.'

Anwen left the hospital, strolling up Station Road to the centre of the village. She came up short, just before reaching the McKenzie Arms, struck by a notion.

Hywel had said Edgar Williams had been off sick. It had been three days now. In fact, his going off sick must have roughly coincided with the time Beadle was assaulted.

She hurried off, not to chapel, but to find Hywel and Gwilym.

–

Anwen was having second thoughts, standing outside the Williams's home, Uncle Hywel banging on the door. They should have gone to get Sergeant Harries first, told him of their suspicions. Yet… Anwen wasn't even sure she could put into words her deep-seated misgiving. The police hadn't been terribly helpful around here lately.

'Do you think they're out?' said Hywel.

'No,' said Gwilym. 'I saw the curtain twitch. Perhaps we'll leave it and tell Harries.'

'No!' said Anwen. 'I want some answers and I think we'll get them here.'

'I agree,' said Hywel. 'There's something fishy going on in this village, and this attack on Beadle is connected.'

Anwen pushed past the men, knocking ten times, then repeated it. Passing people had started to gather round the gate. A couple next door on one side peered over from their path.

Anwen heard the door creak and watched it slowly open to reveal Esther, sporting a velvet jacket and a large-brimmed hat with a feather. 'What do you lot want?' Her imitation of Margaret Meredith had been restored. 'I'm due out on my rounds as Guardian. I have to do these despite my poor Christopher having gone missing. And I have no wish to speak to any of *you*.'

'That's all right,' said Anwen, 'because we've come to speak to your husband.'

'He's not here.'

'The hell he isn't,' Hywel snapped. 'He's been off work three days, ill with the flu we've been told. So why would he be out?'

'He – he's at the hospital.'

'No he isn't,' said Anwen. She barged past Esther, who, not expecting it, stumbled out of the way easily.

Gwilym called, 'Anwen!' but followed her in with Hywel regardless.

Edgar wasn't hard to track down, sitting in the kitchen as he was, slumped on the table. It soon became apparent why. He lifted his head, bleary-eyed, trying to focus on them. On the table beside him was a bottle of whisky, three-quarters empty.

Esther scurried in behind them, shouting, 'How dare you barge into my house! I'll tell Sergeant Harries, you see if I—'

'Oh shut up, woman,' said Williams.

'Have you drunk all that today?' asked Hywel.

'Upset he is, about our Christopher going,' said Esther. 'I told him, he should be out there searching for him.'

'Shut your trap, else you'll get a taste of these, too.' Edgar lifted his hands, balled into fists. They were covered in faded green bruises. There was also one on his chin.

'So it was you who assaulted Cadoc Beadle,' said Anwen. 'And it looks like he tried to fight back.'

'No, of course he didn't,' said Esther. 'Got those hitting the door in frustration when Christopher left.'

'But you told Anwen he'd only just gone last night,' said Hywel. 'Those bruises are older than that.'

'Exactly!' said Esther. 'Our son went last night, but Beadle was assaulted a week back. So Edgar wouldn't have had *any* excuse to attack him.'

A good point, thought Anwen, yet… 'But Christopher tried to leave to sign up before. So he could have assaulted him for giving him the idea.'

'No, no, no!' Esther's voice became ever more piercing with each word.

Edgar wobbled to his feet clumsily, knocking over the chair next to his. His knees buckled before he managed to right himself and he made a grab for the table for support. 'Of course I beat up Beadle,' he slurred.

'No you didn't!' Esther screeched. 'You're drunk and confused.'

'I did it all right, and I'm proud of it. He should pay for encouraging boys to enlist. Bloody war, taking my men, my Daniel, trying to take Christopher.' He pointed at Gwilym with difficulty. 'He can take your brother. Don't bloody care about him.'

Esther had dissolved into a snivelling wreck, her shoulders lifting and falling as she gave full rein to the sobs.

Anwen leant across the table from the opposite side, hands firmly planted on it. 'But if you're so proud of it, why have you let an innocent man get arrested for it?'

'Oh yes, that was a bonus. Couldn't believe my luck when the wife told me she'd seen him on Mafeking Terrace, no one else around.' He staggered back a couple of steps, landing with a thump on his chair. 'Soon as word went round Beadle had been found, I got her to go straight away and report seeing Hughes. Harries was only too willing to take the credit for a quick arrest.' He slumped forward and Anwen thought he'd gone to sleep, till he popped up again, confused at first by his surroundings. 'Ah yes, Idris Hughes. Bloody upstart.'

There was a dull thump from above. They all looked up.

'What's that?' said Hywel.

Esther ran to the door, blocking it. 'Nothing, an ornament falling, no doubt.'

'It was a heavy thud, not like an ornament.' Hywel pulled Esther away from the door with difficulty, so determined was she that he wasn't opening it. Once through, he ran up the stairs, Gwilym following on.

Anwen considered Edgar Williams, slumped once more on the table. Esther was crouched on the floor, wailing piteously.

'And you call yourself a Guardian, Esther Williams. The only thing you've been guarding is your husband's crimes.'

Edgar lifted his head. 'Guardian? She's no bloody Guardian. Made it all up, she did.'

'You rotten bastard, Edgar!' Esther's bawling grew louder. Her husband flopped forward onto the table once more.

Neither were likely to be going anywhere soon. Anwen took the chance and headed upstairs.

In the small bedroom, Christopher was lying on the floor. Gwilym and Hywel were untying his hands and feet, bound as they were with a thin rope. Nearby was a piece of looped fabric, still knotted, which had most likely been round his mouth.

'What happened?' said Anwen.

'Christopher fell off the bed to alert us to his presence,' said Hywel. 'He didn't run away at all.'

The boy twisted his wrists back and forth after the relief of their release. His teeth were chattering. 'They caught me packing a bag to run away and locked me in my room. But I heard the neighbours talking outside in the back garden about Mr Beadle. When I saw Da's hands I guessed what he'd done, so he tied me up.'

'*Duw!*' said Gwilym. 'What will that man not stoop to?'

Once Christopher's feet were unbound, Anwen helped him walk around to get the circulation going, though it was more of a limp.

Hywel got up. 'Gwilym, you go downstairs and keep an eye on Williams and his wife. I'm going up to the fire station. They have a telephone there, so I'll get them to ring the police in Rhymney.'

Gwilym nodded, leaving for his guard duty.

'Will you be all right here, *cariad*?' said Hywel.

'Yes, of course. I'll take care of Christopher.'

He left and soon she heard the front door slam.

All right? She was more than all right now she knew Idris would soon be home. It would be like seeing his return from the army all over again.

Except that hadn't worked out well, had it? She let that thought dampen her spirit for only a moment before placing a blanket over Christopher.

Chapter Twenty-Four

Anwen heard of Idris's release from several people while carrying out her afternoon errands for Mrs Meredith the following day. Her shift at the house now over, she rushed to Alexandra Street, practising the speech she'd devised in anticipation of this event. She needed to make more of an effort with him, as she should have done when he first arrived home, instead of accepting a conclusion settled on by him in the midst of melancholy.

She was brought up short halfway down the street. Idris had stepped out of his front door and was walking in her direction. Spotting her he smiled, an occurrence so rare these days she couldn't help but reciprocate. She expected his soon to fade, but instead it got wider, revealing the dimples that were once so often in evidence.

They stopped two feet away from each other.

'Idris, you're home.'

'Thank you, Anwen. Without your quick wits I might still be in prison. My father told me what happened.'

'I'm sorry you were implicated in this awful business at all.'

'It's young Christopher Williams I feel sorry for. He was a decent enough lad, like his brother, Daniel.'

She recalled Daniel's vague interest in her, embarrassed even though there was nothing in it. 'They left Christopher with Esther yesterday and didn't arrest her for her part in the whole drama. She claimed it was Edgar who tied him up and that she was threatened not to say anything. She also insisted she didn't know until after she reported seeing you in Mafeking Terrace that Edgar had assaulted Mr Beadle. They've taken her word for it.'

'Aye, so I gather. Has Beadle woken up yet?'

'Not the last I'd heard. People have been known to be in a coma for weeks, months or even years. I looked it up at the library.'

He seemed to ponder this awhile. 'Were you going to the allotment?'

'Not in these clothes,' she laughed. 'I was coming to see how you are.'

'That was kind of you. I'm off to the Cottages field. It's time I started helping again. The one benefit of being locked up in a cell is that I've had a rest at least.'

'You do have a bit more colour than you have had of late. I'll walk over with you. I'd like to see how things are getting on there.' They set off down the hill. She'd already stopped by briefly on her way home from work, but it was an opportunity to spend more time with him.

'I'm glad you've decided to join in again,' she said. 'The men respond to your leadership.'

'I don't know about that, but I do enjoy it.' He was quiet for a while before he said in a subdued manner, 'I hear Tom Meredith signed up.'

Did he imagine she was proud of Tom for enlisting, and that by comparison, his rejection from the army made him a failure in her eyes? She wanted to enfold him in her arms, to reassure him.

'Oh yes, he signed up. But not out of any sense of duty, more because he knew he wouldn't get away with not doing so for much longer. And because he made a major mistake in his life and thinks he can escape to some "awfully big adventure".' Anwen thought of the copy of *Peter and Wendy* lying beneath her mattress that she'd intended to give Sara last Christmas.

'Peter Pan,' said Idris.

Anwen stopped abruptly, causing Idris to do the same. 'Yes. A lot of the men who signed up voluntarily thought they were heading for an "awfully big adventure". But Peter Pan was talking about *dying*. And sadly that's what many of them are destined for.' It didn't bear thinking about, all the souls already lost to the war, the ones that would be lost before it was finished.

'What mistake did he make? Tom Meredith. Something to do with you?'

'No, nothing to do with me. He did try to woo me a little but I was never really interested. I can't tell you about his mistake because I promised Elizabeth. Please don't tell anyone.' What had possessed her to mention it?

'Of course I won't.'

As they set off once more, Anwen said, 'Tom has little to be proud of. He only ever helped on the allotments half-heartedly. You, on the other hand, have put your whole soul in. You – you're a hero in my eyes… and Gwilym, and the rest of your group on the allotment.' She was aware her steps were speeding up, fuelled by her nerves and eagerness to get her speech out.

'I'm only doing my bit. I could have perhaps done more on the Front.'

Her words weren't having the desired effect on his mood, but instead had wiped away the smile and painted a frown in its place. They passed over the small bridge that spanned Nantygalon, the tiny stream that trickled down to the valley bottom. She tried again.

'Idris, you can do your bit in your own back yard, with the rest of us.'

He made no reply, sticking his thumbs in the top of his trousers, pulling on the braces which were on show, due to him wearing no waistcoat or jacket over the patched clothes fit only for gardening.

They wound their way round the curve in the path to arrive on the road just below the first row of cottages. Anwen took Idris's arm, stopping him going any further.

'I want to ask you something,' she said.

'Go on.'

'Did you break up with me because you really didn't want to be with me anymore, or because you thought yourself inadequate, being discharged from the army? Because if that's the case, I've never thought less of you since you came home. You really tried to do your bit in that way, and I applaud you for it.'

A few seconds elapsed. A combination of sadness and longing inhabited his deep brown eyes. A swell of love flooded her as she waited to be elated or disappointed. His lips slowly parted.

'Anwen! Idris! What wonderful news it was to hear of your release.' Elizabeth was running down the field towards them, attired as a man in her usual gardening fashion.

Anwen glanced back at Idris. His mouth had closed, watching Elizabeth's progress.

The moment was gone.

–

It had been threatening rain all day, the sky low, as Anwen had gone about her work. It wasn't until she reached her front door that it finally broke, like a cloud tipping out its contents. She held her arms out at the sides, letting the drops wash away the dust of the day. Anyone seeing her would have thought her deranged. Everything was topsy-turvy since Idris's return. Before that, even, right back to when Tomos died. People passed on, left, changed personality, raged wars, on and on as everything good, everything beautiful eventually decayed.

Her father had told her to come the front way in future, not round the back, 'bursting in on my business without a by-your-leave', as he put it. She resented that she couldn't enter her own home whichever way she wanted. Furthermore, Cadi was being dismissed every afternoon when he arrived home from his shift, leaving her mother without help or company, the house only half cleaned, and no preparation made for supper.

Often Cadi sneaked back when she knew her son was else-where. Even she had little sway on him now and had told

Anwen she didn't want to make too much fuss in case he banned her from the house altogether.

After less than a quarter of a minute, the rain stopped as quickly as it had started. She shivered in her insubstantial jacket. The temperature today, like most of the summer so far, was nippy. Still she stood there, stuck in time, not wanting to enter the house. She might have remained there, in a dream world, had the door not opened. Madog was in his smart suit once more, apart from the jacket that hung on the hatstand.

'What the bloody hell are you doing?' he hissed. 'I saw you from the window, just standing there. Get in the bloody house.'

She stepped in, removing her jacket. 'I'll just go and change.'

'No you bloody won't. You can get me something to eat. I'm bloody starving.' He went back to the kitchen, sitting at the table expectantly. 'Get me something quick. Eggs and bacon'll do.'

'But that's for breakfast, Da. There's only one slice of bacon and two eggs left.'

'Just bloody get it!'

Her boots squelched to the scullery and back. She turned up her soaked sleeves, wishing she hadn't been so foolish in the rain. Soon she had the bacon sizzling in a pan, along with two eggs, glad for the warmth of the stove. Madog had fetched a knife and fork and was now sitting down, the cutlery held upwards in each hand. He started grumbling in a mixture of Welsh and English, neither of which Anwen could make much sense of.

'Should be given a bloody medal,' was the first phrase she understood.

'Who should, Da?'

'Edgar – bloody – Williams. That's who. Instead of being handed in to the police like a bloody criminal.'

'Da, he *is* a criminal. Not only did he attack Mr Beadle, he tied up his own son and locked him in his room. That's cruel, that is.'

'He bloody deserved it. Would have done the same to Tomos and Geraint if they'd tried that on.'

She flinched, both at the rare mention of their names and his proposed cruelty to his dead sons. And the fact that both would have been old enough to be called up had perhaps slipped his mind.

'Da, don't.'

He propelled himself out of the chair and took three long strides over to her at the stove. His body hovered over her cowering form, far too close and stinking of something that was probably meant to be pleasant, a type of cologne. But he'd put on too much. 'And it's your bloody fault, isn't it? I 'eard about it, you and your uncle and that bloody friend of Idris's. But it was you told the police the whole story you concocted.'

Anwen was aware the bacon and eggs were on the verge of overcooking. There would be hell to pay if that happened, yet she couldn't risk moving. 'I didn't concoct it. I just worked it out and Edgar Williams confirmed it. Told the whole story.'

'Bloody little liar. How're we going to carry on without Edgar? He organises us, he do.'

'I heard one of the surface overmen, John Bowen, was taking over as under-manager.'

'What're you talking about, you stupid cow? Bowen's got nothing to do with this.'

From above them they heard the tapping of the walking stick Hywel had found for Enid, so she could easily draw attention when she needed it. A distant voice called, 'What's going on?'

'That bloody stick,' said Madog. 'That's going on the fire.' His head shot back. 'Shut up you silly cow!'

Anwen glanced at the food again. Soon it would be too late.

'Everything's useless now because of you and Idris. You're useless. Enid's the most bloody useless of all.'

The bacon was browned to a crisp and beginning to burn. The egg yolks were already hard, which Madog hated.

'Da, Mam can't help it if she fell down the stairs.'

He inched closer. 'If she'd done as she was told, she might not have done.'

Had she slipped on something he'd warned her about? No. Wait. Something Hywel had said the night she fetched him, after she knocked her father out... It was there, at the back of her mind, trying to connect with something at the front.

Oh God. No. 'Da, did you push her?'

'You're a bloody liability you are, and too bloody clever by 'alf. You need teaching a lesson.'

Before she could dart out of the way, he'd lifted the pan with the overcooked food and smoking lard, tipping it over her arm.

'Arrrhhhh!' she screamed, running immediately to the scullery.

Bang, bang, bang, went the stick on the ceiling. 'What's going on, what's happening?' came the faint call.

Anwen hurried to the sink, holding her arm under the flowing tap. It wasn't long before Madog followed her into the scullery, expletives dripping from his lips, the frying pan held high.

On the draining board was a bigger pan. If only she could swing it effectively, she could defend herself, as she'd defended Sara that night.

She lunged for the pan, the tap still running, her arm blistering. She clutched hold of it, Madog shouting, 'Oh no you don't!' He swung his pan, meeting hers as she fought back. Each about to swing again, they were halted in their tracks.

An enormous pounding bang made the house vibrate, followed by a slightly smaller one, then a rumble like that of overhead thunder.

Anwen dropped the pan, running to the back door, leaving Madog in the middle of the room. He lowered his pan, terror invading his face. She opened the door, got two steps outside, surprised to find Abraham Owen there.

'Has something happened?' she said.

'Yes, I'm afraid it has.' The colour had drained from Abraham's face.

'Why are you here?'

'I heard screaming coming from your house as I was passing down—'

Madog appeared in the doorway shouting, 'The pit! It's the pit!' He ran from the house, barging past them, disappearing out of the back gate.

'Oh my God,' said Anwen. 'Let's go, let's go.'

'But your arm,' said Abraham. 'And you're soaking wet.'

'Never mind, it doesn't matter.'

She hurried down the path. Abraham followed on. As they went, people ran from their back gates. By the time they'd reached Jubilee Green many others had joined them. Anwen pulled down her sleeve, hiding the raw skin. It smarted dreadfully. She pushed the pain away, not allowing herself to pay it any heed. From the valley bottom there were plumes of smoke. More villagers poured from the side streets.

Soon the call, repeated over and over, was echoing around the village.

There's been an explosion at the pit.

Chapter Twenty-Five

Idris hadn't wanted to do a double shift. He was sick of being underground, where the air was heavy with carbon and dust. Despite it now being July, the weather had not improved much, yet underground it felt more clammy than usual. It was Gwilym's fault. The foreman had extolled the virtues of getting repairs done quickly so they could keep up with the Navy's demand for coal, asking for volunteers. Gwilym had stepped forward, offering the pair of them, nudging Idris to say, 'Always do with a bit of extra money, can't we, mun?'

So here he was, working in the gloom of lamplight, the space beyond his colleagues a deep void. He craved the light and air. He wasn't in the same area as Gwilym, who was working with his father, Earnest, on Hosea Pimm Heading. Idris was currently with Twm Bach and a haulier called Lewis Jones. They were assisting the timberman, Samuel Bevan, who was repairing props on the main roadway. They'd already fixed two areas and were slowly moving along towards the interior of the pit.

'Well, this makes a change from hewing the old black stuff,' said Twm, his toothy smile in stark contrast to his sooty face. 'But of course, you're an examiner now, aren't you, Idris, *bach*? Better for your back that is, with you being so tall.' Twm stood next to him, putting his hand sideways against his forehead and shifting towards Idris. He barely reached Idris's chest.

'Everyone's tall next to you, even my old mamgu,' Lewis joked, bringing his pony round after unhitching him from the truck they'd brought the wood down in. The animal whinnied and threw her head up twice. 'Steady Bessie, steady.'

'She's thinking she should be back at the stable with her pals,' said Idris. 'Not doing double shifts.'

'Aye, but we've all got to make sacrifices in these days of war. I'm sure Jones the Horse will find some extra bits of hay for a pony what's worked well.'

Idris thought about John Jones the ostler, in the stables at the end of this roadway. It must be a peaceful job attending the horses. When he'd first started work, Gwilym's grancher, Abraham, had been ostler here. He'd retired not long after, following a bad bout of influenza.

'Right lads, let's get started,' called Samuel. They all peered at the prop he indicated as he held the lamp. He pointed at Lewis. 'You give me a hand here holding up the light, while I dismantle the rotten piece. Twm, fetch some wood and a saw. Idris, sort out a dozen nails from my bag. And bring two hammers.'

Idris and Twm went together with their lamps, Idris stopping a few feet away from the truck to put his lamp by the cloth bag, thrown on the floor by Samuel when they'd first arrived. He knelt down to sort through it, finding the box with nails quickly. He heard Twm talk to Bessie as he shifted bits of timber.

At first he thought Twm had dropped a piece of wood into the tram, creating the metallic grumble. But the noise continued like a low rumble of distant thunder.

Except he knew it wasn't.

'Explosion!' screamed Idris. 'Get down.' He saw Twm obey immediately as he hit the ground. Idris lay prostrate nearby, his hands covering his head.

'Don't be daft,' said Lewis. 'It's just a shot.'

The last word was barely out of his mouth when a noise like a hurricane rushed down the tunnel and an intense light flashed. Even with his face down, Idris saw it. Stones pelted him and his ears rang with the colossal clang and clatter of something large and metal crashing down to his right.

Then, nothing.

–

'There aren't so many on the night shift, are there?' Anwen asked.

'A lot more than normal.' Abraham's voice cracked with the effort of running. 'Gwilym and Earnest were doing a double. Repairs. And Idris, I think.'

Anwen's heart squeezed tight; she found it hard to catch her breath. As they ran down Jubilee Green, people poured out of houses and down the hill, like lava pouring down the side of a volcano.

There was a clamour of voices getting ever louder, chanting similar anthems of distress. The shopkeepers stood outside their doors, white starched aprons soiled, staring down towards the pit.

They met Isaiah and Meg Hughes coming around the other side of the park, both their faces filled with blind panic.

At the bottom of Jubilee Green, running out from James Street, was Cadi. Anwen stopped, grabbing her grandmother's hands. 'Mamgu, please, would you go to Mam. She'll be wondering what's happened. Da's in a foul mood. Oh, and I left the tap on!'

'Don't worry, *cariad*. I'll sort it all out.'

Anwen watched for a few seconds as Cadi dragged herself up the hill, against the crowd. Carrying on down once more, she dodged those who were slower, catching up Abraham and the others. On they went, an unstoppable wave of bodies congregating at the pit head.

'It's complete Bedlam here,' said Isaiah. 'No one appears to be in charge.'

'Isn't that the new under-manager, John Bowen?' Anwen pointed towards a fair man who was standing in the doorway of Edgar Williams's old office, watching the chaos, his face pale and baffled.

Isaiah tramped over to him, followed by Anwen and the rest. 'Bowen, lad, you need to take charge, mun. Is Mr Meredith around?'

'No, he went home an hour since.'

'I daresay he heard the noise and will be back down. What's happened?'

'I – I don't know. No one does.'

'Then it's about time someone found out. We need to get down there,' said Isaiah.

The under-manager closed his eyes tight, squeezing his whole face up in concentration. On opening his eyes he said, 'First we need to form a barrier – yes, a barrier, and get non-workers to stand behind it.'

Anwen immediately alerted several people, workers above ground, men and women, gathering them into a group. Many knew her because of the allotments, or because they had worked with her on the screens. They formed a line across the yard, pushing gently forward, persuading the families to step back towards the opening. At the same time, there was an abrupt crunching noise. Anwen turned to see four workers appear from the cages, stumbling out, helping each other up. Their already shabby work clothes were tattered. She ran to them, searching their sooty faces for Idris.

He wasn't there.

Bowen snapped into action and gathered the new arrivals quickly into a group, asking what they knew.

One miner, his sleeve blown off, his arm slightly burnt, spoke first. 'We were working near this end of the main roadway, examining the props, when we heard a rumble, then a crack, like lightening. Then a kind of wind came rushing down the tunnel, knocking us off our feet. It was an explosion, mun, I swear it.'

–

Black. So black. Were his eyes open? Idris lifted his head cautiously, placing two fingers to each eye. Yes, definitely open. Gradually he recalled the bang, the rush of sound, the flash of light. Had it blinded him? He spat on the ground several times, ridding his mouth of grit. The old dread of suffocation threatened to overwhelm him, as it had in the early days, until his father had taught him to breathe slowly, to imagine mountains and grass and eternal skies. He'd done this until he no longer needed to.

The air was devoid of sound. He sat up. Which way was east and the exit? A pony whinnied feebly. Twm had been near her when the explosion happened.

'Twm? Twm?'

'Idris.' Twm's voice was weak, chesty. 'Where are you?'

'Where I was when I fell, I suppose… Samuel? Lewis?' There was no response. 'Stay where you are, Twm and keep talking. I'll get you.' Idris put his hand out, grabbing at jagged rock and pit props as he went.

'I can feel the tram next to me. Reckon I had a near miss there. Did you hear it thud onto the ground?'

'Yes. I think I'm near you now.' It wasn't easy to position sound in the tunnels, though at least they were wider here on the main level and he could walk upright. He patted the air until he located Twm's abundant hair, being careful to keep walking in the same direction. 'Can you stand?'

'I think so. Good job you called the warning when you did. Wonder how Samuel and Lewis have fared?'

'Might just be knocked out.' He could hope.

'Idris, Twm, is that you?'

'Samuel?' Idris called.

'Yes.'

'Are you all right?'

'I don't know. There's a hell of a pain in my arm and leg, maybe where I hit the ground. Hang on… I'm sitting up, feeling round for Lewis, but I can't find him. He was next to me. I think we were both blown off our feet.'

'Can you stand?'

'...No.'

'Right. Keep talking and I'll come and find you. Twm, you stay here, in exactly the same spot. That way we'll know which way is towards the exit.'

'All right.'

It took some time, Idris following what he hoped was the direction of Samuel's voice. Beyond that were other sounds now, a faint echo of voices or a low rumble, it was hard to tell. Eventually, he managed to find his way to Samuel. Reaching around the area, he called Lewis's name.

'It's no good,' he concluded. 'If he can't talk we'll never find him without light. Samuel, if I lifted you, could you walk?'

'I could try.'

Four times Idris tried to haul the timberman up, aware his heart was pounding like a hammer on stone. On the fifth try, he got Samuel to his feet. They struggled towards Twm's voice, Samuel limping with the effort to hold some of his own weight. A few steps along, Twm started singing 'Dafydd y Garreg Wen' in his rich baritone voice, surprising from one so small. Idris thought the lyrics, about the composer on his death bed, were a little too close to home in their present situation. But as Twm sang, Idris's determination to get out increased. He still had a life, whether it was long or short, unlike the doomed soul in the song, playing his harp. Whatever the army had said about it not being likely he'd become an efficient soldier, there were things he could do. And one of them was to take good care of his family. Especially Jenkin.

As they reached Twm, Idris said, 'Let's keep going while we remember which direction we're heading. It would be easy to become disorientated and get lost, without the lights. Hold onto my other arm, Twm.' He knocked it against his friend so he'd know where it was.

Nearby, the pony whinnied a mournful lament, her shoed hooves kicking out.

'What about Bessie?' said Twm. 'She must be stuck on her side.'

'Not a lot we can do about her now,' said Idris. 'Not till we can come back with lights.' A draught of foul air brought the stench of rotten eggs and an acidity that arrested his breathing. He coughed, almost retched. Soon the other two were following suit.

'Afterdamp!' gasped Twm.

Idris knew this mixture of noxious gases, left behind after a mine explosion, could be the end of them.

Herbert Meredith arrived at the pit head just before seven-forty, hurrying along with Elizabeth. Anwen had managed to remain inside the cordon, along with Isaiah, Meg and Abraham, grateful to be in a position to get early news. Mr Meredith stopped to speak with the under-manager. Elizabeth, spotting Anwen, darted to her side.

'Anwen. How many have surfaced so far, do you know?'

'Only five. They were near the cage so managed to find their way easily. Their lamps went out. I suppose everyone else's did too. Idris and Gwilym were on a double shift.' Her resolve to stay strong slipped. A deep breath gave her time to strengthen her spirit once more. 'And Gwilym's father.'

'I'm so sorry. Let's pray for their safe return.'

'The lamp tokens left in the lamp room have been counted. There are still sixty-nine missing.' Anwen concentrated on the hopeful families pressing against the human barrier. 'I know we can't join the search parties, but is there anything we can do, rather than just stand here?'

'There's Dr Roberts and Sister Grey. She might be glad of assistance. I will ask.'

Following Elizabeth, Anwen thought she saw her father moving through the crowd this side of the cordon. Yet the man she saw entered the under-manager's office, so it was unlikely it was him.

'Sister Grey,' said Elizabeth, catching up to the middle-aged woman.

'Miss Meredith. Isn't it terrible? Dr Roberts and I are setting up in the lamp room to attend any casualties.'

'Could you do with two assistants?' said Elizabeth.

'Yes. A few more hands would be useful.'

They followed the nurse to a single-storey gabled building a few yards from the cage. Anwen noticed four policemen arrive, including Sergeant Harries and PC Probert. They joined the workers on the cordon, persuading the onlookers to step further back.

In the lamp room, the five men who'd surfaced earlier were sitting on the floor, bedraggled and silent. The wooden shelves lining the brick walls contained those lamps not yet returned. With the men sat Pastor Richards who, for once, appeared lost for words. He jumped up and walked towards them. 'Is there any news?'

'No,' said Anwen. 'But Mr Meredith has arrived. The first rescue party should be going down soon, I think.'

'Thank God.' The pastor put his palms together briefly, looking up. 'Joseph is down there, and him with a new baby.'

Joseph had married Jenny, the maid Anwen had replaced at McKenzie House. 'I'm sorry to hear that, Pastor.'

Sister Grey went about setting up the medical supplies on an empty table. Elizabeth went to help her.

'Have you family down there?' said the Pastor.

'No, but Idris Hughes and Gwilym and Earnest Owen are there.'

'I will pray for them.'

Dr Roberts entered the room. He regarded the wounded miners. 'They're sending the first rescue party down now so we'd better be ready for more casualties.'

Samuel coughed once more, prompting Idris and Twm to come to a halt. Idris was almost carrying him, he was struggling so much. How long had they been walking? It could have been ten minutes, it could have been an hour. He had a momentary twinge of fear. What if they'd turned about at some point without realising, maybe when he reached Twm earlier, and were now heading the wrong way? No way to know, except by carrying on.

'If only we had our tea tins,' said Idris. 'We could have dampened our handkerchiefs and held them to our noses. It would have helped with this stench.' He wrinkled his nose against another wave of fetid gas, then retched a little.

'Aye, but God knows where they got blown to,' said Twm.

'Let's keep moving or we'll pass out.'

A few minutes had gone by, maybe five, maybe twenty, when Twm cried, 'Stop! Do you feel that? The air. It's cooler, less foul.'

Idris breathed in more deeply than he had been. The air maybe tasted fresher, perhaps wasn't as hot. Or was it his imagination because he was desperate for it to be true? 'I dunno. Could be. Let's keep going.'

He could have closed his eyes as they shuffled along, it would have made no difference. The pitch canvas before them was filled with lights and flashes, the ones seen behind eyelids when eyes were closed at night. A veil of cooler air wafted across his face. Maybe Twm was right. More lights played in front of his eyes, not dispersing as they had done. They seemed to be getting bigger.

'Idris, can you see that?' said Twm. 'Or am I hallucinating?'

'You can see the lights too?'

'Yes.'

'Thank God.' Despite his burden, Idris put a spurt in his step, pulling Twm along quicker too. It wasn't long before the ghostly outline of several men could be spied, and a rumble of voices heard.

'Hello?' called Twm. 'Hello?'

'Is that you, Twm Bach?' said a disconnected voice.

'Yes, it's Twm Bach. Is that you, John Morgan?'

'Aye. I'm with Mr Meredith, and several others.'

'*Diolch i Dduw*. Thank God. I'm here with Idris Hughes and Samuel Bevan.'

That was all that was said until the two groups finally met. When the lamp was held up to reveal them, Idris squinted against the bright light. As his eyes adjusted, he could see Samuel had been burnt on the arm and face, but how badly he couldn't ascertain. He explained exactly where they'd been when the explosion took place, what they'd heard, seen and felt.

'And you couldn't locate Lewis Jones?' asked Meredith.

'No, sir.'

'Morgan, escort these men to the surface, please. We'll carry on to Number One Heading. Tell the next party to make their way to Number Three Dip.' Meredith and the six remaining men carried on.

John Morgan gave the lamp to Twm to hold and he took Samuel from Idris. 'It's not too far now.'

Samuel moaned. Morgan stopped to pull him up a little. It seemed he'd lost the ability to hold any of his own weight. Idris went to Morgan's aid, holding Samuel up on the other side. 'Not long now, mun,' he said.

Five minutes later they were in a cage, going up. A dim electric light took over the illumination from the lamp. The tension seeped out of Idris's pores as he slumped against the wall, relief flooding in to replace it. As they ascended and reached ground level, he blinked against the natural light, even though it had faded into sunset.

It wasn't until Morgan went in front with Samuel that Idris could see the full extent of his injuries. His left arm and his

313

head on that side had been stripped of flesh. Idris looked away, stemming the urge to be sick.

'*O Duw*,' murmured Twm. 'Have you seen—?'

'Yes, I've seen.'

–

Anwen heard the door of the lamp room open. She was concentrating on washing the coal-pitted graze of a miner's arm and paid no heed to who'd come in. It was only when she heard the voice say, 'Please, he needs immediate attention,' that she twisted round to see Idris, ahead of another man, carrying a third whose skin was badly damaged. Samuel Bevan, she thought his name might be. Twm Bach followed on.

'Thank you, God,' she whispered several times. She felt weak with relief, taking a few seconds before continuing with her task.

She diverted her gaze as they got closer. Bevan's injury was appalling, an extensive patch of scorched skin. The fat scald on her own arm, despite the pain, became insignificant in comparison. Idris was walking, talking and seemed unharmed. The comfort of that knowledge fought with the sorrow of the situation.

Several people burst through the door: Isaiah and Meg Hughes along with Rachael and Abraham Owen. Anwen wondered vaguely how Rachael had got past the cordon.

Meg's strident, 'Idris, you're safe, thank the Lord,' clashed with Rachael's, 'Idris, where's Gwilym and Earnest? Have you seen them?'

Sister Grey marched over. 'Please, we can't have everybody in here. You must wait outside.'

Isaiah and Meg retreated, obviously satisfied their son was safe, but Rachael, her voice shrill with panic, said: 'I only want to know what's happened to my Gwilym and Earnest. Idris can tell me.' Abraham was beside her, his arm around her shoulder.

Having laid Samuel down, Idris came over. 'I'm sorry, Mrs Owen, I wasn't working near Gwilym and Mr Owen. They were in another part of the mine.'

Rachael doubled over, the choking sobs hiccoughing from her body.

Sister Grey said, more softly now, 'I'm sorry to hear your men are missing, but I will have to ask you to leave. If they're brought in, we will send word to you.'

'Come along, Rachael,' said Abraham. 'Let's leave these good people to do their jobs.' He led his daughter-in-law out, closing the door quietly.

Idris followed on, shambling towards the door, maybe in the hope that no one would notice. Anwen considered calling to him to stay, but was pre-empted by Sister Grey, saying, 'And where are you going, young man?'

He straightened his posture to address her, as if he were in their old schoolroom. 'To join a search party.'

'Not yet you're not. You may have been breathing in after-damp. You'll stay until I'm happy there are no after effects.'

Idris looked like he was about to argue, but made his way back to the centre of the room, sitting where the nurse indicated. It was only now that he noticed Anwen attending the grazed miner. He nodded his head once in acknowledgement. She returned the gesture before attending once more to her task.

-

During the next hour, two more doctors came to help from the surrounding villages. Several other men had made their way up from underground, or had been helped by one of the search parties. Most of them had been working on repairs towards the middle of the mine, further away from what had now been established as the blast area in the east. Their appearance had been delayed by lack of light and the presence of some afterdamp.

Anwen had washed grit from multiple grazes, placed on this single task by Sister Grey, who was exceptionally organised. Elizabeth had been tasked with bandaging cuts that were bleeding. Meg had been commandeered to help her. Anwen glanced at the old clock on the wall, discovering it was twenty minutes to midnight. Despite the cold night, the room was immensely humid, the windows steamed up. The mingled odours of sweat, blood and coal were unpleasant.

Idris, who'd slumped against the shelves of lamps after Sister Grey had examined him, had slowly risen from this posture to make himself useful. He'd questioned newly arrived groups of men about what they'd seen and heard. And who they'd seen.

'What about you?' Idris asked a lad, no more than sixteen. 'What's your name?'

'Arthur.' He was shivering. 'It was my first month in the pit. Can't rightly say I saw anything. Blinded, I was. Then it was so dark.'

Idris hunkered down, placing his arm around the lad and rubbing his arm. 'It is that.'

Anwen's heart went out to Idris as she watched him comfort the boy, putting aside his own worries about his friends.

'What's been happening?' one of the men who'd come in with the lad asked.

'Managers from other mines have come in, to help the search parties,' said Idris. 'And several mining engineers have arrived to help with safety.'

'That's good,' said the man, nodding, yet distracted. 'How did it happen, do they know?'

'Not exactly. But they think the explosion may have loosened the timber supports and raised the risk of the roof collapsing. So they're having to be careful.'

People had been coming in and out all evening, imparting these titbits of news. All this activity appeared to Anwen as a blur. She was out of place and time, a kind of ghost looking on at an event. She wondered vaguely whether this was what it was like in hospitals on the Front, people coming and going, casualties appearing regularly. Thirty-three men had now been brought to them, some of whom had already gone home. They'd heard of no fatalities so far. Anwen offered up a silent prayer. *Please let it stay that way.*

The door opened, bringing her out of the reverie. It was Abraham, helping a limping man into the lamp room. He'd volunteered to help men at the pit top as they arrived out of the cages. Rachael had been sent to stand with the rest of the onlookers. Abraham took his charge to Martha Simms, a probationary nurse who'd been released from the village hospital to help. Abraham hobbled over to Dr Roberts, whispering something to him. The doctor lifted his spectacles in order to pinch the top of his nose. He shook his head slowly before replacing the glasses. The doctor whispered something to Sister Grey, closed his bag and left with Abraham.

Slowly the word went round. *First victim's been brought up... taking them to the fitting and blacksmiths' shop.*

When the rumour reached Idris he marched from the room, leaving the lad to burst into tears. He sloped back five minutes later, his eyebrows drawn together. Anwen knew his expressions well enough to be sure he had not lost his best friend. Having finished with the man she was treating, she went to him.

'What news is it you have, Idris?'

Luckily he took her good arm and led her to one side of the room, away from where Twm was sitting with Samuel Bevan. His touch gave her a warm assurance.

'They found Lewis Jones. We were working with him, me and Twm and Bevan. We couldn't find him in the dark, see. He didn't answer when we called.' He was almost talking to himself. 'Took the force of the blast, they say. Me and Twm, we got down. He was stretching up to the roof when I last saw him. Think Bevan must have got down, at least a bit, 'cos he's not so, not so...' He tailed off, gazing at the wall.

Anwen wasn't so sure about Bevan. He wasn't in good shape as far as she could see, with one side of his body covered in burns, weeping pus. He should have been in the hospital, but they didn't want to move him.

Sister Grey came over to them. Idris had gone quiet so Anwen explained what had happened.

'You were not far into the mine, either, were you, Mr Hughes?'

'No. No we weren't.'

Anwen was sure Idris had already been thinking this; that if Lewis Jones was dead, those closer to the blast stood no chance.

'I suppose it depends which heading you're in, and how it connects to where the blast was.' Anwen used the knowledge she had gleaned from things her father had said about his job. She didn't want to allow Idris to slip into greater despondency.

'Maybe,' said Idris.

'Miss Rhys, would you fetch the men some water to drink from the tap please,' said Sister Grey. 'I believe there are glasses in the manager's office.'

'Of course. Straight away.'

As she headed to her destination, men were shuffling back and forth, heads down. From one side her father appeared, glancing around him. His presence made her aware of the throbbing in her arm. What was he doing here?

'Da? Do you have any news?'

He jerked his head around, greeting her with a scowl. 'I'm – I'm joining a rescue team,' he snapped. After a pause, he added in an even, upbeat voice, 'Just waiting to be assigned one.' It was as if the fight in the kitchen had never happened. 'What are *you* doing here?'

'Helping the nurses.'

'You'd better get back to it then. Go on.'

She did as she was bid, quickly fetching the glasses of water back to the lamp room on a tray. When she glanced out of the window after, he was gone. Despite what had happened, she couldn't help but be impressed he was thinking of others. She recalled he'd been involved in a pit accident back in 1885, at Maerdy, as a sixteen-year-old. His best friend had died. Her mother had told them about the incident. He'd never spoken of it.

The door opened and three more men entered, one being carried by his colleague. Time to get back to work.

–

It was twelve-thirty in the morning when five more bodies were brought up, found on the main level, further along than Idris and Twm had been. Idris had just consulted the clock on the wall when the news was conveyed to those in the lamp room. Dr Richards left to examine them, along with another doctor.

Idris paced the floor, praying that none of the bodies were either Gwilym or Earnest, but with each minute that passed it seemed increasingly unlikely they'd survived. Yet injured men were still being recovered. Another five appeared as he paced. They were wheezing, their words croaky, their flesh bruised or scarred, or both. He searched their faces as they entered, helping the last of them, who stumbled as he came in. Idris added them to the total in his head. Fifty men had passed through, seven of whom had died. Fifty-seven in all. That left twelve.

Anwen took the arm of one of the men. Idris knew he was in his fifties, but old before his time. She sat him down to bathe his wounds. Idris had managed to stay this side of the cordon by fetching and carrying items needed. All the while he watched his former sweetheart work, comforted by her presence. She was gentle, smiling to reassure, asking questions in a calm manner to illicit information about where they felt pain.

The man Anwen attended suddenly blurted out, 'Joseph's gone!'

'Joseph who?' called one of the men already there.

'Richards. Joseph Richards. Only a lad, really.'

'Oh no, not the pastor's son,' said Anwen.

There were wails of anguish around the room. The pastor had left some while before, to talk to the families affected. Another one of the casualties reeled off the names of the other four dead miners, bringing fresh cries of grief.

The door opened once more, bringing Mr Meredith in, his clothes dirty, the jacket gone, his shirt sleeves rolled up. He considered the men there, now a dozen of them. Others had either been sent home or, in the case of three, sent to the hospital, including Bevan. Idris bounded over to him, hoping for an accurate update of the situation.

'Mr Meredith, sir, we've just heard about the victims. Do you know what happened?'

'We think there was an explosion between Merthyr Heading and Death Road.'

Death Road. Idris's full throat threatened to choke him. He was sure that was the direction Gwilym and his father had been going with their team earlier. He had to pull himself together. 'Sir, I've been helping in here, but I'm sure I could be of more use in one of the parties.'

'I could do with men, but I don't know. Aren't you here because you're injured?'

Sister Grey interjected with, 'He's been very helpful but he's free to go whenever he wants.'

Meredith surveyed him from head to foot, perhaps remembering that he had given Idris an examiner's job because he wasn't capable enough to be a hewer anymore. He prayed that wouldn't prejudice his decision.

'Yes, Hughes, that would be useful. As an examiner you have a good idea of the layout underground.'

'Thank you, sir.' He breathed out a deep sigh of relief and thanks.

'My group's standing down for a rest, but you can join us when we go out again in half an hour. Now, go and get yourself a drink of tea while you're waiting. They're serving it in my office.'

'Yes sir, thank you sir.'

'That applies to everyone here,' Meredith announced. 'If someone would like to fetch the tea for those unable to leave, I would be grateful.'

Meredith went over to Anwen. Idris held back from getting his tea. He was being nosy, straining his ears to hear what was being said. He approached one of the men being bandaged by Miss Meredith.

'Shall I fetch you some tea, Huw?'

'Thank you, mun. That would be very welcome.'

As he moved slowly away, Idris heard Mr Meredith say, '... with one of the rescue parties, but didn't return with them.' When Anwen said nothing, Meredith added, 'Madog Rhys is your father, is he not?'

'He is,' said Anwen at last. 'Did he have a lamp?'

'Of course. We all did.'

'Then I expect he's got his own idea of how to go about it. He usually does.'

If Mr Meredith was surprised at her lack of concern, he didn't show it. 'I will make sure you know of any news concerning him, when we discover what happened.'

'Thank you, sir.' She attended once more to washing a wound.

Idris hesitated, wondering if he should say something to her. No, he'd better get the tea before it was time for him to descend once more into the depths.

—

The rescue group Idris joined had veered off the main level, onto a pathway known as Number Two Heading. Already they had found two fatalities, carried back on sheets which were used as makeshift stretchers by some of the group. Now there were only five rescuers left. Idris looked forlornly at the next set of underground doors as Meredith held his lamp up. They'd been blown clean off, compromising the ventilation. Already, the men were coughing. Idris, carrying the tins of water he'd suggested to Mr Meredith before they set off, wet the men's handkerchiefs for them. It seemed to bring some relief as they held them to their noses.

'We'll need some brattice cloths put up here for temporary ventilation,' Mr Meredith announced, gesturing to the man who'd come along with the necessary equipment. The man nodded and began the job. The rest of the group carried on. They were getting near to Hosea Pimm Heading, where Gwilym and his father had supposedly been working. Idris's body pulsed with trepidation. The further in they'd got, the more injuries the miners had sustained.

They didn't get far before they were brought to a halt by a fall of rock blocking the whole path. There was a group grunt of frustration. Idris's panic grew. If the tunnel had collapsed, what hope did the missing miners have? The engineer they'd brought with them examined the area, poking at the roof, pushing at the rocks and the coal, the shiny blackness picked up by the light's beam.

'What do you think?' Meredith said to the engineer.

'Not sure we've any choice but to try and get through. Digging to the next heading would take too long. I'll need to secure the props as we move the rocks.'

'Let's get to it, men.' Meredith allocated jobs to those there: aiding the engineer with the props, removing stones and carrying them away, which was what Idris was assigned to do.

A sense of time slipped from Idris once more. He was flagging, panting as he worked, but he was not going to give up, not while he had an ounce of energy in his muscles. He built up a rhythm, singing in his head as he did, a method he'd long used to get through the most arduous of jobs.

At long last they cleared the blockage enough for them to step through. They lifted their lamps to see what was ahead. Only yards from the rock fall there were two bodies on the ground. Idris ran to the larger of the two, turning him face upwards.

'It's Philip Hubbard,' he called back. The union representative groaned softly, opening his eyes with effort. One side of his face was scorched and black.

'Hubbard? How do you feel?'

Hubbard released a low grumble in his throat. Idris had to put his ear closer to hear him murmur, 'Bloody Edgar Williams.'

'What do you mean?' Was he saying Edgar was responsible? Idris couldn't understand how.

'Number Four Heading.'

That heading had been closed off and declared dangerous due to the detection of firedamp, a flammable gas, some weeks before. 'What's that got to do with the explosion?'

'Nothing. Edgar got comeuppance though.'

It didn't make sense. Idris placed his hand on Hubbard's forehead. It was damp but cold, not feverish. 'Hubbard, do you know where Gwilym is? Gwilym Owen.'

'Nearby, was working near – by.' His eyelids fluttered. 'Number Four Heading,' he repeated. 'Remember.' There was a last exhalation of breath before he was silent.

'Hubbard? Hubbard?' Idris shook his shoulder but he knew he was gone.

Idris stood with difficulty. The other body was being lifted by Meredith while the man next to him held up two lamps. 'Does anyone know this lad's name?' said the manager.

Despite the smooth features having been disfigured by afterdamp, Idris recognised him immediately. It was like he'd been thumped in the chest, the air knocked from his lungs. Now was not the time to buckle. 'Ifor Ellis, sir. Fourteen, he was. Only started two weeks ago.'

'What a waste of young life,' said Meredith, his voice hoarse. He placed the boy next to Philip Hubbard. 'We've been down here long enough. We'll take these victims to the surface and send another group down.'

Idris's mouth opened to volunteer to stay and keep searching, alone if necessary, but he failed to voice his frustration. He was exhausted. They all were. They couldn't carry on indefinitely, least of all him.

One of the other men laid out two old sheets and the bodies were lifted onto them. They carried them back along the heading to the main level.

–

As the men in Idris's rescue team stepped out of the fitting and blacksmiths' shop, the overman in charge of the shift approached Mr Meredith. His clothes were tattered and he was limping.

'Sir, could I have a word? I've not long got to the surface. At the end of Number One Heading, I was.' He leant forward to let out a barking cough. 'Sorry, still a bit of afterdamp in my lungs. Was out cold for a bit.' He composed himself. 'Someone told me that Jory Damerell, Hector Harris, Fergal McGee and Earnest Owen haven't been located yet. Sir, I was patrolling the area not long before the explosion, between Harries Heading and Death Road. I saw them there together.'

Jory was down there too? 'What about Gwilym Owen?' asked Idris urgently. He realised he was butting into a conversation between his elders and betters. 'Sorry, sir,' he said, when he realised he should have left the talking to Mr Meredith.

'That's all right, Hughes,' said the manager. 'I can understand you're worried about your friend.'

'Don't rightly know about him,' said the overman. 'Didn't see him with them.'

Was that good or bad? Either way, it was becoming less and less likely he'd survived. It was even possible he'd never be found. It happened. Idris's stomach churned.

'Thank you for the information,' said Meredith. 'We will task the next rescue team with searching that area.'

'Sir, can I join that party?' said Idris.

Meredith patted his arm. 'You've worked hard and you should have a rest. Go home, have a sleep. If Mr Owen's there, the next team will find him.'

Idris couldn't argue with that. He did desperately need to sit down, lie down even. 'Very well, sir.'

In the lamp room, Anwen and the nurses were sitting against the wall. Anwen had her eyes closed, as did Martha Simms. There was no one else in the room.

'Mr Hughes,' said Sister Grey, standing. 'What's the latest news?'

Anwen half opened her eyes, snapping them wide when she realised Idris was there.

'We've just brought up Philip Hubbard and young Ifor Ellis.'

'Ifor Ellis?' said Anwen in a strangled voice. 'Oh no.' Her lower lip wobbled as she wept easy tears.

Idris wished it was acceptable for men to weep so readily. He would have shed many a tear. He ducked down, sitting next to her, taking her hand tentatively. She didn't pull away, so he allowed his fingers to surround hers completely. 'Only five left,' he said. 'Let's hope they find them soon.'

'Six, if you count my father.'

'Aye. Has my mam gone home?'

'Yes. She left soon after you did, saying she'd relieve me later.'

Sister Grey took hold of the nearby broom to sweep up some dirty dressings, swabs and bandages from the floor. Nurse Simms slept on, her head leaning almost on her own shoulder.

Idris looked up at the clock: six minutes past four. Outside it was already getting light. He and Anwen spoke no more but simply sat, holding hands.

–

It was gone six in the morning when Anwen and Idris were ordered home to sleep by both Sister Grey and Meg Hughes, who'd returned to relieve Anwen as she'd promised. Abraham had sloped off home, limping, several hours before, but Anwen knew Rachael was still at the front of the crowd outside, waiting for news.

When Idris hesitated, Anwen said, 'I'm sure someone will come and tell you if they find Gwilym and his da.' He was pale, paler than she'd ever seen him, the circles beneath his eyes like bruises.

'Aye,' said Meg. 'I'll come and tell you. Now home with you before I march you there myself.'

Anwen took Idris's arm, escorting him out of the door. The air, crisp and fresh, was a salve on her face after the oppressive lamp room. Beyond the yard, several policemen stood, unmoving. Apart from chirping birds there were few sounds. The diminished crowd was silent, still, a seam of sad faces. She'd never heard it so quiet in Dorcalon, where there was always sound: the pit wheel, someone singing, a baby crying, the chatter of friends or workmates. Always the rumble of noise. Beside her, Idris stopped.

'What is it, Idris, *bach*?'

'I don't think I can go home until they've found Gwilym.'

Quite likely he didn't want to be alone at home, with Meg staying to help the nurses and Isaiah in a rescue party. Jenkin had apparently stayed overnight with a friend. 'Come to my home.' In case this sounded improper, she added, 'Mamgu will be there, and Mam. You can rest on the chaise longue.'

'I don't know...'

At the corner of her eye, Anwen saw a figure appear, carrying another. 'Idris, look!'

Coming across the yard was her father, carrying a prone figure towards the lamp room.

'Gwilym!' Idris shouted, running back the way they'd come. Anwen followed him.

Another voice in the crowd was heard shrieking, 'Gwilym, my Gwilym!' Rachael Owen broke through the cordon, avoiding the outstretched arm of the old constable, and ran across the yard. He didn't pursue her.

Madog stopped at the lamp room door, where he tried to push it open with his back. Gwilym must be alive, thought Anwen, otherwise her father would have taken him to the fitting and blacksmiths' shop.

Idris got to the door, opening it wide for Madog.

'Oh my goodness,' called Meg, running towards them, directing Madog to a makeshift bed made simply of blankets.

'Gwilym, Gwilym? Are you all right?' Idris cried out.

Sister Grey held out her arms to keep them all at bay. 'Please, would everyone step away while I examine him? And would somebody please fetch Dr Roberts, who I believe is in the manager's office.'

'I'll do that,' said Idris, scurrying away.

The rest of the party did as Sister Grey requested, apart from Rachael who knelt on the floor next to her son. 'Gwilym? Wake up, Gwilym.'

Meg leant over to draw her away, holding onto her as Sister Grey bent to feel his pulse. Anwen searched the room for her father, wanting to thank him for bringing Gwilym to the surface. He had disappeared once again.

'He is alive, isn't he?' whimpered Rachael.

'Oh yes, he's very much alive,' said Sister Grey. 'And doesn't seem to have any burns, though he's a bit bruised. A bit over-whelmed with the afterdamp, I shouldn't wonder. But let's wait for the doctor's assessment.'

At this point Dr Roberts appeared with Mr Meredith. Idris, just behind them, pushed to the front, heedless of manners. She knew his main motive in staying up all night was to make sure of his friend's safety, and she loved him all the more for it.

As the doctor examined Gwilym, using a stethoscope to listen to his heart, his eyelids fluttered open and he moaned softly. Dr Roberts leaned back. 'Not too much wrong with this lad, I'd warrant, but we'll keep him here for a while to make sure.'

Rachael burst into joyful tears, hanging on tightly to Meg.

'Mam,' said Gwilym, weakly.

Rachael let go of Meg to dip down to his level. 'Son, where's your da?'

'I don't know,' came the whispering reply. 'I wasn't with him when the explosion happened. Sorry, Mam.'

'Don't be daft with your sorries. You're safe, that's what counts.'

Anwen took Idris's hand. His face was lined with exhaustion. He gazed down at her, smiling briefly. Then his eyes lost focus before they closed and he slipped gracefully to the ground. She tried to catch him but he was too big, too heavy for her. Herbert Meredith caught him instead before he hit the floor. Meg was soon by his side, kneeling next to Anwen.

'Idris? Idris!' cried Anwen. *Oh God, not now, when he seemed safe and well.* She couldn't take much more heartbreak.

'I'm afraid being part of the search team and being up all night has been too much for him,' said Mr Meredith.

Dr Roberts left Gwilym's side, his stethoscope in use once more as he examined Idris, still partly held up by the manager. 'You could be right. But I want to admit him to hospital.'

Meg grabbed Anwen's arm, gripping it tight. She cried out in pain, the burn on her arm forcefully remembered. Liquid seeped through her sleeve as Meg removed her hand.

'What is that?' said Dr Roberts. He lifted her sleeve gingerly to reveal the raw blisters, some now burst, on the length of her forearm. Those standing around exclaimed their horror. 'My dear, how did you get such a bad burn?'

'I spilled hot fat on my arm when I was cooking Da some bacon.' Now it was exposed and she had time to take notice of it, the dull smarting transformed to an unbearable stinging. She bit her bottom lip to stop herself whining.

'Or did he throw it on your arm?' said Rachael. 'Abraham told me you'd been arguing.'

She wouldn't have mentioned it, not now he'd rescued Gwilym, but there was no point in lying. 'Yes. He lifted the pan and spilled it on my arm.' Still she tried to make it sound like an accident.

'Where is he, anyway?' said Dr Roberts.

'He left soon after he brought Gwilym in,' said Sister Grey.

Meg, cradling Idris's head said, 'Where's your uncle Hywel?'

'Hywel Llewellyn?' said Meredith. 'He joined one of the parties, but he went home an hour since.'

'Someone better knock him up. He needs to look after his family.'

Chapter Twenty-Six

The seat was bumpy and had a wonky leg, but Anwen didn't care. She wanted only to sit with her darling Idris, the love of her life, as he always would be, whatever happened between them. Nurse Campbell had been pleased to have someone to keep an eye on him, busy as they were with the casualties of the pit disaster.

Anwen held Idris's hand as he lay on his back, unconscious. She examined his familiar face, still handsome despite its pallor. Meg and Isaiah had been in earlier, departing half an hour before to get something to eat. Cadi had invited them home and was determined to look after them. They'd also wanted to call into Gwilym's house to see what they might do to help there. Anwen moaned softly to herself. So much tragedy in the last eighteen hours.

Outside the sky was overcast, covering the village in a blanket of gloom. The lights had been put on in the ward.

Gwilym was in the ward next door with three other men who'd survived the explosion. There were another two in Idris's ward. The final count of thirteen bodies had now all been removed from the fitting and blacksmiths' shop to the front rooms of their own homes in Dorcalon. There would be a good few days of funerals and mourning to come. The weight on Anwen's heart made her feel older than Cadi.

She was concentrating so much on Idris's face, she didn't notice Dr Roberts at the foot of the bed until he spoke. 'I've been wondering about Idris's discharge,' he started.

Anwen jumped, clutching her chest when she realised it was the doctor. 'Sorry, I didn't see you there. His hospital discharge?'

'No, his army one. I believe he was discharged due to ill health. His mother told me that the army declared him, "Unlikely to become an efficient soldier." Do you know whether any cause was given?'

'Apart from him suffering from tachycardia, I'm afraid I don't.' The doctor's eyebrows rose in an admiring gaze, acknowledging her use of the medical word. She didn't know whether to be pleased he was impressed, or affronted that he was surprised. 'I think he said his heart regularly beats at a hundred and thirty beats per minute.'

'I'm surprised he hasn't requested a visit to investigate a reason and possible treatment.'

'He's a proud man, Doctor, one who doesn't like people thinking he can't cope.' She had always known this about him, but it only now struck her that he might also be keen to keep the full extent of his symptoms from her. She looked down at his sleeping form.

Dr Roberts moved on, speaking in hushed tones to the next but one patient, someone else overcome by afterdamp. There was a low muttering, indistinct words, and Anwen realised Idris was stirring. She waited patiently for him to wake up in his own time, removing her hand from his.

When his eyelids were finally fully open, he stared at her as if he couldn't quite believe what he was seeing. His voice cracked as he said, 'What happened?'

'You passed out, after they brought Gwilym in.'

'Gwilym!' He tried to sit up.

Anwen pushed him gently back. 'Gwilym is fine, in the next ward. They'll be discharging him later today.'

'Your father – he brought him in.'

'Yes, but he hasn't been seen since. Uncle Hywel is at my house now, looking after Cadi and Mam.'

'What had Gwilym been doing – in the mine – on his own?'

331

'He told me earlier he was working not far from Philip Hubbard in Number Three Heading when Hubbard started moaning about Edgar Williams to Ifor Ellis. But Gwilym overheard it and gathered something had been stolen and hidden in Number Four Heading, which had apparently been shut.'

'That's right. Hubbard as fireman reckoned there was some firedamp there. Williams forbade us all from going near it.'

'Gwilym heard Mr Hubbard ask why they couldn't just sell whatever it was and get the money. He asked Ifor if he'd help him sneak some of it out, but Ifor said he wanted nothing to do with it because his mother would kill him.' Anwen gasped at her own words, realising the cruelty of them. 'Poor lad, only fourteen.'

Idris took her hand where it lay on the bed next to his. 'It's just a saying, *cariad*, it's not your fault. What happened next?'

Anwen pulled herself together. 'Hubbard hadn't realised Gwilym was there in the dark, so Gwilym took one of the crossroads to Number Four Heading while he was near it. He said he turned down his lamp to test for firedamp, and there wasn't any. I don't know how that works.'

'When you turn your lamp down, it looks like there's a pale flame above it if there's firedamp in the air.'

'Anyway, he found a huge stash of whisky, spirits and tinned food behind a tall stack of rocks. It was then the explosion happened. The fact he was that much further away, and in another heading, probably saved him, though he lay unconscious for a long while. First thing he knew, my father was pulling him up. They struggled back to the main level together.'

'So, your father is a hero?' *For a change* was left unsaid, but Anwen almost fancied she heard it.

'I dunno about that.' She told him about the things she'd found stashed in Sara's room. 'And why did he break away from the group in the first place and disappear? I can't help thinking he had the same idea as Philip Hubbard, to go and get some of the stolen goods to get them out of the mine.'

'I can't even see how he'd have managed that. Maybe a coupla bottles hidden in his jacket, but that'd be it. Presumably Edgar Williams was planning on getting it out during the night, maybe bit by bit, to sell.'

'Well, since my father has disappeared again and Philip Hubbard is one of the fatalities, there's only Mr Williams to ask. We should pass this on to the police.'

Idris squeezed her hand gently. 'Be careful, Anwen. You don't want someone overhearing you tell the police and taking their revenge.'

Like Da, she thought, a profound loneliness assailing her. If your own father was willing to tip boiling fat on your arm and throw your mother down the stairs, who knew what he was capable of? Her arm smarted constantly, but at least the bandage Sister Grey had put around her arm was hidden by her loose sleeve.

'Gwilym's father! And Jory. And the other men. Oh God. Have they found them?' Idris attempted again to sit up, giving up part-way as Anwen's arms shot out to prevent him.

Anwen had been dreading this question, hoping he would be a little stronger before he remembered. She knew she would cry again by the time she'd finished explaining. She had to give an answer, though. If she didn't, he'd guess anyway. She swallowed hard.

'They were brought up at ten o'clock this morning.'

'Brought up? All of them?' His voice was expressionless.

'I'm sorry. Gwilym's father didn't survive. Nor Jory.'

There was a pause before he said, 'What about the others?'

She shook her head. 'Hector Harris and Fergal McGee were all found with Mr Owen, already... well, already passed on. They reckon it was instant. They were the last four missing. Everyone's accounted for now.' *Except my father.*

'I see.'

'They were where the overman said they'd be, between Harries Heading and Death Road. It's where the explosion took place.' Anwen took a deep breath. 'And there's one more thing. Samuel Bevan. He died a couple of hours ago.' *Please, please don't let me cry.*

Idris shut his eyes tight. The next thing she knew his body was jerking. She wondered at first whether he was having some kind of fit. Then she saw the tears flow down his face and heard the long keening note. It was too much for her: she burst into tears.

They clutched each other's hands, sobbing in unison until they were both spent.

–

Later that day, Anwen headed out to pay a visit to Sergeant Harries. About to turn onto Gabriel Street she noticed Abraham Owen, stooping and ambling along in a way he never had. He'd aged ten years in the last two days.

'Ah, Anwen. I've just been to the field up yonder.' He pointed to a small piece of rough ground beyond James Street. 'Helped bury the ponies, I did. Least I could do to give them a send-off, after all the years I worked with them. Only half of them left, there is.' He wiped a stray tear from his cheek. 'Can't hang around doing nothing, waiting for a funeral, can you? Can't believe we're burying my oldest son tomorrow. It's not right, outliving your children. You're not planning on coming to see Earnest laid out, are you?'

She hadn't been, hating the practice. She could never understand why people wanted to ogle the dead. 'If you'd like me—'

'No! That's just what I don't want you to do. Encouraged everyone to stay away, I have. Not everyone's been put off, though. His face, oh, it's burnt and not fit to lay eyes on. It's not my son. Please, don't come.'

It was a relief to be given permission not to view the remains of Earnest Owen. 'Are you coming round for some supper later?'

'Rachael's going. I can't tell you how much we appreciate your family, and Idris's, caring for us. But Gwilym and I are going to work on the allotment when I get back. We both need to do something, and there's life there, with those vegetables, and they give life and health to others.'

'I'm so grateful that people still want to work on them, despite what's happened.'

'We've still got to eat, *cariad*. And people here, with a few exceptions, are a good sort… Has your father turned up yet? I appreciate him rescuing Gwilym but I don't condone the other things he's done.'

'No he hasn't. I'm off to tell Sergeant Harries about him and Edgar Williams and the stolen goods. If my father does turn up, I hope to God it's not at our house.'

'Aye, me too. Good luck, *cariad*.'

Abraham dragged his old bones up the hill. Anwen walked the half dozen footsteps to the house on the corner of Gabriel Street. She tapped on the door, not wanting to alert too many other people. It wasn't long before Harries came to the door, bags under his eyes, his face drawn.

'What can I do for you this time, Miss Rhys?' he said. 'I had two hours' sleep this morning and have only just got off duty.'

'That's more sleep than I've had. I have some important information, about the recent thefts and where the stolen goods might be. And about my mother's so-called accident.'

'I think you'd better come in.'

–

That was another week Anwen did not wish to live through again. She went over it as she took the road down to the hospital on her way to Sunday afternoon visiting. The sun shone from time to time through the half-hearted clouds, but the stiff wind meant it was no warmer today than on the recent overcast days. She pulled her shawl around herself.

Seven days had passed since Idris had collapsed and the last of the fatalities had been brought to the surface, days in which all the funerals had taken place. Anwen had been summoned to the police station in Rhymney to give a statement, along with Gwilym. The police had been to her house to collect the stolen items. Enid had finally confessed to Sergeant Harries what happened the day she supposedly fell down the stairs. Afterwards, Anwen had hidden herself away in her bedroom and cried. Da was probably far away by now.

Reaching the end of her street and the top of Jubilee Green, she bumped into Winnie Price and Elizabeth, coming out of the greengrocer's.

Winnie launched straight into, 'I was just saying to Miss Meredith here, you've all produced some lovely veggies between you. Nice and fresh, not like that old rubbery stuff James the Veg was fobbing us off with before. And at last there's some good news.'

'I don't suppose the war has ended.' Anwen's hope sprang to life, though it had been misplaced at least once before.

'No, sadly. But they've finally found a new Secretary of State for War to replace the late Lord Kitchener, and it's our very own Mr Lloyd George.'

'That's something,' Anwen said, trying to sound enthusiastic through the disappointment. She'd barely given the war a thought this last week of mourning, still less read of its progress in the newspaper.

'Well I never, what's going on down there then? Oh, and over there.' Winnie pointed down the pavement to the butcher's, then across to the McKenzie Arms. There were police entering both properties. Elizabeth glanced at Anwen, who could guess what she was thinking.

'I wonder if they're going to—' Winnie began. 'Oh yes, there you go... And again. Think it has anything to do with the thefts and the contraband found?'

'Almost certainly,' said Elizabeth.

They watched as Iolo Prosser was dragged from the butcher's shop. His wife, Eileen, was screaming insults, not at the police, but at him, calling him a silly old sod and asking what she was supposed to do now. Straight after, Reginald Moss emerged from the double doors on the corner, his wrists cuffed. He wasn't resisting like Prosser, though his face was contorted with anger.

'You been shouting your mouth off?' the landlord bellowed at the butcher.

'No, have you?'

Moss didn't reply. Both men were bundled into a horse-drawn carriage waiting on the corner by the bookshop, where Joseph Schenck was standing outside his door, looking on.

Sergeant Harries appeared from the butcher's, trekking up to Anwen and the others when he spotted them.

When he was a few steps away, Anwen said, 'I don't suppose you've heard any more about my father's whereabouts? You said you might be able to find out from Edgar Williams.'

'No such luck, I'm afraid,' he replied. 'Mr Williams has happily told us of the hiding places of the rest of the stolen goods and given up the people involved, including those two we've just arrested. Reckoned if he wasn't going to profit, they certainly weren't going to. There's loyalty for you. Since Williams has sung like a canary about everything else, I doubt he's keeping your father's whereabouts a secret. Got it in for the world now, has our Mr Williams. Are you off to the hospital to see Idris Hughes?'

'I am.'

'Give him my best wishes, and tell him I hope there's no lasting resentment over his arrest.'

'I'll do that. Thank you, Sergeant.'

He lifted his helmet in farewell and strode down to the carriage.

–

Idris's ward was busy today with visitors, though the mood was still solemn after the tragic events. Anwen noticed Dr Roberts was standing next to Idris's bed, along with Isaiah. Isaiah spotted her, beckoning her over. Idris was sitting up, the colour in his cheeks warmer than it had been all week.

'Well here's some better news at last,' said Isaiah when Anwen was in earshot.

'Apart from Mr Lloyd George being made Secretary of State for War?' she remarked.

'Has he? Well I never. He'll be prime minister next at this rate. No, it's Idris. He could be cured.'

'Now let's not get ahead of ourselves,' said the doctor. 'It's all very new, but there is hope of a good prognosis for people with Idris's condition.'

'What condition?' said Anwen.

'I'll leave you to explain,' said Dr Roberts. 'I have some home visits to make.'

When he was out of sight Isaiah said, 'Are you going to tell her, Idris?'

As Idris heaved himself up, the pillows slipped sideways. Anwen rushed forward to straighten and plump them up for him.

'Thank you,' said Idris. 'You might as well sit down.'

She took the rickety seat, wishing Idris would get on with it.

'The doctor apparently took some blood from me and had it examined. He thought my symptoms might be due to what he described as an overactive thyroid. It's some gland in the throat that's important. If it produces too much thyroxine, it makes you ill. It's what makes my heart beat so fast. *Graves' disease*, he called it. He says the lump in my throat isn't a large Adam's apple, but a small goitre.'

'Oh,' was all Anwen could think of to say. It was hard to take it all in.

'There's an operation they've been performing the last fifty-odd years,' Isaiah interrupted, unable to contain his hope.

Anwen went cold. Operations were dangerous. Violet's cousin had died during one to remove her appendix. 'What sort of operation?' She heard the wobble in her voice.

'They cut some of the thyroid gland away, so it doesn't make so much of the thyroxine stuff,' said Isaiah. 'They've had lots of success in London.'

'And that's the problem,' said Idris. 'I'd have to go all the way there. And it costs money.'

'Which the doctor said would be covered by the subscriptions,' said Isaiah.

'Yes, but I'd be off work a long while, even after coming home, with no money coming in and you having to keep me.'

'Don't be daft,' said Isaiah. 'We'll manage all right. It won't be long till Jenkin's off to work anyway.'

'That depends on what he does. And you need to put money away for when you retire from the pit. That pension you can get now won't go far.'

'Hark at him,' Isaiah said to Anwen, indicating Idris. 'Anyone would think he didn't want to get well.'

It seemed like that to Anwen too. There was something else behind it all, there had to be.

'We'll talk about it when you come out,' said Isaiah, in a tone that forbade any further discussion. He consulted the clock on the far wall. 'I'm due to join one of the parties repairing the mine. Quicker we get it done, the quicker we'll be back at work.'

'Before you go,' said Anwen, 'you might like to know that they've just arrested Iolo Prosser and Reginald Moss for their part in stealing, hoarding, and no doubt profiteering.'

'I'm not at all surprised,' said Isaiah. 'Top of my list, they'd have been. I'll see you tomorrow, son. It'll be good to have you home.'

'Aye, Da. It'll be good to be home.'

Idris watched his father leave the ward. As he did, an idea came to Anwen, regarding replacing the money Idris would lose with time off work.

'So, what else has been going on in the outside world?' said Idris.

Anwen was glad to be side-tracked from her thoughts, that she'd give more serious consideration to when she was alone.

–

It had been a long day for Anwen. She'd done twelve hours at McKenzie House, plus another two on the allotments, before she'd dragged herself home at sunset. In almost all ways, life was easier without her father around. She had a freedom she'd never experienced before. Uncle Hywel had moved in to contribute to their household but didn't take up the role of man of the house. He was happy for her to make the decisions, as was Cadi, who'd also moved in. Her mother had fallen into an odd mood since Madog had disappeared; jumpy, frenetic, relieved at her new-found freedom, yet fearing it.

Anwen had flopped into bed without any supper well before ten o'clock. She'd been lying awake now for at least an hour, half drifting into sleep several times, but always jerking back to consciousness. She'd tried to give Cadi her room but she'd refused it, insisting she'd share with Enid because she'd cope better with her restlessness. But here Anwen was, disturbed anyway. Three days had gone by since she'd had the idea about Idris's operation, but still it was rattling around her brain. He'd gone home on Monday so it would no longer be easy to speak to him alone.

At last she drifted off to a more settled sleep, punctuated by dreams of the lamp room and the casualties. She knew in the dream it was in the past, yet found herself stuck there, trying to get through the door into the yard. When she finally managed it, there were corpses on the ground, burnt and bloodied. There were muffled yet aggressive words being spoken, ones she couldn't quite make out. She was in the state of trying to wake up, yet unable to move. There was something else, beyond the dream, something that needed her attention.

She awoke with a start: the muffled words were real, inside the house. She jumped from the bed and crept out onto the landing, listening. The sound was coming from Sara's room – Uncle Hywel's room now. She carefully pushed open the already ajar door to find her father with his back to her in the moonlight, cursing with foul words. Hywel had his back against the far wall, his hands up, palms facing out.

'Where are my bloody things, you damned thief?' her father was muttering.

Why was Hywel not doing anything? He was more than a match for Madog, taller, younger. She let go of the door, but it opened a little more on its own, squeaking before it came to a stop. Her father wheeled around, holding a short pistol aloft.

'Da—'

'Get over there with your bloody uncle and keep your voice down.'

She did as she was told, treading carefully, slowly, trying to gauge the expression on his face in the half light. He didn't appear drunk.

'There's a pair of you, informing on me I 'eard from Prosser, before he was arrested. You'll pay for that. Now where are my bloody things?'

'The police took them, Da.'

'Don't bloody *Da* me. No daughter of mine, you aren't.' His oaths became thicker, as he raved in an undertone of her perceived shortcomings.

Anwen spotted something moving behind him. She tried not to look directly at the figure, who could only be Cadi. Her grandmother was holding something up high, though Anwen couldn't work out what. Her father stopped talking. She needed to engage him in more conversation so he wouldn't spot his mother.

'Why did you push Mam down the stairs? What did she ever do but look after you?'

'Bloody look after *me*? I look after myself. Just a bloody millstone she became, like the rest of you. Not like my boys, my lovely boys. Kept on and on she did, about being given more money, about my drinking and gambling. Nothing to bloody do with her, the bitch.'

'That's my sister you're talking about,' said Hywel, finding his voice. He must have spotted Cadi by now. 'She was always too good for you.'

Cadi crept closer, lifting her hand higher. A chamber pot, that's what it was. The urge to laugh filled Anwen. It was hysteria. She bit her lip to contain it, biting down so hard it hurt.

Madog lifted the gun a little, cocking the hammer, aiming it at Hywel's head. 'Shut your bloody yap, you bastard. If I hear another word I swear I'll blow your bloody brains out. Too good an opportunity it was, her standing there at the top of the stairs, yapping on. Thought it'd give her a fright, a small fall. But even better: she lost the use of her legs and can't go following me around anymore, pulling me outta bars, telling people not to take my bets, bleeding me dry of money. I had two daughters who could attend to the house, would do as they were told. What did I need with her?'

'But Sara,' said Hywel, the hatred glowing in his eyes. 'You put too much work on her and it finished her off.'

'One less mouth to feed.'

Cadi's arm rolled back swiftly, clearly in readiness to swing forward and hit her son. Madog was concentrating on keeping the gun aimed at Hywel. Anwen's heart was speeding, making her chest uncomfortable. She wondered if Idris felt like that all the time. She took a deep breath, readying herself to lurch forward to push her father down, once Mamgu struck a blow. Hopefully Hywel would do the same. As Cadi's arm came forward, she took a step and the floorboard beneath her foot creaked.

Madog swung round. The gun went off just before the chamber pot made contact with his skull. Or was it the other way round? Anwen wasn't sure.

All she knew was that at around the same time, her mamgu, her uncle and her father all hit the ground, along with the chamber pot that now lay shattered on the floor.

There were further sounds, from beyond the room. The light switched on.

There was her mother standing, albeit stooped, in the doorway.

'*O Duw, O Duw*, what's happened?' The words were barely out before she crumpled to the ground in a pool of nightie, crying.

On the stairs there were stomping steps, urgent, coming upwards.

Oh Lord, who's that now?

Chapter Twenty-Seven

Idris burst through the bedroom door, narrowly missing Enid on the ground. She was still weeping. He examined the room in horror.

'What the hell happened?'

There came a knock on the front door, loud and insistent.

Anwen was in a dream-like state, her family scattered round the room, with bits of china between them. Her father was sprawled on the ground while Hywel was curled up, groaning. Cadi was on her back. Idris couldn't tell what had happened to whom.

There was a growl from Madog. He lifted his head from the ground, looking around for something before he lumbered to his feet. Anwen stepped back.

'You bloody bastards, I'll get you.' He sprang towards Anwen. She cowered, her arms over her head.

Something snapped in Idris, pouring forth a rage he'd never experienced before. He leapt across the room, lifting his arm and hurling his fist into Madog's face. The older man went down once more, and this time he was silent.

The knocking on the door had already become a continuous thumping. Now it sounded like someone was trying to break the door down.

Anwen surveyed the chaos, then Idris, her expression that of a frightened child. 'Thank you, Idris. Now, would you answer that please?'

He ran down the stairs, shaking his sore hand. Opening the door revealed Gwilym, his mother and several neighbours. The women present were all in dressing gowns and the men hastily dressed.

'We heard a shot,' said Gwilym.

'Are you all right, love?' said Rachael.

'Madog, his mother, Mrs Rhys and Hywel Llewellyn are all on the floor. Gwilym, would you please get the doctor?'

'Of course.' He rushed off.

'And would someone else get Sergeant Harries?'

Two of the male onlookers rushed off to perform the task.

Idris considered the people left. 'Perhaps someone should wait here, too.'

'We will,' said the two remaining men.

'I'll get dressed, then come back to see if you need any practical help,' said Rachael.

Idris nodded gratefully, 'Thank you.' He left the rest standing there, making his way back to the bedroom, treading carefully through the door to avoid the china.

Cadi was sitting up, rubbing her leg. Anwen was hunkering down beside her. 'Mamgu, are you all right?'

'Slipped up I did, on the mat, as I hit him. I'm just a bit bruised, that's all, *cariad*. Don't worry about me.'

Idris went to Enid, who'd somehow moved along the ground and was leaning over her brother, calling, 'Hywel, oh Hywel. Wake up… His leg, it's been shot.'

It was then they spotted the blood seeping from under his thigh.

Anwen clutched her throat, 'Uncle Hywel!'

Idris hunkered down next to Enid. 'Did Madog do this?' He rooted around, finding the gun just under the bed. 'What happened exactly?'

'The gun must have gone off as I hit him,' said Cadi. 'I didn't mean that to happen. I hope Hywel's all right. Oh sweet Lord.'

'Don't worry, Mamgu, you did the right thing,' said Anwen. 'It might have been far worse if you hadn't intervened.'

Hywel groaned, his eyes fluttering open. 'Damn it, my leg hurts.'

He tried to sit up but Enid pulled him back. 'Just keep still, *bach*. You'll be fine. You just need to lie still.'

Idris realised nobody had bothered to see how Madog was, not even his own mother. Could he blame them? They needed to know what state he was in, though, either way. He bent down to him. He was still breathing, his eyes shut, unmoving. A lump had formed on his head, where Cadi had hit him, presumably with the now broken chamber pot, and a black eye was already evident from Idris's own assault.

'What kind of condition is he in?' asked Anwen.

'Unconscious, that's all I can tell you.'

'Let's hope he stays that way until the police get here.'

The doctor arrived first, confirming what Anwen suspected: Hywel needed immediate medical attention and the best place for that was the hospital. She didn't want him to get any kind of infection. She'd heard of men on the Front being shot and dying of gangrene, something that might not have happened if they'd had proper treatment.

Sergeant Harries appeared just after with PC Probert, neither of whom were in uniform. He brought up the two men who'd fetched him, commandeering them to carry Madog downstairs.

Dr Roberts examined him briefly before they left. 'As far as I can tell, he's simply unconscious. But I suggest they get a doctor to examine him in Rhymney. I've got my hands full here.'

'Aye,' said Harries. 'We'll get him downstairs and wait for the carriage there. I rang Rhymney police at the fire station before I got here. Come on men, let's get this lump out of here.'

Probert and the other two men lifted him, none too carefully, and removed him from the room. Harries picked up the gun with a handkerchief, placing it in a sack bag before following them.

Dr Roberts turned his attention back to Hywel. He removed a bandage from his bag, winding it around his leg to stay the blood flow. Hywel whined with the pain. Enid wept as she stroked her brother's forehead.

Anwen experienced an unnatural calmness after the initial activity, detached from the experience, like a bystander. Idris, who'd left the room some minutes before, returned with a brush and dustpan. He proceeded to rid the floor of the broken china. He was talking to the doctor, to Hywel, asking what had happened, doing things she should have been doing, if she could have freed herself of the feeling that she was watching them all from a distance.

The two neighbours who'd helped get Madog into the carriage came back, bringing two more neighbours with them. They lifted Hywel onto a makeshift stretcher, made from a blanket, removing him from the room. Idris opened the front door for them. Anwen followed on behind. Outside, a mist lay across the mountains, obscuring the sunrise that should have been visible beyond the far mountain.

'I'll come and see you later, Uncle,' she told him, clutching his hand momentarily before he was carried away. When he was halfway down the street she reluctantly closed the door. Idris was standing at the bottom of the stairs.

'I can't go to work today,' she told him.

'I'll head over in a bit, tell them what's happened.'

'But Idris, you're not well.'

He treated her to a smile that made her knees weak. '*Cariad*, I'm well enough to walk. I need to keep as fit as I can.'

'Don't overdo it.'

'I won't.'

A thought only now occurred to her. 'Why were you even here earlier?'

'I couldn't sleep. I was standing in the back yard, watching the moon setting. I heard a noise and saw a figure pass by the back gate. I knew it was your father. I was afraid he'd do something bad, so I followed him. When I got to your garden, I saw your back door was open, and crept in. I was in the kitchen when the shot was fired.'

'Thank you, Idris. You put yourself in danger to keep us safe.'

'I wasn't going to risk him hurting you.'

They gazed at each other steadily, intently. She could have spent all morning fixed on his deep brown eyes, but she was the one to break eye contact first. 'I'd better see how Mam and Mamgu are.'

He nodded, following her up. He waited outside the open door.

Upstairs, Dr Roberts was examining Cadi. 'Nothing a trip back to bed won't cure,' he concluded, helping her up from the floor as Anwen stood in the doorway.

'If it's all the same to you, Doctor, I'd rather have a sit down and a nice cup of tea.'

'I'm sure that will do it too,' said Dr Roberts. 'Then later you could pop along to Rhymney police station to see your son.'

She pursed her lips. 'See that good-for-nothing would-be murderer? He's no son of mine. I've got a family here to look after. Come on, *cariad*.' She went to Enid, putting out her hands to help her up.

'I can't,' she said, her face wracked with misery.

'Well you got here all by yourself. Come on now, Enid. I think there's something you haven't been telling us, don't you?'

Enid placed her face into the palms of her hands. A second later she was convulsing with tears.

'Mam? What is it?' Anwen went to her, kneeling down.

'Oh, It's stupid I am. This is all my fault. I've been able to walk for quite a while. Suddenly came back to me, it did, one day, when I got out of bed to use the pot, without even thinking. Before then I couldn't walk, I swear. I just couldn't.'

Anwen recalled the day she'd found her mother sitting on the edge of the bed.

'Hysteria can cause the belief you can't walk,' said the doctor. 'You'd certainly been through a trauma. You should have told us sooner.'

'I don't understand. Why did you keep up the pretence?' Part of Anwen was angry that their mother had left all the work to them, while they were trying to earn a living outside of the home too.

'I – I thought we'd all be safer. I could handle him at one time, but then his moods became fiercer. He'd tried once to kill me. I thought I'd be better staying put, pretending to be helpless. He'd come in and insult me every day, tell me how useless I was. I thought if he got it out of his system, he'd leave you and Sara alone. I – I thought… I thought we'd be – safer.' She broke down into sobs once more.

'Oh, Mam. But when Sara died, didn't you think you'd pretended long enough?'

Enid leant her head on the wall, her cheeks and chin wet with tears. 'I'd got so weak by then. I wanted to get my strength back. I carried on with those exercises Miss Elizabeth gave me, even when he tore the magazine up. I'd memorised them, see. I considered pretending I'd had a sudden recovery, then realised it was a bad idea. Your father might have guessed I'd been pretending and got angrier, or he might – he might have just killed me.' Her breaths were coming in rapid spurts.

'Mrs Rhys,' said Dr Roberts, kneeling on the other side of Enid. 'Mr Rhys will be locked up for many years to come. You need to get back on your feet and look after your family. Your daughter's been keeping the home going, earning the money to keep you all fed. You've got your mother-in-law here to think about, and your brother will need attention while he's recovering. You can't leave this all to Anwen.'

Enid's eyes were narrowed in contemplation. She sighed and it was like she'd drawn a line across her life. 'Right. Now, what are we all sitting around here for?'

Dr Roberts took hold of her arm but she shook him off. 'No, it's about time I started doing things for myself.'

She pushed herself up onto her knees. From there, she grabbed hold of the bed and eased herself up. Soon she was standing. Anwen went to take her arm, but Enid waved her away. The first two steps were halting, like those of a toddler. By the time she reached the door, they were more confident, if slow. She glanced at each of them in turn. 'I'm going to get dressed, have a cup of tea and then I'm going to the hospital to see my brother.'

'But Mam, isn't it too soon to walk that far? And they might not let you in outside of visiting hours.'

'I've gone that far pacing my room. I've had long enough in that one space.'

'I'll examine you, none the less,' said Dr Roberts.

'Very well.'

With that, she hobbled through the door and into her bedroom. The doctor went in after, shutting the door behind him.

'Now, where's that cup of tea?' said Cadi.

–

Anwen accompanied her mother to the hospital that afternoon. Enid insisted on wearing her winter coat, saying she felt bone cold. She allowed Anwen to take her arm lightly as they made their way down the road, stumbling only a couple of times. The high early morning mist had now descended into the valley floor as fog, obscuring the pit. Above, there were leaden clouds. Everyone they met who they knew did a double-take, some so surprised to see Enid they failed to say anything. They kept on going according to the agreement they'd made before they left the house, taking no time out for explanations.

Dr Roberts was in the reception area when they reached the hospital.

'Mrs Rhys! Are you sure you're all right, walking so far?'

'I told you I'd come. Now, how is my brother?'

It was her old Mam speaking, not the weaker, shrinking female she'd become, even before the fall.

'We've removed the bullet. He was lucky it missed the bone. He's patched up now and should be waking up soon. I should think he'll have a limp at the least for quite a while. He's in the ward, but don't expect too much of him.'

Anwen, still holding Enid's arm, felt the tension leave her mother's body. They were directed to the ward Idris had been in. Hywel, far from being asleep, was sitting up in bed, reading a newspaper.

'Hywel, *cariad*,' said Enid, attempting to run to her brother, but losing her footing. Anwen managed to grab her before she went down.

Hywel called out, 'Enid, what are you doing?'

The ward became hushed as everyone stared at Enid. She straightened herself, adjusted her coat, then pushed her arms out to remove the unwanted helping hands. 'I am fine.' She strode on till she reached Hywel's bed. Anwen was close behind.

'Enid, you're walking?' Hywel's eyes boggled in surprise.

'And I should have done so a long time ago. I've let my family down, Hywel. I was so concerned with doing nothing in order to keep people safe, that it didn't occur to me to do *some*thing to make sure of it. Please forgive me. If I hadn't languished in my bedroom for so long, you might not be in hospital now.'

Hywel took his sister's hands. 'Enid, you can't blame yourself for Madog's wrongdoing. Always had a streak of malice, that one.'

'Uncle Hywel, how's your leg?'

'I've been better, Anwen. Quite painful, it is. But the doctor reckons I'm lucky, so I suppose I shall have to take his word for it. They'll probably discharge me tomorrow and he'll call by to see how I am. I feel like limping out now. The nurses are a bit bossy, like.'

'For your own good,' said Anwen. 'Right, I have an errand to run. Mam, I'll come back at four to collect you.'

'What errand have you to do?' asked Enid.

'I'll tell you when I get back.' She leant over and kissed Hywel's cheek. 'I'll see you later. No disobeying the nurses, now. They know what's best for you.'

She left the hospital, still struck by the unnatural quiet of the unmoving pit wheels.

Time to confront Idris.

—

'Anwen! How are you? How's your family?' Idris got up from the chair by the fireplace, laying the book he'd been reading on the table. 'I'm sorry I didn't come back over this morning.'

'Doctor's orders?' said Anwen.

'Mother's orders.' He glanced at Meg as she pinned her hat to her hair.

'You need to rest, *bach*, after what you went through. You've done your fair share of coming to the rescue the last week, and no mistake. Now, I'm going to leave you to it. There are things need doing at the allotments, despite the weather.' Meg had stepped in to do her bit when bereavement had deprived the group of a couple of helpers. 'Make yourself a cup of tea when the kettle's boiled, *cariad*.' She pointed to the stove and promptly left via the scullery.

Anwen and Idris sat at the table opposite each other.

'Now she's gone, would you like to take a turn on Twyn Gobaith?' said Idris. 'I've been dying to get out since dinner time.'

'Yes, I'd like that.'

They went out the back way to get to the hill behind, strolling upwards and diagonally, past the fire station and Institute. It reminded her of walks they'd had here as young sweethearts. There was an abundance of fleabane, willowherb and buttercups. They were halfway up when Anwen came to a halt.

Idris stood next to her. 'Your trip to the hospital – your mother managed to walk there by herself?'

'She had the odd wobble, but yes.'

'Remarkable. I don't think I'd be able to keep still all those months if I could walk.'

'She thought she was protecting us. And I do appreciate that…'

'But?'

'I don't know, Idris. Who can guess what might have been? It's not worth trying. We just need to get on with it, don't we? I daresay my father would have been up to his tricks either way.'

'How's your arm?'

Her injury, small in comparison to those of others, had mostly been forgotten by everyone else. Only Cadi had checked it twice a day, bathing it in a calendula infusion and applying a baking soda paste to it.

'Much better, thank you. The pain is a lot less than it was.' She didn't add that she feared she would be scarred for evermore. Time would tell.

They started walking again, him slightly further down the hill, so they were almost equal height. Her hand went out to the side, taking his as she said, 'And how are you now? And none of your "I'm fine" flannel, either.'

He enclosed his hand round hers, laughing briefly. 'I'm better for knowing what's wrong with me.'

'And that something could be done.'

'Now Anwen, I've explained—'

'Listen Idris, just listen.'

He squeezed his lips together, as if tolerating her need to voice an opinion, then nodded.

'That money you were saving for years, in the bank in Rhymney, for our married life together. Have you spent any of it?'

He jolted to a halt, horrified, removing his hand from hers. 'On what? Do I look like I've been frittering away money since I got back?'

353

He never had wasted his wages on drink or betting, or fancy clothes. Each week, after giving his mother housekeeping, the same amount had been deposited in the bank. It had increased as his wages had gone up. She'd been grateful for his frugality, given that her father had taken most of her meagre wage.

'No, of course you don't. But there must be a pretty penny in there now. More than enough to pay your way while you're off work, without having to inconvenience your parents.'

'But that was for... I thought it was for... I suppose that doesn't matter now.' He groaned, leaning his head back for a moment. 'I did think of giving it to you a while back, as a kind of compensation, to escape from your father. Now I think you'll need some of it, with your father's wage gone and Hywel laid up for a while. As for the rest, I could give some to my parents to make up for me not working right now. Who knows if I'll ever get back to it? Even as an examiner. I daresay I could do something clerical. It's what Mam always wanted.'

'Idris, listen to yourself!' As much as she loved him, he was starting to frustrate her. 'As kind as it is for you to offer me the money, I'm working, Cadi's getting money from her sewing and Uncle Hywel has a bit put by to pay rent. And can't you see that your argument about your parents doesn't make sense? You don't want to leave them out of pocket by having the operation. But if you had it, you'd be well enough to work and earn money. You could go round and round with that argument.

'Look, I want you to get better, see, that's what matters. And you saving that money for both of us *is* still appropriate to me, even if it isn't to you.' She put her hand out to tip his chin up. His eyes were still studying the ground. 'Do you understand me?'

'Aye, I understand. I gave you the chance to walk away, Anwen, to find someone healthy who can take care of you.' He did now catch her eye, if briefly. 'The doctor said the operation is *mostly* successful, but what if it isn't?'

'That doesn't make any sense either... Hang on. Are you afraid of having the operation?'

It was a few seconds before he replied, 'Maybe.'

'Oh Idris. I know it's daunting to contemplate, but if you don't have it, your condition will probably get worse.' There was no probably about it. She'd looked it up in a medical dictionary at the library. Heart problems were among several life-sapping conditions he could end up with. She felt a mounting sense of hopelessness that terrified her. She *had* to persuade him the operation was the best course of action.

'Please have the operation, Idris. It's the best choice. The only choice. And do you know what? Even if there was no operation, you are the only man for me. You always have been and you always will be.'

She leant over swiftly and kissed his mouth before she was able to question the wisdom of it. He was reluctant to respond at first, but soon his lips came to life, taking possession of hers. The heat from them awoke her body, as if spring had arrived after winter, and her heart blossomed with hope. Her soul, only half an entity by itself, was reunited with its mate and all was well with the world.

Slowly he lifted her off her feet, stretching himself up to his full height. She hung onto his shoulders, a rush of satisfaction coursing through her body, making her breathless. He spun her around before lowering her and ending the kiss. They held on to each other, his arms round her shoulders, hers round his waist, her head resting on his chest, his head resting on her hair.

Finally, she tipped her head back. 'Tell Dr Roberts you've decided to have the operation, Idris. Then, when you've had it and recovered, let's get married. We can live at mine, to begin with, and you can use the money saved to help your family out if you like, until Jenkin's bringing some money in.'

'That money was so we could rent our own place, get the bits of furniture we'd need, even if it was second-hand.'

'There might be money left, and we'll save again anyway. When the war finishes, we'll think about it anew.'

Anwen lifted her head, staring at the sky. The cloud had begun to dissolve, allowing the sun to muscle through the fog and create several sunbeams across the valley. A shaft of light illuminated the area around them. Somewhere on the slope a grasshopper chirruped, and a bee buzzed around the white clover.

'There's always hope, Idris, always a bright light somewhere pointing towards the future, however long it takes. And you're the person I want to journey with to get there.'

She gazed up at him, and he down at her, his deep, warm eyes captivating her as always.

'I've been lost without you these past months,' he said.

'You need never be lost again, Idris. I will always be there for you, whatever happens. I've missed you so terribly.'

'Then let's go now and find our families. I'm sure they'll be thrilled to hear our news.'

He took her hand once more and they strolled down Twyn Gobaith towards their future.

A Letter From Francesca

I've always been a keen family history researcher and excitedly mined Ancestry.co.uk for snippets of information about my relatives. One day a 'hint' popped up to tell me that one of the World War One military records might be about my great-grandfather, Hugh Morgan. Although doubting there was a connection, I went and had a look anyway. Much to my surprise, the record was indeed about my great-grandfather, informing me that he'd enlisted with the Welsh Rhondda Battalion in March 1915. However, he was given a medical discharge in the November due to tachycardia. It was the ink stamp claiming, 'Not likely to become an efficient soldier', that caught my eye. How would he have felt about that attack on his manhood, I wondered, having signed up willingly with his pals? What would it be like to go home, feeling you'd failed? And so was born Idris Hughes and the girl waiting at home for him, Anwen Rhys.

We hear much about what happened to the soldiers of World War One, how they lived and died, and rightly so, but little about the home front of that time, particularly in Wales. In researching the mining community, the villages, the occupations, activities and entertainments, particularly through local newspapers of the time, I feel I have learnt much about my mother's family's background. How I wish I'd asked my great-grandmother, Mary Jones, a woman in her twenties in the war, so many more questions than I did. Although it was Hugh's story that started the ball rolling, it is Mary's village of

Abertwyssyg, (rather than Hugh's New Tredegar, just down the road), that forms the basis for my village of Dorcalon.

After all the research and writing, I can't quite believe that *Heartbreak in the Valleys* is now being published. Thank you to Hera Books for giving me the opportunity to share this story of love, struggle and community, but ultimately hope, with the wider world.

If you enjoyed *Heartbreak in the Valleys* and would like to leave a review, that would be lovely. Then maybe others will discover what life was like in the Welsh valleys too.

If you'd like to discuss the novel with me, or discover more about it, I'd love to chat to you on social media here:

Facebook: www.facebook.com/FrancescaCapaldiAuthor/
Twitter: @FCapaldiBurgess
Blog: www.writemindswriteplace.wordpress.com/

Thank you for taking the time to read my book, and if you're interested in finding out what happened next in Dorcalon, a new *Valleys* book will be published in a few months' time.

Best wishes,

Francesca xx

Acknowledgments

First of all, a big thank you to Keshini Naidoo and Lindsey Mooney at Hera Books for their belief in my story and all their hard work during the process of publishing.

I'm indebted to Elaine Everest of The Write Place, who has taught me a lot about all sorts of publishing. She gave me the confidence all those years back to send out my first short story and has encouraged me in my various writing projects since. Thank you to all the other writers I've met through The Write Place, they've been a great support and also huge fun. A special mention to Ann W, Barbara, Catherine, Chris W, Elaine R, Karen, Natalie, Rosemary and Sarah – and also Viv, who, though not part of TWP, has been part of our group at many events.

A special mention to Angela, my Welsh speaking writing friend, who's helped me with the bits of Welsh included in this book. *Diolch yn fawr iawn*. Any mistakes are down to me!

Thanks also to The Romantic Novelists' Association whose New Writers' Scheme and conferences have been invaluable.

Finally, thank you to my family for all their encouragement, particularly my late dad, Giuseppe, whose love of history set me down that path, and my mother, Maureen, who's off-the-cuff stories made me eager to make up my own.